CEDAR CREEK

Book Two

Bronwyn Trotter

Publisher: Inspiring Publishers,
P.O. Box 159, Calwell, ACT Australia 2905
Email: publishaspg@gmail.com
http://www.inspiringpublishers.com

A catalogue record for this book is available from the National Library of Australia

National Library of Australia The Prepublication Data Service

Author: Bronwyn Trotter
Title: Cedar Creek
Genre: Fiction
ISBN: 978-1-922327-14-7

Forward

Four trappers, Joseph Beauford Jones, James Fergus, Brent Garrett and Will Sloan have made their promise to Calahan Cole. They promised to take care of his daughter Sarah if anything should happen to him. The night Calahan gambled their home 'Mountain View Lodge' and all his money on a game of poker, he lost everything, including his life when he got into a fight with Benjamin Crawley, the owner of Cedar Creek's general store.

While in the care of the trappers, Sarah met Frank Mason, the son of wealthy rancher Major Hardy, and against his father's wishes, they became friends. Major Hardy preferred Frank to marry Millicent Crawley. Threatened with a whipping if she continued to see Frank, Sarah tried her best to stay away from him, but Frank was in love with her, and for the next two years, determined to get her to marry him, he followed Sarah to her mountain.

Having declared their love for each other, they tried keeping their relationship secret from everyone, but after returning to Cedar Creek for the winter, they met at a shack on Major Hardy's land, where Sarah told Frank she was pregnant and Frank asked her to marry him. Catching Sarah and Frank together, Major Hardy carried out his threat to whip Sarah, but it was Frank, trying to protect her, who took the brunt of the whipping.

Recovered from his wound, Frank returned to the mountain and Sarah. There, waiting the birth of their child, he made a fatal mistake by going to the High Country to hunt alone. Blaming the trappers for Frank's death, Sarah tried releasing them from their promise, but the promise was made on the mountain where it could not be broken. Giving birth to a baby boy she named Thomas, the trappers stayed with her until she told them to leave. Joe is hurt by Sarah's attitude toward them. However, the men haven't forgotten they have a promise to keep, but conceding to her wishes, they step aside to allow her to raise her son.

Sarah's first winter in Cedar Creek with Thomas proved devastating for her. Blaming Sarah for Frank's death, Major Hardy stole Thomas away from Sarah and refused to relinquish him. Having told the trappers to leave her alone, Sarah felt she couldn't ask them to help her get Thomas back, so it wasn't until she skinned and slaughtered a wolf in the church, scaring the town folk, that the four men themselves figured out a way to get Thomas back.

Raising Thomas alone on the mountain had its drawbacks when Sarah's trapping fell by the wayside. Although keeping herself apart from the trappers, Sarah doesn't mind that Thomas and the men have become friends. The trappers find Sarah stubborn and strong willed, and still posing problems for them.

Foley Andrews, is owed a debt of gratitude. After saving Sarah the night Frank was whipped, the trappers don't mind him becoming friends with her. Only Foley's brother Brady knows he is in love with Sarah, but everyone knows he proposes marriage to her every winter. However, Sarah repeatedly turns him down, because she feels he has nothing to offer her, besides, he works for Major Hardy, a man she despises.

Thomas is twelve years old now and Cedar Creek has a new sheriff, a man with his own past, and Benjamin Crawley's daughter Millicent, having failed to marry Frank because of his love for Sarah, has set her bonnet on marrying him. Even though Sarah and Sheriff Christian Morgan have a confrontation the day she returns to town for the winter, neither waste time before beginning a relationship that proves stormy from the get go…

Chapter One

The school bell rang out loudly, letting everyone know it is time for their children to head off to school. When the bell tolls, it can be heard all over town and the outlying areas of the county. This day, the sound of a gunshot mingled with the peal of the bell and echoed through the air. Two horses, their eyes wide with fear, race along the street, passing startled people at full gallop. One horse is loaded with skins, the other carries a canvas covered load of belongings. Both horse's heavy loads sway precariously from side to side, so much so, they threaten to fall off the horses at any moment. As the two horses gallop down the street, men, women, and children scatter to get out of their way. Buckboards careen off to the side. Horses with riders rear up in fright. Standing on the boardwalk outside the Sheriff's Office, Christian frowned as he watched them race by. Not long after, a third horse went galloping past, following the first two, its saddle is empty and Christian wonders where its rider is. People are running in the direction of the schoolhouse.

Stepping off the boardwalk, Christian lifted his gun up and down in his holster, something he did out of habit, needing his gun to slide out easily for when he confronted men with guns. Making his way quickly toward the schoolhouse he could already see a large crowd gathered outside the building. Pushing his way through the crowd, he glanced over to his left and saw a young boy standing off to one side trying his best to hold a horse that was desperately trying to escape his clutches. In the middle of the crowd stood someone wearing the dirtiest, raggedy, worn out hat and biggest oversized fur coat Christian had ever seen. The coat's hood sat haphazardly on the wearers back, giving the wearer the appearance of bulk, while the rest of it hung to the ground and completely covered the wearers arms. The rifle poking out the front was almost completely hidden, except for part of its long barrel.

The raggedy hat and fur coat wearer, standing in the middle of the street facing toward the schoolhouse, held a double-barrel shotgun aimed squarely at Cedar Creek's new school teacher Jonathon O'Rourke. O'Rourke, being a city man, brought his family to Cedar Creek seven months ago, more than a month after Christian. The previous teacher, having got herself married, left to go to Boston with her new husband, leaving Cedar Creek without a teacher for two years. When O'Rourke was asked if he would like to take her place, he thought it would be a good opportunity for his family to see what the west was like. But his family had never been out west, and some of the people in town frightened them. Upon seeing the wild appearance of the mountain men when they came riding in, O'Rourke, fearful for his family's safety, rushed off to Christian for reassurance. Christian assured O'Rourke, while he was the law in Cedar Creek, he and his family would be safe.

The town folk were happy to have a new teacher and O'Rourke was a good one. It hadn't taken long for the children to get to like him. O'Rourke was proud of his bell he brought with him when he came to town, so when he showed it to the town folk, they eagerly helped erect the pole it hung from. Everyone became used to hearing the bell when it tolled. Now though, it was obvious, the bell for a time, would no longer ring, because the bell-rope had clearly been shot off the bell by the raggedy hat wearer. Now Christian felt like he had let O'Rourke down, because O'Rourke appeared to be frozen to the spot, and Christian thought he looked kind of funny, standing there with the end of the bell-rope firmly clutched in his right hand, and the rest of it coiled around his feet.

Christian pulled his .45 out of its holster and cocking it, moved to stand next to the raggedy hat wearer. Poking it in under the brim of the dirty hat, he felt sure he was aiming his gun at the man's ear.

"Put down your rifle!" Christian's booming voice ordered. The voice that answered took him completely by surprise, causing him to frown, but he didn't move his gun.

"I ain't puttin down my rifle mister! cause this here empty-headed slimy maggot, scared my horses, an they're probably half way to Mexico by now, an he's goin to go get em, besides, me and Thomas there! ...almost fell off our goddamn horses! could've broke our goddamn necks!" The voice spoke in such an aggressive tone, Christian could almost feel the anger oozing out from under the hat.

A trapper standing in the crowd, called out to the raggedy hat wearer. "Hey Cole! ...horses are at the Tradin' Post!" Another yelled. "Yeah! ...got their heads up to their necks in the trough!" While there was a lot of sniggering, another called. "Fillin their goddamn bellies full of cold water, no less!" Someone else was heard saying. "At least they know where the hell they got to go!" When everyone burst out laughing, the raggedy hat wearer cursed, but didn't change its stance. Christian knew by the way the men were talking, he was confronting another trapper, making him wonder just how many more were still to come to town, and if he was going to have any more trouble. "Goddamn son-of-a-bitch!" The voice under the hat cursed. "Someone go get them horses heads out'a that trough will yuh? before they keel over with guts ache!"

Will Sloan hurriedly tethered Cole's horses to the hitching rail outside the Trading Post, then ran back up the street to where the crowd was to watch what was happening. Christian heard a deep, almost calm voice resonate from the crowd. "It's alright Cole, Will tied your horses to the rail, they are doin just fine."

The trapper under the hat didn't look up to see who spoke. This trapper already knew whom the voice belonged to. "Thanks for letting me know that Joe." The rifle aimed at O'Rourke remained steady. Christian recognized the voice as belonging to one of the four trappers he met when they handed their guns in for safe keeping. He had a pretty good memory for names, and memorized every trappers name that came to town.

Keeping his gun poked in under the hat, Christian glanced over at the crowd and found the man the voice belonged to. Will Sloan, James Fergus and Brent Garrett were there watching what was happening alongside Joe Jones, the oldest man of the group. The four men rode in with loaded packhorses a few days ahead of the rest of the trappers. These men had been in town a little over two weeks and he had spoken with them on several occasions.

When trappers started arriving in smaller groups, two and sometimes three at a time, the four men were seen talking to them, but they didn't seem to get the answer they wanted, making Christian confused as to the men riding out of town each day. Leaving at first light, they rode across the bridge, then headed toward the mountains, and didn't come back until late in the afternoon. As time wore on, the men appeared to be getting more restless. By the time the rest of the trappers finished arriving, there were nineteen in all. Joe and the other three men kept watching the trail, and each day, kept riding out, watching and waiting. Christian figured there were still more trappers yet to come off the mountain, but as the days dragged on, no more men arrived.

After arriving in town, the trappers all lived together in one big house. Situated almost opposite the Trading Post, the Ferguson House, as it is called, sits on a ridge just above the Red Cedar River where a road winds past the front porch, ending along a track in a thick stand of trees and brush, giving access to an open grassed area on the riverbank. On the opposite side of the river, a pier has been erected where three small row boats are moored. Upstairs, the house has six bedrooms, downstairs there are five. Downstairs also consists of a huge combined living and eating area. A long table set up in the middle of the vast room has enough seats around it for every man to sit. Three fireplaces keep the house warm all winter. One is open and used for heating, another for cooking. In the washroom there is not only a bathtub but a large metal tub sits atop a stone fireplace, where water for bathing can be heated, giving extra warmth to the house, and where laundry can be done.

When the Ferguson family, who owned the house sold up and moved to Moreton, two weeks hard ride south of Cedar Creek, the trappers pooled their money and bought the house for their own use. Now the Ferguson House only ever gets used during the winter months. The Ferguson House isn't the grandest house in town, but it is the largest. The grandest house is the two storey house known as Mountain View Lodge, and that, is where Christian lives.

Trappers arrive in Cedar Creek well before winter sets in, which is always around the middle of December when heavy snow finally makes its way off the mountain. Snow is already falling high up, and the trappers have made their journey before the mountain pass could become blocked so they wouldn't be cut off from civilization.

Spending winter in and around Cedar Creek, allows the trappers to fill their time working for Major Hardy on his cattle and horse ranch. Only a few of the old trappers wait in town until the Major's men run his horses to the corrals. These men prefer working with horses rather than spend their days breaking their backs branding cattle. Most trappers never fail to find enough work to occupy them until the snow begins to melt the following spring. They wait just long enough for the mountain pass to open up again, allowing them to have another year of trapping.

"Just why the hell did you take so damn long gettin here Cole?' Joe asked the raggedy hat wearer. Christian stood facing the trapper with his gun still poked in under the hat and listened to the exchange. He now at least had the name of the raggedy hat wearer.

"Had things to take care of Joe." Cole didn't waver, the rifle remained aimed squarely at O'Rourke.

"Yeah! …well we got out more than two weeks ago, when we came past your cabin no-one was there, and the goddamn snow was deep then!" Christian could hear the anger in Joe's voice. "You cut it too close Cole! the goddamn pass was almost closed when we came through! …you keep takin' risks like that and we'll be finding your dead body come the spring!" Christian raised his eyebrows at the equally angry reply that followed.

"The goddamn pass was not almost closed when you got out Joe! the goddamn pass was just about closed when I got out! …so, don't you go worrying about me none! …you just worry about your goddamn self!" Christian listened to Cole's angry voice and frowned, because the voice he was hearing no longer sounded deep, nor masculine, like a man's voice. The only way Christian could describe the voice was to say it was sounding, well, feminine!

Ignoring Christian holding his gun under the hat, Joe and Cole kept their angry banter going. "I know when to get out Joe! and you know I know that too! …goddamn it!" Cole continued. "Yeah! well you…!" Joe didn't get to finish his tirade. Tired of the banter between the two trappers, and annoyed with the crowd that was getting larger by the minute, Christian just wanted to end the standoff so didn't give Joe time to reply. "Alright!" he barked. "That's enough! you two can have a reunion later! ...and you lot! ...clear out and let me handle this! now go on! go about your business! ...all of you!" Ignoring Christian, the crowd jostled each other for better vantage points, wanting to see what was going to happen between the sheriff and Cole. They already knew Cole had a temper and could stand up to any man. They just wanted to see if their new sheriff could stand up to Cole.

The trappers especially ignored him, and stayed to watch. Shaking his head from side to side in disbelief that no-one moved on, he moved closer to the side of the hat wearer, and looking to see what he could do to get the rifle, asked Cole to hand it over one more time.

"Let me have that rifle," he demanded as calmly as he could, not wanting to spook the rifle holder into shooting O'Rourke.

"You can go to hell mister! cause you ain't gettin my rifle! ...nobody gets my rifle! ...not ever!" Christian pressed his lips firmly together at Cole's savage answer. No-one was going to tell him to go to hell. "If you think you are going to shoot our teacher, you are mistaken! And if you do happen to shoot our teacher! ...I ...am going to shoot you! ...but I don't think you want me doing that! ...you just might want to go back to that mountain of yours without a hole in you ...so give me that goddamn rifle ...*now!*" he said raising his voice in anger. But his demand was to no avail.

"Like I said mister, you ain't takin' my goddamn rifle, nobody takes my..." Everyone, including Cole, was stunned by what happened next. "Give me that goddamn rifle!" Christian snarled through clenched teeth. Then, without giving Cole time to think, he made a sudden grab for the gun. Taking hold of it around the barrel with his left hand while keeping his six-shooter aimed in under the hat, he jerked the rifle swiftly upwards.

Cole's finger, still on the trigger, caused the gun to suddenly go off. Christian felt the discharge vibrate through his hand and up his arm. There were loud curses and screams from those people refusing to follow Christian's orders to leave. No-one knew where the bullet had gone. Everyone, including the trappers, ducked for cover. O'Rourke closed his eyes and prayed he hadn't been shot.

As Christian jerked the rifle upwards, he pulled it towards him, took a step back and using his size and strength for leverage, tried to take the gun. But Cole held on tight.

Joe ducked when he saw Christian grab the barrel, thinking, 'what sort of fool goes for a gun by its barrel?' Becoming intrigued by Christian right then, he made a vow to himself to find out more about him.

Cole's body slammed into Christians, knocking him backwards. Although managing to keep his balance, he was still caught off guard by what happened. Unable to see the face under the hat, but feeling the body that came crashing against him left him confused. The sudden sharp pain of whatever slammed into his groin made him wince when it dug in.

Forced to let go of the rifle, Cole bounced off Christian, and sailing backwards, landed with a heavy thud on the ground. Christian watched, as one arm swung out wide while the other moved quickly inside the fur coat. When Cole hit the ground, the raggedy hat fell off and rolled to one side, leaving a long braid of light brown hair curled in the dirt. The oversized fur coat laying wide open, exposed a pair of long legs spread out wide.

It all happened so fast, Christian ended up holding the rifle firmly in his left hand and his six-shooter in his right, but he still had the sense to aim his gun at the figure lying on its back at his feet. Taking a couple of quick steps forward to stand next to the body sprawled on the ground, his stomach lurched and his heart skipped a beat, making him surprised as he looked into the face of a woman. He couldn't help but notice her. The woman was not at all what he imagined a female trapper would look like. This woman was way too pretty. Letting his eyes wander over her, noticing how tight her shirt was and how it accentuated her bust, he figured they had to be what hit him in the chest, and he knew exactly what hit him in the groin. He could see she was packing a weapon down the front of her pants.

Staring down at the woman everyone was calling Cole, he caught the sun shining off the blade of a very large knife she was gripping in her hand. He hadn't seen the knife, not until it had been pulled clear of its sheath as the woman fell backwards. Quickly placing his foot on her wrist to hold the knife down, Christian aimed his gun at her head. "Drop the knife!" he demanded loudly. The crowd fell silent as they watched what was happening between Christian Morgan and Sarah Cole.

The knife was huge, it looked sharp, and Sarah was holding it tight. Thinking it must hang from her waist all the way past her knees, Christian wondered how the hell she carried it, let alone held it. "Drop it!" he demanded again, pressing his foot more firmly on her arm. The weight wasn't all that great, but it made Sarah open her hand. Looking into the barrel of his gun she let the knife fall freely to the ground.

Feeling the threat was gone, Christian relaxed, then un-cocked his gun and looked away. That was all it took for Sarah to quickly twist her body around and bring her legs up hard behind his, knocking him off his feet. She moved so fast, it caught Christian off guard. Joe grabbed hold of both Fergus and Garrett when he saw what Sarah was doing. Will's mouth dropped open in surprise. The four men sniggered and kept watching.

Christian let go of the rifle as his legs went up in the air and came crashing onto his back beside Sarah with his legs sprawled. Quickly grabbing her knife, Sarah crawled between his legs and crouched over him. Her eyes pierced into his, her mouth held the hint of a smile. But keeping his wits, Christian re-cocked his gun and pointed it directly at Sarah's face. Sarah stopped where she was, her body hovering above his, one hand resting on the ground between Christian's arm and his chest, the other holding the huge knife that was almost touching the tip of his nose.

Sarah did exactly what the four trappers taught her to do to defend herself, surprising her attacker. It was a tactical move taught to the men while in the cavalry, but they soon stopped sniggering when Christian pointed his gun back in her face.

"Don't even think about using that knife!" Christian warned, looking over the knife into her deep blue eyes. "I don't want to have to shoot you, put the knife down." Now that he was dealing with a female trapper, things had changed. He had to be careful, he was unsure of what this woman was capable of doing.

Sarah wasn't concerned with his threat. He wouldn't shoot her, not like this, not in front of everyone. Instead of putting the knife down she turned it around and put it back in its sheath, then held her hands up to show Christian it was gone. Backing out from between his legs, she grabbed her hat and while he picked himself up off the ground and regained his composure, she hit her hat against her leg to remove the dust, then, pulling it back down to sit tight on her head, smiled over at the trappers and dusted herself off.

Christian's heart was pounding. He couldn't believe he had been outsmarted by a woman. As Christian and Sarah stood facing each other, a gruff voice in the crowd called out. "Hey sheriff! ...I think Cole may have won that round!" When everyone burst out laughing, Christian felt embarrassed. He only lost concentration for a split second, letting her get the better of him. If it had been a man, he didn't think he would have made that mistake, but he felt this woman was cunning and his heart had been racing because he had been thinking just how pretty she was, which, he made the excuse to himself, was the cause of him having a lapse of judgement.

Leaving the rifle lying on the ground where it landed, Christian turned to the crowd. "All of you go about your goddamn business, there is nothing more for you to see here!" His face was burning from having been made a fool of. "I told you to get lost! ...all of you!" He repeated as he waited for the crowd to disperse. "No, you didn't!" A man in the crowd called. "You told us to go about our business." Christian could feel Sarah's eyes on him as the crowd erupted in raucous laughter at the man correcting what he said.

Except for the four trappers, the crowd wandered off talking and laughing amongst themselves. Joe and the other three men moved to one side and leant against a hitching rail where they could keep watching. Ignoring them, Christian turned his attention back to Sarah. "I want that gun you are packing Cole." That was the first time he addressed Sarah by the name he heard the trappers use.

Studying Sarah, Christian could see her eyes were the darkest blue he had ever seen. She had a small nose and full lips, her skin, what he could see of it, was lightly tanned and without blemish. Wisps of curls hung around her face under the raggedy hat she pulled down almost covering her ears. Moving his eyes slowly downwards, most of her was covered by the huge fur coat she was wearing, but what he could see, he liked. Her shirt, open at the top, allowed him to see a hint of her breasts. Her waist was small and her trousers, although not tight, were sitting low on her hips. The sheath hung from her hip, and Christian was right when he thought the knife was too big for her. The knife hung as far as her knees, making him wonder why she would carry such a big weapon. Every trapper carried the same knife and he knew they used them for skinning wolves, but he couldn't imagine a pretty woman such as Cole skinning anything.

"What gun mister?" Sarah could see him studying her and her eyes sparkled with mischief when she spoke. Christian was taking in how tall Sarah was. The top of her head came up as far as his chin. She had to tilt her head a little to see into his eyes. He didn't have to bend his head far to look into hers. Sarah's eyes moved over him as she questioned him about the gun, he knew she was packing.

"The gun you have hidden down your pants ...I want it!" Christian's .45 was now aimed at one of Sarah's legs. If he was forced to shoot her, he would only wound her, but he didn't want to do that, he imagined a pretty woman like Cole wouldn't want to be scarred. The rifle still lay on the ground where it landed when he was knocked off his feet.

"I don't have a gun down my pants!" Sarah said sounding incredulous, while her eyes never left Christian's face.

"Well, you would be a pretty funny looking woman, or a funny looking man, if what I felt dig into me a moment ago isn't a gun, now, either you give it to me, or I will be forced to take it!" Christian held out his hand.

Now it was Sarah's turn to be embarrassed. Her face flushed pink, her smile faded and the tone of her voice suddenly changed. "You put a hand on me mister! ...and you won't have a hand to scratch yourself with!" Sarah said seriously, looking at Christian's crotch while putting her hand to the handle of her knife and leaving it there.

Seeing where she was looking, Christian felt his face burning. "Don't even think about going for that knife Cole! I can take that off you too! there just so happens to be a sign on the other side of the bridge you should have seen on your way in that says, no firearms allowed in the town limits, everyone has to hand over their guns, that includes you, that is the law."

Sarah smirked. "Well what mangy coyote would make up a stupid law like that?" She knew it would be the man standing in front of her that made that law. He was new in town and that sign near the bridge hadn't been there last spring when she left Cedar Creek, besides, he was wearing a badge, right then Sarah wondered where Sheriff Clem was. Christian knew Sarah knew who made the law and all she wanted was to have a dig at him. "I was that mangy coyote that made that law, and it isn't a stupid law as you put it, no-one in town has a problem with it, seems like it is only you ...so, hand it over!" As their stand-off continued and his heart raced, Christian held out his hand waiting for Sarah to hand him her gun.

Instead of handing over her gun, Sarah turned her back on him and spoke to Thomas. "Thomas! did you see a goddamn sign on the way into town? ...cause I sure didn't!" Following Sarah's gaze, Christian could see Thomas had managed to get his horse under control and was standing back quietly while watching everything that was going on.

"Yeah! I saw it! but you were already way passed it when I saw it! so it was too late to tell you about it! ...it's just a stupid sign anyhow!" Christian raised his eyebrows when he heard Thomas denigrate his sign. Noticing the tone of Thomas's voice sounded as angry as Cole's, he figured Thomas and Cole were probably brother and sister, and that Thomas and his sister were blessed with the same angry attitude.

Sarah turned back to Christian. "Well mister, I didn't see your sign, and that there school teacher! ...if that is what you call him...!" Sarah looked passed Christian toward O'Rourke and pointed her finger at him. "Rang that goddamn stupid bell! anyway ...you know what happened then ...so ...what does that sign that I didn't see say?"

"It says!" Christian paused while holstering his gun so he could bend down to pick up Sarah's rifle. Having been fired twice, Christian was satisfied it was empty. Straightening up, he took a deep breath, hooked the rifle over his arm, then continued. "No firearms permitted within the town limits, by order of the sheriff ...and I, Cole, ...am the sheriff!"

Sarah was surprised to learn Clem was no longer sheriff. "Well, goddamn! what happened to Clem? ...he was sheriff when I left here last spring!" Clem had been sheriff for a long time. She could remember when she was a small child Clem being sheriff. He even locked her in the jailhouse more than once, especially the time she shot up the town trying to get Thomas back, the time he was stolen from her.

"Clem is still here, now, you going to give me that gun, or am I going to have to take it?" Christian didn't think now was the time to dwell on Clem not being sheriff. He thought Sarah knew perfectly well he was sheriff, she couldn't possibly miss seeing the star pinned to his shirt, she would have seen it close up when she crashed into him and besides, he thought. 'Why should Cole care who was sheriff? he was sheriff and that was all there was to it, Cole would just have to put up with it!' He stuck his hand out again for Sarah to hand him her gun.

Watching Sarah pull her shirt out of her trousers, Christian caught a glimpse of bare skin before she pulled a long-barreled handgun out of its hiding place and reluctantly handed it over. Taking it, Christian felt its warmth after being next to Sarah's body. Turning the gun quickly over in his hands, he made out the engraved barrel made of silver, and the ivory grips carvings. Opening the chamber, he found it fully loaded with five small calibre shells. While glancing at Sarah, he shook the bullets into the palm of his hand.

Sarah watched Christian put the bullets in his shirt pocket, then shove the gun inside the top of his trousers where it pressed against his bare skin. The barrel was longer than average pistols, making it sit just above his groin, so he wriggled it around a bit to make it sit more comfortably. "Wouldn't want to shoot nothing off now! ... would you sheriff?" Sarah smirked. Christian tried to ignore Sarah's sarcasm, but felt his face burn at her insinuation he had nothing between his legs.

"You got any more guns Cole?" he asked, trying to stop his face from burning. 'Hell,' he thought. 'I shouldn't let her unsettle me.' But Sarah was unsettling him, and he could feel the four trapper's eyes on him too, watching his every move.

"Nope! ...you got 'em all!" Sarah held her coat open so Christian could get a much better look at her not having any guns. Christian got a good look, just before she pulled the coat closed so he could no longer see anything.

Stepping to one side, allowing her to see around Christian, Sarah smiled broadly, put her hand up to her mouth to stifle a laugh, then turned to Thomas standing by his horse. "Hey Thomas! ...that there is your teacher!" Sarah pointed to O'Rourke, then with a smile still on her face, turned back to Christian. Christian couldn't slow his heartbeat thumping wildly against his chest at seeing Sarah's smile.

Forcing himself to look at O'Rourke, who was too scared to move a muscle and still standing where he was when the bell was shot at, Christian had to suppress his own smile. "It's alright O'Rourke ...Cole isn't going to shoot you! ...go inside ...the children are waiting." But O'Rourke was petrified, the female trapper scared him pretty darn good.

"Yeah! ...O'Rourke ...that your name?" Sarah jabbed her finger toward O'Rourke and bellowed. "Well, I ain't goin to shoot you! ...cause now ...I don't have a gun!" She held her hands, palms up, to show they were empty. "But you better not go ringin that bell anytime soon! ...cause well ...now you don't have a rope to ring it with!" Sarah giggled at her own silly comment. "Oh! ...and by the way," she added as an after-thought. "Thomas will be along tomorrow for his schoolin."

Christian wondered what Thomas would be like when he got with other children. Thinking, if Thomas had the same attitude as Cole, he may be too much of a handful for O'Rourke to handle. He looked over at Thomas still holding on tight to his horse and made up his mind to keep an eye on him, and if Cole was going to be trouble, he was going to keep a close eye on her as well.

Christian waited until O'Rourke had gone inside the schoolhouse, before turning back to take one last look at Sarah, then deciding he didn't want to rile her again, and taking her rifle and pistol with him, started walking toward the Sheriff's Office. Seeing him walk off, Sarah quickly fell in step beside him, and Thomas followed with his horse in tow.

"What are you going to do with my guns sheriff?" she asked as she tried keeping in step. "I'm going to lock them up for safe keeping," Christian said, keeping up his pace. "Well, when can I get them back?" Sarah picked up her stride and looked sideways at him. "You can have them back when you leave town." Christian kept looking straight ahead, even so, he felt aware of Sarah walking beside him. "What do you mean when I leave town? ...we don't leave until next spring! you can't keep my guns until then! ...I need my guns! ...goddamn son-of-a ...bitch!" she said, cursing loud enough for Christian to hear.

Thinking it not very ladylike for a woman to be cursing, Christian tried to ignore her outburst, but then, he wasn't sure if Sarah was a lady, at least not of the city variety. Shaking his head from side to side he stepped onto the boardwalk in front of the Sheriff's Office, and looking back, saw Thomas and his horse had stopped behind Cole. "Anytime you decide to leave town Cole, you can come in and get your guns ... you just have to sign them out as you leave, then sign them back in when you come back ...that is how my law works." Looking down on Sarah from the boardwalk, Christian couldn't stop himself from thinking how pretty she was, while at the same time, thinking how infuriating she was too.

"So, what you are saying sheriff is ...if Thomas and I are out of town, we can have our guns ...that right?" Sarah narrowed her eyes but her voice remained calm. Christian's ears pricked when hearing the difference in Sarah's voice. Having dropped her aggressive tone, her voice sounded more feminine. "That's right," he replied, stepping back off the boardwalk so he could study Sarah more closely. "Well, Thomas and I will be setting up camp down on the riverbank ...out of town ...so after we put our skins in, and get supplies..." Taking a step back from Christian, Sarah paused for effect. "I will be coming for my guns!" Again, there was a threatening tone to Sarah's voice as she turned and started to walk off. Thomas glared at Christian and followed Sarah.

Feeling a little confused at Sarah's about face in attitude, Christian watched Thomas's horse as he led it away, and saw something he probably shouldn't have been able to see, and it was hanging from the saddle on the other side of his horse. "Cole! ...stop where you are! ...right now!" he bellowed. Both Sarah and Thomas stopped abruptly and turned to face him. "You forget something sheriff?" Sarah said looking bewildered. Walking around the far side of Thomas's horse, Christian pulled a small rifle out of its holster, then carrying it, stepped up to Sarah.

"What is this, Cole?" he asked, not realizing asking what it is made him sound like he didn't know it was a gun. Knowing full well what Christian was asking, Sarah looked at the rifle then Christian, and raising her eyebrows, thought she would have a dig at him anyway. "If you don't know what that is, sheriff …then perhaps you shouldn't be sheriff!" Christian, couldn't ignore her sarcasm. "Don't get smart with me Cole, I asked you if you had any more guns and you said you didn't! …you lied to me!"

Not liking that Christian accused her of lying, Sarah's eyes grew dark with anger. "I am not a liar!" she snapped, one hand wrapping instinctively around the handle of her knife as she pointed to Thomas's horse. "That is *not* my horse! …that is *not* my gun! …*that!* …is Thomas's horse! …and *that!* …is his gun!" Realizing he should have been more careful with what he said, Christian stared in astonishment at Sarah's angry retort. His face burned for the second time, and trying to ignore Sarah's hand going to her knife, he turned to Thomas. Still feeling foolish about making one mistake after another, Christian wasn't prepared for the next mistake he made. "Why didn't you tell me you had this gun son?"

"Don't call me son!" Thomas snapped. "I'm not your son! …besides, you didn't ask me if I had a gun!" Taken aback by Thomas's sudden outburst, all Christian could do was stare open mouthed at him. After closing his mouth, he concentrated on sizing Thomas up. Thomas was solidly built. His curly hair was nothing at all like Cole's, and it hung over his ears and over the collar of the fur coat he wore. But he looked a little like Cole, and he sounded angry, just like Cole.

Trying to ignore the both of them, Christian cracked Thomas's rifle to see if it was loaded and found it empty. Walking along the side of Thomas's horse while Sarah and Thomas kept glaring at him, he felt inside the saddlebags, and running his hand along the inside of the bedroll tied to the back of the saddle, came up with nothing. "Can we go now sheriff? We have a lot to do before it gets too dark to set up camp." Tired from their four-day trek, Sarah lowered her voice and put her arm around Thomas's shoulders as they waited for Christian to give them permission to go.

Christian stepped back onto the boardwalk. "Sure, you can go, but you better not have any more guns," he warned, picking up Sarah's rifle. Not happy with Christian threatening her, she called after him. "Sheriff!" This time when she spoke her voice reflected how tired she was. "What is it Cole?" Christian asked, turning to see Sarah and Thomas had stopped again. "You better take real good care of our guns! ...especially that pistol! ...because if anything happens to them..." Sarah narrowed her eyes before continuing, "...I will make you pay!"

There was no mistaking the threat in Sarah's voice. Stepping back off the boardwalk Christian strode quickly towards them, forcing her to step back. "Are you threatening me Cole?" he questioned, stepping right in front of her and pulling himself up to his full height. Sarah tilted her head a little and looked him squarely in the eyes. "No! ...trappers don't make threats ...they make promises ...and that! ...sheriff! ...is a promise!" Looking into Sarah's eyes Christian saw how they suddenly dimmed, almost becoming sad when she spoke. Christian's heart pounded, unsure whether she was serious with her threat or not.

Turning away together, Sarah and Thomas headed toward the Trading Post where their packhorses were waiting. Christian stood in the middle of the street, watching them go. The oversized fur coat Sarah wore, brushed the ground as she walked. Thomas's coat covered his legs just below his knees. 'He looks just like Cole,' Christian thought again. Unable to tell how old Sarah was, he figured she wasn't much older than Thomas. Were they brother and sister? It didn't really matter, he thought they were both going to cause him a lot of grief anyway. Still standing on the boardwalk, Christian watched four trappers walk past him and follow Sarah and Thomas toward the Trading Post, convincing him, they were the late comers the men had been waiting for.

Returning to his office, he placed the two rifles on his desk, lifted the pistol out from where it sat down the front of his trousers, and holding it in his hands, felt its warmth after resting next to his skin. Thinking of Sarah having the gun stashed down the front of her trousers made him smile. Sitting in his chair, he pulled open the top draw of his desk, took out a bottle of ink and a quill, then extracted a large book and opened it.

First, he studied the pistol. Turning it over in his hand he could see just how beautiful a gun it was. Small enough for a girl, or woman to handle, although it could do reasonable damage to a man, he didn't think it was any good for hunting large animals. He figured Cole carried it for protection, probably to protect herself from trappers. She was a good-looking woman, and as far as he was aware, the only female on the mountain. She would need to protect herself from any advances the men made toward her. He imagined Sarah would get a lot of proposals.

Vines and leaves covered the long barrel, its chamber plain silver. The grip, made of ivory had exquisite engravings on the sides. The letters SC, engraved below a mountain scene with the sun peeking out behind it graced one side. An engraving of a wolf with the letters FM below it was on the other. Now the letters SC got him thinking. They surely were Cole's initials, but what was her first name? The trappers called her by her last name, and who was FM?' The boy's name was Thomas, so FM didn't make sense. He tagged the pistol with a tag numbered 108 and put it in his desk draw. Remembering he put the bullets for the pistol in his shirt pocket, he dug them out, sat them alongside the pistol, then closed and locked the draw. Christian picked up the quill, and dipping it in ink, wrote the description in the ledger. Number 108 - small .36 calibre pistol, vines and leaves on silver barrel, ivory grip, engravings - mountain and wolf with letters SC and FM - owner S Cole.

Next, he picked up the shotgun Sarah used to shoot the bell rope with. It was a heavy, long, twin barreled gun with a wooden stock, more a man's choice of weapon. Christian wondered how Cole managed to hold it let alone fire it. Carved into the stock were the initials SC making it obvious this gun belonged to the female trapper. Turning the rifle over, Christian frowned when seeing on the other side burnt into the stock the initials CC.

Putting the rifle down, Christian wrote in the ledger, Number 109 - twin barrel shotgun - wooden stock - initials CC and SC - owner S Cole, then tagged it.

The smaller rifle, Cole angrily told him, belonged to Thomas. He felt his face burn again as he thought of his confrontation with Sarah. This rifle would be suitable for a woman to use as well. It had a single barrel and a wooden stock. On one side of the stock was a carving of a wolf and the initials TM carved roughly under it. Now these initials threw Christian completely. He thought Sarah and Thomas were brother and sister, but they had different last names. Thomas for certain was Thomas M and Cole, was either C Cole or S Cole. But because he reckoned the shotgun was a man's weapon, she wasn't C Cole. Besides, the initials SC had been crudely cut into the stock of that rifle, and another thing, Cole carried the pistol inside her pants, and that gun was definitely S Cole's. To Christian none of the initials made sense. 'Maybe' He surmised. 'Thomas and Cole weren't related at all.' Christian turned the rifle over. This side was blank except for two small letters neatly engraved near the bottom of the stock, the same as what was on Sarah's pistol. This rifle once belonging to FM, now belonged to Thomas. Christian wondered just who FM was.

After writing in the ledger - Number 110 – Yager .54 calibre rifle, wooden stock, wolf carved on side, initials TM and FM - owner Thomas M, he tagged this rifle, then picking up both rifles he carried them into the gun-room.

The gun-room had, once upon a time, been one of the jail-cells. The jailhouse used to have four cells now it only had three. After becoming sheriff, Christian reinforced the cell with stone, and to stop anyone from breaking in, installed a heavy door with an enormous steel padlock. The two rifles were locked in this room for safe keeping, along with other rifles and hand-guns that had been handed in.

Chapter Two

The trappers were crowding around outside the Trading Post when Sarah and Thomas walked up. Seeing her horses tethered to the hitching rail where Will tied them, and her skins still loaded on the back of her packhorse, she breathed a sigh of relief. If anyone touched her skins, she wouldn't stand a chance at taking part in 'The Pot.' Every trapper knew the rule about touching anyone else's skins, but that didn't mean one of them might do something to stop her taking part in the competition. If someone other than herself touched her skins she would be disqualified. But there was no rule made to say Will couldn't hold her packhorse for her.

When Sarah's father Calahan, and Joe Jones reckoned there were enough men trapping on the mountain to set up a competition to find out which man was the best trapper, every man wanted to take part, and now each year they put in a portion of the money they got paid for their skins into a pot to be won by the trapper with the most skins. Calahan and Joe made rules and each man had to abide by those rules. The rules state, he has to trap or shoot his wolves himself. He has to skin them, mark them and load them onto his packhorse, that goes for partners as well. These rules apply to Sarah, she is a trapper, and if she wants to take part in the competition she has to abide by those rules. Each year since trapping on her own she stood little chance of winning against the more experienced trappers. Even though she was as good a trapper as any of the men, she had Thomas to think about.

After bringing their skins in, Fess, the man running the Trading Post counts them, gives them a chit so they can be paid, then writes their names on a board out the front so everyone can see who is leading the competition. The only name left to go on the list this year is Sarah's. Sarah has kept the men waiting impatiently for more than two weeks for this day.

Sarah pushed her way through the crush of men. "Hurry it up Cole!" One of the trappers called. "Get your skins in so we know who won the pot!" Another said. "Yeah, hurry it up goddamn it!" Someone else snarled impatiently. "We been waitin long enough to know you ain't got a chance at takin the money!" A bunch of men laughed when they agreed with the man's comment, and the comments kept coming thick and fast.

"Why don't you all just shut the hell up! I will get my skins in when I am good and ready!" Sarah spat back at them. The men muttered their disapproval at being kept waiting as they jostled each other for position as they watched Sarah untie her skins and unload them onto the boardwalk. "Get the goddamn hell back!" she cursed as they came close to her skins. Last year she had to fire her gun over their heads to make them stay back. That year she didn't win the pot either. She was ten skins short and her name was written up somewhere in the middle of the board. Now, she didn't have a gun to threaten the men with, all because the new sheriff took them.

"Any of you touch my skins, damn you, I will use my goddamn knife on you!" Sarah snarled, standing on the boardwalk facing them. Taking her knife out of her sheath she held it up to show she meant what she said. The men knew not to mess with her, but they only stepped back a little, giving her just enough room to pick up her skins.

"Don't worry Cole, we'll hold them back … but hurry it up will you, and get in there!" While holding his arms out wide and pushing the men back, Joe glanced over his shoulder at Sarah. When he said we, Sarah knew Joe meant himself, Will, Garrett, and Fergus.

Thomas stood with the men watching Sarah struggling to pick up her skins. He could see she was tired and wanted to help, but knew she would lose her chance at the pot if he did, and this year he reckoned, she had a good chance of winning with her two white skins.

Holding the skins tight while some still threatened to fall from her grasp, Sarah glanced up at the board with the trapper's names on it. "Whose name is on top?" she asked whoever wanted to answer.

"Whose do you think Cole? Joe's of course!" Reece, one of the trappers standing off to one side said. "I should have known," Sarah muttered, not at all surprised. Joe had been on the mountain the longest and everyone knew he was the best at trapping. He taught a lot of men how to trap. He taught Frank and Frank had become adept at it. Except Joe hadn't stressed enough to Frank about the dangers of trapping alone up in the High Country, and Frank paid with his life for not knowing. Now she and Joe didn't get along as well as they used to.

Sarah carried her first load inside. "Howdy Cole, you're late comin in," Fess drawled as she threw the skins on the table for him to count. "Howdy Fess," she replied, hurrying straight back outside to get a second lot. Her third trip out to her horse, she undid a securely wrapped bundle, then gathered the rest of her skins and carried them inside. "Don't forget to look at this when you finish counting," she said, sitting the bundle on the table.

As the four trappers came through the door behind her, Thomas came rushing in with them, a huge smile on his face, making it obvious he had been getting reacquainted with Joe and the other three men. "There's coffee on the stove if you want it Cole," Fess offered, going to the table where Sarah's skins were to count them. Sarah went over to the fire and poured herself a mug of coffee. While waiting for Fess to start counting, Joe and the other three men crowded around the stove with her. "How do you think you went this year Sarah?" Joe only ever called her Sarah when he wasn't angry with her. "I think I did alright ...this time," Sarah said, taking a mouthful of coffee. It tasted good, smooth and creamy, just how she liked it.

Swallowing it in gulps, she poured herself another.

"You shouldn't have stayed behind so long ...you know we were worried about you," Joe said, standing opposite her.

"We? ...or just you Joe? ...I told you not to worry about me." Sarah looked into her mug before putting the mug up to her mouth.

"We were all worried about you Sarah lass," Fergus put in. Will and Garrett, standing quietly beside the fire warming their hands, both nodded in agreement.

Not appreciating Sarah's attitude toward them, Joe started to get angry with her. "What about Thomas Sarah? Don't you ever think about him other than yourself? What about the dangers you could have put him in?"

"I think about him all the time Joe!" Sarah snapped. "And don't you go starting with me! I've had one hell of a day!" Feeling tired and worn, it wouldn't take much more after Sarah's run in with the bell-ringer and the sheriff to make her mad, she hoped the coffee would pick her up.

"We had wolves chase us uncle Joe, we had to ride for our lives, Ma hasn't had any sleep since..." Thomas smiled up at Joe, excited to tell him about the wolves and him shooting one, but he didn't get to finish what he wanted to tell Joe before Sarah cut him off. "Thomas don't!" she snapped sharply. Thomas looked over at Sarah, his smile fading. Putting his head down, he didn't say another word. Joe glared at Sarah for scolding Thomas. "Goddamn it! Cole! you don't travel alone, you hear? and don't you go putting Thomas in danger!" Joe pointed his finger at Sarah in anger. Not having had much sleep worrying about Sarah and Thomas still on the mountain when he and the other men had come down safely, he was tired too. "Next time you may not be so fucking lucky!" When confronting Sarah, Joe hardly ever cursed, he raised his voice, but never cursed, so when Joe suddenly cursed, Sarah knew he was tired and angry. Joe went on scolding Sarah until he got interrupted by Fess yelling. "Whooee! Look at this here! Holy jumpin coyote!" Everyone's attention turned to Fess.

"What is it Fess?" Joe asked, going to the table to take a look at what he was hollering about. "Look at this Joe! take a good look at this!" Fess said sounding excited, and laughing out loud, slapped his hand on his leg. "Come take a look boy's, look at what Cole's brought in!" The three men followed Joe to the table where they stood crowded together with their backs to Sarah and Thomas. Sarah stayed by the fire drinking her coffee, and when Thomas looked at her, she winked at him. Knowing his Ma didn't mean anything bad by scolding him, he immediately forgot about it, and smiled back at her. Both knew what the men were looking at. "Shit!" Sarah heard Garrett say. "Fuck!" Fergus cursed, lowering his voice. The men tried talking amongst themselves, but Sarah heard them mention the pot. "If this don't beat all!" Will said sounding happy about what he was looking at.

"Yep, they sure beat em alright!" Fess said, laughing out loud again. Joe went back to Sarah. "So that's why you stayed behind?" He knew she beat him and won the pot, but he wasn't about to congratulate her, he was still angry with her for staying behind and putting her and Thomas's lives at risk. She was a trapper just like the rest of them and should know the dangers. Deep down he was happy she finally won, but he wasn't going to admit that to her. "That's right Joe, some things just take time." Sarah turned her back on him and finished her coffee. Not pleased about her turning her back on him, Joe stormed to the door.

"Fess, write Cole's name up so everyone can stop waiting and wondering!" Reverting back to calling her Cole, treating her as an equal with the rest of the men, he pulled the door open savagely and storming out, slammed the door closed behind him.

Fergus and Garrett smiled and congratulated Sarah on her win. Smiling, Will leant toward her and whispered, "congratulations, I'm happy you won," then gave her a wink, and still smiling, all three men filed out behind Joe. Sarah heard them telling the men waiting outside, "Cole got two white skins and won the pot!" There were shouts of disbelief mixed with cursing, but all in all the men were pleased Sarah had finally beaten Joe.

Going over to the fire, Fess handed Sarah her chits for the bank. "You got a good thousand for your skins Cole, and here's the chit for the pot." Fess wasn't sure how much money was in the pot being held at the bank, all he knew was, it could be equal to a thousand dollars. "Goddamn if that don't beat all! I'm glad you finally got it Cole." Fess stood in front of the fire next to Sarah and rubbed his hands together.

"Thanks Fess, I figured I didn't have a hope of winning with the greys I got, but when I got the whites, I knew I had a chance …I didn't know if anyone else had been lucky to get whites too though." Fess ruffled Thomas's hair. "No-one got any whites, you are the only one, your Ma did good, didn't she Thomas?" Fess continued to talk to Sarah before Thomas could answer. "Wouldn't have mattered how many greys you got Cole, you would win the pot with a white skin every time, I better go write your name up on that board and put those men out of their misery, and you better get those chits to the bank."

After thanking Fess for the coffee, Sarah and Thomas followed him out the front where they watched him write her name on the board above all the other names.

It didn't matter to Sarah what Fess was writing, just knowing he was writing above Joe at the top made her feel good. Some men called, "congratulations Cole," as they walked away. Samuels though hung back. "Thanks," Sarah said, after he congratulated her. Samuels in past years had proposed marriage to Sarah, but felt afraid to ask again after she turned him down last time. Having witnessed the beating Logan received from Joe when he tried helping himself to Sarah in her shelter, was warning enough for him to stay away from her. Samuels staying behind gave Sarah the feeling he wanted to say something else, but after a moment of hesitation, Samuels tipped his hat and stepping off the boardwalk, walked away with a group of men.

Feeling a little overwhelmed by the attention she was receiving, gave rise to thoughts that some of the men weren't too bad, but there were those she was dubious about, especially Logan, who was still making advances toward her on the sly. Sarah unhitched her horses and put her arm around Thomas's shoulders. Their next stop was Morley's Bank.

Chapter Three

Thomas held the door to the bank open and letting Sarah go in first, had to stop when Sarah pulled up in front of him. Looking through dim light toward the counter, Sarah's mouth fell open at seeing a stranger standing behind it, the likes of which she had never seen before.

He was young, maybe around the same age Frank had been when she met him. This stranger looked like he came straight from a big city. His hair was red and his face was covered in freckles. He wore a high-collared shirt. A cravat was tied around his neck and he wore a black coat. He didn't look like he should be standing behind Morley's counter. He looked more like he should own the whole bank. Sarah hoped that wasn't the case, she didn't want to have to do business with a total stranger. Morley knew her and she liked it when he helped her with her account.

Feeling wary of the young man, Sarah put her hand on her knife as she always did when threatened. When the young man saw Sarah enter the bank, his eyes went immediately to her hand, and watching her wide eyed stammered, "m ...m... may I ...h ...help you?" with either surprise or fright, Sarah couldn't tell which.

"Where is Morley?" she asked, keeping her eyes firmly fixed on the stranger. Thomas stayed behind Sarah, letting her handle this new situation. "Mister Morley is busy, may I help you?" The young man repeated, his mouth suddenly going dry.

Pulling her knife quickly from its sheath and striding across the floor toward him, "no! you can't!" she said a bit too sharply. Having dealt with two strangers already, she was not happy. Here she was having to deal with a third, making her wonder, just how many more strangers had come to town since last winter and what else could possibly happen. All she wanted was to get her chits in, get some cash so she could get her supplies and set up camp. The day was getting away from her and she was so damn tired, she didn't know how much more she could take. "What have you done with Mister Morley? You son-of-a …a …goddamn!" Sarah stopped herself short of cursing, but felt she wasn't going to take any more trouble from anyone.

The young man stepped quickly away from the counter and held up his hands in surrender. After calmly dealing with nineteen wild looking trappers when they came to the bank, he wasn't prepared for this equally wild looking woman and boy that suddenly appeared in front of him. "Mister Morley! Mister Morley!" he shouted at the top of his lungs. "Mister...!" He stopped yelling abruptly when Morley came rushing out of his office to see what the commotion was.

"What the blazes is the trouble! ...Sarah! Thomas!" Morley smiled broadly when he saw Sarah and Thomas standing in the middle of his bank. "Well, how are you both? you certainly took your time coming to town." Morley looked over at the young man behind the counter and waved his hand in dismissal. "Michael, put down your hands, Sarah won't hurt you ...maybe you should put that thing away!" he nodded, looking wide eyed at Sarah's knife.

Sarah put her knife back in its sheath, and stepping up to Morley, stretched her arms out wide to take in Morley's huge belly. Morley wrapped his huge arms around her, and Sarah almost disappeared in Morley's hug. Seeing it was obvious they knew each other well, Michael stepped back to the counter and watched the exchange between the wild woman and Morley. When Morley let Sarah go, he gave Thomas a bear hug too. Lifting him off the ground caused Sarah and Thomas both to laugh when Thomas disappeared completely in Morley's embrace.

Lewis Morley was a huge man who wore a neatly coiffured beard all of the time, and his moustache curled up at the ends. In all the year's Sarah had known Morley she had never heard him curse or seen his hair unruly, and he was always impeccably dressed.

Morley's family lived in Cedar Creek for as long as Sarah could remember, arriving when the town was just starting to flourish. Trapping had taken off and the Fur Trading Company needed a bank to handle their business, so Morley, a teller in Boston at the time, volunteered to start up a bank using a makeshift tent. When the Lumber Yard commenced trading, and houses were required, timber hewn from cedar trees and various other trees growing plentiful along the river were used to build the very first commercial building, which was Morley's bank, and Morley was proud of it. As the town grew, men found work all year round, and Morley held their accounts in his bank. Morley and his wife Esther, raised their young family of four children, three boys and one girl, in a beautiful little town on the edge of a river where land was fertile and where several farms had begun to produce crops. Produce grown on the farms kept the town supplied with fresh food all year round.

The Morley's children are all grown up now and have left town to make their own way, spreading out all across the country. Morley and Sarah's father had done business together and Morley's wife Esther was a friendly woman whom Sarah had come to like. Whenever Sarah came to town she often visited with the Morley's at their home, just like her and her Pa had done many times before. Sarah didn't mind it when Morley called her Sarah, he was a friendly jolly giant of a man.

Morley introduced Sarah to Michael. "Imagine how pleased I was to find he once worked in a bank in Chicago and is very good with money, I employed him as my teller straight away, he will be able to attend to all your needs." Morley stepped up to the counter. "Michael, get Cole's book and the Fur Trading Company ledger please." Michael hurriedly found the two books and opened them up on the counter. Sarah handed Morley her two chits. "Goddamn Sarah! you won the pot!" Morley's smile grew wide at being surprised by Sarah finally beating the men, but before Sarah could speak, Thomas piped up. "Sure did, Mister Morley! Ma got two whites! that's why we were late coming to town, they beat everyone's skins!"

"Well good for you …Michael, write Sarah's chit in her book for her greys, deduct a thousand from the Fur Trading Company ledger, then write up another thousand in Sarah's book with the word 'Pot' beside it. Sarah, how much cash would you like to take?"

Morley was all business when it came to money, and Sarah was feeling too tired to know how much money she needed.

"I don't know! I want to get Thomas some new clothes, he is growing so fast, what would you suggest Morley?" Sarah didn't think she might need new clothing, the shirt she was wearing was almost threadbare. She searched Morley's eyes for his answer.

"How about a hundred, that ought to do for now, if you need any more you can come in and get it anytime." Morley reached out his hand to Michael and snapped his fingers. Michael reached into a draw behind the counter and took out two bills.

"I reckon that would do, thanks Morley," Sarah agreed. When Michael handed Sarah the two bills, Sarah noticed how Michael's hands were shaking and frowned. She didn't think she was that scary. "You need to sign your name in your book Sarah," he said, pushing the book toward her. When Sarah suddenly glared at him, Michael looked at her nervously, his eyes going wide at the sudden realization he made a mistake thinking he was entitled to call her Sarah. "I don't sign! …and my name is Cole!" Sarah informed him curtly, her hand going to her knife again, only this time as a matter of habit. Morley ignored Sarah telling Michael he was to call her Cole. Michael looked to Morley for support but got none. He wondered why Morley was able to call this wild woman standing in front of him and commanding the floor Sarah, when she insisted on him calling her Cole. Michael felt offended, after all, he considered himself as good a man as Lewis Morley, and demanded respect for himself, but he thought it best to keep quiet, at least for now, he didn't like the look of that big knife, and he certainly didn't want Cole waving it at him.

"Sarah it is bank policy that when you take money out you sign for it, that way we know you are the person who took your money and not someone else, just make your mark like you always do." Sarah hadn't understood what Michael meant by signing, but when Morley explained it was the same as making her mark, she felt more at ease. Morley turned the book around and Sarah made a rough snake like 'S' near where Michael indicated.

"How is Esther these days Morley? Last time I was here she wasn't feeling the best." Not liking to rush out of the bank as soon as she had her money, Sarah asked after Morley's wife as a matter of politeness, even so, she felt her mood could have been better.

"Esther is fine, if I remember when you were here last, she only had an upset stomach, I'll let her know you have arrived, she'll look forward to a visit I'm sure." Sarah didn't want to commit herself by saying she would visit straight away, there was a lot to do before she could get around to visiting friends. "I will visit with Esther as soon as I can, right now I have to get our supplies and set up camp." Thomas didn't mind that Morley had his arm around his shoulders. Walking Sarah and Thomas to the door, Morley ruffled Thomas's hair, and bid them farewell. Once they left the bank, they made their way up the street to Crawley's General Store.

When Michael was sure Sarah and Thomas wouldn't be coming back, he called Morley over to the counter. "Mister Morley, have you had a look at that woman's book?" he said without a hint of fear in his voice. Thinking perhaps he should have dealt with Sarah's account himself, Morley snapped. "Michael! that is confidential!" "But Mister Morley she is a rich..."

"*Michael!*" Morley snapped again, cutting him off. "Cole's book is of no concern of yours, it is strictly to be kept quiet, you hear me, *nothing* about Cole, is to leave this bank! *ever*! or you will surely face the consequences!" Knowing if anything were to be leaked about Sarah's account the trappers would have his skin, Morley made his eyes round as he glared at Michael. "Yes sir, Mister Morley!" Michael muttered in response to Morley yelling at him.

When Morley went back to his office and closed the door, Michael studied Sarah's book more thoroughly. Noting the deposits that had been entered each year, going back fourteen years, not only from Sarah's own trapping, but from others, Michael scratched his head and wondered why each year, nineteen men deducted a sum of money from their own accounts and deposited it in Sarah's account. Morley knew why, he had been privy to setting Sarah's account up.

The night Calahan Cole gambled everything on a game of poker the stakes were high. When Sarah's father died his account had been cleaned out and closed. Calahan lost the game and everything he worked for. Calahan and Sarah's home and all his money went to Benjamin Crawley, leaving Sarah with just the cabin on the mountain. The money the trappers put in her account was there to help her survive when her own trapping wasn't doing so well, and when she had Thomas, the men continued putting money in her account to help her raise him. Joe swore Morley and the trappers to secrecy. Sarah was never to find out what the men were doing. Michael didn't know the story, and Morley wasn't about to tell him. Sarah, Michael was told, was the only female on the mountain and his thoughts right then were of another more undesirable possibility.

Sarah was unaware she had the money. As far as she knew, her account only held what she earnt from her skins. She was frugal when spending her money, buying only what she thought necessary for her and Thomas to survive.

Michael stared at the balance at the bottom of the page. Sarah Cole was a very rich woman, making him wonder why a woman with so much money only took one hundred dollars to live on and had to camp on the riverbank.

Chapter Four

Christian had been back in the Sheriff's Office a couple of hours. After tagging Sarah's guns, he stored them in the gun-room and started to pour himself some coffee when his deputy came charging in out of breath. "Sheriff, you better come quick!" Clem's chest heaved as he tried to catch his breath. "There's trouble …over at Crawley's," he puffed. Christian tried to calm him down. "Slow down Clem, what kind of trouble?" Clem took a deep breath and not stopping to tell Christian what kind of trouble was happening, expecting Christian to stop doing whatever it was he was doing and follow him, he started back out the door.

Clem was glad he wasn't sheriff any more, he was only too pleased to have passed trouble Sarah created over to Christian. "You better come now, there is no way I can stop it, you are the sheriff, you have to put a stop to it!" By the time he stepped off the boardwalk, he had stopped talking. Christian put down the coffee pot and his mug, grabbed his hat off the stand behind the door and followed Clem outside. Clem was halfway across the street when Christian caught up to him.

"What is going on Clem? Who did you say is causing trouble in the store?" Christian lifted his gun up and down in his holster a couple of times as he walked quickly along the street beside Clem. Clem kept up his pace, although he was getting on in years and had a limp, his limp didn't slow him down any, when he got going, he could move.

When Christian first came to Cedar Creek, he was curious about the men that trapped wolves, but after being there a few days, he thought the town was just another dead-end town he would simply pass through. Until four cowhands became boisterous and started a punch up in the saloon.

Sheriff Clementine tried to break up the fight, but was finding it beyond him. Because his wife was ill, Clem no longer had the heart for being sheriff. Finding it impossible to have a quiet drink, Christian stepped in to help Clem get two of the men to the jailhouse to sober up overnight. Clem thanked Christian for his help, and straight away asked him to take over his job as sheriff. Christian thought about taking the job for all of two minutes, thinking, how much trouble could there possibly be in such a small town? so he accepted the job. Grateful when Christian agreed to take his place, the two men worked together to find a replacement to be Christian's deputy, but unable to find anyone, Christian asked Clem to stay on as deputy until such time as he could find someone that wanted the job, and Clem agreed.

Needing to find out what kind of man Clem was, especially how good he was with a gun, Christian took him out to the dry gulch behind Major Hardy's land, where he tested Clem's eyesight by stacking bottles on tree stumps, and Clem, firing a shot at each bottle, didn't miss a single one. Sticking out his tongue, he took careful aim, then shot a twig off a tree that was barely visible to the naked eye. Although Clem wasn't fast at the draw, he held his own with straight shooting. Clem was an amicable man, and during the eight months Christian lived in Cedar Creek they had become friends.

Hurrying toward Crawley's store, Christian thought Clem hadn't heard him when he asked who was causing trouble, so after asking him again, didn't expect the answer he got. "It's Cole! goddamn it!" Clem slowed down as they drew nearer the store. "That woman causes trouble every time she comes to town, especially where Crawley is concerned!" Surprised to learn it was Cole Christian cursed. "Shit!" But he shouldn't have been surprised, he had the feeling earlier on that Cole and he were going to clash again, he just didn't think it would be this soon.

Christian and Clem reached the store to find a small group of men and women outside looking annoyed while waiting to get inside to get their supplies. Four horses stood tied to the hitching rail out front, one still heavily packed with its load. Loud cursing and name calling could be heard coming from inside. Stepping quickly onto the boardwalk, Christian grabbed hold of the door. "You stay here Clem, and keep everyone out!" he said over his shoulder. Just about to enter the store, he spotted Thomas leaning against the wall with his arms folded and his legs crossed. Christian and Thomas stared at each other, but while neither spoke, Christian frowned and wondered about the look Thomas was giving him, then shrugging slightly, pulled open the screen door, and stepped inside.

As he stepped inside, Sarah and Crawley could be heard hurling abuse at each other. "Get the hell out of my store Cole, you goddamn stinking whore, every time you come in here something gets broken, if you think I'm going to give you supplies, you are fucking mistaken!" Crawley closed his mouth when he saw Christian.

Inside the store, everything was covered in what looked like a fine layer of snow. Confronted by a mess, Christian ran his hand over a shelf just inside the door, then rubbing his fingers together, was able to tell the snow like substance was flour. Flour covered everything in the vicinity of the counter, including Crawley. His hair was covered, his face, his clothes, even the counter was white. Christian looked over to where Sarah was standing. Although her hat didn't have flour on it, flour balanced precariously across the bridge of her nose. Christian figured she must have shaken the flour off her hat but didn't know she still had flour on her face. When Sarah saw Christian, she quickly removed her hand off her knife and stepped back from the counter.

Produce lay scattered about the floor. Potatoes rested against the counter where they rolled, and bunches of carrots were tipped onto the floor off a stand where onions and other produce were on show. A tray of eggs hadn't been disturbed. 'Thank goodness,' Christian thought. 'If they had been knocked over, they would have made one hell of a mess.' After taking a quick looking around, Christian stepped between the counter and Sarah. Sarah started yelling back at Crawley who remained safely behind his counter. "You better give me my supplies, you murdering, thieving maggot, you …slimy river scum, give me my supplies or I'll…"

"That's enough Cole!" Christian demanded, putting one hand on his hip, and the other on his gun. Straightening himself up to his full height to show Sarah he meant business, he felt a sudden jolt rush through his body when she looked into his eyes. Now the two of them were inside out of the sun, he could look more closely at her. However, he couldn't take his eyes off the flour balancing on her nose. Even though Sarah's face was flushed pink from arguing with Crawley, the flour didn't budge, making Christian feel tempted to reach up and brush it off.

Sarah looked closely at Christian, thinking it must have been the sun blinding her when she looked at his face outside the schoolhouse. She thought him handsome at the time, but now they were inside out of the sun, she could see he was more handsome than she first thought.

"Tell me what is going on ..." Christian paused, but kept gazing at Sarah. Sarah opened her mouth to answer, but he beat her to it when he said. "Crawley?" Sarah shut her mouth, and pressing her lips tight in a scowl, kept her eyes firmly fixed on Christian's face.

"This bitch, mountain whore...!" Crawley started, making Christian cringe at hearing what he called Sarah. Sarah didn't like what Crawley called her either. As her face flushed a deeper pink, she suddenly lunged around Christian, and tried to jump the counter. Scrambling Christian grabbed her by the back of her fur coat, and stretched his arm across the front of her. "You son-of-a-bitch Crawley! you are nothing but a murdering, thieving, maggot!" Sarah yelled. When Crawley dived away from the counter, his back smashed into the shelves behind him, causing the shelves to shake violently, sending several large tins falling dangerously close to his head. They narrowly missed his shoulders and crashed loudly onto the floor, then rolled behind the counter. "This bitch trapper comes in here every winter and destroys my store! I don't want her in here sheriff, you do what you get paid to do and keep her out!" Crawley snarled, kicking the tins when they rolled against his feet.

"Why is that you stinking slimy...? I will gladly get out of your rotten stinking store, just as soon as you give me my supplies!" Sarah was so angry at Crawley she couldn't think what else to call him.

"I don't have to give you anything Cole, I own everything in here! there is no way I will give you anything after the way you come barging in and destroy everything!" Crawley continued his rant by telling her to go to Moreton for her supplies. Sarah replied, saying she would not be going all the way to Moreton, and she would take what she wanted, whether he liked it or not. They continued speaking vehemently back and forth until Christian had had enough.

"Shut up the both of you!" he yelled, loud enough so everyone outside could hear. Both Sarah and Crawley shut their mouths and glared at him. Thomas straightened up. He was used to his Ma and Crawley going head to head, but curious to see what the sheriff was doing, peered in through the store window to see Christian's arm, across the front of Sarah, the only thing keeping her from getting at Crawley.

"He's got my money! ...right there!" she said pointing to the counter "My money is as good as anyone's ...isn't it?" Sarah looked up at Christian hoping for support, her dark blue eyes questioning. Christian felt his knees going weak when he looked back at her.

"That's right Cole, your money is as good as anyone's, I'll tell you what is going to happen." Moving Sarah back a few steps, he folded his arms, then, while continuing to look at her, addressed Crawley.

"Crawley! ...Cole is going to tell you what supplies she needs ... without cursing ...or name calling ...and you, are going to get them for her, then ...you will take Cole's money and give Cole her change ...then she will leave your store ...quietly ...agreed?" Christian kept his arms folded and his back to Crawley while waiting for him to answer. It took a moment for Crawley to agree. Even so, Crawley sounded defeated when he answered, "agreed sheriff!"

Satisfied with Crawley's answer, and keeping his eyes on Sarah, Christian addressed her. "Now, Cole! ...you are going to tell Crawley what supplies you want ...without cursing or name calling ...and Crawley will get them for you ...he will take your money and give you your change, then you will leave his store ...you curse ... or call him names while getting your supplies ...I will stop you and make you leave without your supplies ...agreed?" Christian's arms remained folded while waiting for Sarah to answer. He waited, and he waited some more.

"Cole," he said, still waiting for her answer. Sarah was looking at him but didn't seem to be seeing him. Christian felt his body growing warm. Colour rose on his face.

"Cole!" he said a little louder this time.

"I'm thinking!" Sarah suddenly snapped. After a moment more of hesitation, she spoke purposefully.

"Sheriff ...you mean ...I can't call Crawley a murdering, thieving, maggot?" Sarah stared into Christian's eyes. Christian felt his stomach flutter. Unable to help the way he was starting to feel, he looked into Sarah's deep blue eyes when he answered. "No, you can't."

"I can't call him ...a slimy snake?"

"No."

"What about mangy coyote?" Sarah's eyes sparkled while daring to name call. By asking Christian if she could not call Crawley names, she was getting away with calling him names. By the time he realized Sarah was toying with him Christian was feeling hot.

"Nope!" he said, watching Sarah's eyes crinkle at the corners when knowing her own cunning. Catching on to what she was doing, his mouth curled ever so slightly at the corners. Crawley's name calling had been disgusting, and Christian didn't think it necessary or appropriate so he thought it only fair she should get away with calling Crawley names. "What about creepy maggot guts? I can't call him that either I suppose?" Sarah added for good measure.

"No, Cole, you can't ...now, are you going to agree to my terms? or do you want to leave without your supplies?" Christian said unfolding his arms, after all, he could only let her go so far. "Well Cole, what do you say?"

After another tense moment Sarah quietly answered, "I agree." Christian sighed with relief. Finally, he felt he could get on with getting this mess sorted out and the people waiting outside could come in to get their supplies.

But before starting to get her supplies, Sarah stepped around Christian and went to the door. While watching her carefully for another attempt to get at Crawley, she suddenly called for Thomas to come inside. Thomas came hurrying in and Christian listened carefully as she spoke to him. "Go get yourself a pair of trousers, and a shirt, and see if there are any boots that will fit you, make sure you can wriggle your toes in them, and don't take too long, we have a lot to do before dark." Without saying a word, Thomas disappeared into the far reaches of Crawley's store. Back at the counter, Sarah began telling Crawley what supplies she wanted. Crawley picked up a sack to put Sarah's supplies in and Christian moved out of the way to watch the exchange.

"I want coffee, sugar, milk powder, dripping, treacle, a couple of tins of those peaches from off the floor." Sarah rattled off a whole lot more things, making Crawley rush around getting each item and writing the cost down on a piece of paper. While Crawley was busy writing, Sarah picked potatoes up off the floor, sat some on the counter and the rest back on the stand from where they had fallen. Crawley wrote them down on the list and put them in the sack. Christian watched as Sarah picked up a bunch of carrots and put them on the counter. She picked up the rest and stacked them back on their stand. Apples and onions were placed in front of Crawley. Crawley wrote the cost on the list and they went in the sack. As Sarah made her selections, Crawley had to get another sack for all the supplies to fit, and Christian kept watching. Sarah didn't pay him or Crawley any attention as she rummaged through iron pots and tins. Finding a tin pot with a handle and a lid, she lifted the lid, looked inside, then held the tin up to show Crawley. He wrote it down on the list.

Sarah stood in front of the tray of eggs. "I want some of these eggs," she said out loud. Crawley didn't look up from the counter where he was busy writing. "How many eggs you getting Cole?" he asked. When she didn't answer he looked up. "I want this many," Sarah said pointing along a row. "One dozen eggs," Crawley said and wrote them down. "One dozen eggs," Sarah repeated. Christian frowned. Sarah started carefully putting the eggs in the tin. When she was up to the second last egg on the row, she picked it up and it slipped out of her fingers and smashed on the floor. *"Son-of-a-*

bitch!" she cursed loudly. Crawley's head shot up quickly, and he glanced across at Christian. Christian glanced over at Crawley, then looked at Sarah. She had been warned if she cursed or name called, she would be out of the store without her supplies. Sarah's back stiffened and she froze on the spot. Christian looked at the egg laying smashed on the floor. The store was deathly quiet. Sarah waited, Crawley waited, Christian, while deep in thought, waited.

Deciding Sarah was not name calling, he let her continue. "It's alright Crawley, Cole was cursing herself for dropping the egg, keep going Cole." Sarah and Crawley continued on with their tasks although Crawley looked unhappy about the fact Christian let Sarah get away with cursing. Sarah picked up the last egg in the row then took one from the next row to make up for the one she broke. She carried the tin over to the counter.

"Is that the lot Cole?" Crawley asked her. "I'm not sure yet, I'll have to check, you can get me a bag of that candy." She pointed to the candy jars sitting further along the counter. Getting a paper bag, Crawley quickly scooped several scoops of candy into it. Christian watched as Crawley wrote the cost down and placed the bag on the counter.

"How you doing in there Thomas? You got your trousers and shirt yet?" Sarah made her voice rise a little so Thomas could hear her. Christian, standing back near shelves full of produce with his arms folded, heard Thomas's reply clearly.

"Got em Ma! ...but still tryin on boots!" Christian felt his stomach lurch. 'Thomas just called Cole Ma!' That Cole was Thomas's mother was the last thing he expected. Unfolding his arms, he let them hang by his sides, thinking surely, he must be mistaken. Studying Sarah more intently, he tried to gauge her age. 'Cole is far too young to be the boy's mother' In fact earlier today, when he was lying on the street with her hovering between his legs, he thought her far too young for him to be interested in. At the time, he never thought she could be the boy's mother, now trying to figure out just how old Sarah must be, he figured she would be close to the same age as himself.

"Hurry it up then will you!" Sarah called. "We have to get going or it will be dark before we get our camp set up!" As Sarah returned to the counter and Crawley, she looked fleetingly at Christian and wondered why he was watching her so closely. The flour still balanced precariously across her nose and Christian felt his heart skip a beat when she looked at him.

Thomas came from the other side of the store carrying the shirt and trousers in one hand and his old boots in the other. "Will these do Ma?" he said, wearing the new boots. Christian hadn't been mistaken. 'Goddamn!' he thought, 'Thomas *is* Cole's son!' Christian watched Sarah kick the front of the boots with her foot.

"Can you wriggle your toes?"

"Yeah Ma! they fit good!"

"Ok then, they will do, go get yourself some socks …and be quick!"

Thomas looked like Cole, but being solidly built, Christian imagined he took after his father for that. Standing back, he took in the both of them standing at the counter with their backs to him, giving him an opportunity to study them more closely. When leaning toward each other, whispering, they both leant on the counter the same way.

"Have you got everything Cole?" Crawley asked. Sarah leant in close to Thomas and said quiet loudly. "What do you think Thomas? Have I got everything?"

"I don't know Ma …what did you get?" Thomas asked nonchalantly.

"Well …let …me …see!" Sarah started naming everything slowly. Crawley watched them with his lips pressed tightly together, fuming because they were deliberately wasting his time. "Come on Cole! hurry it up!" he said looking over Sarah's head to Christian as if to ask for help. Christian stood silently by and let them continue. The longer they took, the longer he could study Sarah.

"I know!" Sarah suddenly exclaimed. "I did forget something!" Running her hand along the counter, she scooped up flour, lifted her hand up to her mouth, held it open, then blew the flour off her palm so the flour floated toward Crawley. Crawley coughed and fanned his hand to wave away the cloud. "I need a bag of flour!" Sarah announced proudly. Crawley scowled at Sarah and called for Henry his helper to bring him a bag of flour. When Henry came from the storeroom carrying a large bag, Sarah and Thomas greeted him pleasantly, then looked at each other and giggled, pleased because they fooled Crawley again. Crawley brought the bag of flour to the counter and angrily shoved it in Sarah's bag.

"That's all Crawley, how much do I owe you?" Sarah turned serious again. "And don't you go cheating me!" she added for good measure. Crawley could fool her about money but he couldn't fool Thomas. Thomas had schooling and knew how to add up and take away. Crawley added up the cost on his list and told Sarah the amount, then taking one of the bank notes off the counter, worked out the change and put the change on the counter in front of her. At that moment Clem stuck his head through the door to see how everything was progressing. "How is it in here sheriff? a lot of folk are waiting to get in for supplies." Christian opened his mouth to answer but before he could, Sarah answered Clem herself.

"We won't be much longer Clem …Thomas and I are just about done here." Glancing at Christian, Sarah blushed, then turned back to the counter.

"That's good …um …Cole." Clem looked across at Christian, raised his eyebrows then pulled his head back out the door and closed it.

Christian watched Sarah slide her change off the counter and shove it in her pants pocket. Then watched as they picked up a bag of supplies each and headed for the door. Holding the door open, Christian addressed Thomas as he stepped outside. "Your Ma will be along in a moment Thomas, she has something else to do first." Before Thomas could protest, Christian shut the door and stood in front of Sarah, baring her way out.

The sack of supplies was already heavy and the bag of flour wasn't helping. Holding the sack with both arms stretched out in front of her, Sarah just wanted to get going and glared at Christian. "What now sheriff?"

"Crawley has a bag of flour spread all over his store, and a broken egg that he can't sell …you busted that bag of flour and broke that egg …so you have to pay for them." Christian looked over Sarah's head to Crawley. "Crawley, how much for a bag of flour and one egg?" Looking back at Sarah, he waited for Crawley to tell him how much he wanted for his damaged goods. Sarah was not happy and scowled up at him.

To get back at Sarah for name calling and the damage she caused, Crawley upped the price of the flour and egg. "A dime for the flour and a nickel for the egg, fifteen cents all up sheriff." Happy when thinking Cole wasn't going to get away with the damage she caused, Crawley almost sniggered out loud. He looked over at Christian and smirked.

Thinking the price was a bit too steep, Christian made his own decision about what to charge Sarah. Standing in the doorway with his arms folded so Sarah couldn't leave, he said. "You need to give Crawley a dime Cole." Crawley scowled at the both of them, disgusted and not happy he hadn't got away with overcharging Sarah after all.

Sarah wasn't happy she had to pay Crawley at all for the damaged goods. "Fine!" she huffed, carrying the heavy sack back to the counter and plonking it down. Digging around in her pants pocket, she pulled out all the crumpled notes and coins and tossed them onto the counter. "You take your dime Crawley! and hurry up so I can get out of here!" Crawley shuffled through the money, found a dime and shoved the money back across the counter. "Alright Cole, now get the hell out!" he barked. Sarah grabbed her money, shoved it hurriedly back into her pocket, picked up her sack of supplies and headed back to Christian waiting at the door. What Crawley said next shocked Christian to the core. "You keep that whore bitch and her bastard son out of my store sheriff, those two aren't welcome here ...not unless you come with them."

While Christian held the door open, Sarah came to an abrupt stop beside him, her face bright red with embarrassment at Crawley's disparaging words. Christian didn't blame her, even he was shocked by what Crawley said. Sarah was embarrassed, Crawley called her a whore plenty of times before and it never bothered her. Christian distinctly heard what Crawley called her, and for some reason she couldn't figure out right then, she didn't want him thinking she was one. Still, she managed to reply before she left the store.

"Lucky my hands are full …you …slimy horse turd, cause my knife would look real pretty sticking out of your rotten maggot filled guts." Before glaring back at Crawley, Christian put his hand in the middle of Sarah's back and shoved her out the door. He had believed Crawley to be one of the better upstanding citizens of Cedar Creek. Since coming to town, he had enjoyed being invited to dinner with Crawley and his daughter Millicent many times, but this was a new side to Crawley he hadn't seen before. Christian let the door slam shut behind him.

Once outside, Christian thought he might help Sarah with her supplies. After sitting the tin with the eggs and the bag of candy on the boardwalk, Sarah hoisted the sack onto the back of one of her horses. Thomas's supplies were hanging on one of the packhorses already, and before Christian could help Sarah, he hurried over to help her. Christian however, wasn't ready to leave, not until he found out what was going on between Sarah and Crawley. "What just happened in there Cole? What was all that trouble between you and Crawley about?" Only Sarah's answers were elusive.

"What trouble sheriff?" Sarah didn't look up at Christian while she fastened a rope around the supplies to keep them on the back of her horse.

"You know what trouble I mean! … all that cursing and name calling in there?" He wanted to know why a woman had gotten into an argument with the only store keeper for hundreds of miles. Crawley's was the only place any of the town folk could get supplies. Supply wagons came to Cedar Creek only once every few months. It was a two-week horse ride to the nearest city of Moreton and Christian was sure none of these people wanted to have to go there. He was sure Cole wouldn't want to ride all the way to Moreton to get her supplies either.

"Nothing for you to worry about sheriff," Sarah replied, glancing over at a group of children milling about. All of them were well known to everyone. Some were old enough to attend school, but their parents didn't seem to care if they were educated or not. No-one worried about them hanging about town on their own.

"Any disturbance in this town is something for me to worry about Cole." Christian wanted answers, but he wasn't getting anywhere.

Sarah grabbed the bag of candy and handed it to Thomas. Thomas opened the bag and started passing it around to the children who eagerly dug their hands inside and helped themselves to a sweet. "Crawley and I just don't get along …that's all, it isn't anything for you to worry about," Sarah repeated, tying the rope tighter.

Before replying to Sarah's not caring about what happened in the store, Sarah turned her back on Christian, making him feel frustrated by her attitude toward his authority. "Well, if I have to go with you every time you need supplies Cole! it is not nothing! …it is something! …I am not here for your beck and call!" A little girl with long braids, her leg in a brace and on crutches came hobbling up to Sarah. "Hey Becky …my …haven't you grown? must be three or four inches since Thomas and I were here last winter." As Sarah squatted to speak to the little girl, Christian couldn't help notice the change in her attitude as well as how her voice had softened, she no longer sounded like the trapper she appeared to be when she first arrived in town. The little girl smiled at Sarah as she sucked on a candy.

"Cole, we heard you got two white skins and won the pot." One of the boys standing next to Becky said. Sarah was well aware news travelled fast in Cedar Creek. News about her and Frank being together out of wedlock spread quickly. Over the years her hatred toward Crawley for what he did to her father never waned, and everyone knew she would never give Crawley any peace while ever she was in town. Other than that, Sarah tried keeping herself away from gossip and trouble.

"That's right Sam, I did, why don't all of you go along to the Trading Post and ask Fess to let you have a look at the skins, did you all get candy?"

"Yes, thank you Cole." They all said while none of them made to go.

"Go on then …off you go!" As the children ran off, Sarah watched Becky hopping along on her crutches after the other children. Christian watched Sarah watching the children, and couldn't help notice how attractive a woman she was. Another thing came to his attention too. She seemed to like children more than she did adults.

Sarah kept watching the children as they raced down the street and turned the corner toward the Trading Post. When they were out of sight she turned back to Thomas and her packhorse. "Thomas, you can have the rest of the candy, we better get a move on! we still have a lot to do!" Unhitching her horses, she pulled them around so they faced the trail leading to the river. Christian wasn't finished talking to her, but letting her go, started heading across the street toward the Sheriff's Office. Before getting too far away though, Sarah called out to him, bringing him to a stop.

"Sheriff! …when Thomas and I get our camp set up, we will be coming for our guns!" Keeping Thomas and their horses behind her, she slowed but kept moving. Christian turned to face her. "I don't think so Cole," he said matter-of-factly. Sarah stopped walking, forcing Thomas to pull up behind her. "I will be the one to decide if your camp is outside town," Christian informed her. "Don't worry sheriff, our camp is on the riverbank …down there …out of town!" she pointed along the street leading past the Ferguson House and down the trail. "We will be coming for our guns!" she repeated sternly. Christian could see the fire in Sarah's eyes from where he was standing, and 'Cole' he thought right then, 'was going to be a force to be reckoned with.'

"How long will it take for you to get your camp set up?" he asked, trying to ignore her last remark. Keeping his voice low, Thomas said something to Sarah Christian couldn't make out. Sarah took a moment before answering. "A couple of hours …maybe." Christian noticed Sarah seemed a bit hesitant when she answered. "Two hours Cole," he said back to her. "You have two hours, and then I will be along to check to see if your camp is in town …or not!" he added for good measure.

Sarah glared at him, and Thomas's face held a look of suspicion. "Then you better bring our guns with you! …because I wouldn't want to have to send you back to your jail to get them when you find out we are out of town!" Sarah's voice took on an angry tone as she started walking toward the trail. Christian watched her go, unable to work out why Thomas was giving him that suspicious look as he followed Sarah across the street.

Christian had two hours to fill. Going back to the Sheriff's Office, he sat behind his desk, and rummaging around in some drawers, found an old faded map of the town that would do for his purpose. Clem came in and said he'd be off home to have dinner with his wife. His wife still wasn't in the best of health and she was at him to leave Cedar Creek and move to Moreton where their son and daughter-in-law lived with their grandchildren. Clem was thinking about it but hadn't yet made up his mind, he didn't like to leave Christian without a deputy.

Clem's farm, situated along the road leading to Moreton, sat high above the river where a waterfall fell into a deep waterhole, and the river dropped into the valley before meandering further south, making its way to Moreton and further on. His land was fertile but Clem, being sheriff, never got around to ploughing it to grow crops. There was a beautiful farmhouse with a porch running right around the outside and a big barn, and if Clem left Cedar Creek, he more than likely would sell up. Christian thought about buying it for himself with the idea of raising a family, but he didn't have enough money saved to offer Clem what he thought would be a fair price.

Telling Clem about having to check Cole's camp to see if she was within the town boundary and that he would do this in a couple of hours, Clem informed him, Cole always stayed on the riverbank and that the place she camped was out of town. No-one minded that she camped where she was, in fact, Clem said, it was convenient for the town if Cole camped there. Christian asked him why it was convenient, but all Clem would say was. 'They could keep her and the boy out of trouble.' Christian smiled. He could believe that.

Christian wondered why a woman and a young boy would want to camp on the riverbank all alone, and wondered why they weren't staying in the Ferguson House with the rest of the trappers. From what he had seen, trappers stuck together. He wondered too, about something else. He wondered where Sarah's husband was. He hadn't seen or heard of anyone else coming to town with the name Cole.

Clem knew everything there was to know about Sarah, but, just like everyone else, Clem would not talk about her in case she found out. Sarah hated gossip and over the years had taken her wrath out on people speaking ill of her, still, talk about her amongst men drinking at the saloon was rife. Christian didn't question Clem about Sarah, instead simply said, 'maybe Cole's camp would not be out of town after he drew up the map,' then after telling Clem to come back in two hours, and that he would be on the night shift, he sent Clem off to have dinner with his wife. When Clem left, Christian got a pencil and drew an outline around the town on the map, starting at the corrals. The line went past the church and cemetery, crossed the road leading to several farms, and Major Hardy's ranch, then continued behind the schoolhouse and houses where vacant land was still available for houses to be built. Christian's line went behind the Trading Post, across the road that led south toward Clem's farm and around the back of the Ferguson House.

Christian continued drawing the line beyond the Ferguson House and across the other side of the river to the pier where the little row boats are moored. He had walked on the pier and even rowed one of the boats up and down the river when he and Millicent Crawley had been on one of their picnic's. Rowing up the river, passing under the bridge leading in to town from the direction of the mountain was easy, but no-one could row the opposite way, toward the waterfall. The river south of the pier consists of deep holes where large jagged boulders form part of the river system. After storms, the river becomes a torrent, rushing over the boulders, creating rapids that run all the way to the waterfall where it falls into the waterhole the town folk use as a swimming hole. He has been eight months in Cedar Creek and has not taken the time to go to the swimming hole for a swim.

Dragging the pencil along the paper, Christian drew a line back up the opposite side of the riverbank to the bridge. Joining it back up at the corrals, he put a heading in bold letters at the top. 'CEDAR CREEK TOWN LIMITS.' After underlining the heading, he studied the map. If Cole's camp was anywhere inside the line he drew, he was adamant, she would not be getting her guns. Satisfied, Christian folded his map and put it in his pocket.

Right on two hours, after making it home with just enough time to have dinner with his wife, Clem came back. Christian unlocked the gunroom, and retrieving Sarah's and Thomas's rifles, carried them to his desk where he lay them down on top. Unlocking his desk draw, he retrieved Sarah's pistol and pushed it down the front of his trousers, deciding at the same time, on leaving the bullets behind, because he was sure, he would be bringing her guns back!

The cold steel of the pistol's barrel as it slid against his bare skin, made him wince. The gun felt uncomfortable and the barrel dug in, so he moved it around until it sat comfortably above his crotch. "OK Clem, I'm off to inspect Cole's camp …I will be back soon," he announced, picking up the rifles and opening the door. "Good luck with that," Clem said as Christian shut the door behind him. "Because you are going to need it!" Christian didn't hear the rest of what Clem said.

Chapter Five

It was dark when Christian, carrying the two rifles under his arm and keeping his gun-hand free to swing beside his holster, walked down the street. Turning left at the Ferguson House, he headed toward the river. Passing the street where the lodge was situated, he turned onto the track winding down the riverbank. Smooth, round rocks and small pebbles littered the ground along the riverbank making walking on them difficult. He passed trees growing in clumps along the ridge, hiding the line of buildings up in town.

As he approached the clearing and Sarah's camp, he could see light flickering upward into the canopy of trees. A cool breeze blew across the river, causing the tops of the trees to sway. As he got closer, Sarah's firepit came into view, lighting up the area around it. One side of the firepit facing the river, he noticed, was built high with rocks, creating a windbreak that stopped the wind from fanning flames and spreading sparks into dry brush. A wire rack positioned over the fire, held a blackened pot. Steam escaped from under its lid. A coffee pot, also steaming, sat to one side.

Christian looked to where a canvas shelter had been erected amongst a stand of trees. Glancing to one side, he saw Thomas, sitting in one of the trees busily tying ropes fastened to the canvas shelter around the branches he was sitting on. Turning his attention toward the firepit directly ahead, he could see Sarah standing with her back to him, no longer wearing her oversized fur coat, and her hat was gone. Loose strands from her long braid, fastened haphazardly on top of her head hung over the collar of her shirt. Her arms were extended above her head as she held on tight to the canvas shelter.

The cool gusts blowing in from across the river, fanned the shelter, and every time it blew, Sarah's shirt lifted up her back. Sarah didn't seem to notice, but Christian did. Sarah's trousers, were now sitting low on her hips. The strap of the sheath holding her hunting knife sat around her bare waist. Her body appeared smooth. The line of her backbone disappeared where her buttocks began. Christian couldn't help staring, because it was obvious to him, Sarah wasn't wearing underwear.

His heart began beating faster as a sudden surge of excitement ran through him as he stared. "Hey! Ma! ...sheriff's here!" Thomas called loudly, startling Christian back to reality. Thomas gave Christian a quick sideways glance, before going back to tying ropes to branches. Had Thomas noticed he was staring at his mother, Christian wondered, looking over at Thomas then back at Sarah. "Sheriff!" Sarah said, not at all surprised that he was there. "Do you think you could give me a hand with this?" she asked, tugging at the canvas and turning slightly so she could see him better. A sudden gust of wind blew Sarah's shirt up under her arm, giving Christian a quick glimpse of more than just bare skin.

Almost too quickly, Christian lay the rifles down, dropping them on the stones, before stepping over the rocks and standing behind Sarah. "What do you want me to do Cole?" he asked, trying to keep his voice steady. "Can you take hold of this and pull it towards you? I want to tie this rope around that branch and it just won't reach." Reaching above Sarah's head where she indicated, their hands touched, sending a sudden warmth surging through him. Pulling back hard, the canvas gave easily under his strength, causing Sarah to stumble backwards between his arms. Her hair brushed his face, her head came to rest on his shoulder, her back hit his chest and her backside pressed into his crotch. Christian felt the pistol he was carrying down the front of his trousers dig in.

Christian hadn't been this close to a woman in a long time, and Sarah's touch sent a wave of wanting coursing through him. Sarah was in his arms for only a moment, before ducking away to grab a rope hanging loose. Stepping around the tree, she started to tie the rope off. Watching Sarah over his shoulder, Christian saw how her face was flushed with colour, telling him she felt what he felt when his body pressed against hers.

Sarah finished tying off the rope. "You can let go now sheriff," she said, keeping her eyes on Christian as he eased the canvas back and let go. When the canvas settled into place, Christian stepped back to study it. The shelter consisted of a roof and three sides that didn't quite reach the ground. Ropes hanging along the bottom of each side were fastened haphazardly around large rocks to keep the sides from moving in the wind. Two flaps of canvas at the front formed the entrance. Christian thought Sarah could have erected her shelter further back towards the ridge at the rear of her shelter where it would give them much more cover from the weather. He didn't think the shelter was very sturdy at all, and that it would not stand up to a storm, after all, it was winter, and the weather was unpredictable.

Sarah though, seemed pleased with her shelter. Leaving it, she hurried over to the firepit to check her pot simmering over the fire. Jumping out of the tree, Thomas ran to the fire and stood beside his mother, all the while keeping his suspicious gaze on Christian, making Christian feel uncomfortable. Christian watched Sarah pick up a cloth and wooden spoon and lift the lid to stir the contents. The aroma wafting from the pot made Christian's stomach rumble. Not having eaten yet, Sarah's cooking smelt delicious.

Putting the lid back on the pot, Sarah stood up. "Well sheriff, as you can see our camp is outside town!" She waved the wooden spoon she was holding around in an arc, taking in the whole camp.

"No, it isn't Cole …it is inside the town boundary." Christian put his hand in his pocket as Sarah began to argue with him.

"We are out of town sheriff! this is the riverbank! the town is up there, on that goddamn ridge!" She waved her hand towards the ridge behind the shelter.

"Yes, you are right, the town is up there …and it is also down here." While Sarah grew angrier, Christian fished in his pocket and pulled out his map.

"This is not the town, sheriff!" she emphasized angrily. Thomas continued to glare at Christian.

"Look at this map …it will show you where the town boundaries are," Christian urged, holding out the folded map toward Sarah.

Sarah stared at it. "I don't want to look at your stupid map ...you probably just drew it while waiting to come down here so you could tell us our camp is inside town!" Christian couldn't believe what Sarah just said. She was right, he had just drawn it. Cole was smart, she knew exactly what he had done.

"Please, look at the map." When Christian unfolded the map and tried handing it back to her, she snatched it out of his hands. 'Alright, now we are getting somewhere,' he thought. 'Now she will see her camp is in town.' But Sarah screwed the map up without looking at it and threw it back at him. Taken aback by her action, Christian tried to catch it but missed, and it fell to the ground. "You keep your goddamn map! this part of the river is not in town! ...it never has been! ...no-one from up there..." she pointed to the ridge "...comes down here! ...Thomas and I always camp here! ...this is not the goddamn town!" Sarah had been camping on the riverbank, out of town, ever since Thomas was born, and no-one was going to tell her she was in town. She cursed silently and kept insisting she was not in town. "I want my guns!" she ended, folding her arms in front of her while her face turned red with anger, and if looks could kill, Christian felt he had just died.

He could feel his face starting to burn as he bent down and picked up the map. "This is part of the town Cole, the boundary...." He stopped speaking abruptly when Sarah angrily interrupted him. "It is not!" she yelled, her voice so loud it echoed across the river making Christian think the trappers might hear her up in their house.

"Let me finish Cole!" he continued. "The boundary runs behind the Ferguson House, I have a sign, up there ...the same kind of sign you didn't see when you came across the bridge. The boundary down here runs in line with that sign." He pointed over the top of her shelter. "Down along here..." he said, pointing to the riverbank, then across the river. "It goes up behind that pier..." He kept pointing. "Then up along that side of the river, passing the bridge and back to the corrals." He ended with putting his arm down by his side. Sarah kept her arms folded until he finished.

"It does not sheriff!" she ended in disagreement. Christian felt defeated. "Please, ...just look at the map!" He tried one last time to get Sarah to see reason. "You are right, I did just draw the line around it as you said, but the map already existed and it shows you where everything is." He uncrumpled the map and held it out to her again.

Sarah reached out and taking the map, held it up in front of her. Christian watched in amazement as she took her eyes off him and looked at the map upside-down. Sarah didn't attempt to turn the map the right way up to read it. Thomas however, saw it was upside-down, and so standing beside her, turned the map the right way up. With Thomas pointing things out, they both spent some minutes studying it. Watching them, Christian came to the realization Sarah couldn't read, and that was why she said she hadn't seen the sign on her way into town. Cole had seen the sign alright, she just couldn't read it, which also meant, Christian surmised, Cole couldn't count and that was why she didn't know how many eggs she was getting in Crawley's store. Cole wasn't stupid, he knew that, but he figured she had no education. Thomas and Sarah whispered amongst themselves while Christian, suppressing a smile, stood back waiting patiently.

When they were done, Sarah handed Christian back his map, and for a moment, he thought he had gotten Sarah to agree their camp was within the town boundary, but that was not to be the end of it.

"We are not camped in town sheriff ...I don't care what your map says ...the town is up there and we are down here ...it has always been that way ...that is it ...finished! ...I want my guns ...now!" Sarah's voice quietened, but anger etched her face. Having thought they resolved the issue, Christian stared at her in disbelief, but Sarah was like a dog with a bone, she wouldn't let it go.

"It's the same as your stupid gun law ...you made that up to suit you and now you made up this stupid town boundary ...how can the town grow if there is a boundary?" Sarah's question seemed reasonable, but Christian had an answer. "I redraw the map Cole!"

Sarah stopped talking, her shoulders slumped and her mouth fell open. "Goddamn!" she cursed. Then folding her arms again in defiance, glared at him. Wanting to be fair, Christian kept his voice calm when he proposed a resolution. "I will go up there, on the ridge, and take another look at the boundary …but I am sure, I am right." It was the next thing Sarah said that got Christian's back up. "You go with him Thomas! …that way he can't cheat us!"

Now it was Christian's turn to glare at Sarah. "I do not cheat Cole! …I am the law!" Keeping her arms folded while they faced each other angrily, Sarah replied. "Yes! …well! …we all know there are those that are crooked …don't we sheriff!"

Astounded by her remark Christian replied angrily. "I am not crooked!" Then to himself. 'How dare she accuse me of cheating and being crooked! and besides, why should I have to justify my fucking self to her?' Turning sharply, he cursed out loud. "Goddamn it!" Then taking the rifles with him, he headed back along the riverbank the way he came.

"Where are you going sheriff?" Sarah called after him.

"To the ridge to check the boundary …any objections?" he answered glancing over his shoulder while still walking away. Sarah smiled at his back. "No! …but why don't you let Thomas take you up this way?" Sarah pointed to the ridge behind the shelter. Christian stopped and looked at where she was pointing. "There is a track leading up here behind the Ferguson House, it's much quicker than walking all the way round."

Feeling stupid that he didn't know the track was there, and looking sheepishly at Sarah, he came back to the firepit. Thomas stood silently by while Sarah and Christian argued, now he spoke excitedly. "Come on sheriff! I can show you the way!" Heading toward the clump of trees growing behind the camp, he pushed his way through thick undergrowth with Christian pushing his way through behind him. Scrambling up the side of the ridge, Christian had to hurry to keep up. Coming out at the top of the ridge next to the Ferguson House outhouse, Christian could hear voices and laughter coming from inside the house. The trappers, back from their days work at Major Hardy's were relaxing, getting themselves food and bedding down for the night.

When Christian stopped at the top he looked down on Sarah's camp, and could see her shelter sitting between the trees. He also saw what looked like another canvas, covering what he thought could only be their supplies, not far from the firepit. The firepit in full view where Sarah was standing lit up the open grassed area. She still had her arms folded, waiting for them to return. Christian thought her an attractive woman, and although sometimes looked sad, he wondered why she was so angry. He also thought she was waiting to let fly with another tirade aimed straight at him.

Somewhere behind Christian, Thomas called out, "over here sheriff!" and Christian hurried over to stand next to the sign beside the road leading past Clem's farm. "Let's walk in a straight line toward the edge of the ridge." Christian said to him. Walking side by side, they both stopped at the edge and looked down on top of the shelter. The town boundary Christian drew on his map, ran right through the middle of the tree Sarah and Christian tied the shelter to. Thomas could see they had a problem. "Ma's going to be real mad sheriff!" he said keeping his eyes on his mother. Christian stared at Sarah now stirring her pot at the firepit. Thinking of her stirring trouble, all he could think to say was. "Yeah."

Heading back down the track to the camp, Christian tried to prepare himself for another onslaught of Sarah's anger. Thomas decided not to say anything, instead, left it to Christian to tell his mother the bad news. As Christian came toward her, Sarah stood up, and folding her arms, still thought him handsome. His body looked solid, he swung his muscled arms defiantly, and his legs were long. Giving Sarah a fleeting glance, Christian walked straight past her and went and stood in front of the tree her shelter was tied to, then turned to face her. "This tree stands in the middle of the boundary," he said, slapping his hand on the trunk for effect. "In other word's Cole! …except for the back corner of your shelter, the rest of it is inside the town limits." Keeping the palm of his hand resting on the trunk, he watched Sarah's reaction to this news.

Sarah didn't speak. Thomas squatted at the firepit and looked across at Christian. Christian continued. "If you are standing on this side of the tree." He took a step back to stand outside what he deemed the town boundary. "You can have your guns." He stepped forward. Now he was standing inside the boundary. "But! …if you are standing here …you can't have your guns." Sarah stared at him. She wasn't stupid, she understood perfectly what he was telling her, but she still didn't say anything. Thinking she didn't understand what he was saying, Christian stepped back outside the boundary.

"Guns," he said. Then stepped inside the boundary. "No guns," he said. Getting quicker and hopping from one foot to the other. "Guns ...no guns ...guns ...no guns," he repeated while continuing to hop back and forth. Thomas burst out laughing. Christian laughed too when he saw the funny side of what he was doing. Sarah didn't laugh, she couldn't see the funny side of it at all. This was serious! The sheriff wasn't going to make a fool of her! She hurried over to where Christian was standing and stood in front of him, her eyes dark with anger, her back to the river. Christian stopped hopping and faced her, his smile faded, Sarah seemed to be studying him, her eyes travelled down to his groin and back up again. Christian wondered what she was up to.

Sarah didn't speak. Turning her back on Christian, she looked off into the dark, toward the river, seeming to be looking for something. Christian stood with his back to the tree while trying to prepare himself for whatever Sarah was about to do. But he was so unprepared for what she did.

Turning without warning, both Sarah's hands shot out towards him. Her left hand pressed hard against his stomach, pushing him back against the tree. While he sucked in his breath, her right hand closed around the grip of the pistol sticking out the top of his pants. Pulling the gun straight up, Sarah got it out of his trousers in one swift movement.

"Cole!" Christian yelled as he fell back, stunned at the swiftness she acted. Ignoring his yelling, Sarah turned toward the river, raised the pistol and squeezed the trigger. 'Click!' Nothing happened. 'Click!' Again, nothing happened. Sarah kept squeezing the trigger. 'Click! click! click!' Lowering the gun in disgust, she turned to face Christian. "Goddamn it sheriff! you brought our guns back ... empty?" she questioned, holding the pistol up as if he hadn't seen it. Christian watched Sarah's pupils dilate. The anger in her eyes so overpowering for a moment it stopped him from speaking. "You took my gun with bullets in it! you should have returned it with bullets in it! but oh! I forgot! ...you are afraid you might shoot, nothing, off!" Sarah's face flushed as her eyes darted to his crotch.

Feeling the colour rise on his face, Christian tried to ignore her sarcastic remark about his private parts. Finding his voice, he returned her anger with his own. "I figured your camp was in town Cole! That is why I didn't bother bringing the bullets, because I figured I would be taking your guns back with me! …and I will be taking them back when I leave here!" he said sternly. Without taking her eyes off Christian, Sarah addressed Thomas. "Thomas, get the bullets for my gun …please." Thomas didn't hesitate, he ran to the canvas covered supplies and opening a box, dug around inside. "What are you going to do Cole?" Christian asked suspiciously. Thomas came running back with a handful of small calibre bullets. Sarah ignored Christians question. "I only need one, thank you." Opening the chamber, Sarah shoved a single bullet inside.

"Cole?" Christian questioned with a note of anger in his voice. Having been caught in these situations plenty of times before, he weighed up the odds of him taking a bullet if she tried shooting him. They were standing pretty close for a shoot-out, but he would give it his best shot. While waiting to see what Sarah intended, he put his hand on the grip of his gun as a precaution.

"Don't worry sheriff," Sarah said seeing his movement. "I'm not going to shoot you!" Closing the chamber, she spun it then listened. When it stopped spinning, she moved the chamber one more place. Christian frowned. 'What the hell? Where did Cole learn to do that?' he asked himself. 'Not too many people can tell which chamber is loaded after spinning it.' He was able to do it, but was amazed when he saw Sarah do it.

It was on the mountain. Back when Sarah was ten years old. Garrett and Sarah, sitting with their backs against a tree, were resting after a long day of trapping. Her father Calahan, along with Joe, Will and Fergus, were sitting around a campfire drinking coffee. Garrett emptied his hand-gun of bullets, leaving just two in the chamber. Closing the chamber, then spinning it, he listened carefully until it stopped. Sarah was watching when he pulled the trigger, but it still made her jump. Garrett spun the chamber again, listened, then pulled the trigger again. The four men looked over at Garrett and Sarah as Garrett's shots hit a tree opposite to where they were sitting. He wouldn't deliberately aim his gun at the men, so they weren't concerned where Garrett's bullets were landing. He reloaded to do the same again, only this time, he handed his gun to Sarah, who by this time was watching him intently. Without saying a word, she took the gun and spun the chamber, then pulled the trigger. Nothing happened. "You have to listen to the noise the chamber makes, when there are bullets in each chamber the sound is heavy, if it is empty, you get a hollow sound," Garrett explained. Sarah spun the chamber and listened. Still unable to make out the difference in the sounds the chamber was making, and without taking aim at anything, she pulled the trigger. The gun went off making everyone jump. The bullet, luckily, didn't hit anyone. "Jesus Christ Garrett! you want Sarah to kill one of us?" Calahan cursed, while the other men, getting up from where they were sitting got themselves clear of the shots. "She'll learn," Garrett laughed. Winking at Sarah and taking his gun back, he said, "with practice."

While Christian watched, Sarah turned her back on him, and while she looked toward the river, he waited. What was she looking for? Christian couldn't see anything! In a blink of an eye Sarah raised the gun and fired, causing Christian to jump when the gun went off. The echo reverberated across the river and was gone. Sarah didn't seem to aim at anything, and just as quickly, she turned back to Christian, shoved the gun into his stomach and let it go, forcing him to grab it with both hands. "Damn it, Cole!" he exclaimed, not happy at being made a fool of. Ignoring him, Sarah headed toward the river. When she disappeared in the dark, Christian searched for her, but unable to see where she had gone, he asked Thomas where she had gone. But all Thomas said, looking intently toward the river was, "Ma will be back soon." A short while later Sarah appeared out of the dark, her right arm extended away from her body. Coming closer to where Thomas and Christian were standing, Christian could see she was holding something.

Held tight in Sarah's fingers was a long tail, and on the end of that tail hung the ugliest, hairiest, biggest river rat Christian had ever seen, and he hadn't seen it moving around on the riverbank.

Keeping the rat out in front of her, the rat's legs dangled, its head hung limply, its bulging eyes stared. The bullet had gone through the rat's head near its ear. The bloody hole dripped blood onto the rocky riverbank. Sarah came to a stop in front of Christian. "This is what Thomas and I have to deal with sheriff ... these ugly, stinking vermin come out to see what they can gnaw on, believe me when I say, you don't want to be what they gnaw on!" Sarah continued to hold the rat up for Christian to see. "This is why I need my guns, if I just had my pistol, I can fend these off, Thomas and I can't be without our guns, not down here." Sarah kept holding the rat up in the air in front of Christian. While waiting for him to reply, blood kept dripping out of the rat and onto the rocks. Christian knew all about the rats from camping in this very spot when he first came to Cedar Creek. He couldn't have been more relieved when he moved into the lodge, satisfied he no longer had a problem with fending off marauding river rats every night when he tried to get some sleep.

"You made the choice to camp down here Cole ...maybe you should be up there in town like everyone else ...I will not let you have these guns." Christian and Sarah's eyes met. Unhappy with his reply, Sarah's eyes turned dark with anger, so before stepping away from Christian, she swung the rat hard and let it go. A stream of blood spurted from the rat's body, hitting Christian's trousers below his knees. The rat sailed through the air and disappeared into the dark. A moment later there was a loud splash as the rat landed in the river. The rat's body, would undoubtedly float downstream in the current and end up washed up somewhere along the riverbank, or end up going over the waterfall into the swimming hole. Christian looked down at his trouser legs and pursed his lips. Even though he was furious at Sarah for ruining his trousers, he wasn't about to give her the satisfaction of making him angrier, so he didn't comment on the spatters.

Ignoring the fact she stained Christian's trousers, Sarah walked back to the river where she scrubbed her hands with grit and small pebbles from the riverbed. Shaking the water off her hands, she walked back to the firepit where her pot was steaming and knelt down in front of the fire. Christian watched her pick up a cloth and wooden spoon, then lift the lid and begin to stir the contents of the pot.

"Cole?" Christian began, making to move toward Sarah and the firepit.

"We are done sheriff," Sarah said calmly, concentrating on her cooking. After enduring one hell of a day she was tired. She was over arguing with the sheriff. He could have let her have her pistol, but no, he had to be stubborn! Sarah was done with him, if he wanted trouble, he was going to get it.

Although Christian was able to see reason for her wanting her guns, he shoved her pistol back down the front of his trousers, then stooping down and picking up the two rifles, started past the firepit toward the trail. Stopping abruptly, he tried to justify why he couldn't let her have her guns, even though right then, he wanted to hand her the pistol.

"I can't let you have them Cole ...I made the law to keep the town safe ...if I give you your guns, I have to give everyone their guns ...and I am not prepared to do that." He waited for a reply that did not come. Putting both rifles under his left arm, keeping his gun-hand free, because he didn't trust Sarah with his back turned, after all, she still carried her hunting knife, and he didn't want it in his back, he started back up the trail. Sarah stood up suddenly and without a trace of animosity in her voice called, "sheriff!" Christian stopped where he was. Thinking, 'this woman was determined to have the last word,' and preparing himself for another argument, he slowly turned to face her. "Thank you for helping me with our shelter," Sarah said from behind the firepit.

Christian's eyes travelled over parts of Sarah's body the glow from the fire accentuated. There was that wanting feeling inside him again. He didn't answer, he couldn't. After arguing with each other, Sarah had just thanked him, so instead of saying anything to spoil the moment, he simply nodded, walked off along the trail, and carrying the two rifles, headed back to his office.

Chapter Six

After taking the rifles back to the jailhouse, and leaving Clem in charge, Christian retired to the lodge for the night. Renting the bottom floor of the two storey house called Mountain View Lodge from Benjamin Crawley, made Christian wonder why Crawley and his daughter Millicent lived at the back of their store, in a small attachment, when they owned a grand house such as 'The Lodge'.

Crawley told him the house was furnished, but he still got a bit of a shock when he moved in. The house was furnished all right. The furniture consisted of an old wooden table and four battered old chairs. The table sat in the middle of a large open living area while the original formal dining room stood empty. There was an old wooden bench in one corner of the room that served as a preparation area for cooking. An enamel dish sat on the bench and was used for washing dishes. The open fireplace had an area built in it for sitting pots. This fire was used to heat water for washing oneself as well as heating the downstairs area.

In the original, large kitchen, the sink was still there, but the hand pump for water had been removed and sealed off. There was an enormous stove with an oven and closed in firebox that Maria, his housekeeper, used for cooking his meals. Maria, a Mexican woman, did laundry and cleaning for several families around the district and offered to cook for Christian four times a week. She also washed his bed sheets and clothes once a week for a small sum. The rest of the time he cooked for himself or ate at the eatery next door to the saloon. Although Maria was paid to do housework, she became persistent with making other advances toward him, but he kept brushing her off, telling her he wasn't interested in having a relationship with anyone at this time. Maria was not the woman he was looking to settle down with. Still, he was glad to employ her, she kept his living area spotless.

The room he slept in, he figured, had never been a bedroom. The room had a stone fireplace built in one wall, but it couldn't be lit because it had been sealed up too. There were marks on the walls where he thought a number of shelves or cupboards may have stood. He slept on an old cast iron bed with squeaky springs, and the mattress was lumpy, although now he had settled into it, the bed had moulded into his shape and was comfortable.

A badly dinted round metal tub sat in the middle of what he thought was the original washroom. There was a small cupboard where a china basin and jug sat. An old chair, the same as the ones around the wooden dining table, sat just inside the door that he used to throw his dirty clothes over, and there was a full-length timber framed mirror standing in one corner. The stone fireplace under the washstand, again, had been sealed, so whenever he needed a bath, he had to boil water outside in a large iron pot over an open fire, then he had to haul the water inside to the metal bathtub. This job he hated, but did once a week, whether he needed to or not.

Crawley had been adamant when he told Christian he didn't have access upstairs. That area, Crawley insisted, was private. But curiosity got the better of Christian, he didn't like being told he couldn't do something, so after only one day in the house he went upstairs to take a look, and was disappointed when there was nothing to see. Four doors lined either side of a long hallway and every one of them had a huge steel padlock bolted to a steel bar across its door. Christian wondered what could be so important in those rooms they needed to be locked with such heavy locks.

Christian sat in the ugly green winged chair. The chair had been in the house when he moved in and at the time, he thought it a hideous green velvet thing, with a high back and padded arms. The big, ugly, green winged chair, had pride of place in front of the fireplace, and proved to be the most comfortable chair he ever sat in. He often fell asleep in front of the fire while sitting in it, and tonight he sat in it and thought of Sarah.

The woman infuriated him, she also intrigued him. He would like to know what her first name was so he didn't have to address her as Cole all the time. Arguing with her seemed to be a losing battle. Today being her first day in town, she already knocked him off his feet and argued with him over his firearms law. Then there was the trouble in Crawley's store. 'Damn!' he thought. 'What was that all about?' When he asked her about their viciousness toward each other she wouldn't tell him, except to say they didn't like each other. He knew there had to be more to it than just dislike, a whole lot more.

Sarah made him smile too, because she also had a sense of humour. Christian laughed when remembering her asking him if she could call Crawley names, and repeating each name loud enough for Crawley to hear, which infuriated him. The mischievous twinkle in her eye, made his heart race. His smile faded when remembering what Crawley called her, thinking it uncalled for, but then his smile returned when he thought of Sarah having busted the bag of flour and sending it all over Crawley and everything else. He thought about how the flour sat on the bridge of her nose and how he desperately wanted to brush it off. He smiled some more when he thought about how she left asking for flour until the very last minute, and how Crawley was not amused.

He pictured her long hair pinned on top of her head and the wisps of soft curls falling around her shoulders. Earlier in the day he thought Sarah pretty, but after seeing her this evening in the glow of her campfire, he thought her beautiful. A feeling of desire came over him when thinking about her. "Hell" he said out loud, remembering Sarah saying she and Thomas couldn't be alone on the riverbank without their guns, he assumed she was saying they would only be alone until her husband showed up. "I can't be thinking of Cole like this, her husband may be on his way, he probably just sent Cole and his son on ahead to set up camp."

Going to the washroom to ready himself for bed, Christian stripped off his shirt, then, throwing it over the chair, poured warm water into the dish and washed his face and neck. Lathering a cloth with soap, he wiped it over his chest and over his stomach. Undoing the front of his trousers and dropping them to the floor, he suddenly remembered Sarah pulling the pistol out of them. Standing naked in front of the full-length mirror, he looked at his crotch, then ran his fingers through the thick mat of hair surrounding his manhood, searching for the mark he thought Sarah made with her gun. When he couldn't find anything, he kept looking at himself in the mirror.

Sarah said he was scared he was going to shoot 'nothing' off, twice she said it. He wasn't looking at 'nothing' he thought. 'What I have between my legs Cole, is not nothing!' Standing with his hands on his hips, he flexed his muscles and smiled at his reflection, then, walking out to the fire, loaded it with wood to keep it burning. The house was already warm and he wanted to keep it that way. Hating the confinement of night attire, especially when they became twisted around his body while he slept, he took to sleeping naked, that way he got a better sleep. He didn't like long-johns under his trousers either, they just made him sweat.

The bedroom was comfortably warm, so laying on top of the blankets, Christian put his hands behind his head, and for a moment looked up at the ceiling, his mind still on Sarah. She didn't wear underwear either, he knew that for a fact. Watching the breeze lift her shirt allowed him to see her smooth, silken body, and the lower part of her breast. Sarah had a hell of a body and a real pretty face. Her eyes, when he looked into them, were as blue as the water in the swimming hole, and just as deep. Her nose was a nice shape, not too long, not too short and not too wide, it was a perfect nose. Her mouth looked soft, her lips full, and Christian wondered what it would be like to put his mouth on hers.

Closing his eyes, he tried to imagine kissing Sarah. His arms would be around her, his hands touching her smooth, bare skin. He opened his eyes quickly when he felt an ache start between his legs. Getting out of bed, he hurried to the washroom where he grabbed the washer and wet it with cold water. Holding it to his crotch, he waited for the throbbing ache to go away. After his body calmed down, he went back to bed, thinking if he wanted to sleep tonight, he would have to think of something else other than Sarah. He turned his thoughts to another woman he had come to know.

Millicent Crawley befriended him soon after he arrived in town, inviting him several times to dine with her and her father. Christian asked himself again why they didn't live in the lodge. He never asked the Crawley's, it wasn't any of his business the way they chose to live, but it still puzzled him. Millicent was a plain looking woman who always wore her jet-black hair pulled back in a tight bun. Her nose was long and thin, as was her mouth. Her skin was pale, as if she had never been out in the sun. She always carried a parasol with her whenever she ventured outdoors. Millicent was thin, almost to the point of looking starved. The dresses she wore were elegant, but hung loosely from her thin frame, as if they belonged on a woman who at the very least had some shape about her. 'And,' his thoughts turned immediately to Sarah, 'breasts like Cole.' Millicent didn't appear to have either. "Shit!" he cursed for thinking of Sarah. He turned his thoughts back to Millicent, and the day she invited him to go on a picnic.

It was a beautiful summers day. They took the buckboard along the road south of town, passing by Clem's farm, and stopped at a place where a thicket of trees grew on the ridge high above the waterfall. Standing at the edge of the ridge, they looked down into the river below where they could see the river flowing in torrents over boulders until it reached the waterfall where it spilled over the edge, sending up a spray of fine mist before falling into a deep blue pool. After the pool, the river dropped further into the valley and meandered over more boulders and continued on its way in the distance. It had been Millicent who informed him the pool was called 'The Swimming Hole' and that town folk took their children there in the summer for picnics. It was a pretty sight, looking down on the pool of water.

He remembered they spread a blanket out in the shade under the trees. Millicent kept herself in the shade and kept her parasol over her head for extra protection, there was no way she was going to get sunburnt. 'Not like Cole, her skin was lightly tanned.' It was obvious, to Christian, Cole had been out in the sun at some stage without clothes. "Damn!" Christian said aloud, there he was again, thinking of Cole. Forcing his mind back to the picnic, he remembered they ate a lunch of chicken legs and small vegetable cakes, and they drank lemonade Millicent made. The lemonade, he remembered, tasted bitter. Millicent talked about herself a great deal, telling him she spent a lot of her childhood attending an all girl's school and lady's finishing college in Philadelphia. She made a point of telling him her father ordered her dresses she wore from one of his many catalogues he kept in his store. Her dresses she said, came all the way from Paris, and she got a new dress every year for her birthday, making him wonder at the time, because Millicent was so thin, why Crawley hadn't ordered Millicent's dresses a size smaller so they fitted her properly. He still wondered.

He wasn't at all attracted to Millicent, even though he thought she wasn't a bad sort of woman, she wasn't the type of woman he was hoping he would one day meet and fall in love with. Millicent wasn't the only eligible woman in town. There were saloon girls, and farm girls, but he wasn't interested in any of them.

Millicent seemed overly happy the day they went on their picnic, talking incessantly and seeming more than friendly, constantly touching his arm and smiling at him. He had, almost without thinking, leant over and planted a kiss on her. He still doesn't know why he did that, and he cringes whenever he thinks about it. He thought it may have just been the day, the sun was shining, it was warm, and he felt relaxed.

Kissing Millicent came as quite a shock to him, her mouth felt cold, uninviting. He immediately regretted kissing her, becoming only too pleased when Millicent herself pushed him away and said she wouldn't be having a man touch her in any way, at least not until she was married, she hastily added. She then glanced demurely at him as if to say, it would be him she would be marrying. Thinking fast, Christian told her it was just a friendly kiss, to thank her for making him feel welcome, and she seemed to accept his excuse. He certainly had no intentions of making Millicent his wife. Thinking of that kiss with Millicent put his body and mind at ease. Pulling the bedcovers up, he finally fell asleep.

Christian didn't know how long he had been asleep, but it was still dark when he woke to the sound of what he thought was thunder. Thinking the sky had been clear when he went to bed, he frowned. *Boom! Boom!* the noise thundered, causing the house to shake with every blast. *Boom! Boom! Boom!* continued to reverberate through the house. All of a sudden there was a lull. Christian relaxed, but then. *Boom! Boom!* the noise started again. Having a good idea what the noise was and where it was coming from, he threw the covers back, flew out of bed and almost tripped when his foot caught the bedsheet. "Goddamn it all!" Cursing out loud and stumbling, he raced to the washroom where he grabbed his blood-stained trousers and yanked them up his legs. Grabbing his boots, he pulled them on, then hastily pulling his shirt up his arms, made a quick decision not to do the buttons up as he raced to the door, where necessity made him stop to do up a couple of buttons on his trousers to stop them falling down and exposing him. "Goddamn son-of-a-bitch!" he cursed at the time he was wasting. *Boom! Boom!* the noise continued echoing up from the river.

Before running out the door, he grabbed his gun out of its holster, and quickly checking that it was fully loaded, ran down the street to see lamps coming on in the Ferguson House. Christian figured the trappers would hear the noise louder than anyone else, their house being right above the river where it was coming from. Lamps came on above shops in the main street, making it obvious the noise could be heard all over town. The noise grew louder as he got closer to the river.

Turning right onto the track leading to the riverbank, he passed Clem walking along at a brisk pace and overtook the four trappers, all heading down the track toward Sarah's camp. 'Why are they always around where Cole is?' Christian asked himself. But he didn't have time to dwell on them. Stepping quickly across the rocky riverbank near Sarah's camp, he stopped only when he neared Sarah's firepit. The sight that greeted him was one of utter carnage. Clumps of fur, mangled rat bodies and legs, severed heads, guts and blood, were scattered all over the rocks. Christian saw Sarah standing beside the tree he helped her tie her shelter too, inside the town limits. Seeing Christian coming toward her, Sarah darted to the other side of the tree. 'Aha!' he said to himself. Sarah was now outside the limits. 'Cole was cunning' and Christian guessed she thought he wouldn't do anything about the gun she was holding with both hands if she was outside town, but she was wrong.

Glancing around the camp, Christian saw Thomas standing near the back of the shelter where the stand of trees grew thickest, holding a long piece of tree branch, he was using to belt rats with. Christian watched Thomas swing the branch, and send a rat flying through the air to land amongst the trees.

Leaving Thomas belting rats, Christian turned his attention to Sarah, just in time to see her reloading a gun. "Cole, goddamn it!" he yelled. "Don't you dare fire that gun!" While he clambered over rocks trying to avoid blood and guts strewn everywhere, Sarah raised the gun into the air when a hairy river rat scurried out from bushes near where she was standing. Trying to make her hear him clearly, Christian yelled louder. "Goddamn it! Cole! you fire that goddamn gun! I will shoot you!" Sarah shot the rat. *Boom!* and blew it in half.

At the same time as Sarah shot the rat, Christian lifted his gun and fired. What happened next shocked him as well as the four trappers, and Clem, who stopped in their tracks in disbelief at what they saw. Christian's heart skipped a beat and his stomach dropped.

Turning her head at the precise moment Christian's bullet slammed into the tree, sending pieces of wood and bark splintering off the trunk and flying through the air, a splinter hit Sarah in the face, cutting her under her left eye. Christian heard the men behind him suck in their breath and utter an oath as they witnessed what happened. Before slumping to the ground, Sarah let go of the gun she was holding with both hands and put one hand up to her face. Christian was of the belief he hadn't shot her, but seeing her go down, he wasn't so sure.

"*Ma!*" Thomas screamed, and holding up the branch ran towards Christian. Still shocked by what happened, Christian pointed his gun toward Thomas. Thinking the sheriff was going to shoot him, Thomas's eyes widened with fear causing him to stop in his tracks. That was when Joe saw red.

"Don't you dare raise your gun to that boy sheriff! ...not if you want to keep breathing!" Joe's threatening voice boomed loudly. His hand moved to his hip to draw his gun, but realizing he didn't have his gun, pursed his lips in anger and stopped where he was. Christian brought his gun around and aimed it at the trappers, and for a split second saw a hint of a threat in the men's eyes. The three men with Joe opened their coats giving Christian a glimpse of the knives they were carrying. Even if they didn't have guns, he wouldn't be able to take on four men with knives. He had no intentions of shooting Thomas, he just wanted him to stop where he was, so he could deal with the situation and the gun Cole was holding. When he lowered his gun and turned back to Sarah, the men closed their coats and stayed on the trail. They weren't going to get blood and guts on their boots, not if they didn't have to. "Did the sheriff just shoot Cole?" Garret asked, unsure of what he witnessed. "I don't know!" came a worried reply from Will. Christian, facing Sarah where she crouched heard their worried queries. "I didn't shoot her! ...I fired a warning shot, that's all!" he said. Joe asked Sarah if she was alright. Keeping her head down, she let her hair cover her face and didn't answer. Her cheek began to sting. Christian couldn't see how badly hurt she was so stepped closer to take a look.

"Goddamn it, Cole! answer me! ...*are you hurt?*" Joe spoke much louder this time. Holding her hand out in front of her to look at it, she answered, "I'm ...I'm alright Joe!" Seeing her fingers covered in blood, Christian felt his heart give off a sudden thump. He had never shot a woman before and didn't think he shot Sarah.

Joe was satisfied with Sarah's answer, she wouldn't say she was alright if she wasn't, making his concern for her less worrying. Over many years Sarah learnt how to take care of herself, but still, Joe didn't want her to be hurt, if she were, he had a promise to keep, the sheriff would end up paying with his life if he caused Sarah to be hurt bad. Before Thomas was born Sarah shot herself while out hunting, and Frank Mason tried to fix it, almost killing Sarah in the process. At the time, Joe wanted to kill Frank, but Sarah didn't want Frank punished. Nor would Joe let anyone hurt Thomas. He had good reason to watch over him too.

"Thomas! are you alright son?" he called. Thomas wiped his eyes before answering.

"I'm alright uncle Joe." Hearing Thomas's reply, Christian had another puzzle. Now it seemed, Joe was Thomas's uncle. Was Joe related to Cole? If so, how were they related? Confused more than ever, Christian asked himself what was going on between these four trappers and Cole?

Keeping his eyes on Sarah, he asked her to get up. Sarah ignored him. "Get up Cole! ...I want that gun!" he asked again, this time more sternly. Reaching back, Sarah pressed her bloodied hand against the trunk of the tree and got to her feet. Her arm hung by her side as she struggled to hold what looked like a black Colt .44. As she stood, it wasn't the gun that had Christian staring.

Sarah's clothes looked as though they had been pulled on in a hurry and didn't cover her completely. One button, holding her shirt closed over her breasts, looked like it would give up that job at any moment. Christian's eyes travelled over her abdomen, then her stomach. His eyes took in her navel at the opening of her trousers, where one button she managed to do up in her haste, kept her trousers from falling over her hips. Letting his gaze travel down Sarah's legs, he saw she was barefoot. Unable to keep from staring, it became apparent, Cole slept naked, just like he did, but then, she was sleeping naked in a shelter right there on the riverbank. When he looked up, Sarah's eyes met his. He wasn't dressed any better than she was. 'But shit,' he was thinking. 'He was a man, and it didn't matter if his body was slightly uncovered.'

Blood seeping from the small cut under Sarah's eye, made its way down her cheek to her jaw, down her neck and inside her shirt. "Everything all right sheriff?" Clem asked from where he was standing next to the trappers. Christian looked over at the men. "Everything is fine Clem ...Cole's ok ...I can handle this ...get those men out of here!"

"Sure! ...come on Joe, Garrett, the rest of you too, sheriff has it under control, let's go." Relieved Christian had everything in hand, Clem herded the men into a group and started marching them up the trail, but not before Joe had a parting word. "You go easy sheriff ...shootin rats ain't against the law."

"Shooting guns off in town is Joe," Christian said to Joe's back. Joe didn't answer, he was satisfied Sarah wasn't hurt bad and Thomas was fine. What did it matter if Sarah shot a few rats? She did it every year when she camped on the riverbank, except back then, she used her pistol, that gun didn't make near as much noise as Frank's .44. Nobody in town was ever disturbed by her gunshots, not until tonight, and that was the sheriff's fault.

"We'll be seein you later Thomas, laddie!" Fergus called before the men made their way back up the trail, muttering their protests as they went.

"See you uncle Fergus," Thomas called. Hearing Thomas call Fergus uncle too, Christian figured Thomas called all the men uncle simply because trappers stuck together.

"He should've let her have her goddamn pistol!" Joe muttered to the other men as they walked away.

Christian could feel Sarah studying him while he was dealing with Clem and the trappers. When he turned his attention back to her, she lifted her eyes to look at his face.

"You missed sheriff!" she said softly, trying to keep her eyes off his exposed body.

"I never miss what I aim at Cole!" he said back to her. "I want that gun," he demanded, stepping closer. Christian looked closely at the cut on her cheek. It didn't look too deep, but there was a lot of blood smeared over the side of her face. "No sheriff! you can't have it!" Sarah was not about to let him have Frank's gun. "You said, if I was on this side of the tree, I could have a gun." Suddenly feeling tired, after having endured a very long day coming straight from almost two sleepless nights. One at 'The Wells' and the second, out on the prairie, along with everything that happened since arriving in town, Sarah was beat, but she wouldn't give in, not to this man who thought he was going to change the town.

"I am the law Cole, I can take that gun off you anywhere, and at any time, if I think it is being used unlawfully." While reminding Sarah of the fact he was the law, he took another step towards her. Standing between her outstretched legs, their bodies only inches apart, he reached out and put his hand on her arm, then slowly, running his hand down to where she was holding the gun, closed his hand over hers. The sudden thrill he felt as his hand covered hers was unexpected.

"I'm taking this gun," he said softly, trying to gauge her reaction to his demand. When Christian's hand touched hers, Sarah felt her stomach flutter as a warm feeling surfaced between her legs and surged through her body. Giving in, she opened her hand, and let Christian take Frank's gun.

"You are a hypocrite sheriff," Sarah replied, stepping away from the tree and Christian. On her way across to the firepit, she glanced toward the ridge, all the while, being careful to avoid the mutilated pieces of dead rats with her bare feet.

"And you are a liar Cole," Christian said to her back. Thomas sat next to Sarah in front of the fire and put his arm around her while glaring over at Christian. Speaking quietly to Thomas, he stood up, then going to get a cloth, glanced up at the ridge. Taking a pot to the river, he half filled it with water, brought it back, sat it on the rack over the fire, then sat beside Sarah to wait for the water to heat up.

Looking around at the carnage littering the camp and the riverbank, Christian could see clumps of rat's bodies floating in the river. The smell of flesh burning in the firepit permeated the air. Stepping gingerly over fur and entrails trying not to get any on his boots, he brought himself over to where Sarah was sitting. "How many rats did you kill Cole?" he asked, squatting in front of her. "All of them sheriff!" Sarah said, thinking that a stupid question. Everyone knew she was a good shot. "You must have missed some?" Christian smiled, trying to ease the situation. But Sarah wasn't amused. "I never miss what I aim at!" she answered bluntly. 'Touche' Christian thought, as Sarah repeated what he said earlier. Looking closely at the wound, he realized how it must have hurt, but there was nothing he could do about it, she would have to let Doc Harris deal with it.

"Whose gun is this Cole?" he asked, holding the colt up as if Sarah hadn't seen it. Asking her about the gun had an immediate impact on the atmosphere around them.

"Whose do you think?" she answered curtly.

"Then you lied to me! when I asked you earlier today if you had any more guns! you told me you didn't! so…!" Sarah would not abide anyone calling her a liar and interrupted him. "I told you the truth when I said I didn't have any more…!" she snapped. But Christian interrupted her interruption. "Where did you have this gun hidden?" Sarah answered angrily. "It was on my packhorse! and my packhorse was at the Trading Post! so I didn't have it on me! …did I?" Christian could understand her reasoning, but the packhorse, even though it wasn't with her when he asked her if she had more guns, was still her horse, and the gun, being on her horse, meant she didn't tell him the whole truth about not having any more guns. Not wanting to get into further argument with her, because he figured he would lose, he let the guns whereabouts slide.

The water in the pot began to steam. Taking the cloth, Thomas lifted the pot off the fire, then put the cloth in the water to wet it. Christian watched Thomas wring the cloth out and hand it to Sarah. While Sarah began to wipe her face, Christian weighed the two guns in his hands. The black Colt .44 was a lot heavier than his own gun, his being a Colt.45. Sarah had to hold it with both hands to fire it, but she still managed to reload the gun quickly each time she fired a round. Sarah obviously knew what she was doing when it came to guns, and Christian thought she must have had a good teacher to have taught her how to use them.

Trying to wipe blood off her face, but unable to see what she was doing, only made it worse. Putting the guns down, Christian took the cloth from Sarah. Moving himself closer, so he could use the glow from the fire to see what he was doing, he gently wiped the cloth over her cheek and along her jaw. Rinsing the cloth, then while trying to move her collar aside, his fingers brushed her neck, causing a sudden warmth to course through Sarah that she hadn't felt in a long time. Frowning, she grabbed his hand. "Don't go there, sheriff," she said softly. A quiver of excitement ran through Christian from her touch. "I'm going to have to search your camp Cole," he said, keeping his voice low and handing her the cloth. "What for?" Sarah's voice was barely audible when she answered. "For guns," Christian said looking into her eyes. "There aren't any," Sarah said back to him.

While staying focused on each other, their quietly spoken banter passed back and forth. "Why don't I believe you Cole?" he whispered, struggling to keep himself in check. Christian's face was so close to Sarah's he could have moved forward a fraction and kissed her. Watching Christian move closer, Sarah focused on his mouth. Seeing how inviting it looked, she thought if she moved her head forward a fraction, she could kiss him. When Christian suddenly moved away and began to get up, the moment was lost and Sarah's eyes bore into him. "You do what you have to do sheriff! but don't you go putting your dirty boots where Thomas and I have to sleep!" she said, her voice becoming harsh.

Carrying both guns, Christian stopped outside the entrance of the shelter where he lay both down to do up his shirt and the buttons on his trousers. After sitting in the entrance to remove his boots, he shoved his gun down the front of his pants, then, picking Sarah's gun up, he crawled inside.

A lamp sitting on an upturned box at the back of the shelter allowed him to see everything. Crawling across blankets and furs piled on the ground, he found a rucksack next to a small wooden box with a lid. After tipping the rucksack's contents out and studying each item, he could see this part of the shelter was where Thomas slept.

As well as two other books, there is a reading book, its pages tattered and curled at the corners. There is a small knife in a sheath. He picked up a few small decorative stones, then dropped them. Flicking through pages of a writing book, he could see, even though the writing is in a child's hand, it is very neat. Putting all the items back in the rucksack, and picking up a much larger book, he flicked its pages and came across beautiful sketches of wolves and other animals, scenes of forests, mountains and a river. He stopped at a picture of a cabin. Going by the drawing, it is well-built. Flicking the pages further, he stopped when he came across pictures of people. There were the four trappers, Joe, Fergus, Will and Garrett. How important these four men are to Thomas and Cole Christian does not know, but seeing the drawings, he is going to make it his business to find out.

Christian felt his face burning when he came across several sketches of Sarah. They are a good likeness. Her long hair drapes over her shoulders, wisps of curls frame her face. Sarah's mouth is curled in a smile, her eyes appear soft and seductive. Who is she smiling at? The next picture is a full figure of Sarah, standing on a boulder, holding her rifle against her shoulder, aiming at something, and again, she is smiling and looks very happy. All the sketches appear to have been drawn a long time ago. Joe, Fergus, Will and Garrett all appear younger than now. Christian came across one more sketch of Sarah. This one, like all the others, had been drawn a long time ago, only something had changed. Christian believed it had been drawn by the same person who drew the other pictures, but Sarah herself was different. In this picture her eyes are sad, the light had gone out of them, like tonight when he looked into her eyes. She isn't smiling and her long hair is short. It looks as if Sarah has lost her spark. Something obviously happened to cause her to become sad. Christian turned the book back to the cover.

Someone had written in the front, 'This book belongs to Frank Mason.' The name Frank Mason had been crossed out and under it was written 'Thomas Mason'. There it was! The initial's FM carved in the grip of Cole's pistol belonged to Frank Mason, Thomas had to be Frank's son. But then Christian wondered, why didn't Cole go by the name of Mason instead of Cole? The only answer he could come up with was, Frank Mason and Cole weren't married. Thomas was born out of wedlock and that was why Crawley called her a whore and Thomas a bastard. Still, Christian thought, Crawley had no right calling them those names. 'Where is Frank Mason now?' Christian asked himself, closing the book and putting it back in the rucksack. At least some of his earlier questions had been answered.

Opening the small wooden box, Christian found Thomas's new clothes folded neatly inside. His new boots sit next to a pair of thick socks. Rummaging around under the socks, he found a silver timepiece wrapped between a piece of cloth. Opening the timepiece, he read the inscription. 'Frank, Happy 16th Birthday Love Mother.' Convinced the watch once belonged to Thomas's father, he closed the watch and put it back under the socks and closed the box. It didn't go unnoticed, how the shelter was divided in two. Hanging from a rope stretched along the middle and fastened to each end of the shelter, were blankets anchored to the floor the same way as the sides. Cole and Thomas slept beside each other, but separated by blankets for privacy.

When Christian crawled out of the shelter and glanced toward the firepit, Thomas looked up and said something to Sarah. Christian figured he was telling her he was going in her side. Which he did, closing the flap behind him.

Thomas watched Christian come out, saw him glance toward them, then crawl back inside. "He's going in your side, Ma." Sarah kept her face to the river. "He's going to be going through everything!" Sarah felt saddened. The sheriff would look through her rucksack and find Frank's bible. She hoped he would leave it alone when he saw it, but somehow, she knew he wouldn't. He was an inquisitive man, and would want to know why she had a ribbon tied around a bible. Thomas leant over and put his head on Sarah's shoulder. "You are tired Thomas, as soon as the sheriff is gone, you can go back to sleep." Thomas kept his head where it was. "I'm ok Ma, I can wait until he's gone." They both went quiet for a moment. Christian stayed inside the shelter. "Ma, we killed a lot of rat's, didn't we?" Thomas giggled quietly. "Yeah ...I didn't know Frank's gun would blow them to pieces like it did, look at the mess they made." Sarah glanced around at the slaughter that surrounded her camp. "You belted them pretty good with that stick Thomas, I saw one go all the way over there in the trees." Sarah giggled then too. "Yeah, I bet I gave that rat a pretty good headache." They both laughed quietly so Christian couldn't hear them.

Sarah's side of the shelter was laid out much the same as Thomas's, except her wooden box was bigger than his. After up-ending Sarah's rucksack, Christian perused the contents spread out on the blanket. There is a wooden handled hair brush, and some hairpins, also two lengths of ribbon, one a faded pink and the other a pale blue. Two small calibre bullets, that he can tell are for Sarah's pistol, sit among the hairpins. When a small black book with a faded yellow hair ribbon tied with a bow wrapped around it fell out of the rucksack, Christian picked it up and saw it was a bible. Why he wondered, did a bible need to have a ribbon tied around it? To satisfy his curiosity, he untied the ribbon and flicked through the pages. What surprised him were stains all through the book. The stains were so bad, some of the pages couldn't be read at all. He had seen stains like these before. Someone's blood had been spilt to be all over the bible. Flicking back to the front, he read on the inside cover, a message written in a neat hand, but badly faded.

> '*To my darling son Frank, on your Christening*
> *May this book guide you through bad times*
> *Your loving mother*'

Scrawled in pencil under the first message was another message, stained with blood.

'My darling Sarah, know that I loved you with all of my being
I never wanted to leave you this way
I know it will be difficult, but I beg you,
forgive me for what I am about to do
Believe me when I say, my love for you will last forever

Frank'

Christian closed the book and thought about Frank's message addressed to Sarah. 'At last!' he thought. 'The initials SC etched on her pistol stood for Sarah Cole and the bible belonged to Frank Mason. He was Sarah's lover, and the father of Thomas. But where is he? What has happened to Frank? Is it his blood staining the bible? Why did he leave her? What was it he was going to do that he needed to ask her to forgive him?' The bible gave Christian one answer but left him with so many more questions.

Sarah was a mystery to Christian and he wanted answers, but it was too soon to delve too deeply into her life, he had only just met her, but he knew right from the very moment he met her he wanted to get to know her more.

After re-tying the ribbon around the bible as best as he could, and putting it back in the rucksack, he opened the wooden box and looked inside. Boxes containing bullets for the shotgun, the pistol and Thomas's rifle were stacked neatly in this box. Christian couldn't see bullets for the .44. 'Where were they?' he asked himself. While closing the box, and before leaving the shelter, Christian noticed something else. There wasn't any man's clothing. To him, this could mean only one thing, and that was, Sarah was alone.

Feeling around the bedding and furs, he came across something hard under the blanket. Uncovering Sarah's large hunting knife, he gave it a quick glance and covered it back over, then, as he crawled out of the shelter, he noticed her boots, standing just inside the entrance, convincing him she dressed quickly when the rats invaded her camp.

Walking towards the firepit, he noticed two small boxes near the tree where Sarah had been standing when she shot the rats. Picking up the two boxes, he found one completely empty, and half the ammunition was gone out of the other. If his calculations were correct, and one box had been full and each box contained twenty shells, then Sarah shot around thirty rats. He thought this an incredible number to kill in such a short period of time. Sarah said she didn't miss any. That made her a perfect shot. Was she that good? Christian hoped he never had to find out.

"Well, sheriff …did you find what you were looking for?" Sarah asked, holding the cloth to her cheek as he came over and stood near the fire in front of her and Thomas. The fire had a fresh lot of wood on it and was throwing off good heat and bright light. Thomas looked up at Christian sleepily, making Christian think Thomas needed to go back to bed. Having put their furs in, got fresh supplies and set up their camp, all after travelling from the mountain, both Thomas and Sarah appeared worn out. He surprised himself by thinking of Cole as Sarah. Aware too, he had to be careful. He didn't think she would appreciate him calling her Sarah when everyone called her Cole.

Eager for Thomas to get back to sleep as soon as possible, Christian tried not to waste any more time, however, Sarah had other ideas.

"I didn't find any guns …but you should know Cole …I could lock you up for what you did here tonight, however…" he started to say.

Sarah rose quickly to her feet. "You want to lock me up and leave a child on his own, without someone to keep him safe! …is that the sort of man you are sheriff?" she snapped. At that point Christian thought. 'If you want an argument Sarah, I will oblige you!'

"If you let me finish …Cole!" he snapped back. "What I was going to say is, I am not going to lock you up, I am going to fine you instead." Even though fining people for breaking the law was in practice in other towns and cities across the country, Christian was pleased he came up with the idea for Cedar Creek.

"Fine me!" Sarah said, raising her voice and looking bewildered. "What in tarnation is that?" She had never heard of such a thing as a fine, and so folding her arms, waited for Christian to explain what it was. Looking at the cut on her cheek, and thinking Doc Harris would have to stitch it up, Christian silently kicked himself for thinking he had scared Sarah's pretty face, then went on to explain what a fine was.

"Instead of spending time in a cell, you pay money for the damage you caused." Pleased with his idea, he thought Sarah would understand. "Money!" she exclaimed. "You want me to pay you money for shooting vermin?" She laughed incredulously while holding her hand up to her injured cheek.

"You don't pay me Cole!" Christian said, trying to ignore her mocking him. "Yes, I collect the money, but it goes into the public purse and is spent for the betterment of the community, say for instance, it could be spent on the church, or the new Town Hall that is being built, or the school may benefit from it." Even though standing in front of Sarah was unnerving, he kept his voice steady. Sarah muttered she didn't mind her money going to the school if the children were to benefit from it, but she wasn't going to have her money going to the church, she wouldn't give them a dime after what the god-fearing town folk did to her. Her trousers were sitting low on her hips, and if they fell any further, what was hidden between her legs would become exposed. Taking hold of the sides while Christian was still speaking, she pulled them up, then let them go. Christian watched them fall back over her hips to sit at the exact same place they had been before.

"How much do I have to pay sheriff?" Christian was staring and didn't realize Sarah had spoken to him. "Sheriff! ...how much do I have to pay?" Sarah frowned at Christian not taking any notice of her. Having heard Sarah this time, Christian lifted his eyes and looked at her face. "I ...I have to work that out ...um ...you ...you better let Doc see to that wound, then come by my office and I will be able to tell you."

"Oh no! ...I have to clean this mess up first!" Looking around at the carnage littering the camp, Sarah folded her arms. "That may take me most of the day! ...then I will go see Doc ...maybe then I will go by your office ...if I have the time!" she finished defiantly. Christian knew if he let her say more, he wouldn't get away from there any time soon. "All right Cole, after you do what you have to, come and see me and I will tell you how much the fine is." Leaving Sarah and Thomas in front of their firepit, Christian started to walk off.

"Oh, and Cole!" he said, as he side-stepped over rocks covered in rat guts, blood and bits of fur. "Just so as you know! ...no! ...I am not the type of man to leave a child all alone on the riverbank to fend for himself!" Then, not giving Sarah a chance to answer, and while paying careful attention to where he was stepping, and carrying the last of Sarah's gun's away with him, he left her camp quickly.

Chapter Seven

After the four trappers left the riverbank with Clem, they didn't go back to the Ferguson House right away. Joe took the three men around the back of the house and stood on the ridge overlooking Sarah's camp. Standing side by side, looking down at Sarah and Thomas sitting by their fire, they watched as Sheriff Morgan squatted in front of Sarah, and took the cloth she was wiping her face with off her. Joe wasn't happy, neither were the other men standing silent as they watched him wipe Sarah's face. Sheriff Morgan hurt Sarah, and now it looked like he was trying to fix what he had done. The four men couldn't hear what Sarah and Sheriff Morgan were talking about, they kept their heads close together, too close for Joe's liking, and their voices low.

The men watched Sheriff Morgan stand up and walk toward Sarah's shelter. Joe couldn't see exactly where he went, but figured he had gone inside to search for guns. Standing quietly on the ridge, the men waited for Sheriff Morgan to come back out, but it was a long time before they saw him again. When he went back to Sarah and Thomas still sitting at their fire, Joe could hear his voice, but unable to make out what he was saying, paid particular attention to Sarah as she got to her feet and said something back to him. When they started to have a disagreement, both their voices grew louder. Not wanting Sarah to know they were standing there watching, all four men tried their best to hear what was being said, but they couldn't make out the words without getting too close to the edge of the ridge.

Joe was pleased though, because Sarah seemed to be giving Sheriff Morgan as good as what he was giving her. Joe smiled over at Fergus and the two men laughed quietly. Sarah was good at giving people a lashing with her tongue. When Sheriff Morgan started up the trail, Joe had seen enough. He headed back to the Ferguson House and the other three men followed.

Thomas was looking forward to going to school. Needing to be rested so he could concentrate in class, he went to the shelter to get some much-needed sleep. Glancing up at the ridge and finding the four men gone, Sarah got busy gathering mangled rat bodies that were scattered all the way from the shelter down to the river. After digging a hole as far away from her camp as she thought would do, she scooped the remains into the hole and buried them. Using her bucket, she threw water over rocks around her camp, and washed blood and any small pieces of remains she missed away. It was late when Sarah finally went to bed.

While undressing, thoughts of Christian came to mind. He was going to cause her no end of trouble and she knew it. After lying on her furs and pulling a blanket over her shoulders, she thought about him sleeping naked too, that being obvious when he turned up at her camp half dressed. She reckoned he must have pulled his clothes on fast when he heard her gunshots. He got a good look at most of her too, and she made no apology for taking a good look at him. She smiled to herself as she closed her eyes.

Sleep didn't come easily though. She had been so damn tired before she was woken by Thomas's yells, now she was wide awake, and unable to stop thinking about Christian and what passed between them. Thinking him a handsome man, his body firm and muscular, and his touch when he wiped the blood from her face gentle, made her chest pound. The feeling coursing through her when he tried to take the gun from her was indescribable. With her eyes closed, she could see him standing in front of her with his shirt open, giving her the urge to reach out and run her hands over his body.

It had been a long time since she touched a man intimately and a man touched her. Except for Foley Andrews, who was the only man she showed any interest in, because he proposed to her every winter, she hadn't given any thought to being with anyone. She almost said yes to Foley's last proposal, but after thinking what it meant to be married to Major Hardy's gun-hand, she turned him down again. Besides, Thomas took up all of her time and she pushed all thought of having a relationship behind her. No other man since Frank had turned her head. Not until now.

Christian didn't get much sleep after being woken by Sarah blasting away at the river rats. What followed between them was on his mind when he got back to the lodge and it took a long time to get the thought of Sarah and the way she was dressed, or rather the way she was undressed, out of his mind. The very thought of seeing her partially naked hadn't left him easily. He tossed and turned and only got a couple of hours sleep, but still managed to get up at the same time as usual when daylight streamed through the window and fell across his bed.

Stoking the coals in the fire, he stacked it with wood and waited until flames took hold, then went to the washroom where he washed his face and hands to help wake him up. Leaving the blood-stained trousers for Maria to wash, he dressed then cooked himself breakfast of bacon and eggs, and finished it all off with a mug of coffee. By the time he finished eating, Sarah and her mostly naked body had taken over his thoughts again. What he saw he liked, and while smiling to himself, he thought about the times he had ridden all over the country, meeting lots of women, but never meeting any remotely like Sarah.

After finishing breakfast and before making his way to the Sheriff's Office, he needed to get Sarah out of his mind, so he took a walk around town. Walking up one side of the main street taking in Ham's Livery, he crossed the road by the bridge, and walked past the corrals, the church and the cemetery. He crossed to the other side of the street to the schoolhouse, turned down the boardwalk on the opposite side to the Sheriff's Office, strolled past Doc Harris's Practice, the Eatery, the Saloon, and Crawley's General Store. As he walked, his thoughts kept returning to what happened between him and Sarah. Crossing the road leading toward Clem's farm, and making his way behind the Ferguson House, he stood at the edge of the ridge overlooking Sarah's camp, and could see she had partly cleaned up the gruesome mess from the night before. It was still early, Sarah he imagined, was still asleep in her shelter. 'Would she be naked? or lying there with her clothes on?' he wondered. Christian stayed for a few minutes, then walked back along the street to his office. Clem hadn't arrived yet. It was still too early for him.

The first thing Clem did each day when he arrived, was get himself a hot drink, so Christian lit the fire in the potbelly stove and put on a fresh pot of coffee. Clem came in about an hour later and informed Christian his wife, still feeling ill, was at him again to move to Moreton to see their grandchildren before it was too late. Christian told Clem he was free to leave whenever he wanted, he would not stop him. However, he said, he needed at least one deputy to back him if there were any trouble. Clem thanked Christian and said he would make every effort to find someone to replace him as soon as he could. They discussed the day and what they both planned on doing.

Light shone through the opening of the flap at the front of the shelter and Sarah woke up. The day dawned too soon, but Sarah was rearing to get started. She dressed first then went to the river to wash her face and hands. Getting the fire going, she heated the coffee pot and it wasn't long before the smell of hotcakes wafted through the air. Thomas was dressed and sitting by the fire eating the first of the hotcakes to come out of the pan. Pouring treacle over the hotcakes, he drowned them in the sticky substance. They ran out of treacle at their cabin months ago and Sarah proposed to get extra tins of the sticky sweet substance before returning to the mountain so they had enough to last them until the following winter. Sarah couldn't help laughing at Thomas as she watched treacle ooze between his fingers as he shoved the warm cakes in his mouth.

Thomas's first comment to Sarah when she woke this morning, was that her cheek looked really nasty. It felt sore, even though the sheriff said it didn't look bad, she had her doubts. After convincing Sarah he was old enough to take himself to school, Thomas raced off, leaving her to clean up the rest of the river rats from the riverbank.

Digging another deep hole near the first, and using her small spade to pick up the pieces, she scooped the pieces into her bucket and dropped them in the hole. Filling the hole with dirt, and piling rocks, leaves and bark along with tree branches over the top so the remains couldn't be dug up by other animals, she threw numerous buckets of water over the stones along the riverbank to wash away blood and any remains she couldn't scoop. It took Sarah several hours to complete the clean-up. Standing by the river, she looked back at her camp, and felt pleased with how she managed to rid the area of all the gory bits. Snares would have to be set now if she wanted to catch rats to stop them from invading her camp.

Quickly running her hands through grit and pebbles in the river to clean them, and after tidying herself up as best as she could by brushing her hair and braiding it, it was well after midday when she set off for Doc Harris's Practice so he could check her health and take a look at the cut on her cheek.

To get to the main street and Doc's, Sarah had a couple of choices in which way she went, but she decided to walk past the Ferguson House. Major Hardy's horses were due in sometime that day, and some of the trappers, waiting to start breaking them, were whiling their time away by sitting on the front steps relaxing with a cheroot. When Sarah drew level with the house, they couldn't help seeing the cut on her face. Logan, the nastiest of trappers and Sarah had been friends once, but after what happened between them, Sarah no longer trusted him.

Thomas was just four years old when he and Sarah camped in the same place they were camped now. Sarah always camped in the same place when she came to town. Everyone knew the riverbank below the Ferguson House was her place. Sarah had been asleep in her shelter when she suddenly felt Logan's hand sliding up her leg under her blanket. Trying to fight him off, she found him too strong and he soon overpowered her. Luckily the four trappers were there in an instant. After beating Logan within an inch of his life, Joe made Logan apologize for his drunken behaviour, but a few months later, he had the audacity to propose to her. Sarah turned him down flat, she wasn't the least bit interested in him, she wasn't in love with him, in fact, she disliked him a great deal.

As Sarah approached the house, Logan sniggered. He didn't care that Frank Mason had beaten him to bed her and got her pregnant. He didn't care that Joe nearly beat him to death when he tried taking her in her shelter. He still thought her worth having, and was determined to pursue his desire for her to that end. "Who have you been fighting with this time Cole?" Logan knew very well what happened. When the four trappers got back to the house, after loud gunshots woke everyone, Joe informed the men Sarah was shooting rats as she always did, only this time she had to use Frank's gun.

The way Logan spoke to Sarah just now, put her on the defensive. "That is none of your business Logan!" she snapped. "You would be better off if you didn't smoke those goddamn horse shit cheroots you suck on! …maybe then some girl would be able to get near you!" Sarah smiled when some of the men laughed at what she said, although none of them were prepared for Logan's reply. "I'd like to suck on you Cole." Then running his tongue around his mouth, he grabbed his crotch and laughed. The men stopped laughing and looked embarrassed at Sarah. To them it seemed, Logan hadn't learnt his lesson last time, because just as he made his remark and crude gesture, Joe and Fergus stepped out onto the porch.

Sarah could tell by the look on Joe's face Logan was in serious trouble again. Joe didn't like it when the men spoke to her in a derogatory way, not even when they were joshing. Sarah looked at Joe then continued heading toward Doc Harris's Practice.

Doc's practice was quiet when Sarah walked in and found Gerda and Doc in their front room busy cleaning up after the day's patients. They hadn't heard her come in and they both looked up to see who had entered, and when they saw Sarah's face, both were taken aback by her appearance. "Good heavens Sarah, what on earth has happened? you look awful!" When Doc approached Sarah to take a look at her, he kissed her on the opposite cheek to her injury then sucked in his breath when he got a better look at the cut.

"Sarah, darling girl!" Gerda exclaimed, clasping her hands together then drawing Sarah further into the room. "What have you been doing to yourself?"

"I had a bit of trouble when I was shooting rats, sheriff…whatever his name is! …tried to shoot me but missed, said he was firing a warning shot and hit the tree close to my face, a piece of the tree got me …I guess I looked around at the wrong time." Sarah left out the part where both she and Christian were practically naked.

As Gerda and Doc started gathering things together, Doc told Sarah a little about how Christian came to be sheriff. "You know he lives in the lodge!" he finished. Trying to decide what it meant for Christian to be living in the house that once used to be her home, Sarah stared at Doc. After a moment passed, Sarah shrugged her shoulders. "Why should that bother me? The lodge isn't my home anymore, it's Crawley's, he can do what he wants with it …if he wanted to burn it down …he could." Mountain View Lodge was a grand house, standing high above the river. Its upper floor, with its beautiful big bay windows, could be seen along the trail on the approach to town. Sarah hoped Crawley would never burn it down. Doc heard a note of sadness in Sarah's voice when she tried covering up what it meant for someone else to be living in her home. Gerda made Sarah sit on the edge of their examination bed while Doc got a bottle, and opening it, wet a swab with its liquid contents.

"This is going to sting a little Sarah, but I have to sterilize that wound to stop any infection."

"What is that Doc? What is in the bottle?" Sarah didn't like it if she didn't know what it was.

"Just alcohol!" Doc said with a shrug, quickly dabbing the cut on Sarah's cheek before she could refuse it. It stung, causing Sarah to flinch.

"Ow! alcohol! it won't make me smell like I've been drinking, will it Doc? …Ow! " Ignoring what Sarah said, Doc quickly dabbed her face again, this time, it didn't sting as much.

"We heard the commotion last night and thought it was you, so we didn't bother getting up to see what was going on," Doc said, busying himself at his tray of instruments.

"There wasn't anything to see." Sarah answered as Doc stuck a piece of tape over her wound. "Your face is bruised and you have a black eye, but that should clear up in a week or two, the cut isn't very deep, thank goodness …I won't need to stitch it." When Gerda held up a mirror, Sarah could see a bruise spreading out in the corner near her eye and around the tape. Like he always did from the time Sarah was born, Doc finished with giving her, her usual check-up. Sarah was grateful for Doc making sure she was healthy. Although he didn't deliver Thomas, Doc checked his health every winter too.

"You send Thomas over so I can check on him, I want to see how he is growing and if he is healthy, Sarah don't you forget." Because she was anxious to get to the Sheriff's Office to see Christian, she told Doc she wouldn't forget, and left him and Gerda just as a farmer was carried in by his two sons with a cut to his leg.

Chapter Eight

Clem took his usual walk to the saloon to see what was happening there. With men already gathering for the day, he found the place rowdy. No doubt he would take the trapper called Bear back to the cells to spend the night. Bear always ended up spending several nights a week locked up and it was costing money to feed him. Christian was still trying to figure out a way to stop him from spending so much time in his jailhouse.

Bear, a mostly placid giant of a man who has a wild bushy beard covering his face, wears a thick fur coat and hat of which makes him resemble a bear, this being the reason everyone calls him Bear. No-one knows what his real name is. Bear likes keeping to himself most of the time, but he likes his drink, a good fight and a decent meal, so, he spends most of winter causing trouble for the free food he gets every time he gets locked up. The trappers reckon when Clem was sheriff, he liked having Bear in jail so he had someone to talk to on those quiet winter nights. But things are different now there is a new sheriff. Sheriff Morgan isn't keen on locking people up, he wants to fine them, and keep the cells empty.

Having told Sarah, he would have her fine worked out for when she came in to see him, Christian pulled out the bottom draw of his desk, and reaching in, lifted out a blank piece of paper. He was looking forward to her visit, and hoped they could both talk more amicably instead of arguing, but he doubted when she found out how much he was going to fine her if she was going to be very happy about it, still, he thought, he would like to see her.

After sitting for a long time, and crossing off a lot of figures, he decided he needed another break, so heading out for another walk, this time retracing his steps in the opposite direction, he walked towards the Ferguson House first then crossed the road to the Trading Post. Walking up a street behind the main street, passing private homes, he walked toward the schoolhouse, and as he drew near, he could hear children playing outside. Coming around the side of the building, he saw a group of children playing catch with a ball, and another group chasing each other around the yard.

Smiling at the sound of laughing children, Christian was about to continue his walk when he spotted Thomas sitting by himself under the shade of a tree with his legs crossed, holding a small stick in his hand that he was using to scratch in the dirt. Billy Henderson was sitting on the schoolhouse porch, swinging his legs back and forth over the side. Every now and then, Billy glanced over at Thomas, and to Christian it looked like Billy was trying to work up the courage to talk to him. Feeling certain they had to have known each other before now, he wondered why the two boys weren't already playing together.

As he watched, two older boys, Jamie Finch and Daniel Connell, ran past Thomas and kicked dirt in his direction. Thomas leant back, keeping away from the dirt, but didn't do anything about it. As the Finch and Connell boy's ran back the other way, they kicked dirt up again, and again, Thomas continued to sit there and take it.

O'Rourke, appearing oblivious to what Jamie Finch and Daniel Connell had been doing, called the children inside. Thomas got up and ran quickly to the porch ahead of the other boys. Watching Billy Henderson as Thomas approached, Christian thought Billy was going to say something to Thomas, but as Thomas rushed past, Billy obviously decided against it, and followed Thomas inside.

While wondering why Thomas and Billy sat by themselves and why Thomas let the older boy's kick dirt at him, Christian made his way back to his office. Thomas didn't seem like the same boy who threatened him when he thought he was going to shoot his mother.

Christian had only been back in his office for a couple of minutes when Foley came barging in. Major Hardy's men, while rounding up strays came across several dead steers, and dead steers meant the Major was losing money. Foley rode to town with strict orders to bring Christian to the dry gulch. The dry gulch was at least two hours ride to the far reaches of the Major's ranch, which meant Christian would have a long ride back to town. Studying Foley's face, Christian wondered just what sort of fight Foley had been in to get a scar all the way from his forehead to his chin. Being hired to keep control of rowdy cowhands and anyone else that threatened the Major or his cattle and horses, Christian thought it possible that was how he got it. Christian informed Foley his role as sheriff didn't include looking at a couple of dead steers.

"The Major sent me to get you because it's more than a couple, it's more like twenty," Foley said seriously. "The Major said I wasn't to come back without you sheriff," he added.

"Well then ...Foley!" Christian said, grabbing his hat off the rack behind the door and stepping outside. "We had better go take a look." As he pulled his hat on, he decided Sarah's fines would just have to wait.

Sarah hurried across the street and up to the Sheriff's Office, hoping when Christian saw her, he would be sorry for the damage he caused to her face. Pushing open the door, she entered. Except for one prisoner being held in the cells, the office appeared to be empty. Clem came barging in behind Sarah standing in front of the desk. "Hello Cole, what can I do for you?" he asked jovially. "I'm looking for the sheriff, he around?" Sarah asked, seeing Bear asleep in a cell. "No, he's out at the Major's, something to do with dead steers, he won't be back 'til later today, not something I can help you with is it?" he asked as he moved around the desk. "He was going to tell me how much I have to pay for shooting off my guns and getting rid of all those vermin ...don't suppose he told you how much I have to pay?" Sarah was disappointed Christian wasn't there. He told her to call in, so she thought he should have been waiting for her. They had gotten off to a bad start and she wanted to talk more civil to him to see what he was really like, but now she was mad at him all over again.

"Nope! ...maybe you ought to come back later ...when he comes back." Clem informed her.

"I am not chasing after him Clem! you tell the sheriff, if he wants me to know what fines I have to pay, he can come to me, he knows where my camp is!" Sarah opened the door and stepped outside into what appeared to be a storm building up. The sky had turned dark, the wind was picking up, leaves and small twigs were starting to be blown from trees.

The two men rode in silence all the way to the dry gulch where the river formed one boundary of the Major's land and high cliffs another. Arriving at the spot where the dead steers were, Christian found the Major, and another of his gun-hand's Brady, waiting for him. Before looking at the steers, Christian took a moment to look about the area. Except for tall trees and low growing shrubs covered in red berries growing along the edge of the river, the ground in the gulch where the dead steers were, was bone dry. The hills surrounding the gulch, were barren of trees. Walking amongst some of the steers, Christian tried to find signs as to the cause of their demise. But there didn't appear to be any. They looked very much like they had dropped dead where they were feeding. Christian suggested they cut one open to see if there was anything in its gut that may show what caused so many steers to die.

"We don't carry knives with us to cut them open, sheriff," Foley said, bringing that fact to Christian's attention. Foley sat tall in his saddle. His repeater rifle in its holster, hung near his saddle-horn. The six-shooter strapped to his hip sat low like Christian's. Christian wore his gun low to enable him to draw fast without having to lift it too far. He wondered about Foley, and Brady. The two men, similar in appearance were always together and he couldn't figure out what it was about them that puzzled him. "I will have to come back and bring a knife with me to…" Christian started to say. "I reckon you will need one of those skinning knives the trapper's use to slice through these tough hides," Foley interrupted. Major Hardy, sitting quietly by, watched Christian with a furrowed brow, while Brady, whom Christian had never heard utter a word the whole time he had been in Cedar Creek, sat quietly on his horse while he and Foley talked.

"Yeah, I think I just might." Christian almost said to himself, wondering why these men didn't carry knives with them. 'They slaughtered steers for food, didn't they?' he asked himself. Maybe they just relied on their guns, either way, he didn't pursue the matter.

"You wouldn't happen to know where I might get one would you?" Christian laughed, trying to making a joke to ease the tension. There were plenty of trappers in town he could borrow a sharp knife off, but the three men didn't crack a smile.

Major Hardy thought Christian arrogant. He didn't allow his men to carry hunting knives, not since the incident twelve years ago where his expensive prized longhorn bull had been slaughtered. He still had no idea who the culprit was, and he didn't trust anyone, not even his own men. All knives were kept at the ranch for when fresh meat was required. A steer would be brought to the corral nearest the ranch-house and slaughtered. If a steer became sick it would be shot, then burnt, and the remains buried. However, here was a large number of steers, dying for no apparent reason, and it was costing him money. He wanted to know now, not later, what was killing them. "When do you plan on coming back here sheriff?" Major Hardy asked without feeling. "Maybe in two or three days," Christian offered, wanting to get back to town. He had better things to do besides look at dead steers. "Come back tomorrow, I don't want more steers dying in the meantime," Major Hardy ordered. Then to make sure the carcasses couldn't attract wolves, he ordered his men to oversee the burning and burial of the remains.

Having met Major Hardy not long after coming to town, Christian thought him a decent man, but his arrogant attitude just now bemused Christian. Major Hardy pulled on his reins, making his horse turn suddenly, and without so much as a buy your leave, rode off. Both Foley and Brady nodded to Christian and followed him. It seemed to Christian, when Major Hardy spoke, everyone was expected to jump. Well not him, he didn't jump, not for anyone.

After Major Hardy and his men left, Christian walked amongst the dead steers. Some were decomposing and their stench lay thick in the air. Others appeared to have dropped dead just a few hours earlier. Mystified as to the cause of their death, he scratched his head and headed back to town the way Foley had taken him out to the gulch. While riding along, he wondered if there could have been a quicker way to get back. Thinking if he crossed to the other side of the river, there might be an easy trail he could follow, but not wanting to be caught out after dark when he wasn't wearing warm clothing, he decided not to look for another way right then.

Night-time temperatures were dropping, he felt snow would not be far away now that it had fallen on the mountains.

Instead of riding straight back to town, Christian took the opportunity to stop along the way at some of the outlying farms and ranches to see how folk were coping. Compared to the Major's twenty thousand acres, the Anderson's had a very small spread. Their ranch was a thousand acres and they ran a few head of cattle and grew corn. Several fields were ploughed ready for planting. The Anderson's welcomed Christian happily. Joan made a pot of coffee and laid out a nice plate of freshly baked cookies. Becky, their five-year old daughter joined them on their porch. Becky was born with a twisted leg, Joan explained. Doc Harris put a steel brace on her leg to straighten it, although still on crutches this allowed her to get around easily. Christian remembered seeing Becky when Sarah rode into town. Watching Sarah give the little girl and other children candy outside Crawley's store, he saw her whole demeanor change, becoming gentle in her approach to the children, particularly toward Becky.

Leaving the Anderson's, he headed over to the Barker's, a few miles closer to town. The road Christian rode along ran from town, past the Barker and Anderson farm's, all the way to Major Hardy's ranch where green paddocks made way for dry, barren land toward the back of his land. The Barker's yards were fenced, and horses ran freely in paddock's where grass was long and lush. Their farm was the smallest, only a hundred acres. The few horses they ran were used for ploughing their own fields. As he rode up the trail between fences on both sides, a crop of corn swayed in the breeze. He passed a field planted out with carrots. Potatoes grew in another. This was one of the farms that supplied the town with fresh produce.

On seeing him ride up, the Barker's welcomed him and invited him to stay for lunch. He was happy to oblige them as Tom Barker was a pleasant man to talk with, and his wife Mary, was a good cook. While sitting on their porch, at a table in the sun, talking about everyday things while they ate, Christian fished for information about the only female trapper he heard of, without sounding like he was too interested in her. "What can you tell me about the Cole woman Tom?" he asked while putting fresh cooked vegetables straight from the Barker farm on his fork. "Can't tell you nothing about her sheriff," Tom answered in his dry country drawl, clamping up all of a sudden. "We don't talk about Cole, Sheriff Morgan, it wouldn't be proper," Mary offered, taking a fleeting glance at her husband before smiling at Christian and continuing to eat her meal. Refusing to get into a conversation with Christian about Sarah, the Barker's changed the subject and talked about the different crops they were growing. Tom and Mary Barker weren't the first people to refuse to talk about Sarah. Everyone Christian spoke with wouldn't tell him anything about her. That only served to make him all the more curious.

It was well into the afternoon when he left the Barker farm. The ride back to town took him through to late afternoon when dark ominous clouds started to appear in the sky. A storm was brewing. As he approached the outskirts of town, lightning streaked across the sky and the sound of thunder rumbled off in the distance. Spots of rain began to fall.

Chapter Nine

While waiting for Thomas to come from school, Sarah watched the sky nervously. Dark clouds were building and rolling in across the river. It was too early to prepare dinner, so, worried her camp wouldn't withstand a severe thunderstorm, she checked it was in order.

Seeing the ominous looking clouds gathering, O'Rourke sent the children home early to beat the storm. Thomas came running down the trail toward their camp. "Ma! looks like a storm's coming!" he yelled excitedly.

"Looks like it, Thomas, how was your first day at school?" Regardless of the storm, Sarah wanted to know if he made new friends.

"It was good Ma, do you want help tying down our shelter to make it stronger?" Thomas didn't let on how his first day back at school went. He didn't want his Ma to know he didn't have any friends, or that he sat on his own in the yard while Jamie Finch and Daniel Connell kicked dirt at him. They did the same every year, they weren't afraid of him, they weren't afraid of his Ma either. When he threatened them with telling her, they tormented him, and called him a cry baby. It didn't matter that he didn't have any friends, he liked school. He liked to learn all about the faraway places he hoped one day he would get to see. Sarah could only believe Thomas's first day went well.

The wind was picking up and Sarah needed to get their camp organized before she could prepare their meal. "Help me move our supplies in under the shelter first please," Sarah urged, pulling the blankets off the ropes dividing the shelter down the middle, and spreading them out on top of the blankets and furs they slept on. They worked quickly, Sarah's shovel and axe, along with their supplies were stacked in the middle of the shelter by the time rain began to fall. When they finished moving everything, Thomas and Sarah could only stand toward the back of the shelter, watching as the wind started to blow stronger. Ropes tied around stones holding the sides down, worked loose, causing the canopy to billow as gusts of wind blew in under it. The sides suddenly lifted as a gust of wind caught them and blew them over the top of the shelter, making the shelter open to the wind and rain. When lightning streaked the sky and thunder became fierce their situation became worse. Powerful gusts of wind snapped branches off trees and sent them flying toward the canopy. When a branch flew in where Thomas and Sarah were standing, Sarah grabbed it and dragged it out into the rain. All around the camp, leaves and branches littered the ground. Larger tree branches started crashing around them and the sky grew dark. Rain coming in sideways under the shelter fell in torrents, putting out their fire. When a huge tree crashed on top of the firepit crushing it, Sarah knew it was time to find a safer haven. Thomas looked frightened, he had experienced storms before, but not as bad as this. 'This storm was going to be bad,' Sarah thought as she put her arm around Thomas's shoulders to reassure him.

"Thomas, get your rucksack and put it outside!" Before diving out in the rain, Thomas grabbed his drawing book and timepiece out of his wooden box and shoved them in his rucksack. He came charging back in under the shelter just as the canopy whipped up and smacked back down with a loud 'thwack'. As wind and torrential rain roared towards them from across the river, Sarah grabbed her rucksack and put it outside next to Thomas's. "Get your knife and help me drop the canopy!" Sarah yelled. Racing around, they cut ropes holding the canopy to the trees. Thomas though was having trouble reaching ropes tied higher up, so Sarah cut those and the canopy dropped, falling in a wet heap over their belongings. Watching Sarah pull at the canopy to straighten it, Thomas got in and helped.

"Get some stones Thomas and throw them on the canopy to hold it down!" Thomas couldn't hear what Sarah was saying, so she grabbed a rock and threw it to show him what to do. By the time they finished tossing rocks on the canopy, they were both soaked through.

Quickly picking up her rucksack, she put it on her back. Copying what she was doing, Thomas put his rucksack over his shoulders. "Come on, let's go!" Sarah yelled, pointing toward the riverbank. Taking Thomas by the hand, they ran along the edge toward town. The wind was so strong blowing across the river it made running against it difficult, but Sarah felt grateful. Trees swaying violently, and their broken branches, were being tossed away from them.

The sky grew black, night came early. Sarah and Thomas made their way as fast as possible along the riverbank. Sarah suddenly stopped running. Already drenched to the bone and freezing cold, it made no difference for them to stand and wait until a flash of lightning lit up the area around them, enabling her to find the track leading to the alley beside Hams Livery. When she saw the track not far ahead, she didn't have to say anything to Thomas. When she moved, Thomas knew to go with her. Fighting their way through tree branches and wet foliage lashed by wind, they came out behind the Livery.

Watching lightning streak across the sky and thunder rumble overhead, hoping he would make it back before the storm hit, Christian pushed his horse faster. By the time he passed the corrals and rode at a gallop into the Livery it was raining. Pulling his horse up quickly before it went charging into the stalls and hurting itself, Christian dismounted. Making the boardwalk across the alley in a couple of strides, he walked briskly down the boardwalk back to his office where he found Clem waiting anxiously for him. Clem had been watching the storm building and had begun to worry about his wife being on her own. He told Christian how his wife hated storms and didn't like to be left alone. Christian told Clem to head home before the storm got too bad and he couldn't get home to his wife at all. Clem didn't argue with Christian, he said goodnight and disappeared out the door.

After Clem left, Christian made his way to the eatery for dinner. The storm being responsible for keeping everyone in their own homes, he found the eatery empty, so ate his meal alone, then against the wind and driving rain, and carrying a covered meal on a plate for Bear, he made his way back across the street to his office.

Lightning flashed, thunder rumbled overhead and the wind grew stronger. Rain poured in through the open barred windows of the cells, making Christian work fast. Pulling bunks out from under windows so they wouldn't get wet, he unlocked the cell where Bear was trying to get out of the way of the rain and gave him the bunk in the back room to bed down on for the night. Christian could tell it was going to be a long night.

Pouring himself a mug of coffee, he stood at the window to watch the storm. A little way down the street Doc Harris's sign for his practice swung wildly back and forth under the awning. A flash of lightning, followed by a loud clap of thunder, shook the buildings. Small twigs and branches from trees growing along the river flew through the air and slammed into the walls of buildings across the street. It was a vicious storm and Christian wondered about Sarah and Thomas camped on the riverbank. Well aware their shelter wasn't capable of withstanding this kind of storm, he could only hope they would be alright.

Tired of being cooped up inside his office while the storm raged outside, Christian decided to brave the storm and do his rounds. Deciding to only go as far as he could without going out in the rain, and not bothering to wear his coat, he stepped outside, and shivered when a blast of cold air hit him. Keeping to his side of the street where he was sheltered, he made his way along the boardwalk. An alley running toward the river separated the Barber Shop from the Livery. The street where the lodge was situated joined the alley halfway along, making it perfect for wild gusts of wind to converge with gusts blowing from the direction of the lodge. Christian walked as far as the Barber Shop. Holding his hat to stop it blowing away, he stuck his head out into the storm and watched leaves and small branches blowing along the alley towards him.

Thomas shivered violently as he stood alongside Sarah at the back wall of the Livery where a small access door was padlocked. Holding the padlock in her hand as water ran down her face and into her eyes making it hard to see, Sarah pulled her knife from its sheath, and jamming it in behind the steel bar holding the padlock, rammed her knife down hard, then, after forcing the knife down a second time, the timber splintered and the steel bar came off the wall. The door flung open and Sarah grabbed it before it could crash against the wall. Holding her finger up to her mouth, she indicated to Thomas not to make a sound, then, pushing him through the door, followed him in. Finding a lantern, Sarah made her way along the stalls. Thomas's teeth chattered loudly as they moved into a stall where dry straw, spread out on the floor ready to accommodate a horse, greeted them. Hanging the lantern on a nail, and after helping Thomas get his rucksack off his back, Sarah put her rucksack down and took out her drying towel.

Before he could walk back to his office, Christian heard a loud banging coming from the alley. The wind, howling as it blew along the alley made it almost difficult to hear other noises. Putting his head back out into the storm, he listened carefully. The continual pounding sounded like a door being blown back and forth in the wind. Christian stepped into the storm to investigate.

As rain whipped him and wind blew hard against his body, he gripped his hat tight to keep it on his head, and keeping close to the wall, he hurried down the alley to the back of the Livery. Watching trees swaying violently towards him, he rounded the corner, and spotted a small access door being bashed by the howling wind back and forth against the building. Taking hold of the door to stop it banging, he could see the padlock where it had been secured to the wall had been torn off. A fresh cut in the timber indicated it happened not long ago. Lifting his gun out of his holster and cocking it, he stepped gingerly through the door.

Inside, the Livery was dark. Ham's forge where he made horseshoes and other metal fixings glowed dully, its light only just enabling Christian to see his horse in a stall along with Sarah's four horses and a number of other horses. Most of the trapper's horses were left in the corrals where they could get in under a shelter, allowing the Livery to keep stalls free for anyone needing a stall overnight. Slowly making his way along the stalls, looking in each as he went, he came to a stall where dull light shone from a lamp hanging from a nail.

Holding his gun up in front of him, he stepped into the opening. What he saw wasn't what he expected. Un-cocking his gun so as not to startle the pair, he pushed his hat back on his head with the tip of the barrel, and leaning on the post at the entrance, watched Sarah vigorously drying Thomas's hair.

Rubbing Thomas's hair briskly and talking quietly about their camp and the storm, Sarah heard Christian's deep voice behind her. "You do know it is against the law to break in to private property? ...don't you Cole?" he asked. Angry at herself for not hearing Christian before he came into the stall, Sarah removed the towel off Thomas's head and turned to face him. Christian was wet too, but not nearly as wet as Thomas and herself. Thomas shivered while waiting to see what trouble he and his Ma was in. Noticing how Sarah's wet shirt accentuated everything through the thin material, Christian holstered his gun without taking his eyes off her.

"There is a storm outside sheriff! ...if you hadn't noticed!" Sarah answered, making her voice sound angry, although she wasn't angry, not at him, just surprised to see him standing there. Trying not to focus too much on Sarah's wet shirt, Christian replied, "I noticed." Sarah didn't appear to be shivering, even so, it was obvious she was cold, her nipples stood out like two sentinels guarding the gates of Eden, making Christian feel warm inside. Knowing full well what he was looking at, Sarah lifted the towel up in front of her, forcing him to look at her face and not her shirt. "Why didn't you come to the Sheriff's Office Cole? ...you could have taken shelter there," Christian asked, disappointed now he couldn't see anything. Thomas' teeth chattered as he shivered. "Oh! you would just love to lock us in a cell, wouldn't you?" Sarah replied sternly. Christian was about to say he would have given her a blanket and a hot drink and Thomas a bed near the fire, when a door opened and a man's voice called, "whose there?"

Out of the dark recesses of the Livery, Ham appeared carrying a shotgun. "It's alright Ham, it's me ...Sheriff Morgan ...you have company." When Ham saw it was definitely Christian, he lowered his gun. "Cole! Thomas! what the hell!" he said, surprised to see Sarah and Thomas. "Sorry Ham," Sarah said, adjusting the towel across her chest so neither man could see anything. "Our camp is ruined ...we needed to take shelter somewhere, and I thought this was the best place." Sarah's body shivered suddenly.

Trying to ignore the storm raging outside, because there was a storm raging right there in the Livery between him and Sarah, Christian desperately wanted to make it stop, but first, he wasn't going to let her get away with the trouble she was causing. His gaze never left Sarah when he spoke with authority. "As well as breaking in here, which is against the law, Cole broke your lock, and that is destruction of private property …and you know Cole? …I can arrest you for that!"

"Sheriff!" Ham said holding up his hand to stop Christian saying more. "I wouldn't leave the devil out on a night like this …Cole's shelter, like she said, could not have stood up to this storm." Just then a loud clap of thunder shook the Livery and they all looked at each other.

Feeling the heat between her and Christian beginning to surface, Sarah glared at Christian. "I will pay to have your lock fixed Ham, Thomas and I just need to stay until the storm has passed, then we will go!" But Christian wasn't ready to drop it. "It is not that easy Cole! …you can't buy your way out of this!" Everything it seemed was simple to Cole, and Christian wasn't having any of it. "Well, while you two argue, Thomas here is catching his death …come on Thomas, you too Cole, come on in and I'll get you a warm drink and a blanket, you can't stay like that all night," Ham beckoned. When Sarah and Thomas made to follow Ham, Christian stepped between them and blocked their path. "You take Thomas with you Ham …Cole and I have things to discuss." He put his hands on his hips to show he meant business. Ham looked at Christian then Sarah, then shrugged his shoulders. If they had business to discuss it was no concern of his. "Come on Thomas …we'll bring a blanket back for your Ma." Thomas walked around Christian and gave him his suspicious look. Recognizing that look, Christian wondered why Thomas needed to feel suspicious of him. Did he think he was going to hurt his Ma, or him?

Christian waited until he heard the door to Ham's residence close, then hanging his hat on the post at the entrance to the stall, ran his hand through his hair before turning his attention back to Sarah. Taking a step toward her, Sarah stepped back and Christian stopped. "I just want to talk to you Cole," he said barely above a whisper. When he took another step, Sarah stepped back again and ran out of room to put distance between them. Christian stepped closer, bringing them so close they were almost touching. Christian looked into Sarah's eyes and she looked up into his. "What did you want to discuss sheriff?" Seeing a wet strand of hair clinging to Sarah's face, Christian lifted it away and gently ran his fingers down her injured cheek, stopping them under her chin, where he studied her black eye and the bruise he caused, taking in the small piece of tape that covered the cut. "I'm sorry I hurt you, Cole," he said softly. Leaning forward, Christian took a chance when thinking Sarah wouldn't use her knife on him. When Sarah could see what he was about to do, she opened her mouth slightly to welcome his kiss and instinctively put her hand to the handle of her knife.

Christian's heart thumped against his chest. What he thought when he had been alone in his bed was right, Sarah's mouth was soft and inviting. He gently pushed his tongue between her teeth and into the warmth of her mouth. His mouth too was warm, and Sarah's tongue found Christian's. Taking her hand off her knife, she let the towel drop to the floor and brought both hands up to rest on his chest as she eagerly returned his kiss. When they stopped kissing, Christian stepped back, surprised at his eagerness to take what wasn't his.

Suddenly, and without warning, Sarah grabbed hold of Christian's shirt, and pulled him towards her. Coming together in wild abandonment, their mouths worked feverishly, their hands groped for clothing. At the same time Sarah reached for Christian's shirt, Christian pulled Sarah's shirt out of her trousers. Sliding his hand around her waist, he groaned at feeling the silky-smooth coolness of her skin. Hurriedly undoing Christian's buttons, working her way down to his trousers, Sarah slid her hands back over his bare chest, and felt the firmness of his breasts. When Christian moved his hand up the outside of Sarah's shirt, Sarah covered his hand with hers and held it against her, keeping it there for a moment before letting him move his fingers to the buttons. Undoing her shirt, Christian let his fingers slide downward, sending a surge of desire coursing through him. Pushing her shirt open, he cupped each breast, and massaged them until her nipples stood hard against his palms. Christian's body responded to the firmness he was creating. Keeping Sarah against him, his tongue delved deeper within her mouth. Sarah pushed her tongue against Christian's. Their bodies pressed against each other. Their wanting increased with each touch and kiss.

Lightning and thunder continued to rage outside. The temperature inside the stall was rising. Christian helped Sarah loosen his holster and undo his trousers, letting her slip her fingers inside to feel the warmth of his body against her hand. It had been a long time since Christian had been with a woman. Sarah's touch sent waves of wanting surging through him, and he wanted her badly. Christian worked fast. Undoing the front of Sarah's trousers, he pushed his fingers between her legs. Sarah hadn't been with a man since Frank, and hadn't realized how lonely she was. Longing for someone to caress her, she let Christian's fingers make her body come alive. They both knew this was what they wanted, and they were prepared to go all the way for it.

Although working feverishly at touching each other, both Sarah and Christian had the presence of mind to hear a door open. Ham and Thomas were on their way back. Sarah and Christian stopped what they were doing and looked at each other's clothing in disarray. "Fuck! Christian uttered as he rested his head against Sarah's. Her shirt, hanging out of her trousers was wide open. Her breasts were out there for Christian to see, and he was looking. There was no way they could get themselves buttoned up before Thomas and Ham came into the stall. They would surely catch both of them in a very compromising situation.

Sarah looked pleadingly at Christian. He was almost naked. His shirt hung open, exposing his body and his trousers were undone. A line of dark hair ran from his navel and disappeared into the opening. His holster was twisted to one side. Judging by the look on Christian's face when he stepped back and looked at her, she was no better dressed.

Christian was taking all of Sarah in with his eyes when he made a quick decision. Stepping over to the lamp, he blew it out, and plunged the stall into darkness. Sarah quickly buttoned her shirt, then working fast, tucked her shirt back in and buttoned up her trousers.

Chapter Ten

"What the hell happened to the goddamn light?" Ham asked. Sarah jokingly said a big gust of hot air blew it out. Christian almost laughed out loud when he heard Sarah's insinuation that he was full of hot air. Ham went off looking for another light and came back carrying another lamp. Studying Christian in the light, Sarah could see his shirt was now buttoned up and tucked back into his trousers. Christian pushed the belt holding his holster through its buckle and did it up just as Ham and Thomas came into the stall. While Sarah and Christian kept their eyes on each other, Sarah could feel her face burning, and she didn't feel cold anymore, Christian had succeeded in warming her up.

Ham didn't seem to notice anything out of the ordinary. "You can sleep in the loft Cole, you and Thomas will be warm up there, there are plenty of sacks of feed and bales of straw to make beds out of," Ham was saying. Sarah was thinking about what she and Christian had been doing and didn't acknowledge him. Thomas was excited about sleeping in the loft.

"I'm not finished with you Cole," Christian said putting his hands on his hips. Pushing the fact, he and Sarah had just aroused each other to the very brink of sexual gratification to the back of his mind, he reverted back to his authoritarian manner. "There is still the matter of fines to be paid, and now I will have to add another to the list." Sarah thought she knew what he meant when he said he wasn't finished with her, and it had nothing to do with fines. Grabbing his hat off the post, and saying goodnight to Ham and Thomas, Christian gave Sarah a knowing look, then with a nod, stepped through the small side door and back out into the raging storm.

Sarah let Thomas climb the ladder ahead of her. Holding blankets and a plate of cookies, she climbed up a few rungs where she was able to pass them up to him. "You go on up Cole," Ham said behind her. "I'll come up and hand you the coffee pot …it's hot and I wouldn't want you burning yourself."

"Thanks Ham," Sarah said, climbing the ladder. Lying on her stomach, she reached down and took the pot off him. "Here's the mug Cole!" he yelled when he climbed back down. If they were trying to be quiet, it wasn't working. A timber wall was all that separated Ham's Livery from his residence, and it was getting late. Sarah hoped they weren't making too much noise so as to disturb Ham's wife Patrice and their daughter's Sissy and Lilly.

Holding her hands over the edge, Ham threw her the mug. After catching it first try, they smiled back at each other. "Pull the ladder up, you'll be safe up there, and before you leave in the morning, you and Thomas come and have breakfast with Patrice and the girls …goodnight." Ham pushed the ladder up and Thomas helped Sarah pull it all the way. "Good night Ham …and thanks," Sarah said, but Ham had already disappeared. Hearing a door close, she was satisfied he had gone.

"Get out of your wet clothes," Sarah ordered Thomas quietly, watching him sitting on the floor eating a cookie. "Alright Ma …but don't look." Thomas stopped letting Sarah bath and dress him when he turned five, and their shelter was divided in two so they both had their privacy. After taking off his wet clothes and wrapping a blanket tightly around himself, he shuffled over to where Sarah was removing her boots. "You getting out of your wet clothes Ma? you don't want to catch fever," he asked, concern in his voice. Gathering Thomas's wet clothes, Sarah hung them over the railing to dry in the heat rising from Ham's forge. After placing his boots near his clothes, she picked up the blanket Ham gave her, and disappeared behind the stack of feed bags and bales of straw to get undressed. Unbuttoning her shirt, she thought of Christian and what they had been doing, and to get a feeling of what he felt, she closed her eyes and covered her breasts with her hands. Her breasts felt firm, her nipples, hard. Her face began to burn at the memory of his touch. Hastily taking off her shirt and draping it over a sack of feed, she undid her trousers, slid them down her legs and lifted her feet out. Standing naked in the dark for a moment, she thought how Christian's touch made her feel. Closing her eyes again, she pushed her fingers between her legs and gave herself a feeling she hadn't felt in a very long time.

"Ma! you alright?" Sarah jumped from the sudden sound of Thomas's voice bringing her back to reality. Quickly wrapping the blanket around herself and tucking it under her arm, she scooped up her wet clothes and went back to Thomas.

Thomas poured coffee into the mug and handed it to her. "Do you want a cookie Ma? they are nice, not as nice as yours, but they are nice," Thomas smiled. Sarah smiled too. "I'm not hungry Thomas, why don't you have them." Thomas ate the cookies while Sarah sat quietly holding her mug. Finishing her coffee, and seeing Thomas's hair was dry, she brushed her hands through his curly strands, making it curlier. "Oh! Ma! don't make it curly! I like it straight!" Sarah rubbed her hands harder when he complained and they both laughed. "Don't be ashamed of your hair Thomas, your Pa had curly hair and he was a good man." Sarah became sad thinking about Frank, she loved his curls and ran her hands through his hair when they made love. Thomas saw how his mother had become sad, and able to tell she was thinking about his Pa, didn't want to be the cause of her sadness. "I'm not ashamed of it, Ma!" He tousled his hair and it made Sarah smile.

Two bags of feed were pushed end to end to make a bed for Thomas, and after wriggling himself into a comfortable position, Sarah covered him with hessian sacks to keep him extra warm. Empty sacks were rolled up to make Sarah a pillow. Blowing out the lamp and lying on the floor next to Thomas, Sarah wasn't prepared for what he said before he went to sleep.

"Ma? ...did Sheriff Morgan hurt you?"

"What do you mean Thomas?"

"Well ...when I came back with a blanket, Sheriff Morgan was standing close to you ...what was he doing Ma?" Thomas stopped talking for a moment to yawn. "Was he cuddling you?"

'Damn,' Sarah cursed under her breath, Thomas had seen them. 'But how much had he seen?' she wondered. "He wasn't hurting me Thomas," was all Sarah could say.

"Do you like Sheriff Morgan Ma?" Starting to sound sleepy, Thomas yawned again. Sarah didn't know how to answer his question. Did she like Sheriff Morgan? She could answer yes, she did like him, but she only just met him, she didn't know anything about him. When he kissed her, she liked it very much, she liked that his hands were gentle when he caressed her. Sheriff Morgan's body, when she rubbed her hands over him, felt nice. Sarah didn't answer Thomas's question.

"Ma …are you asleep?" Thomas said sleepily. "Almost Thomas," Sarah answered, grateful to hear his steady breathing. Thomas had gone to sleep, and in the morning, hopefully he would have forgotten that he asked her about the sheriff. Sarah however, lay awake thinking. Why had she been attracted to Sheriff Morgan when there were so many men in town, and on the mountain, she could have her choice of? She had many offers of marriage. Foley Andrews kept asking her, and she thought if she were to marry again, Foley would be her choice, only she pushed him away and now he is seeing Maria. To Sarah, Maria seems a nice woman, and she is glad Foley is finally seeing someone rather than always asking her to marry him. Even so, she feels a little put out with him showing interest in someone else.

Sarah knows nothing about Sheriff Morgan. Where did he come from? Does he have a family? he could be married for all she knows. She hadn't thought to ask him. 'Why?' she asked herself. 'After all these years of being alone, have I suddenly felt the need to let a complete stranger touch me?'

Christian stepped out of the Livery and into the alley. The storm was still raging violently, wind howled along the alleyway, making him hold onto his hat. Racing back to the boardwalk, he stepped quickly under the awnings where he was sheltered and hurried back to his office. The potbelly stove was still throwing out good heat making the office warm and he was grateful for it. His clothes were saturated just from running across from the Livery to the Barber Shop, and his body shivered from the cold. Christian thought of Sarah and how wet she had been, thinking she must have been freezing, but she hadn't let on. Quickly pouring himself some coffee, he sat in his chair in front of the fire to get warm and let his thoughts return to Sarah and how beautiful, and sexy a woman she was. He could still feel her body under his hand. 'Hell' he thought. 'I nearly went all the way with her. If Thomas and Ham hadn't come back when they did, Sarah and I may have become intimate right there in the Livery.' His thoughts turned to the possibility of Sarah being a whore. She didn't hesitate to take him on when he made advances to her, sure, he made the first move, but it was Sarah who grabbed him and started undressing him. Christian put his mug to his mouth, then remembering when Sarah was at Crawley's store, and how Crawley called her a whore, and seeing her face go bright red from embarrassment, he concluded Sarah was like him. Neither of them had been with anyone for some time, and they just wanted to be loved. The sound of Bear snoring in the back room brought him out of his reverie, reminding him he was on duty.

When Thomas and Sarah woke in Ham's loft the next morning, the storm had finally petered out. The sound of Ham hammering away at his furnace making horseshoes already was noisy, and it was only just on daylight.

Wrapping the blanket securely around herself, Sarah checked Thomas and her clothes. Relieved at finding them dry, she took her shirt and trousers and went behind the bales of straw to get dressed. After Thomas dressed, they helped each other lower the ladder and climbed down. Ham stopped working when he saw them. "Morning you two, storms gone, go on through and have breakfast before you go." He winked at Thomas and held the door to his residence open for them. "Ma!" Thomas whispered, jiggling from one foot to the other. "I have to go." Sarah almost laughed. "Me too Thomas …Ham!" she pleaded, looking at Ham and sounding urgent. Ham laughed at the two of them. "You can go through to the outhouse from here."

After washing in Ham and Patrice's washroom, they found Patrice had already set them a place each at their table. Lilly, their youngest daughter was already seated when Sarah and Thomas came in. Sissy, the older of the two girls, was helping get breakfast. Sarah said good morning to everyone and sat in the chair offered her. Thomas, sitting on a seat next to Lilly, listened to Patrice and Sarah talk about the storm and their camp while they ate. When Patrice asked Sarah about Christian in front of their children Sarah clamped up. "Well, come on, what did you and the sheriff …talk about?" Patrice persisted with a glint in her eyes.

"Nothing! really! just about me breaking in here, and paying fines!" Explaining to Patrice what Christian meant by fines, she glanced over at Thomas, and seeing him frowning, felt her face begin to burn. Thomas knew she and the sheriff hadn't been talking.

When Patrice sent Lilly off to school with a packed lunch, Thomas remained sitting quietly at the table. He wouldn't have anything for lunch now their shelter had been hammered by the storm. Their supplies were under the canopy and Thomas wasn't sure if they had a camp anymore. He was surprised when Patrice handed him a packed lunch. "Off you go Thomas, go with Lilly," Patrice said. Thomas looked at Sarah to see if it was alright for him to take the bag Patrice was offering him. "It's alright Thomas, I packed one especially for you," Patrice said with a smile. "Go on Thomas," Sarah said, taking the bag from Patrice and handing it to Thomas. "Thank you, Misses Hammond," Thomas said taking the bag, and jumping to his feet. Hurriedly kissing Sarah on her cheek, he called, "see you Ma!" then raced out the door trying to catch up to Lilly. "See you Thomas ...at the camp this afternoon!" Sarah called as he disappeared out the door. Patrice shook her head and smiled at Sarah.

After Thomas and Lilly left, Patrice sent Sissy out to do some laundry, leaving Sarah to her mercy. Patrice wanted to know everything that happened in the Livery between her and Christian, and she wasn't about to let Sarah go without telling her the details. Sitting down and pouring them both another mug of coffee, she smiled sheepishly at Sarah. "Now! you know we are best friends Sarah, anything you tell me won't leave this house ...tell me what happened with you and Sheriff Morgan ...and don't leave anything out!" Sarah didn't want to tell Patrice she and Christian had almost become intimate, she felt it was none of her business. "I don't know what you mean Patrice, nothing happened." Her face burned, giving her away. "Oh! I suppose Thomas came back from taking you a blanket and looking all embarrassed for no reason, just like you look now ...I wasn't asleep you know ...come on girl, you can tell me, I won't tell a soul, you know I am good at keeping secrets!" Patrice folded her arms and waited for Sarah to answer.

"He..." Sarah looked coyly at Patrice, her face turning a brighter shade of pink. "He ...kissed me!" She didn't know if she should elaborate on other details or not. "And!" Patrice didn't seem at all surprised at Sarah telling her Christian kissed her.

"And what?" Sarah said back to her. Patrice just kept staring while waiting for more information. "And we …we!" Sarah shrugged. "We …may have touched each other in a certain way." Sarah didn't know where to look when Patrice exclaimed excitedly. "Ah huh! you go girl! it's about time you came back to the land of the living! a woman can only go for so long without a bit of loving! …so, tell me, how do you feel about him?" Patrice was settling down to have a long conversation, but wanting to see what sort of mess the storm left her camp in, Sarah wanted to get going. She would have a lot of work to do and she wanted to get started. "I don't know how I feel! I have only just met him …tell Ham thank you for letting us stay, I will pay for the broken lock, and thank you for breakfast …and Thomas's lunch …I have to go." Sarah stood up to go, but hesitated. "Let me just say this …Sheriff Morgan seems a nice enough man, but what happened last night …well …it will never happen again …nothing will come of it." Sarah moved toward the door.

"You could let it become something Sarah …if you wanted it too!" Patrice muttered after she left.

Chapter Eleven

Patrice and Ham came to Cedar Creek from Alabama as free settlers. Ham, having been trained as a Liveryman and Blacksmith knew everything there was to know about horses and was in great demand for fixing wagon wheels, so started his own Livery and Stable. When Sarah was a young girl, she had taken a liking to Ham and Patrice because they were different to the people she knew. Besides Doc Harris and Gerda, they were Sarah's closest friends. But Patrice, Sarah sometimes felt, even though she didn't spread gossip, could be nosey. Sarah brushed what Patrice said off and saying goodbye, left Patrice wondering about her and Sheriff Morgan.

The sky was clear of any clouds and the sun was shining, it was a beautiful day for winter. The ground however, was saturated and a cold wind blew across the river from the mountains, snow was heading their way. Sarah walked down the alley beside the Livery to the track leading through the trees to the river where she was forced to cut her way through fallen branches to get on the riverbank. Once there, she had to climb over trees that came down in the storm. The river itself was high and running fast.

As she came up on her camp, she was shocked to see the tree Christian helped tie her shelter too had been uprooted and now lay where her shelter used to be. She couldn't see her shelter at all for thick tree branches and foliage littering the ground.

Sarah looked across the river to the pier. It was still there, but the three little row boats had fared worse. One had sunk, one was lying upside down with a huge hole in it on this side of the river and one, Sarah guessed, must have been swept away altogether.

After setting about clearing her camp of debris by gathering up all the small branches and twigs and throwing them into the bushes, she rebuilt the rock wall across the back of the firepit. Cleaning the leaves out of it, she came across her coffee pot lying in the bottom with the steel grill and black cooking pot. Her coffee pot was dented but thankfully still serviceable. Thinking if she could reach under the tree lying across her shelter, to cut her way through the canvas, she might be able to find her axe and her coffee. She could go without food, but couldn't work all day without coffee.

Twisting her long hair in a bunch and fastening it on top of her head, she rolled her sleeves up above her elbows, undid some of the buttons on her shirt and tied a knot in it under her bust. Leaving her stomach exposed to the air, helped keep her cool. Taking her knife out of its sheath, she began hacking at the smaller branches of the tree. When she began to work up a sweat, she undid more buttons, exposing the top of her breasts which cooled her down even more. Sarah continued cutting away at the tree until she made enough room between the branches and twigs to allow her to see her shelter. Pushing her knife into the canvas, she cut a hole, then reaching in, felt around for her axe. When her hand closed on a handle, she tugged at it until it came free. It wasn't her axe, but her small spade. 'Excellent' she thought. Her axe should be right next to where her spade was. Feeling around again, sure enough, she found her axe, and now able to cut larger branches off the tree, she hoped she could remove enough branches to allow her to lift the tree off her shelter. Sarah had her head down swinging her axe wildly at a branch when Christian came walking towards her.

Checking around town, making sure everything and everyone survived the storm, and finding there was nothing he could do to help with repairs, Christian made his way down the trail to Sarah's camp to check out what damage the storm had done there. Sarah was holding her axe in the air ready to bring it down on a branch when she saw him approaching.

"What a mess Cole!" Christian said, putting his hands on his hips and looking around. Watching him for a moment, Sarah noticed how strong his arms were and remembered how gentle he had been with his hands when touching her. Resting her axe on the trunk, a bead of sweat ran between her breasts and continued down her stomach. Standing on the opposite side of the tree, Christian watched the bead slowly slip down her skin to the top of her pants. 'Damn' Sarah thought. 'Why did he have to look at me like that?' She felt a little undressed, but no more undressed than when she shot at the river rats. Right now, she was less undressed than she had been in the Livery, but Christian was looking at her now, the same way he was looking at her then.

"What do you hope to achieve by cutting off all those branches?" Christian forced himself to take his eyes off Sarah's bare stomach to survey the tree. 'Damn' he was thinking. 'Why does she have to be dressed like that.' His desire for her rose in the pit of his stomach.

"I plan to chop the branches off to make it easier for me to lift the tree off my shelter." Sarah thought her plan was a good plan, but she could tell by the frown on Christian's face, he didn't think it was.

"You are not going to lift this tree ...not even I could lift this tree!" He bent down and tried lifting it. When it didn't budge, he stood up and pushed his hat back on his head. "Whew! What you need are some really big men to lift this." Sarah had an idea what he was going to say but hoped to stop him. She didn't want him getting the trappers to help her, she didn't need their help, and would never ask for it. She didn't need his help either.

"I can manage by cutting it up as much as I can," she said swinging her axe at a branch. When the axe got stuck in the wood, and she struggled to pull it back out, Christian suppressed a smile and raised his eyebrows. Sarah thought he was mocking her and that made her mad. "I will get the trappers and be back in a..." Christian turned to walk back up the trail, but before he could leave, Sarah angrily interrupted him. "I wouldn't want you wasting your time sheriff! so don't you go asking for their help, I don't need it!" she snapped. Christian was taken aback by her sudden outburst. "How is it a waste of time Cole?"

"Because I said I don't need their help!" she repeated savagely, lifting her axe above her head.

"They are men, they will help you." Christian insisted. Men always help women in distress, it was the proper thing to do. But not knowing the reason Sarah wouldn't accept their help, he was going to get their help whether she liked it or not.

"They won't help me sheriff!" Sarah said, as her blood boiled. Angry at his insistence, she hit the axe savagely at the tree causing a branch to break off and fling into the air.

"Just why won't they help you?" Christian watched the branch go flying and wondered why Sarah insisted the trappers wouldn't help her. Sarah swung the axe again, and didn't answer. Christian's persistence to get her help didn't alter. "I will be right back!" This time, when she didn't answer, he walked quickly up the trail and disappeared. "Goddamn it!" Sarah was really angry at Christian. "They won't help me!" she snapped through clenched teeth. "But what if he manages to get them to come down here? goddamn it!" She embedded her axe in the trunk of the tree and taking her hair down, quickly braided it and tied it off. Untying the knot at the front of her shirt she did up all the buttons, quickly tucked it back in her trousers, then rolled down her sleeves. She felt hot, her body was sticky, her clothes were clinging to her. She pulled her axe out of the tree and started cutting another branch.

While Sarah continued to hack at the tree, Christian knocked on the door of the Ferguson House.

"What can we do for you sheriff?" Joe asked, when Will opened the door. Along with the other trappers, Joe was getting ready to ride out to Major Hardy's to bring horses back to the corrals. Once the horses were brought in, the men would be busy for the next couple of weeks and wouldn't have time for looking out for Sarah, or Thomas.

"The storm brought down a huge tree and it fell on Cole's camp she..." Joe stopped Christian before he could fully explain what happened. "Cole and Thomas! ...they alright?" The other men visibly tensed when they heard what Christian was telling them.

"Yeah, they are fine, they camped at the Livery last night." Seeing the men appear relieved when their shoulders suddenly relaxed, Christian frowned.

"But Cole needs a hand to get the tree off her shelter, I thought you men might be able to help her move it." Christian waited while all four men glanced fleetingly at each other.

"Cole does not need our help sheriff, she can move the tree herself." Joe lifted his coat off the hook near the door and the other three men moved to go out the door with him. Christian was mortified when the men said Sarah didn't need their help. "She can't possibly lift that tree on her own Joe, it's huge! ...I thought the five of us might lift it."

"We are not helping her Morgan." Joe's voice was low as he opened the door. Christian was stunned. 'Cole was right, they weren't going to help her.' Christian asked himself again what was going on between the trappers and Sarah. First, they were concerned she was hurt when they thought he shot her, and after telling them a tree crashed on her camp, they were visibly shaken thinking Sarah and Thomas may have been hurt, then relieved when he told them they weren't, now here they are saying they won't help her remove that tree. "Cole said you wouldn't help her." Christian wasn't going to leave though, not until he had an answer. "Why?... why won't you help her?"

"The reason is none of your concern ...just leave it alone!" Joe answered quietly, as he stepped out the door.

There was no way Christian was going to leave it alone, anger reflected in his voice when he spoke. "I watched you men ride out each day for two weeks before Cole came to town, and when they rode in, I figured it was them you were watching for ...you men worried every day for those two weeks, waiting for the two of them to come off that goddamn mountain, and you were there in an instant when she shot those rats ...and now you won't help her move a ...*fucking tree*!" Christian was angry and confused. "What is going on Joe? What is it between you men and Cole?"

"I told you Morgan ...it is none of your concern!" Joe repeated sternly. The other men didn't give up any information either and followed Joe out to the porch. Christian's mouth was agape as he watched them file out the door one by one. He had to think fast before they left town and he couldn't get Sarah any help.

"Alright! if you won't help Cole..." Christian's mind ticked over. For some obscure reason they wouldn't help Sarah, but just maybe they would help him. "Then help me move a tree that has come down on the riverbank!" Speaking loud enough for the men to hear him out on the porch, he went out and looked Joe squarely in his eyes. "There is a large tree on the riverbank that needs moving, will you help me move it?" Christian repeated, then waited to see if it made a difference to the men. Christian could see Joe thinking. "Alright! ...show us where this tree is." Joe's answer confused Christian. He cursed under his breath but let it go so he could get the men down to Sarah's camp.

Sarah was concentrating on cutting branches off the tree when Christian came back down the trail. Looking up, she was surprised and a little taken aback when she saw all four trappers striding toward her. 'He actually did it! Sheriff Morgan got the men to come and help me.' Remaining behind the tree holding her axe in her hands, she watched Christian frowning as he came walking toward her and guessed it was because of the way she was now dressed.

Joe was thinking while he was walking down the trail. 'Sarah said when Frank died, she would never ask me, or the other men for their help, at least with Morgan asking us to help him, we can help her without her feeling she went back on her word.'

"These men have come to help me move this tree Cole." Christian informed her while studying her change of dress. He liked the way she looked before. It aroused a feeling in him he hadn't felt in a long time. The four men stood behind Christian and didn't speak, their faces unsmiling while they looked at Sarah. "You better get out of the way and let us move it, go stand up there somewhere," Christian ordered, while pointing toward the ridge and keeping his voice steady. 'So that's it, he got them to help him, not me.' It was just as Sarah thought, they wouldn't help her, not without her asking, and that was something she was never going to do. Sarah stepped out from behind the tree and went and stood where Christian indicated.

Holding her axe in her hand, she folded her arms, then watched the five men spread out along the trunk of the tree. "Right! we'll throw it over there!" Christian commanded, pointing to where he wanted the tree to go. "When I count to three, we lift together." All five men bent down and put their hands under the trunk. Christian counted, and while there were a lot of grunts and groans and a lot of cursing, they lifted it. Staggering under the trees weight, and stumbling when two of them had to walk over Sarah's ruined shelter, they carried it to the edge of the stand of trees and together, threw it into the bushes. The log rolled and crashed its way down through the undergrowth where it came to rest against tree trunks, causing the trees canopies to shudder. The men watched as it came to rest, then laughing, patted each other on the back at a job well done.

After Christian shook their hands and thanked them for their help, they started back up the trail, but not before each man gave Sarah a quick glance. Putting her head down, Sarah looked at the ground until they were gone. Still unable to understand the men's and Sarah's attitude toward each other, Christian frowned as he walked over to Sarah and stood next to her.

"You could have thanked them Cole," he said in dismay at her attitude.

"Why? they didn't come here to help me …they came here to help you!" Feeling uncomfortable having him standing so close, Sarah kept her arms folded in front of her. Christian didn't say anything in response to her remark. "Do you need help getting your shelter back up?" he asked. Sarah should have been grateful for Christian's help, but she wouldn't let herself accept anyone's help, not even his. "No, I can do it," she said. Christian was silent for a moment. "You know Cole? …it wouldn't hurt to ask for help occasionally," he said almost to himself as he started to walk away. Sarah let him get as far as the trail before calling him. "Sheriff!" Christian stopped where he was and turned to face her. "I guess …I could use help to move it."

Only too eager to help now she asked, Christian hurried back and stood facing her. "Where would you like it moved to?" Sarah pointed with her axe to where she wanted the shelter to go. "Up here towards the ridge, it might give Thomas and me more protection from the weather." Christian looked at the very spot he thought her shelter would have been better off being erected the night he helped her tie it off to the tree he and the four men had just moved off her shelter.

"Alright, let's roll it up and get it up there." Working together, they moved stones off the canvas, then standing either side, rolled it up, then picking it up, they carried it to a spot amongst a thick stand of trees closer to the ridge.

"I'll give you a hand to put it up, may I suggest if you make it smaller, the sides will hang on the ground and you will be able to stake it down to keep it from moving in the wind." Listening to Christian's voice, Sarah thought he sounded nice, when he wasn't angry. "You may suggest it sheriff, but whether I agree with your suggestion is another thing." Christian stopped unrolling the canvas, and looking seriously at Sarah, was convinced he made her angry again. Seeing the look on his face, Sarah's mouth curled in a smile. When she laughed, Christian was relieved and laughed along with her. Sarah had a nice smile, when she wasn't angry at him. "You should still have enough room for you and Thomas to have your privacy," he went on. Working together to attach the canvas to the trees, in no time the shelter was up. Christian being tall, was able to tie the canvas high enough without having to climb onto branches, allowing Sarah and Thomas room to walk around under the canopy.

Inside the shelter Christian could see Sarah struggling to tie the last rope through a loop that held blankets that divided the shelter in two. Hurrying to stand behind her, their bodies brushed together. When a sudden warmth radiated between them, Sarah let go of the rope and put her arms down, but stayed where she was. Reaching above her head, Christian finished tying off the rope, then slid his hands down Sarah's arms.

Sliding his hands around her waist, he gently turned her to face him. Reaching up, Sarah put her arms around his neck and moved her body against his. Christian's mouth covered Sarah's. As the air in the shelter became heated and their wanting surfaced, Sarah closed her eyes. Christian's tongue delved deeper inside Sarah's mouth. His arms tightened around her. Their bodies came together.

"Sheriff Morgan, you here?" came a voice outside the shelter. "Sheriff!" The voice called again. "Shit!" Christian cursed, not happy his and Sarah's encounter had been interrupted for the second time. "I'm here Clem," he said loudly. Stepping away from Sarah, and noticing how her nipples poked out under her shirt and how her face was flushed, he tried suppressing a smile, but was aroused too. Sarah could tell Christian had become aroused from his kissing her. Having felt his arousal surfacing while their bodies pressed against each other, Sarah smiled back. "Ask Ham for some spikes to hold down the bottom of your shelter Cole, you want about a dozen …

six for each side …that should do it." Christian spoke slowly and deliberately, giving himself time to compose himself. Sarah knew it was not only for Clem's benefit but for his. She folded her arms across her chest trying to hide her arousal and smiled at Christian, who smiled back before stepping outside.

"What is it Clem?" Sarah heard him say to Clem standing just outside the shelter. A moment later, she came out and stood behind Christian.

"Howdy Cole," Clem said when he saw her.

"Howdy Clem," Sarah returned. Knowing her face was still pink from Christian kissing her, she was glad Clem didn't seem to notice she had become fully aroused.

"Major Hardy's man has come to see you, says it's urgent, he's waiting for you up at the jailhouse." Christian turned to Sarah. "Right, see you another time, Cole." He nodded and walked off with Clem.

"Thank you for helping me put the shelter back up Sheriff Morgan!" Sarah called to his retreating back. Christian looked over his shoulder. "You're welcome, Cole," he smiled as he strode away.

After Christian left, Sarah moved her belongings to her new shelter, built a new firepit outside the entrance by digging a hole and lining it with river rocks, and to keep the wind from fanning the flames, the wall at the back of the pit was built high. Sarah decided, when it begins to snow, they would use this firepit closest to the shelter for both cooking and heating.

That afternoon when Thomas came from school, he was pleased with the shelter too, and commented on how much sturdier the shelter looked from the one they had erected the first time. Sarah was pleased too, especially with Christian for helping her.

Thomas and Sarah spent their first night in a much more comfortable shelter. Lying under her furs and blankets, Sarah thought about her and Christian's last kiss and what happened to their bodies when they held each other. It made Sarah think perhaps their first encounter in the Livery hadn't been just a whim.

Chapter Twelve

After coming from helping Sarah put up her shelter and going with Foley back to the dry gulch to study another lot of dead steers, Christian spent a quiet night at the lodge. His thoughts, when sitting by the open fire were about him and Sarah and what happened in the Livery and their kissing each other in her shelter. Sarah hadn't stopped him either times, convincing him they were interested in each other. Lying in bed awake, thinking how he would like to make love to her, he decided he wouldn't rush into it. Sarah was a mysterious woman and he would have to tread carefully when around her. He didn't want to rile her by coming on too strong. Sarah had to be the one to invite him to get into bed with her. As the night wore on, Christian tried putting all thought of Sarah out of his mind, but after falling into a deep sleep, his dreams when they came were of her. Her face appeared close to his. Her mouth beckoned him. Her naked body nestled against his, enticing him when she lay in his arms. Her beautiful blue eyes crinkled at the corners when she smiled at him. He saw her time and time again, until finally he awoke to daylight streaming through his window.

Ordered out to Major Hardy's for the third time to look at more steers that had mysteriously dropped dead, neither the Major, his two gun-hands, Foley and Brady nor Christian could figure out what was killing them. To see what had caused a steer's death, Christian tried cutting it open with the only knife he thought would be sharp enough to cut through tough cowhide, only to have the blade break when it hit bone. He told the Major he would have to come back yet again, and bring one of the trapper's knives with him. Christian still didn't understand why the Major or his men didn't carry knives with them. The Major carried a whip, and Christian thought a knife would have been more appropriate than a whip.

After coming back to town, and leaving his horse at the Livery, Christian made his way down the street, only to have Billy Henderson come running flat out along the street toward him. Billy wasn't watching where he was going and barreled straight into him.

"Whoa! Billy! Where are you going in such a hurry?" Christian asked, grabbing him by both arms to stop him getting away.

"I'm going home to get my reader, cause Mister O'Rourke said I could cause we are having a reading test, and I forgot my reader!" Billy was puffing, his face was turning bright red from exertion. "Well then, you better run along," Christian laughed. Billy made to run off, but Christian held him firmly by his arms. "Just a moment!" Christian said as he squatted in front of Billy. Billy was twelve-years old, the same age as Thomas. But he was shorter than Thomas and thin framed. His hair was blonde, and where Thomas was slightly tanned, Billy's skin was fair. Christian guessed that was because Thomas spent most of his time out of door's running around on the mountain.

"Billy, I want to ask you something."

Billy tried to get his eyes to focus on Christian. "Sure, Sheriff Morgan, what do you want to ask me?" he said, closing one eye to the sun.

"Why aren't you and Thomas Mason Friends?" The look on Billy's face changed in an instant. His eyes and mouth opened wide in surprise at Christian's question. "I ...I can't be friends with Thomas!" he said, putting his head down and looking at the ground.

"Why not Billy? Are you afraid of Thomas?" Christian pushed. "I ain't afraid of Thomas!" Billy said angrily, trying to pull away from Christian. "I want to be friends with him ...but I can't!" Billy said looking nervous. It was obvious that day at school, when Christian saw Thomas sitting alone when the older boys ran past, kicking dirt at him, that Thomas didn't have any friends. Billy didn't appear to have any friends either. Seeing Billy sitting alone on the schoolhouse porch watching other children at play, Christian thought Billy and Thomas would make perfect friends, if only they would get together, and right now, he would do anything in his power to make that happen. But first, he wanted to know what was stopping them from being friends. Christian smiled at Billy to reassure him.

"It's alright Billy, I'm not going to hurt you, just let me ask you, is it because of Jamie Finch and Daniel Connell? Are they stopping you from being friends with Thomas?" Billy gave Christian the answer he expected. "They torment us, they told us to stay away from Thomas, they said Cole would skin us if we played with Thomas and something happened to him!" Christian eased his grip on Billy's arms. "You don't believe that do you Billy? Cole wouldn't hurt you or any of the other children." Christian saw how kind Sarah was with children when she gave them candy and they eagerly took it from her, making it obvious they liked her. He didn't believe Sarah would hurt any of them.

"I guess Cole wouldn't hurt me, but I can't make friends with Thomas at school, the older boys won't let us," Billy said sounding worried. Digging around in his pocket, Christian found some coins and decided, because of Billy's answer, he was going to give him an incentive to make friends with Thomas.

There was a time in Christian's life, growing up in an orphanage, where older boys gave him money to fight another boy. The fight ended with him losing, but gaining a new friend, and the money. Battered and bruised, he was able to buy a book he needed to help with his schooling. He even had enough money to buy a pair of boots. Christian couldn't see anything wrong with paying Billy to be friends with Thomas.

"Billy if I give you this money, will you make friends with Thomas?" Christian held out five one-dollar coins in his palm. Billy's eyes widened when he saw the money. "I can't take your money!" he said staring at the coins. "You don't have to make friends with Thomas at school, just after school, and on the days when there's no school, you and Thomas could play together all day when school is out." What Christian was saying made sense to Billy. He looked at the money again.

"There must be something you would like to have from Crawley's store?" Christian smiled. "I guess so," Billy said, thinking about the knife he had seen, the one that folded up inside itself and can be carried in a pocket. Billy wanted one but didn't like to ask his Ma and Pa for anything, but if he had his own money, he could buy the knife and still have some money left over. "I will make friends with Thomas after school, I have to go now," Billy said taking the money. Christian tousled his hair, and stood up. "Good boy Billy, now go get your reader and get back to school before you get in trouble with Mister O'Rourke." Carrying the five gold coins clenched in his hand, Billy ran home as fast as he could. Neither Christian nor Billy noticed Jamie Finch and Daniel Connell watching them from inside the schoolhouse. Both boy's seats were near a window facing onto the street, allowing them to see the exchange between Christian and Billy, making both boys curious to find out what their meeting was all about.

Billy was taking far too long to get his reader and was sure he would be in trouble with Mister O'Rourke when he got back to school. Not having time to stop to tell his mother he was home, he raced up the stairs to his room. Martha, in the backyard hanging out washing, heard the front door open and footsteps running up the stairs, and thinking surely it was Billy, stopped what she was doing and went up to Billy's room to investigate.

"Billy is that you?" she called, entering his room. "Yeah Ma!" Billy's face was red. He had run home really fast and was out of breath, talking to Sheriff Morgan had taken up precious time. He dropped the five coins in a small box that held his most treasured possessions. There was his first baby tooth that he lost when his second tooth came through.

A lock of hair from his head that was his first ever haircut from the barber. A piece of string that was not for any particular reason, he just thought he would keep it. Along with everything else in the box, was a faded nine of club's playing card he found when he saw one corner sticking out of the ground where it was buried in the street outside the saloon. The card looked like it had been buried a long time, and when he held it up to the light, he could see tiny holes punched through one of the clubs in the corner.

Billy decided to leave the gold coins in the box until he could buy his pocket knife. Then he planned to hide the knife in the box so his Ma and Pa couldn't find it. They wouldn't like him to have the knife, they would think he would hurt himself with it.

"What are you doing home love?" Martha said coming into his room. Billy quickly grabbed his reader off the top of his chest of drawers. "I forgot to take my reader to school." He was still puffing from his run. "Sir is going to test us, so he let me come home to get it," Billy puffed. "I have to get back now Ma." Martha moved aside as Billy tried to go around her. "Don't go running so hard Billy, you may fall over and hurt yourself." Martha fretted over her only son. "I won't fall over Ma!" Billy ducked around his mother and started down the stairs. Martha followed quickly behind.

Billy suddenly stopped before going out the front door. "Ma …seeing how there isn't any school tomorrow, can Thomas come here to sleep tonight?" He looked up at his mother with his big blue eyes. Martha loved Billy with all her heart, and she would do anything for him, so would Dave, Billy's father.

"By Thomas, I take it you mean Thomas Mason, Sarah Cole's son?" She crossed her hand's in front of her. "Yeah Ma," Billy laughed. "There is no other Thomas that I know of."

"Why do you want him to stay here with us dear?" Martha worried Sarah Cole's son might be too wild for her delicate son to be friends with.

Billy had to think fast. 'Was it because Sheriff Morgan paid him a whole five dollars? or was it because he really wanted to be friends with Thomas?' He had wanted to make friends with Thomas for a long time, but was too scared to approach him. Thomas would be the best friend ever, because he heard stories about the mountain, and Thomas came from the mountain. Living up there would be exciting, and interesting, and he thought Thomas was lucky to live there. The money was important too, but Billy decided it was because he wanted to be friends. "Thomas and I are friends Ma and friends sleep at each other's houses, can we Ma, can Thomas sleep over …please?" he begged his mother. "Well, you had better go ask your Pa, he's out in the garden."

Racing past his mother, Billy jumped off the back porch and ran to his Pa where he was digging in the vegetable patch. "Pa! can I have Thomas sleep here tonight? Ma said I could!" Billy knew full well his mother hadn't agreed, but he hoped they both would say yes. Dave looked up from his digging.

"Thomas Mason?" Dave didn't question why Billy had come home from school, he looked over Billy's head at Martha who had come up behind Billy.

"I don't see why not …did you say yes Martha?" Dave was an easy going, middle aged man, who at last had the perfect family he had yearned for. He and Martha waited a long time to have Billy, and when Billy was born, he was on top of the world. He looked at his wife whom he adored and smiled. "I didn't say anything of the sort, but if you say yes, then it will be fine with me." Billy watched both his parents as they moved a little way away from him and put their heads together. Billy couldn't hear what they were saying, and it was taking him a long time to get his reader and get back to school. "Hurry up Ma! hurry up Pa! I have to get back to school or I will be in trouble for taking too long!"

Martha and Dave discussed the fact Thomas was Sarah Cole's son, and if something should happen to him while he was in their care, what Cole would do to them? They both knew she was capable of taking out vengeance on anyone that hurt her or her family. Both had been witness to her vengeance many years before when Thomas and Billy were babies.

But they were good kind people, and Billy was a good boy, he wouldn't hurt Thomas, they were sure of that, besides, Cole will probably so no to her son staying overnight, because he would have to be away from her, and except for going to school, Cole wouldn't let her son out of her sight. Cole knew where her son was at all times. Deciding nothing could possibly happen to Thomas while he was in their care, they turned back to Billy with their answer.

"Alright Billy, if Thomas asks his Ma if he can stay overnight, and she says yes, then we don't see why not." Billy grinned and jumped up and down with glee. "Thanks Ma, Thanks Pa," he said excitedly. Giving his Ma and Pa a quick hug, he raced back through the house, out the front door, which he left open, and didn't stop to close the front gate behind him either, he didn't have time. As he sprinted down the street toward the schoolhouse Billy smiled, glad he came up with the idea of inviting Thomas to sleep over, now all he had to do was find the courage to ask Thomas without letting Jamie Finch and Daniel Connell know.

Billy was busy thinking. His mind wasn't on the reading test, he wanted desperately to be friends with Thomas, and Sheriff Morgan had paid him a whopping five dollars to make friends with him, so he would do it, he would come straight out and ask Thomas to come home with him, but he would have to wait until the afternoon when Jamie and Daniel left school before them. Billy bounded into the classroom. "What took you so long Billy Henderson?" O'Rourke asked as he sat back down red faced and puffing at his desk. "I couldn't find my reader sir," he huffed. Billy came up with that answer on his way back from home too. His seat was opposite Thomas in class. Thomas looked over at Billy's red face. Billy looked back at Thomas and smiled.

Chapter Thirteen

Wanting two trout for dinner, one for Thomas and one for herself, Sarah spent several hours fishing. After fashioning a hook out of a small pin and tying it to a long piece of thin twine tied to a fishing pole she made out of a thin branch, one trout lay on the bank already, now all she had to do was get another on her hook. As she continued to throw the line out and pull it back in, the fish followed, but didn't take the hook.

She had just thrown the line back in the water when Thomas came bounding down the trail toward her. "Ma! Hey! Ma!" He called, red in the face and puffing. School was out, and thinking he was hurt, Sarah threw the pole on the ground and hurried toward him. "Thomas what is it? What is the matter?" she said sounding worried. Thomas came to a stop in front of her and tried to catch his breath. "Nothing's the matter Ma! …Billy Henderson asked me to stay at his house …tonight …can I Ma? please …can I?" Thomas begged with excitement.

"What do you mean Thomas? …Billy asked you?" Sarah folded her arms and looked questioning at her son. Thomas knew from his mother's stance he had to be truthful. He and his Ma never had reason to lie to each other. Thomas held his hand over his heart as he breathed deeply. "Yeah Ma! he wants me to sleep at his house, and tomorrow, we are going to snare rabbits, and maybe even build a fort! Ma can I stay, can I?" Thomas was so excited he was almost jumping out of his skin.

"Wait just a minute Thomas, did Billy's folks say you could stay at their home? Or is this just you and Billy making this up?" Thomas had never asked to stay with one of his friends before and Sarah was dubious about him asking now.

"No Ma, you know I wouldn't make something up, Billy's folks said I could if it was alright with you, they told me to ask you and if you said it was alright, I was to come straight back, please Ma!" Thomas didn't draw breath.

Thomas had never been away from her, not since he was a baby anyway. The memory of him being taken from her remained foremost in her mind. She kept Thomas close for twelve years, not allowing him to be out of her sight except to go to school. When they trapped on the mountain, he was always with her for safety, now here he was wanting to go stay overnight with a friend. When Thomas had been taken, she almost died from her loss, causing her to put the fear of the devil into the town to get him back, and she vowed she would never let something like that happen again. Now here they were, facing each other with Thomas wanting to go stay with Billy Henderson. Joe warned her this day would come, and here it was. Sarah felt it was far too soon.

Sarah waited until Thomas had his breath back. His face however, remained flushed, his eyes studied her. "Please Ma, its only for one night!" He knew the story of that time and knew it was why she was hesitating. Sarah didn't want to disappoint Thomas when he sounded excited at the prospect of spending a night with one of his friends "Well …I suppose it won't hurt you to spend one night at Billy's." Thomas threw his arms around Sarah's waist. "Thank you, Ma! …I love you!" He let go of her and began to head back up the trail. "Hold on a moment Thomas! where are you going?" Sarah called after him. "I'm going back to Billy's, they said come straight back!" Thomas wanted to get going, he had never stayed overnight at a friend's house, he had never stayed with anyone, his Ma would never let him out of her sight.

"Give me a moment Thomas and I will walk you back." Sarah wouldn't need to catch another fish now Thomas wouldn't be with her for dinner. But she had to clean the one she caught, and she wanted to speak with the Henderson's. Slicing her knife swiftly from the fish's bowel to its head, she scraped the innards out and washed the fish in the river, then wrapped it in a wet cloth before placing it in a long cast iron pot. Putting the lid on the pot, she sat heavy stones on top, then sat the pot in the water on the riverbed. The stones would keep water out of the pot, and the river would keep the pot cold until she was ready to cook her fish. Once this was done, she washed her knife, put it in her sheath and scooping pebbles from the bottom of the river, rubbed them over her hands to clean them off. Standing up, Sarah looked around for Thomas, and found him up at the shelter carrying his rucksack. "What are you taking with you Thomas?" she asked as she walked towards him. "Just my drawing book Ma, Billy and I might draw pictures before we go to sleep." Sarah thought that was a good thing, at least she would be comforted to know he would be safe indoors. "Alright, are you ready to go then?" Thomas nodded, but sensing how she felt, held her hand and looked up at her. "It will be alright Ma, I promise." Sarah took his hand in hers and squeezed it gently. "Remember what I told you Thomas …never make a promise you may not be able to keep," she said solemnly. Thomas could see she was serious, and his face turned bright with colour. "Alright Ma, I won't promise, but it will be fine I... I." He couldn't think what else to say, so he shrugged his shoulders, and they both laughed.

Walking up the trail together, they passed the Ferguson House. The house looked deserted. Trappers weren't men to sit idly by when there was work to be had. Branding and castrating cattle kept them occupied every day. The Major's horses had been rounded up and brought to the corrals so they could be broken. Both cattle and horses would then be herded to Moreton for sale. Joe, Will, Fergus and Garrett and maybe one or two others were most likely at the corrals. Joe was getting too old to get down on his knees to brand steers so he left that to the younger men. Joe would also want to keep an eye on Sarah.

Passing by Crawley's store, Sarah and Thomas made their way up the street on the opposite side to the Sheriff's Office. Thomas hurried along in front of her, and when she told him to slow down, he stopped and waited for her to catch up to him, then fell in step beside her. People walking about hurried to the opposite side of the street when they saw Sarah approaching. Putting her hand on the handle of her hunting knife as they scurried away was an action Sarah had no control over. If someone she was wary of even looked in her direction, she took hold of her knife and lifted it up a fraction to show she meant business.

The Henderson's lived not far from the schoolhouse and Thomas and Sarah had no choice but to walk past the saloon to get there. After running horses to the corrals, some of the Major's men, and some trappers, were milling about outside the saloon with drinks in their hands. When Sarah drew level, the men greeted her cheerfully.

"Howdy Cole!" Yates, one of the trappers was the first to speak. "Howdy Yates!" Sarah returned, stopping and facing the group of men.

"You got a couple of good skins Cole," Parker, one of the Major's robust cowhands commented. Sarah squinted up at him. "Yeah, but they took some getting." After hearing someone say Sarah was outside, Foley stepped out. "Hello …Thomas," he said, glancing at Sarah first, then Thomas. Thomas has known Foley long before he was old enough to go to school. When Thomas looked up at Foley, he smiled and studied his face. Foley's moustache and whiskers covered the scar on his jaw, but they couldn't cover it on his cheek and forehead. Thomas was thinking, anyone that didn't know Foley would be scared of him. He was aware Foley asked his Ma to marry him every winter, and even though she said no every time, they were still friends. "Hello Foley," Thomas said back to him.

"Is that the reason you came in late Cole?" Yates was saying. "Yeah, kinda had to chase em around a bit before I could trap em, then I had to get their skins." The men laughed when she told them she had to chase the wolves to catch them. It was usually the other way around for trappers, having to run for their lives when wolves chased them.

"Skin's look real nice Cole, good job of skinnin there." Samuels, another of the trappers commented. A while back Samuels too asked Sarah to marry him and it was easy for her to turn him down. He was from the mountain and she wouldn't marry any man from the mountain. They were wild, none of them cared about the foul language they spoke, nor their state of cleanliness. She wasn't in love with the men around Cedar Creek either, the closest one she came to falling in love with since Frank was Foley, she liked him a great deal. Sarah was thanking Samuels when another lot of men came out of the saloon, and their talk about her getting the two white skins became jovial.

"Hey Cole, heard you won the pot!" Lomax, one of the men that had been at the shack the night Frank was whipped suddenly said. Lomax never smiled, and Sarah figured that was the reason. Sarah didn't hate him, because like Foley and Brady, he had just been following orders. Both Foley and Brady became her friends, but none of the other men present that night would ever be considered friends. "Yeah, I did Lomax, want to make something of it." By this time Sarah's hand was gripping her knife. "No, I was just sayin!" While keeping their eyes on Sarah, Sarah's and the men's banter went back and forth. Glancing up and down the street as she talked, she spotted Christian leaning on a post with his arms folded outside the Sheriff's Office, looking in her direction.

"Come on Ma, we got to get going!" Thomas said grabbing her hand and tugging her. "Where are you going in such a hurry Thomas?" Foley asked seriously. "I'm going to ...." Sarah cut in before Thomas could say too much. "None of your business Foley, we just got things to do ...that's all!" It wouldn't have mattered if Foley knew where Thomas was going to be spending the night. He was a decent man, and wouldn't try anything. Except he was standing with other men, and Sarah didn't want the rest of them to know she was going to be alone at her camp, besides, except for Lomax, all of the men in the group had proposed marriage to her. Some of the men would be drunk later in the night and Sarah would have to be watchful. Sarah knew them all too well, and none of them were welcome at her camp. Even though the men knew not to mess with her, she couldn't take any chances.

Standing outside the Sheriff's Office watching Sarah standing outside the saloon where a large group of men had congregated, Christian watched as more men came out and gathered around to talk to her. He could see the men laughing at something she said, but he was too far away to hear the conversation, but he could see why the men were drawn to her. Sarah was an attractive woman, and it stood to reason some of those men would have propositioned her. Before going back inside the saloon, the group of men watched Sarah disappear around the bend in the street. When Christian saw Sarah and Thomas were out of sight, he went back inside his office.

After leaving the men, Sarah and Thomas continued up the street until they came to the Henderson house. The Henderson's had a picket fence along the front of their house and pretty flowers grew in the front yard. Dave Henderson was a keen gardener and a very good one. He had a lemon tree as well as a variety of vegetables growing in his back yard. Thomas pushed open the gate and stepping onto the porch, didn't wait for Sarah before knocking loudly on the door. Sarah came through the gate just as the front door opened and Martha Henderson stepped out and smiled at Thomas. "Well, Hello Thomas?" Martha's smile faded when she saw Sarah. "Hello …Cole," she said as Sarah stepped closer. "Hello Misses Henderson, Thomas tells me you said he could stay with Billy tonight …is that right?" Sarah thought she must have sounded threatening because Martha looked nervous. "Dave, could you come here please?" Martha called, keeping her eyes on Sarah. "Billy asked Dave and I if Thomas could stay tonight, and we told Thomas if you said it was alright, then he could stay." Martha's voice wavered as she spoke nervously. Dave came out the door and pushed past his wife. "Hello Cole," he said jovially. Standing behind Thomas with her hands on his shoulders, Sarah smiled. "Hello Mister Henderson, I was wanting to make sure Billy asked you if Thomas could stay," she said, trying to make light of what she said to Martha. "Yes, he did, and we asked Thomas if he would like to stay for a while tomorrow, if that is alright with you, we will send him home well before dark," Dave said honestly. Martha felt more at ease now Dave was standing beside her. "Would you like to come in for a moment?" she said smiling at Sarah. "Oh, no, thank you …I best be going." Sarah squeezed her hands resting on Thomas's shoulders.

Dave turned and called, "Billy, Thomas is here!" Billy's footsteps could be heard as he came bounding down the stairs from his room. "Hey Thomas!" he yelled. "Is it alright for you to stay?" Thomas grinned at Billy. "Yeah, Ma said I could." When the two boys made to run upstairs, Sarah called Thomas back. "Yeah, Ma?" he questioned. "Be sure to use your manners now, won't you?" Sarah whispered so Martha and Dave couldn't hear. "Sure Ma." He gave Sarah a hug, and as he ran back inside to Billy, called over his shoulder, "see you tomorrow Ma!" and was gone.

"Don't worry Cole," Dave said, noticing the worried look on Sarah's face. "Thomas will be fine." Before Martha and Dave could go back inside Sarah stopped them. "Misses Henderson, could I speak with you a moment?" Martha looked at Dave. Dave went inside and closing the door slightly, stood behind it listening. Dave would never leave Martha alone with Sarah, if anything were to happen to his wife, he would do his utmost to help her. Martha stayed on the porch looking nervous. "Thomas doesn't have night wear, he sleeps in his trousers at our camp," Sarah informed her, feeling embarrassed at having to tell Martha something that was between herself and Thomas. "Oh!" Suddenly realizing Sarah wasn't going to do anything to harm her, Martha beamed. "Goodness me! I'm sure we can find something for Thomas to sleep in, there is no need for you to worry about that."

"Thank you, Misses Henderson, and you be sure and make Thomas behave," Sarah smiled back at Martha. "I'm sure he won't be any trouble," Martha replied, feeling more at ease. Martha was a good deal older than Sarah, and Billy had been born only a few months before Thomas. Feeling there was nothing for her to worry about, Sarah bid Martha good day and made her way back down the street to her camp.

It was the first time since Thomas had been taken away from her as a baby that she would spend time alone at their camp. Sarah felt like crying. Her camp was going to be far too quiet.

Chapter Fourteen

arah cooked her fish, and even though her appetite had gone she forced herself to eat it. Not feeling sleepy at all, she sat by her fire, her mind in turmoil thinking about Thomas being at the Henderson's. 'What is he doing now?' she worried. 'I hope he is alright!' Then she scolded herself for worrying needlessly. Unlike the Finch's and the Connell's, who stole Thomas from her when he was a baby, the Henderson's were good people. 'Martha Henderson is a good woman, and a loving mother, she worships her son. Dave is an upstanding man of the community, surely they won't harm Thomas,' she thought, trying to convince herself Thomas would be fine. The reflection of the moon shone brightly across the river. Sarah watched tiny fish jumping out of the water to catch bugs in the moonlight, creating perfect rings of silver that slowly stretched across the water.

Christian was doing his final check around town, making sure buildings were secure and no-one was sneaking about. After checking the Trading Post was secure, he headed down the trail to Sarah's camp. Because it was late, he expected Sarah's camp to be in darkness, but as he approached, he saw the glow from the fire and Sarah sitting by the pit. Unsure if he would be welcome, he slowed his walk. Sarah watched him coming toward her. "What are you doing all the way down here sheriff?" she asked, staying where she was and looking up at him. "Just doing my rounds Cole," Christian replied, subconsciously resting one hand on his hip and the other on his gun. Something Sarah noticed to be a habit similar to hers. Christian stayed standing on the opposite side of the fire. "Your rounds! ...down here?" Sarah exclaimed with surprise.

"Your camp happens to be a part of the town Cole, and yours and Thomas's safety happens to be my concern," Christian said seriously, keeping his hands where they were. "I wouldn't concern myself with that if I were you sheriff! because by the time you get down here… from up there …you would be too late!" Sarah giggled to show how ridiculous the thought was. She was more than capable of keeping herself and Thomas safe. Christian didn't want to fight with her. Glancing around the camp, he could see everything was fine. "I would do my best," he replied before bidding her good night and walking away.

Sarah felt sorry she laughed at him. She didn't want him to go, not this way. "Would you like some coffee Sheriff Morgan? There is enough in the pot for two." That! Sarah thought, was what she always said to Foley when they met up out on the prairie, and now here she was, saying it to Sheriff Morgan. She wondered just then what his first name was. Christian stopped, and walking back, looked at the pot steaming away on the fire. "Does the coffee come with an argument?" he asked, curling his mouth in a smile and looking at her. Figuring he was being good natured, Sarah smiled up at him and made light of the moment too. "It can …if you want." Deciding this was a good opportunity to talk to Sarah amicably, he replied, "I was going to make myself a pot when I finished my rounds so …yeah! …thanks!"

While Christian made himself comfortable by the fire, Sarah poured their coffee. As Christian took the mug, his fingers covered Sarah's, making his heartbeat quicken. Taking a mouthful of hot liquid, and tasting how rich and smooth the coffee was, Christian raised his eyebrows. When he complimented Sarah on the taste, she blushed and thanked him for his compliment, grateful it was dark so he couldn't see her blushing. But the glow from the fire lit up her face, putting a sheen on her cheeks that gave her an air of innocence. Christian liked that she blushed. Falling silent while they drank their coffee, Christian waited for Sarah to say something, but Sarah didn't know what to talk to Christian about now he was sitting so close.

"How come you are still up? …it is rather late," Christian asked, looking sideways at Sarah and taking another mouthful of coffee. "I couldn't sleep …where are you from sheriff?" Sarah said in the same breath. Christian took a moment to think about her question. "All over," he said, looking into his mug. Then, because he didn't want to tell her about his past said, "no place really."

Sarah didn't think that was a good enough answer and wondered what Christian had to hide. She turned to face him. "You must be from somewhere …everyone is from somewhere …do you have a family?" Christian turned to face Sarah. "I was brought up in an orphanage." That much he could tell her. Sarah frowned. She had never been away from the mountain, or Cedar Creek, and didn't know what an orphanage was. There was never the need to go away from her home, so had never travelled to the city of Moreton. Not wanting to seem ignorant, she didn't pursue what Christian told her. Christian waited for Sarah to ask him about the orphanage but when she didn't, he sat quietly and finished his coffee. Not wanting to seem rude by leaving straight away, he held his empty mug and remained where he was. "What about you Cole? Where are you from? Where is your family?" Christian hoped he would get answers to his many questions. Maybe now she would tell him about Frank Mason and what his relationship to her was.

Sarah nodded her head in the direction of the mountain range looming out of the moonlight in the distance. "I was born up there, on the mountain," then turned to Christian. "Thomas is my family." On saying that, Sarah grew sad. Frank would have been her family too if they had married. The trappers, once considered her family were not now, too much had passed between them for Sarah to call them family. When her eyes dimmed, Christian could tell he wasn't going to get any answers tonight. "I better go," he whispered.

"Why?" Sarah whispered in return.

"Why what?" he said back to her.

"Why do you have to go?" Sarah said softly.

"It is late Cole …I wouldn't want to wake Thomas by making too much noise." Christian's heart began to race as he suddenly thought about their fondling each other in Ham's Livery and their kissing in her shelter.

"Thomas isn't here." Thinking about what they had been doing in the Livery and in her shelter sent Sarah's heart racing. Christian's kisses had been tender and made her feel warm all over.

"Where is Thomas?" Christian asked innocently.

"Billy Henderson invited him to spend the night at his home, he won't be back until tomorrow." Realizing the two of them were alone and no-one else was likely to come along, Sarah kept her eyes focused on Christian for his reaction to what she said. Christian Frowned, he hadn't meant for Billy to take Thomas home, he just wanted the two boys to become friends. "I better go," he said sitting his mug on the side of the firepit. But neither of them made to move.

Putting her hand on Christian's arm, Sarah asked seductively. "Are you going to finish it, Sheriff Morgan?" Knowing exactly what Sarah was referring to, Christian reached over, pushed his fingers into Sarah's hair and pulled her toward him. With his heart thumping wildly, Christian's tongue slipped between Sarah's lips into the warmth of her mouth. While Sarah's tongue brushed against his, her hands tugged at his shirt. Getting it free of his trousers, she pushed her hands inside and slid them over his back. With their wanting growing, Christian lowered Sarah onto the ground beside the fire. Moving his hand to her breasts, he ever so gently felt her nipples through her shirt's flimsy material. As their kissing became feverish, Christian's hands worked to undo the buttons on Sarah's trousers.

"Wait! sheriff, these stones are hard on my back." Sarah giggled softly pushing him aside. Standing, Christian got to his feet too, but before Sarah could move away, he wrapped his arms about her and lifted her off the ground. Hooking her hands around his neck, and her legs around his body, he carried her, stumbling over rocky ground to her shelter, where they tumbled through the entrance onto Sarah's furs and blankets. Laughing quietly, they lay for a moment, tangled in each other's arms. "We need to take our boots off, I don't want to get dirt where I sleep," Sarah said breathlessly. "How is the shelter?" Christian asked, taking his boots off. "It's a lot warmer than before," Sarah said softly. Christian replied he was glad the shelter was better.

After sitting their boots aside, Sarah crawled further into the shelter. Removing his gun-belt, Christian crawled to Sarah. While Christian's hands worked quickly to undo the front of Sarah's trousers, Sarah opened his shirt. Sliding her hands over his chest, feeling his breasts becoming firm under her palms, heat began rising in Sarah's body as his nipples rose to their fullness. Their kissing became passionate, their tongues came together in a fury of desire. Quickly pulling his hands out of his sleeves, Christian threw his shirt to one side then, reaching for Sarah, brought her against him. Feeling aroused already, Sarah couldn't wait any longer. She pushed Christian back a little, moved her hands between them and started undoing the front of his trousers. Christian stopped kissing her and taking hold of her hands stopped her going further. "Not fair Cole," he said softly. "It's my turn."

Looking deeply into her eyes, he could see desire for him in them. Hooking his fingers inside the front of her shirt, undoing each button, touching her breasts as he moved his fingers downwards, he quickly pulled her shirt out of her trousers, pushed it over her shoulder's and exposed her, then removed it altogether. As Christian's eyes took in Sarah, his heart quickened, his body reacted to the sight in front of him. The lamp burning dully from where it sat on the wooden box, cast a shadowed light over Sarah's body. Her breasts looked firm, her nipples pink. Spreading his fingers over her breasts, he felt her nipples hardening as his hands gently massaged their fullness. Covering her nipple with his mouth and gently moving his tongue over it, made it harden further. Sarah's heart raced. While he continued to suckle, she closed her eyes to savour the moment.

Helping Sarah get his trousers over his hips, Sarah smiled at seeing all of him. Sitting back, Christian slipped his feet out of his trousers and tossed them aside. But Christian could only let Sarah look at him for so long. He pushed her gently onto her back, and taking the top of her trousers in his hand's, tugged them over her hips. Christian's body reacted fully at seeing the place he wanted to be.

Throwing her trousers behind him, he gently moved Sarah's legs apart, and crawling between them, rubbed his hand over her womanhood. Curling his fingers and while keeping himself above her, he gazed into her eyes and let his fingers arouse her further. Lowering his body, Christian gave in to his desire. Lifting Sarah against him, he let their rhythmic back and forth thrusting bring them both to an explosive level of sexual release.

The pent-up tension Christian carried with him for many years disappeared. Warmth flowed from him as he came. Moving back and forth along the length of him, Sarah gasped audibly as her orgasm broke uncontrollably. Not wanting her to stop, Christian held her. Sarah brought her legs over Christian's, and kept their bodies working, until both felt fulfilled.

Lying on his back beside Sarah, Christian reached for her hand and held it. "What are you thinking Sarah?" His voice broke the silence between them, but Sarah didn't answer.

"Sarah?" he repeated, raising his head a little and frowning when he saw she had her eyes closed.

"I am to be called Cole, sheriff." Sarah answered curtly, keeping her eyes closed. Christian couldn't believe it. They had just fucked and here she was being formal about it. Taken aback, Christian thought, now they had gone so far as having sex, it was only natural they call each other by their first names. "You don't have to call me sheriff Sarah, my name is Christian." Sarah had wanted to know what his first name was, and now she knew. His was a nice name, but it didn't matter, she would never change her attitude to what people called her, not for anyone.

Rolling onto his side, Christian propped himself up on one elbow so he could see her. "Alright ...Cole!" he said, bringing his face close to Sarah's. Opening her eyes, Sarah focused on him, but didn't speak. "I can't stay," Christian whispered, waiting for her to reply. When she didn't answer, he leant down and kissed her. "I can't stay," he repeated softly.

"You got someplace to be sheriff?" Sarah answered keeping her eyes on him. "You worried what people might say?" This time Christian didn't answer, instead, he let his eyes travel over her. Studying her breasts, still pink from him touching them, his eyes moved over her stomach to her legs then back up until they reached hers. 'Cole has beautiful eyes' he said to himself. 'Deep like the swimming hole at the bottom of the waterfall.' So deep, he could feel himself drowning in them when he stared into them. "I'm not worried about what people may say about me Cole," he whispered. But he was sheriff, and had a reputation to uphold. Town folk expected him to set an example. Fucking Sarah in her shelter on the riverbank when he had only just met her, was not setting a good example.

"Then stay …at least until I fall asleep," Sarah whispered, holding his gaze. When she looked up at him, Christian couldn't help himself, he wanted to stay. "I'm thinking of your reputation, not mine, but I will stay, just for a while, then I have to go." Christian lay back down.

"I already have a reputation in this town."

Hearing Sarah's quietly spoken admission, Christian turned his head in her direction. "What do you mean?" He didn't want her telling him she was a whore. Crawley called her that, and outside the saloon he witnessed a lot of men talking to her, he imagined a few of them could well have been with her, and here he was having sex with her, it was not what he wanted to hear.

"Don't worry sheriff, it isn't as bad as you think." Sarah rolled over on her side away from him. Christian didn't like to ask her again what she meant. "How long will it take for you to fall asleep?" he asked, moving his body closer so his legs rested behind her knees, and stretching his arm over her to cup her breast. "Not long," Sarah said softly, holding his hand while feeling him making himself comfortable behind her. Christian liked that Sarah's back pressed against his chest and her backside nestled against his crotch. He gave her breast a gentle squeeze while listening to her steady breathing, and then promptly fell asleep.

Waking with a start, Christian lifted his head and looked around. He was still lying behind Sarah with his arm still in the same place he put it before going to sleep, but when he looked toward the shelters opening, he could see daylight. "Shit!" he cursed quietly, slowly removing his hand from Sarah's breast. When Sarah didn't stir, Christian picked up his clothes and put them on as quietly as he could. Grabbing his boots and gun-belt, he stepped outside. The sky was beginning to lighten, the sun would soon be up.

Carrying his boots and gun-belt to the firepit, he found hot coals still glowing in the fire. Piling small sticks and pieces of wood onto the coals, he sat down and pulled on his boots. The hot coals soon caught the sticks and the wood began to burn. 'At least Sarah will have a fire when she wakes up,' Christian thought, while watching the fire take hold. Thinking of Sarah still asleep in her shelter with her body uncovered, her skin should have been cool, but when he removed his arm from around her, she felt warm.

Standing, and while buckling his gun-belt around his hips, he saw movement outside the shelter. Looking up, he saw Sarah at the entrance, a blanket wrapped around her, her long hair tousled, hanging in strands over her bare shoulders. As Christian walked back to her, he glanced beyond the shelter when he thought he saw movement on the ridge. Not seeing anything, he stood in front of Sarah and finished buckling his gun-belt. Sarah, her eyes still trying to focus as she woke up, looked at him. "Sheriff," she said sounding sleepy. "I told you Cole …my name is Christian." Even if she wasn't going to let him call her Sarah, he wanted her to call him Christian. He couldn't see why they couldn't use their first names now they had gone further than just kissing.

"I will keep calling you sheriff and you keep calling me Cole." Sarah didn't bat an eyelid when she told him how they should address each other. It was what everyone called her, and that was the way it was. Christian cringed. "I shouldn't have stayed so long," he said softly. "You regret staying sheriff?" Sarah questioned, turning her face up to his. "No …I don't regret staying …not at all," he whispered, pushing his hand into her hair and kissing her passionately. Finding an opening in the blanket, he slipped his hands inside. Sarah's body still felt warm and he felt himself responding to the silkiness of her curves. When Sarah opened the blanket slightly, he gently gripped her buttocks, and moved her to stand against him.

"I have to go," he said, forcing himself to let her go. The town would be waking up soon, and he didn't want anyone knowing he was seeing Sarah.

Sarah helped him solve his problem of getting back to the lodge without being seen. "Go along the riverbank," she said, pointing past the trail leading to town. "You'll come to a track between the trees near Ham's Livery, double back behind the buildings and you will come to the lodge, no-one will see you, if that's what you are worried about." Christian was silent for a moment while he studied her face, then replied. "I told you, I'm not worried about me, I'm worried about you." Sarah raised her eyebrows. "Well you needn't

…like I said, I've already got a reputation in this town, and what these people say, or think about me, doesn't bother me." Christian wanted to ask her what she meant by reputation, but the longer he stood there, the harder he was finding it to leave. "See you Cole," he said walking toward the riverbank. Sarah remained where she was, watching him until he disappeared from sight. Christian didn't look back, if he had, he would have seen they were being watched.

Chapter Fifteen

oe made an early morning trip to the outhouse. He liked getting up well before the other men to go first, otherwise he would have to wait until a bunch of men went before him. Coming out of the outhouse, he strolled over to the edge of the ridge above Sarah's camp. Something he did every morning without Sarah knowing. He just wanted to make sure Sarah and Thomas were safe.

When Joe made his promise to his best friend Calahan, he had no idea just twelve years later, he, along with his other three friends, would take responsibility for looking after Calahan's then fifteen-year old daughter. After Sarah met Frank Mason, he let her and Frank become friends because he wanted her to have someone around her that was near her own age. Joe couldn't have known, when after two years of Frank chasing Sarah, they would take their friendship as far as they did, resulting in Thomas being born a month after Frank died on the mountain. He stepped back from Sarah after she blamed him for Frank's death, telling him she hated him for letting Frank go to the High Country on his own. Even though Frank died by his own hand after being attacked by wolves, he took the blame. But he didn't step back too far. He made his promise, and because of it, managed over the years to keep a lot of men away from Sarah. Those men, who thought they could bed Sarah simply because she was by herself. He would not let any man take advantage of her, but now here she was, getting herself involved with Cedar Creek's new sheriff, a man no-one knew anything about.

This morning as he stood at the edge of the ridge above Sarah's camp, he saw someone come out of her shelter. Watching the man put wood on Sarah's fire, and pull his boots on, then stand up to fasten his gun-belt, was when he figured it was Christian, him being the only man in town wearing a gun.

Becoming curious, he kept watching. After seeing Sarah come out of her shelter, wearing nothing but a blanket, it was obvious Sarah and the sheriff had been together. But! 'Had Sheriff Morgan forced himself on Sarah?' was Joe's first thought when he saw Christian. If he had, Joe was going to make Christian pay dearly for it. Joe suddenly had to step back when Christian, making his way back to Sarah, glanced up toward the ridge. Standing just out of sight but allowing himself to see what was happening, Joe saw Christian kiss Sarah. His kiss was not just a friendly peck, it was deep, and meaningful. When Christian put his hands inside the blanket, Joe pursed his lips in anger. Then raised his eyebrows in surprise when Sarah opened the blanket and Christian held her against him, convincing him Sarah had invited Christian to her shelter.

Joe had seen enough. He went back to the Ferguson House and went inside to find the rest of the trappers just waking up. Joe managed to get to the washroom before all the other men to splash cold water on his face, not only to wake himself up properly, but to try to get the image he witnessed out of his mind. He came out of the washroom feeling fresh but the image of Sarah and Christian and the thought of what they had been doing hadn't gone. Joe went to the fire, and stoking it, shoved hot coals around in anger at Sarah's sudden loose attitude. After shoving a piece of wood in the hot coals, he shook the coffee pot vigorously. Fergus wandered over to the fire and standing beside Joe, scratched his crotch while yawning. Joe glanced over at him. "Goddamn it, Fergus, I hope you're going to wash before you touch anything." Fergus sniffed his hand. "Yep, I'll wash, don't worry about it ...what's been happenin? ...you check Cole's camp as usual? ...everything alright down there?" Fergus scratched his crotch some more. Joe had to tell him what he had seen, but he would also have to tell Garrett and Will. It was no good telling Fergus before telling the other two. He didn't want to have to repeat what he had just now witnessed. "Something's up Fergus, wait 'til the others are up."

Will had his turn at the outhouse and headed for the washroom. Garrett came out of his room and headed straight outside. Joe would have longer to wait for him to come back before telling the three men what he saw.

"What do you mean she's been with the sheriff? How with the sheriff?" Garrett said, rubbing the sleep out of his eyes. He hadn't had his turn in the washroom yet. Joe wasn't able to wait any longer so grabbed him as he came through the house from outside. The men leant in close around the table while Joe recounted what he had seen. "Sarah and the sheriff are..." He paused, because he didn't want to say they were fucking. He wanted it to sound at least a bit nicer than that. "You know... they are ...goddamn it!" Joe smoothed his hand over his beard in dismay as he leant in further. "Sheriff Morgan came out of Sarah's shelter this morning ...and Sarah came out with just a blanket around her, what does that tell you?" Joe thought he explained it clear enough for the men to know what he was telling them.

"You mean they are fucking!" Will said a little too loudly. Some of the other men getting their breakfast turned their heads in their direction when they heard Will's profanity. Joe clipped Will up the side of his head with his hand, causing him to flinch. "Sorry Joe, but is that what you are trying to tell us?" Joe kept his head down and his voice low.

"Yes! goddamn it!" The men sat back, then leaned in again. "Is that a problem Joe? maybe they like each other," Garrett said. "Christ! she's only been in town what, three, maybe four days! How could they possibly know if they like each other?" Joe was trying his best not to get angry with his friends. The men had been party to what happened with Logan when he tried to force himself on Sarah while she was sleeping in her shelter, with Thomas just a baby right alongside her. It was Garrett and Will held Logan up while Joe beat him senseless. Logan spent almost a week laid up at Doc Harris's after his beating. Joe hadn't any trouble from Logan for a long time, but he had to warn him again just recently when he was rude to Sarah while on her way to Doc's to get her cheek seen to after the sheriff shot at her. That was another thing that got Joe's back up. The sheriff seemed to like taking his role as sheriff way too seriously by not letting Sarah have her pistol. 'Well that!' Joe thought. 'Backfired on the sheriff after Sarah got Frank's forty-four and blasted the rats apart and woke the whole goddamn town!'

When Clem was sheriff, he never took his role as sheriff seriously. He would only ever take their guns if they got drunk and fired them off inside the saloon. Both the trappers and Sarah got away with a hell of a lot when Clem was sheriff. And Logan, he was a damn fool, and didn't know when enough was enough, so Joe kept reminding him.

"We just have to keep an eye on what's going on, see if Sarah and the sheriff are going to get serious." Joe got up from the table.

"You don't call that serious Joe?" Will asked. All three looked at Joe for an answer.

"It's not too serious that we can't let it go for now, Sarah's been a long time on her own, and maybe she just found someone to... " Not knowing quite what to say, Joe let his voice trail off.

Major Hardy's men ran in a herd of wild horses and the four men had solid work for a good two weeks. They didn't need any distractions, especially from Sarah. All four men finished their breakfast and headed for the corrals. While leaning on a railing looking through the fence watching until all the horses were in the corrals, Joe thought back to a time before Thomas was born.

It had taken Frank two years to get Sarah to accept she was in love with him. Frank wasn't going to give up on her, he was a trier, Joe gave him that much. Joe grew fond of a decent young man who had fallen for a young girl devastated by the death of her father. Frank tried his best, even giving Sarah that horse of hers. Joe could see from the start Frank had fallen in love with Sarah, and if Frank's father had stayed out of it, Frank and Sarah would be married now, living happily together with their son. Joe was sure they would have had more children, if they had married. As far as he had been concerned, Sarah and Frank were meant to be together, but as things turned out, it wasn't to be. Joe put his head down. Not only had Sarah's life changed dramatically when Frank died, so had theirs. Joe was sorry for Frank having to shoot himself. He thought it stupid of Frank thinking he could go off hunting wolves alone, only to get himself hunted. Frank had been the first trapper to die on the mountain, and the first to use his spare bullet.

Although Joe thought Sarah fell in love with Frank as soon as she met him, she kept Frank at bay because the Major threatened to whip her if she didn't stay away from his son. Even though Joe thought it bad Frank had been whipped instead of Sarah, he was grateful Sarah hadn't been. But Joe could never forgive a man that was as cruel as the Major. The Major denied the young couple years of happiness. Joe witnessed first-hand how Frank's death affected Sarah and he had taken the brunt of Sarah's wrath. Now Joe didn't know what to make of what Sarah and Christian were getting themselves into. Sarah would most definitely be going back to the mountain at the end of winter, and Christian? Joe didn't know what to make of him.

Joe made up his mind to find out all he could about Christian. He had an old friend in Washington whom he had not heard of for more years than he cared to count. After leaving the cavalry to take up trapping, Joe severed all contact with people he had been friends with. Last Joe heard, his friend had become a Senator, but he wasn't sure how to contact him or, if he was still a Senator, even so, getting a letter to him was going to be difficult. There was no U S mail office or stage-coach running between Cedar Creek and Moreton to carry people nor mail. Mail from town went on the supply wagons, and the wagons only came to town every eight weeks or more, depending on what they were bringing. Cedar Creek, Joe reckoned, was at the end of this godforsaken earth, and he expected it would take months for a letter to find its way to Washington and for a reply to come back, but he decided he would send one anyway.

Joe sat down that night, and with help from Fergus and Garrett, penned a letter. He enquired at Crawley's store and was told the supply wagon was, all being well, due in town in a week's time, and so, Joe's letter was going to be sent away on it.

Chapter Sixteen

After Christian left Sarah at daybreak, she didn't get dressed right away. Keeping her blanket wrapped tightly around her, she carried her bucket down to the river and filled it with water. Taking the bucket back to the fire, she poured some of the water into a large tin, then put the tin on the fire to heat up. While waiting for the water to get hot she sat at the fire and thought about Christian.

"I'm glad Christian stayed," she said, feeling fulfilled for the first time in a long time. Ever since Frank's passing, she hadn't wanted another man to touch her. Her body felt dead inside and that was another reason why, when Foley proposed marriage to her, she refused to accept him. Sarah closed her eyes and imagined Christian's body nestled against hers. Still able to feel his strong arms around her and his body nestled between her legs as he sent the same thrill surging through her she experienced with Frank. She felt she had grown up since being with Frank, and now, as a full-grown woman, knew what she wanted and welcomed it with open arms. Sarah tightened the blanket around her as she continued to remember Christian's touch.

The water boiling in the tin brought her back from her thought's. After pouring the water back into the bucket, mixing it with cold to make it just right, and carrying the bucket into her shelter, she dropped the blanket, and standing naked with the bucket of steaming water at her feet, could see where Christian had slept beside her. Christian was different from the men she knew. He had a way of making her think about what she wanted.

Thomas was spending the day with Billy Henderson and wouldn't be back until later that afternoon, so once she finished washing and getting dressed, she found she had lots of time to fill. After hanging blankets in the sun to air so the shelter would smell fresh, she busied herself making cookies and cleaning the camp. The day wore on, Sarah looked up to see where the sun was and sighed. It was noon, and still a long time to wait for Thomas to return.

Deciding to catch two more trout for dinner, she took a walk along the river. Going under the bridge and passing the corrals, she came to a good-sized waterhole where the current was flowing gently over small stones on the riverbed.

Having spent the next couple of hours catching and cleaning the two fish she needed, she carried the pan sized trout back to her camp. The fish were placed in a damp cloth inside her pan with a lid and after placing stones on top, the pan was lowered into the river to keep it cold.

Just as Sarah finished sitting the pan in the water, she heard a sound she had not heard for a long time. Straightening up, she looked along the riverbank and saw Thomas running toward her. Thomas had no reason to cry, not since he thought he lost his Pa's timepiece she entrusted to him for safe keeping. Thomas made a promise to take care of the precious keepsake, only to leave it lying on the porch at their cabin. She found it and kept it from him until he realized what he had done. It hurt Thomas to think he broke his promise. Thomas never left the timepiece lying about after that day.

Seeing Sarah on the riverbank, but instead of running to her, Thomas ran to the shelter. "Thomas!" Sarah called, trying to head him off. "Thomas! what happened?" Thomas quickly disappeared into the shelter before Sarah could get to him, and throwing himself on the furs, buried his face in his hands. "Thomas, what is it? What is wrong?" Sarah asked, kneeling down beside him. "Tell me Thomas, please, tell me, what has happened?" Sarah begged, but Thomas kept crying and Sarah couldn't help feeling something bad had happened to him. "I can't help you Thomas, not if you won't tell me what is wrong." Sitting up suddenly, Thomas threw his arms around Sarah and tried to tell her what happened.

"He didn't want to be my friend Ma, it was all a lie," he sobbed. "He was paid!" Thomas sobbed harder. Sarah didn't understand what he was saying. "What do you mean? Who are you talking about Thomas?"

"Billy!" he sobbed. "Billy Henderson! ...he was paid to be my friend!"

Sarah lifted Thomas away from her so she could look at him. "What do you mean Billy was paid?" Thomas's face was red, his eyes swollen. He could hardly talk for the sobs that racked his body.

"Thomas, tell me everything, from the beginning," Sarah urged. Thomas took a deep breath and while sobbing, related what happened.

"Billy and me were havin fun, we snared some rabbits and we let em go, cause Billy didn't want me to kill em, we were buildin our fort in the trees." He stopped and took another breath and sobbed. "It was good too, then two bigger boys, Jamie Finch and Daniel Connell came along, and they chased us 'til they caught us, Daniel grabbed hold of Billy and sat on his back!" Thomas tried to stifle a sob. "Jamie held me while Daniel twisted Billy's arms, he twisted his arms back until he talked, Billy was screamin and cryin Ma!" He stopped to take another breath. "He asked Billy why Sheriff Morgan gave him the money!" When Sarah heard mention of Christian, her heart lurched, and her stomach dropped. Listening carefully to what Thomas was telling her she couldn't believe what she was hearing, her eyes widened in shock. Thomas started to cry again. "Go on Thomas," Sarah urged.

"Sheriff Morgan paid Billy to be my friend Ma ...Billy didn't want to be my friend ...he was paid to be!" He sobbed uncontrollably and buried his head against Sarah's chest. "I hate them, I hate them all ...I want to go home!" While Thomas continued to sob, Sarah grew angry. Her mind went over yesterday and particularly what happened between her and Christian in her shelter. Sarah wondered just when did Christian pay Billy Henderson to be Thomas's friend? "Thomas ...do you know when Sheriff Morgan paid Billy?" she asked softly. Thomas wiped his nose on the back of his sleeve. "Sure Ma ...it was yesterday, Jamie Finch and Daniel Connell saw Sheriff Morgan give Billy five whole dollars when he went home for his reader ...yesterday!" He snorted and sobbed. "And Ma! ...I punched Billy in the nose and made it bleed!" Thomas's eyes overflowed with more tears. Sarah got a wet cloth, and after wiping his face, made him lie down while she got a blanket off the rope line and covered him with it.

Sitting with him until he fell asleep, Sarah seethed with anger at the thought of Finch and Connell's involvement, and at Christian, and how he came to be at her camp, using the excuse that he was doing his rounds of the town. "Goddamn rounds! ...like hell! ...goddamn it!" Sarah cursed. "He knew Thomas wouldn't be here ...goddamn it! he came here with bad intentions ...planned the whole goddamn thing!" The more Sarah thought about the reason Christian happened to come along, the angrier she got, and she was getting angrier with every minute that passed.

'Sheriff Morgan paid Billy to get Thomas out of the way simply so he could bed me. Just like Logan tried when Thomas was a baby, only Sheriff Morgan used a different tactic, and it worked!' That was the thought going through Sarah's mind as she paced back and forth in front of her firepit. "Goddamn son-of-a-bitch!" she cursed. Sarah had herself convinced Christian knew Thomas was staying at Billy's, because he paid Billy to take Thomas home for the night. Even though it was she who asked Christian to stay, it must have been Christian who planned it. Sarah thought of another, more distasteful reason Christian came to her camp, and that reason, was so Christian could treat her like she was a whore.

Looking in on Thomas, and seeing him sobbing in his sleep, Sarah fumed to think her son had been used and she had been treated like she was a piece of meat. No-one uses her son to get to her, and no-one treats her like she was nothing. Sarah now planned how she was going to retaliate against Christian. After checking Thomas once more, she stormed up the trail and along the main street. People going about their business saw her and could tell by the way she was strutting, something happened again concerning her, and whatever it was, it made her real mad.

Sarah's arms swung back and forth, her knife bounced at her hip, her mouth was pressed tight in a scowl. As she approached the Sheriff's Office, everyone hurried to get out of her way. Stepping on the boardwalk outside, Sarah shoved the door open forcefully, then stepping inside, saw Clem sitting behind the desk, with Christian nowhere in sight. "Where the goddamn hell is the sheriff, Clem?" There was no mistaking the anger in Sarah's voice. "Up at the corrals Cole ...what do you…?" Sarah didn't wait for Clem to finish. Hurrying back out the door, slamming it behind her, she stormed up the street toward the corrals. Her stride was defiant, she swung her arms more forcefully. As her hips swayed, she gripped her knife, and her ponytail swished from side to side. When two men saw her coming towards them, they walked quickly across the street to get out of harm's way. Men and women walking along the boardwalks stopped and stared. Some put their heads together and began whispering. "There goes Cole!" and others. "Looks like someone is in big trouble again!" and everyone waited to see where Sarah was going to see who it was that was about to receive her wrath.

Chapter Seventeen

After spending the night with Sarah, Christian was feeling good. It had been the first time in a long time since he had been with a woman. Although he couldn't remember the last woman he slept with before Sarah, he had frequented a lot of saloons while chasing outlaws, and was sure she would have been a saloon girl. Spending two years at the mission in Les Rios and another five 'searching for his niche,' as Brother Abraham called it, by his own reckoning, until he met Sarah, he hadn't been inclined to take any other woman to bed.

Having left Sarah standing outside her shelter, wrapped only in a blanket, Christian smiled, his body felt relaxed, with Sarah's help, the emotions and tension he had bottled up inside him had finally been released. As he made his way along the riverbank from her camp, he was thinking Sarah was one hell of a sexy woman. Quietly making his way behind the buildings lining the street where the lodge is situated as Sarah suggested, he came to the house. When he got inside without anyone seeing him, he thought how childish it seemed to be to have to sneak about. He was a grown man and Sarah a grown woman, and if they wanted to fuck, it should not be anyone's business. But then, Cedar Creek is a small town, and gossip spreads fast. Christian does not want the town talking about him, or Sarah.

After bathing, he dressed in a clean shirt, and trousers, made himself a huge breakfast of bacon, eggs and beans with fried bread and drank two cups of coffee. 'Hell' he thought, 'I haven't eaten like this in a long time. What I did with Sarah last night sure has helped me work up an appetite.'

Having found out her name was Sarah, after finding her name written inside a bible in a message from a man named Frank, he wanted to call her Sarah. But it was after they finished making love, when he asked her to call him Christian, that she refused. Even though he hated it, he resigned himself to sticking with what she wanted. He held a vivid image of Sarah in his mind, recalling every inch of her body. There was that scar on her left shoulder, which he knew straight away was a bullet wound, and it made him wonder just who, and why, she had been shot. He didn't like to ask her while they were fucking, but made a mental note to himself that he would somehow find out how she got the scar.

Sarah was a beautiful woman, she intrigued him, and he wanted to see her again. He would like them to spend the whole night together without worrying about having to sneak about. 'Maybe' he planned. 'Sarah could come to the lodge …perhaps one night when Thomas stays at Billy Henderson's again.' He thought that a stroke of luck, Billy asking Thomas to have a sleepover. He hadn't told Billy to invite Thomas to his house, but was glad he did. Even though Christian knew it wasn't the right thing to do before getting married, he had no qualms about fucking Sarah, and it seemed to Christian, Sarah didn't have any qualms about fucking him. He smiled to himself and then thought how disgusting his thoughts were. He liked Sarah a great deal, and was surprised at just how much he did like her after only knowing her a few days.

When he left the lodge to go to the Sheriff's Office he was smiling and feeling happy. The sun was shining, taking the bight off the cool breeze blowing up from the river. All in all, it wasn't a bad day for a winter's day. Even the town folk seemed happier. Several people said howdy to him as he walked along the street, and he tipped his hat back to them, making him feel pretty darn good. Sarah and his union had been perfect.

Standing outside his office, he heard someone say the Major's horses had arrived and that the trapper's job of breaking them had begun. Christian had done this type of work along with working on cattle drives when he drifted from place to place, long before he became a bounty hunter, and even longer before he became a lawman, but that was a lifetime ago. Now he was sheriff of a town he reckoned he could raise a family in, being with Sarah got him thinking more seriously about settling down. Those thoughts had only been fleeting up until now. Feeling his future in Cedar Creek looked promising, he wandered along to the corrals to watch the men work.

Will and Fergus were sitting on top of one of the corral fences watching Garrett trying his best to break one of the horses. Christian stood alongside Joe, and both peered through the railings to watch Garrett working.

This wasn't the first time Garrett had broken horses, he was an old hand at it, having worked for the Major every winter for the best part of his life. The stallion Garrett was working stood tall, bucking around the corral, twisting, turning, and kicking, making it difficult for Garrett to get a rope on it. The men laughed when Garrett finally got the rope on and then got unceremoniously pulled off his feet and dragged through the dust and horse manure on his back. The stallion kept bucking wildly forcing Garrett to let go of the rope. The men continued to laugh when Garrett stood up and held his back. He felt old all of a sudden, but not letting the men have the satisfaction of seeing him give up, he took hold of the rope and held on. Joe and Christian laughed while the men whooped and hollered and waved their hats as they cheered Garrett on.

The bridle and bit, was bad enough, it was taking the horse some time to get used to it, and it continued to let Garrett know he wasn't happy. When Garrett got the saddle on, Joe and Christian stopped laughing and talked jovially with each other about horse breaking.

"Sheriff Morgan!" someone called behind Christian's back. Turning from watching Garrett to see who it was that called him, he didn't see the fist that slammed into his jaw. The impact made him bite his lip. Blood spurted from his mouth and ran down his chin. He stumbled back, falling hard against the railings. When the fence shook violently, Will and Fergus hung on to stop themselves from falling. Sarah stood facing Christian, her eyes wild.

"You son-of-a-bitch!" she yelled. Yelling so loud, all the men stopped what they were doing and turned to watch. Joe stared at Sarah. 'Here we go,' he thought. Will and Fergus turned to see what the commotion was about. People in the vicinity of the corrals stopped and stared.

"What the hell?" Sarah's punch made Christian's eyes water. Putting his hand to his jaw, he straightened up and glared at her.

"You son-of-a-bitch!" Sarah repeated so savagely, she couldn't find suitable words to describe what she was feeling.

"Goddamn it all Cole!" Christian yelled back. "What did you do that for?"

"You know damn well why I did that! …sheriff! …you think you can get rid of my son so you can use me? you rotten goddamn! …son-of-a-bitch!" That was the third time Sarah called Christian a name he disliked.

"Don't you go calling me a son-of-a-bitch Cole!" he replied angrily, stepping away from the fence. "My mother was not a bitch!" Christian never knew his mother. He told Sarah he was raised in an orphanage. She should have remembered that.

Ignoring what Christian said, Sarah went on. "My son doesn't need you buying him friends …he has all the friends he needs!" she yelled in his face.

Still holding his jaw, Christian figured he knew what Sarah was talking about. "Your son does not have any friends! he sits by himself in the schoolyard while kids kick dirt at him!" When he let Sarah know that information, he watched her eyes soften for a moment, but it was only a fleeting moment before the fire returned and she started in on him again.

"You thought you could get rid of my son so you could use me! That's what you thought, didn't you? that was your plan, wasn't it? you came to my camp saying you were doing your rounds, but you weren't, were you? …you …stinking, slimy …shit crawling maggot!" Being brought up around trappers, Sarah heard some pretty nasty words, but it was usually Crawley, who was the person on the other end of her tirade. Christian ignored her disparaging remarks and brought himself under control. "Just what are you saying Sarah?"

Suddenly becoming interested in what was happening between Sarah and Christian, Will and Fergus climbed off the fence and stood side by side to listen to the exchange. After what Joe told them about the two of them, they weren't expecting Sarah's sudden angry outburst.

"You know perfectly well what I am saying! don't pretend that you don't! …when you came to my camp last night you knew Thomas wouldn't be there!" Sarah's eyes welled. "How dare you think you can send my son away so you can use me for your own gratification!" When her hand went to her knife, Christian knew she was serious. Trying to take them away from the prying eyes of the men so he could talk some sense into her, he grabbed her by her arm and dragged her protesting down the alley alongside the Livery.

Not letting them get out of earshot, the trappers followed them into the alley. Seeing the men out the corner of his eye watching and listening to their every word, Christian shoved Sarah against the wall and leant in close to keep what he was saying between them. "I did not use your son Sarah, and I did not plan for Billy to ask Thomas to spend the night at his home …and I certainly did not use you!"

"Oh yes you did!" Sarah yelled. Struggling to break free of his grasp, she looked at the blood on Christian's lip and was glad she made him bleed.

"I did not!" he yelled back. Christian's lip hurt and he could feel it beginning to swell. 'So much for keeping his voice down so the trappers couldn't hear them' he thought.

Sarah lowered her voice but remained angry. "You knew Thomas wasn't there, you damn snake! you planned it! that was why you came to my camp, wasn't it? you knew exactly what would happen!" Sarah could see Joe and the other men too, and by this time Garrett had joined them. She didn't care, let them hear, she looked angrily into Christian's face.

"I did not plan it Sarah," Christian repeated more softly, not wanting to fight with her. "I didn't know Thomas wasn't going to be there …if you recall, it was you who asked me to stay …you wanted what happened between us last night to happen just as much as I did …besides …when we were in your shelter, I didn't hear you telling me to stop!" Feeling humiliated that a woman hit him in front of the men and drew blood, he ran his tongue along the inside of his lip and could feel where it was cut.

Sarah thought about what Christian was saying. 'Yes, she had asked him to stay, and yes, she liked that they had sex,' but by her reckoning she believed she wouldn't have asked him to stay if he hadn't come to her camp and found her alone, therefore, making up her mind, Christian planned it.

"You are a liar sheriff, you paid Billy Henderson to get Thomas out of the way so you could bed me!" Sarah's eyes darkened with sudden recollection that Christian had slept with her, because after they finished fucking, he had stayed all night. 'And yes,' Sarah remembered. 'It definitely was her that asked him to stay.' But still, what happened to Thomas and Billy was his fault. Sarah pulled her foot back against the wall and kicked out, collecting Christian on his shin bone. Christian jumped back in pain and let her go. "God! …damn! …I am not a liar Sarah! goddamn it! you… " he stopped himself from calling her a bitch while continuing to hop around holding his leg and thinking to himself. 'Fuck! …now I have a sore leg as well as a split lip! Damn it Sarah! how am I to blame for us fucking and liking it?'

When Christian let Sarah go, she ran to the trees at the far end of the alley, and once at a safe distance, turned to face him. "You stay away from me!" Tears were clearly visible in her eyes. "Stay away from me! …and stay away from my son!" With one last parting thing to say before disappearing down the track leading to the riverbank, she called. "And don't you dare call me Sarah!"

Christian hobbled around holding his leg. "With pleasure …Cole!" he said angrily to her receding back. It had only taken Sarah a few minutes to reduce his earlier sense of euphoria to zero. Now he just wanted to head back to his office to think about what just happened. But before he could, he found himself standing in the alley face to face with four angry men blocking his path. The men didn't want to interfere, but they would if it meant keeping Sarah safe. There were a lot of men who thought they were entitled to have their way with Sarah. Logan was by far the worst. Now here they were, listening to Christian try and justify he hadn't used Sarah for his own gratification. When Joe smirked, it was a look that told Christian Joe wasn't surprised at what just happened. "Well sheriff, looks like you just became another victim of Cole's."

"What do you mean by, victim Joe?" Christian asked, holding his hand to his mouth. Instead of answering Christian's question, Joe asked him one. "Are you involved with Cole sheriff?" Joe stood face to face with Christian waiting for his reply. "I am not 'involved' as you put it Joe." Christian wiped blood from his now swollen lip as he limped toward the men. One night of fucking didn't mean he was involved, even though he harboured a feeling he would like to be, right now he wasn't so sure. Christian tried pushing past Joe and Fergus, but Joe and Fergus stood directly in front of him baring his passage. Will and Garrett circled around behind him and stood so close he could feel their hot breath on the back of his neck. Christian was beginning to feel trapped. 'Maybe this is what a wolf feels like when it is trapped by these men!' he thought

"You think you are not involved sheriff? You come out of Cole's shelter early in the morning, and you think you are not involved! …well you better have been invited there, because if you weren't …you! …are in so deep a hole! …the shit is over your head!" Stepping up to let his huge body touch Christian's, bringing his face within inches of Christian's, Joe could see clearly where Sarah made Christian's lip bleed. 'Good,' he sniggered. 'It's no less than what he deserves.' Having thought no-one had seen him and sounding incredulous, Christian asked, "you saw me?" Joe stared into Christian's eyes. "You're damn right I saw you! …I almost beat a man to death for a lot less than what you did last night."

"You Cole's protector …Jones? …Or do you just like spying on her?" Christian bravely asked, wondering why Joe was always around when something happened where Sarah was concerned. Deep inside though, he was shaken to know Joe had seen him. He hadn't known what these men had to do with Sarah and Thomas, but now, he was getting a sense these four men were their guardians.

Christian thought he and Sarah had been discreet, even she told him to go along the riverbank. But it was too late for him to worry about that now. All four men knew what he and Sarah had been doing, making him wonder how long it would take for the rest of the town to find out.

Ignoring Christian suggesting he spied on Sarah, Joe wanted to know why Sarah and Christian's argument involved Thomas.

"Cole's a grown woman, she knows how to protect herself ...so ... what's this I hear about you using Thomas?" Christian had no choice but to tell the men he paid Billy Henderson to be Thomas's friend. After explaining what he thought must have happened, Joe put his head back and laughed uproariously, then suddenly turned serious. "Well that was a goddamn stupid thing to do, paying a kid to make friends! ...you must have thought it was your lucky day when you turned up at Cole's camp to find Thomas wasn't there!" Will and Garrett moved in closer. No man was going to use Sarah without her honest say so. Christian could feel the men standing right up against his back in a threatening manner. "I didn't plan it Jones, believe me, what happened between us just happened, Cole and I..." Joe didn't let Christian finish. "Let me tell you something! ... sheriff! ...Cole and you are nothing! ...you stay away from her!" he ordered, poking his finger at Christian's chest. "Cole doesn't need you causing her trouble, she has enough to contend with in this town without you adding to it." Joe hadn't wanted what happened between Sarah and Christian to end like this, but it had. This time he would just give Christian a warning, then he would wait and see where his warning went.

"That a threat Jones?" Christian asked, standing up to Joe. Having dealt with some pretty tough ombre's over his lifetime, these men, even if they were Sarah's protectors, weren't going to make him feel afraid. Christian knew from what Sarah told him when they clashed on the first day they met, trappers didn't make threats, they made promises, and he wondered if Joe was going to make him a promise to do him harm if he continued to see Sarah. "Not yet sheriff! I'm just telling you for your own good!" With that, Joe stormed back to the corrals.

After giving Christian an eyeful of their disdain, the other three men followed Joe. Joe on reflection, thought he may have just broken his promise he made to Sarah's father again by interfering, but he didn't care. He had broken his promise before and reckoned he would have good reason to break it again in the near future. There was another promise Joe made before Sarah was born, one which always got him feeling Sarah was his responsibility and his alone. Christian limped back to the jailhouse. Joe sent his letter off to Washington.

Chapter Eighteen

Limping into the Sheriff's Office, Christian sat behind his desk and pulled his trouser leg up to look at the damage Sarah did to his shin. His skin was broken and bruised where she kicked him. A trickle of blood ran down the front of his leg and ran into his boot. It wasn't so much the kick or the punch that hurt him, it was his pride. It made him feel stupid that the trappers witnessed Sarah hitting him, and to let her get the better of him again. Cursing Sarah under his breath, and keeping his trouser leg pushed up, he limped to the back room where a bunk bed was pushed against the wall. A dish, and jug of cold water sat on top of a cupboard in a corner of the room. Pouring water into the dish, then while looking in the mirror at his mouth, he wet a cloth and wiped blood off his chin. Still holding the cloth to his lip, he pulled his lip out and saw the small cut on the inside where his tooth had gone through. Putting his foot on the side of the bunk, he felt the bruise that was forming around the small cut.

"Goddamn it all Cole," he said out loud. "I did not plan for Billy to take Thomas home for the night! why can't you believe that?" Christian could have arrested Sarah for hitting him, no-one hits a lawman and gets away with it. He read that in one of the law books he studied while recuperating at the Les Rios Mission. But he let her get away with it just like when she shot the river rats and breaking in to Ham's Livery. Sarah was starting to get out of hand, and couldn't be allowed to get away with too much more. Accusing him of using her when he knew he hadn't, but he wanted her, right from the moment he met her in the street near the schoolhouse, right about the time she knocked him off his feet, and sometime between that moment, and when they had been together in her shelter, Sarah had wanted him, and they both knew it. Throwing the towel back on the bench in disgust, he pulled down his trouser leg, and going to his desk, went over in his mind how he and Sarah came to get together. 'I went to Cole's camp to check everything was in order like I did all around town. I was about to leave when Cole offered me coffee, we sat and drank coffee together, then I said I had better go. That was when Cole asked me to stay. Her exact words 'you going to finish it sheriff' were pretty darn clear when she looked at me with those beautiful blue eyes of hers, and I knew exactly what she meant. She meant what I started in the Livery the night of the storm, so ...I obliged her ...I finished it!' Christian went over it once more to be certain of what happened.

Satisfied it was all Sarah's doing, he couldn't understand why she thought he planned it just because Thomas found out he gave Billy money to be his friend. Christian couldn't see anything wrong with giving Billy money if it meant the two boys became best friends. His thoughts went back to a time when two boys from the orphanage he was raised in, paid him and another boy, Max, to fight. These two older boys thought he and Max hated each other because sometimes they got into arguments. But they were wrong. After their fight, instead of becoming enemies, he and Max became best friends. Both of them were often punished with beatings for things he thought were insignificant. Beatings were a regular part of their young lives and at age fourteen, he and Max ran away from the orphanage, and the beatings. After picking up odd bits of work, they saved enough money to buy their first horses. The horses were old, but they got them as far away from the orphanage as they could get. Riding out west, they spent the next four years working on cattle ranches and going on cattle drives, both learning how to brand cattle, and break horses. Some ranchers were kind to them, others not so. It was a tough life. Both he and Max learnt how to survive the hard way.

He continued thinking of Max, who thought he was a good fighter, and of when he joined a band of men who gambled on organized fights. Max signed a contract agreeing to fight, but after taking a severe beating he wanted out. When the men refused to let Max go, he stepped in and agreed to fight for Max's freedom. Badly beaten, and clearly losing, he won the fight by knocking his opponent into unconsciousness with a lucky blow, but the men still refused to release Max from his contract. Making a run for their lives, and thinking they had made a clean get away, they began to relax. Freedom though, had not come easy. Hired to track them down, a gunman drew Max into a gunfight. Never having been good with a gun, Max didn't stand a chance.

Holding Max in his arms until he died devastated him. He wasn't good with a gun either, but he practiced until he became so good, he never missed anything he aimed at. Hunting down the man who killed his best friend, and drawing the man into a gunfight, he was satisfied he had revenged his friend's death. Taking the body to the nearest town, he expected to be arrested for murder, and had resigned himself to spending the rest of his life in prison. Being told the man had a price on his head, came as a surprise. Feeling relieved that he wouldn't be spending time in jail, and not caring about his own life, after collecting the reward, he took up Bounty Hunting for a living. Losing the one true friend he ever had, he spent what seemed a lifetime chasing the worst of the worst all over the country. And then, seven years ago, he chased his last outlaw.

Christian remembered why he stopped Bounty Hunting. It was because of an outlaw known as Sam 'Wild West' Weston. He planned on taking Weston alive and collecting five thousand dollars reward. The biggest price on a man's head Christian ever heard of. After chasing Weston from New Mexico and all through Texas, he caught him holed up in a mission a few miles this side of the Mexican border. 'Les Rios Mission and The Brothers of the Holy Father, was what the mission was called. But things didn't quite go the way he expected. Ambushed by Weston and his gang, he managed to kill one man before killing Weston and taking two bullets in his back from another. The last outlaw, now on his own, decided he didn't want to die that day, so made good his escape, leaving Christian fighting for his life.

Unable to thank him enough for rescuing them, the Brothers made him welcome, telling him he could stay for as long as he wanted. It was then, while recuperating from his wounds, he found the Brothers had an extensive library, so he took to reading a collection of law books until he could recite the laws backwards.

Before leaving the mission, Christian was sent to see one of the Brothers. This particular Brother they said, was blessed with the 'knowledge' and could tell Christian his future. Doubtful of the Brother's abilities at the time, Christian remembered Brother Abraham's exact words to him that day. Brother Abraham told him he would find what he had been searching all his life for. He told him he had *goodness in his heart* and that he would *find his niche.* A final more puzzling prediction was told. '*Three would become four.*' Christian wasn't a bad person, he hated being a Bounty Hunter and only turned to it because of his best friend Max being killed. He never wanted to go down the path of lawlessness. He didn't understand what Brother Abraham meant by *'three would become four.'* This last part of his prediction has left Christian still feeling puzzled.

Having found a new zest for life he rode away from the mission and never returned to Bounty Hunting. Instead, he travelled the country searching for his niche and trying to find what Brother Abraham told him he was searching for. But for seven long years, nothing ever came of it. He never got over the loss of his best friend Max. Never forgetting the one true friend he had, and all because he had been offered money to fight him and he had taken it.

Billy's left arm hurt really bad when Daniel Connell twisted it behind his back, and when Thomas Mason hit him in the face his nose bled. He ran home crying and gagging as blood ran down the back of his throat, flowed down his face and soaked the front of his shirt. Billy reckoned he was in a whole mess of trouble with his Ma and Pa. His Ma would be mad because he dirtied his shirt, and his Pa would be mad and make him tell him about taking money off the sheriff. But he didn't care, he was hurting and he needed his Ma and Pa badly.

Billy raced inside with blood still pouring from his nose. Martha and Dave were in their back garden tending their vegetable crop when they heard Billy's cries and the front door banging shut. Billy ran through the house and onto the back porch. Martha, seeing Billy's bloodied face and the blood covering the front of his shirt, screamed for Dave. Dave dropped the spade he was holding and both he and Martha ran to Billy.

Ushering Billy back inside, Dave held his head up to stop the bleeding. Martha handed Dave a wet cloth and he put the cloth to Billy's face and made him hold it there.

"What happened Billy?" Dave asked. But before Billy could answer, Martha tried to take Billy's shirt off him. "Don't take it off Ma, I don't want to take it off!" he cried, and with his good hand, held on tight to the front of his shirt. Martha couldn't get Billy to let go so she left his shirt alone. Billy told his parents, between sobbing and gagging on blood still running down the back of his throat, what happened to him and why it happened.

Dave and Martha waited for Billy's nose to stop bleeding. "Where is the five dollars Billy?" Dave asked when it had stopped. "It's in my room Pa." Billy's face was smeared with blood, snot and dirt, his eyes were red from crying. "Go and get it please son." Dave wasn't mad at his son, he realized Billy had just learnt a valuable lesson in that 'you can't buy friendship, you had to earn it.'

The door to the Sheriff's Office opened and Billy came in followed by his father Dave and his mother Martha. Christian looked at them as they stood in front of his desk and knew straight away the reason they were there, but still, he was shocked at Billy's appearance. The front of Billy's shirt was dirty and covered in dried blood, his face was smeared with dirt mixed with blood, his nose looked like it had been bleeding and his eyes were turning black in the corners near his nose. Billy held up his right arm and sniffling, wiped his sleeve across his face.

"Sheriff ...Billy has something to give you." Dave Henderson gave Billy a gentle nudge and Billy stepped toward Christian's desk. "Go on Billy." Billy held his right hand over the top of Christian's desk and opening it, dropped five one-dollar coins onto his desk. "I don't want your money sheriff." Fresh tears ran down Billy's face. "I don't need it, I told you I just wanted to be friends with Thomas, but now we can never be friends." Billy stepped back to his parents as his tears continued to flow. Dave put his hand on his son's shoulder. "You do know why we are here sheriff ...don't you?" Dave looked disgusted at Christian. Christian nodded. "I think I know Henderson." Although Christian didn't know how Billy came to have a bloodied shirt and black eyes.

"That was an awful thing to put our son through, we had no idea you had given Billy money to make friends with the Mason boy, if we had, we never would have invited him to stay at our house, now Cole knows what has happened!" Dave scolded Christian. Martha added. "You have put us in a terrible position sheriff, Cole can be very vindictive when it comes to anything happening to her son." Christian listened to Dave and Martha's concerns without interruption. Martha, holding a handkerchief to her nose and sniffling, gripped a tin with a flower pattern all over it. "Nothing happened to Cole's son," Christian said, trying to pacify them while looking at the tin. "His pride was hurt that's all." Dave studied Christian's face, and could see he had a busted lip. "Pride! this has nothing to do with pride sheriff! this has got to do with Thomas Mason! Cole is a trapper! her son has been tormented and made a fool of! we have to go now and try to apologize to Cole for what you have done!" Dave frowned when Christian put his hand up to his swollen lip. "Have you seen Cole sheriff?" Christian looked at Dave then at Billy who was still sniffling. "I have already had a visit from Cole, yes," he said, rubbing his finger over his mouth. "If that is all Cole does to you, then you are damn lucky!" Dave retorted. He and Martha were not going to leave the Sheriff's Office until they got an apology for Billy from Christian first. Christian turned his attention to Billy. "What happened to you Billy? How did Thomas find out about the money?"

Billy took a deep breath and repeated his story.

"Thomas and I were building a fort, we already snared a rabbit, and we let it go cause I didn't want to kill it, we built a good fort too, and Jamie Finch and Daniel Connell came along and smashed it down and chased us 'til they caught us, Jamie held Thomas and Daniel pushed me on the ground and sat on my back, he pulled my arms back and twisted em." Billy stopped and snorted. "He twisted my arms until they burned and I had to tell." Billy sobbed at the memory. His arms had burned really bad, and his left arm still hurt.

"Go on Billy, please," Christian urged, speaking softly. Dave and Martha stood quietly by and let Billy talk. "Well, Jamie and Daniel saw you give me the money and they wanted to know why you gave it to me, Jamie was holding Thomas by his arms and Thomas heard me tell them you paid me to be his friend, Thomas got real mad and got loose from Jamie, he pushed Daniel off me and he punched me in the nose and made it bleed, then he ran off." Billy stopped talking and wiped his sleeve over his face again. "I guess he ran home to tell his Ma." Billy looked at Christian. Christian got up and going around to the front of his desk, squatted in front of Billy. His leg ached, reminding him that Sarah had kicked him. "I'm really sorry Billy for what happened to you, I just wanted you and Thomas to be friends, I thought maybe the money would help, it seemed to have worked for me when I was your age, I didn't mean for any of this to happen, I am truly sorry." Dave was satisfied with Christian's apology but couldn't help feel afraid at what they had to do next with regard to Sarah. Billy didn't say any more, he just sniffled. Christian stood up and turned to Dave. "Do you want me to come with you to talk to Cole?" Dave looked aghast at Christian. "I think you have done enough already sheriff! ...but we expect you to talk to the Finch and Connell boys!" With that, Dave herded Martha and Billy out the door.

After the Henderson's left, Christian wondered how Jamie Finch and Daniel Connell had come to see him give the money to Billy. Watching them kicking dirt at Thomas, and Billy telling him they picked on the younger children at school, it was obvious the two boys were trouble makers. Christian was definitely going to talk to them, but first he wanted to wait to see what happened when the Henderson's visited Sarah at her camp.

Chapter Nineteen

After having the fight with Christian at the corrals and returning to her camp, Sarah was shaking so much she thought she was going to be sick. When she got back, she went straight to her shelter to check on Thomas and found he was still sleeping, so leaving him alone, she sat in front of her fire to think about what she had done. Looking at her hand where it was bruised along her knuckles from hitting Christian, she felt disgusted with herself at having acted like a mad woman, but Thomas had been upset, and feeling she had been used, she lashed out without thinking about the consequences.

She was still sitting at her fire when a man and a woman with a small boy came down the trail toward her. Sarah recognized Martha and Dave Henderson, and their son Billy walking along in front of them. As the trio approached her cautiously, Sarah stood up, and although she didn't expect any trouble from the mild-mannered Henderson's, she instinctively put her hand on her knife. When Dave saw Sarah reach for her knife, his hands immediately went to Billy's shoulders and all three of them stopped where they were. Hoping they had a safe distance between them, Dave addressed Sarah. "Cole ...I guess you know what happened ...Thomas has told you?" Sarah could see the worried look on Dave's face when he spoke. "He told me." Sarah looked from Dave to Martha and could see Martha had been crying, she held a handkerchief to her face and clutched a tin of some sort close to her chest. Sarah wasn't concerned about the tin, it looked harmless enough, it was round and too small for a gun to be hidden in.

Billy shrugged off his father's hand and stepping forward, started to cry. "I'm sorry, I didn't want to take the money from Sheriff

Morgan, I really did want to be friends with Thomas, but I was too scared."

"Why were you scared to be friends with Thomas, Billy?" Sarah asked confused.

"The older boys told us younger boys, if we played with Thomas and something happened to him, you would skin us, and you carry that big knife all the time." Sarah wasn't surprised by what Billy was saying, there were a lot of people in Cedar Creek that were afraid of her, because she had made it that way. Wanting Billy to be able to tell her everything, and not wanting Billy to become frightened, Sarah kept her voice calm. "I'm not going to skin you Billy, I have never skinned anyone except wolves with my knife, why don't you tell me what happened from the beginning."

Billy repeated his story twice already and hoped he wouldn't get anything wrong when he told Cole his version of what happened.

"I went home to get my reader and I run in to Sheriff Morgan. He asked me why me and Thomas weren't friends and I told him Thomas didn't have any friends." Sarah was surprised at this revelation about Thomas, Christian said the same thing after she hit him. She thought Thomas had lots of friends and that was one of the reasons he loved going to school. Billy kept talking. "Jamie Finch and Daniel Connell pick on everyone and we can't be friends. I told Sheriff Morgan that, but he still gave me the money, he said just make friends with Thomas after school and on days when there's no school. I didn't want to take the money, but Sheriff Morgan asked me if there was something I wanted, and well, there's a knife at the store that folds up inside itself, and you can carry it around in your pocket, and I thought it would be good to have, cause I wouldn't cut myself with it, Ma is always frightened I will hurt myself." Sarah thought when she saw the blood on Billy's shirt and his dirty face he had certainly got hurt today. Billy continued.

"I got the idea of asking Thomas home when I was looking for my reader, I thought it would be good if Thomas stayed with me for the night, that way Jamie and Daniel wouldn't know." When Sarah heard Billy confess to coming up with the idea of asking Thomas to spend the night, it wasn't Christian at all, that came as quite a shock. Letting go the handle of her knife, she dropped her arms by her sides. "You came up with the idea of Thomas sleeping over Billy?" Sarah asked, to make sure of what he said.

"Yeah, when I got home, I thought, why couldn't Thomas sleep at my house, that way Jamie and Daniel wouldn't know and Ma and Pa said yes." Just like Sarah wouldn't allow Thomas to tell lies, Martha and Dave would not hear of Billy lying. Convinced Billy was telling the truth and Christian hadn't used her at all, Sarah wished she hadn't been so hasty in her decision to confront Christian. She had ruined everything that happened between them.

Billy went on telling Sarah what they had done when Thomas stayed at his house. "Thomas and I had fun drawing lots of pictures, Thomas is good at drawing pictures of wolves and things, he showed me his Pa's book and we snared a rabbit and I didn't want Thomas to kill it so he let it go, and we built a fort and ...." Billy's voice trailed away when he looked beyond Sarah. Sarah followed his gaze toward the shelter. Dave and Martha looked too. Thomas had woken, heard Billy's voice, and came out of the shelter to listen to Billy explaining what had happened.

"I gave the money back Thomas," Billy said when he saw Thomas. His nose ran, his face grew wet with tears, he swiped his sleeve across his face to wipe away the mess. "I wanted us to be friends, but I was too scared to ask you because of Jamie and Daniel." Walking carefully over the stones and up to the grassed area outside the shelter, Billy approached Thomas cautiously. Thomas took a few steps toward Billy and they stood facing each other. Sarah, Dave and Martha watched the exchange between the two boys.

"I still want us to be friends Thomas, but I understand if you don't want to be friends, I didn't think it would hurt if I took the money." Sarah watched as more tears ran down Billy's face. 'This is still Christian's fault,' she thought.

"But I punched you in the nose," Thomas said, his eyes watering. He already cried buckets of tears, and still a tear ran down his cheek. He swiped it away quickly with the palm of his hand and sniffled. Billy looked at the ground at his feet. "I deserved to be punched for what I did."

"No you didn't, but I was mad when I heard you say you were paid to be my friend, you didn't have to be paid, you could have asked me to be your friend and I would have been." Thomas and Billy both sniffled. "Can we still be friends Thomas?" Looking into Thomas's red tear stained eyes, expecting Thomas would say no, Billy drew back a sob because he had messed everything up.

Watching their son trying to make friends with Thomas, Dave and Martha, standing opposite Sarah, moved closer to the firepit. After everything that happened, both Dave and Martha didn't expect the two boys would make up. Thomas looked over at Sarah. "Ma?" he said, questioning her. Sarah knew what Thomas was asking.

"It's not my decision to make Thomas, it's something you have to decide on." The three parents waited. Thomas thought about his decision for all of two seconds. "I still want to be friends with you Billy," he said tearily. "You mean it?" Billy's face broke out in a tearful smile. "Yes," Thomas smiled back at Billy. The two boys stepped forward and reaching out, hugged each other.

Sarah heard Martha sob and glanced at her. Dave put his arm around his wife and looked at Sarah. "Well I'll be," he said with a smile on his face. Looking back at the two boys, Sarah watched them closely. Thomas had both arms around Billy's shoulders, and Billy had his right arm around Thomas. Billy's left arm hung limply by his side making Sarah frown. Going over to the two boys, Sarah crouched beside them. Worried about what Sarah might be going to do, the smile disappeared off Dave's face as both he and Martha watched her carefully.

"Thomas, let Billy go for a moment." Taking Thomas's arm, Sarah moved him away, and placing both hands on Billy's hips, turned Billy to face her. "Billy does your arm hurt?" Sarah looked into Billy's dirty tear stained face. Billy looked into Sarah's eyes. "No," he whimpered unconvincingly. Putting her hand on Billy's arm, she squeezed it ever so gently, causing Billy to scream as pain shot up his arm. Dave let go of Martha and stepped quickly over the stones toward Sarah and Billy.

"Don't hurt him Cole, please, don't hurt our son!" Dave's voice broke with fear for his son's safety as he begged Sarah not to hurt him. Dave and Martha tried for a long time to have a child. Every time Martha got pregnant, she had trouble carrying her unborn babies. When finally getting pregnant with Billy she was almost at the end of her child bearing years and they were ecstatic when she gave birth to the only child they would ever have and they adored him. They called Billy their miracle baby.

Still crouching in front of Billy, Sarah held her hand up to ward off Dave. He stopped where he was but shook with fear at what Sarah had done. Martha could be heard sobbing in the background. "I'm not hurting him, Mister Henderson, Billy is already hurt." She turned to Billy, and trying to push his sleeve up to look at his arm couldn't without hurting him further. "I'm going to take your shirt off you Billy," she said softly. While Thomas looked on, Billy whimpered some more. Reaching up, Sarah undid the blood covered buttons. Pushing his shirt over his shoulders, she noticed how white Billy's skin was. Unlike Thomas who spent his time without a shirt, climbing trees, and frolicking in the river with Star, Billy had never been outside in the sun without a shirt.

Working Billy's good arm out of his shirt, then sliding the sleeve slowly down his left arm, Sarah could see, between his elbow and his wrist, bruising and a break. When Sarah took his shirt all the way off, Billy sobbed and so did Martha.

"Oh Dave, they hurt Billy!" she cried. Dave sucked in his breath when he saw the break. Thomas stared at Billy's arm. "Is it broken Ma?" he said sounding worried.

"Yes Thomas, it is broken, Billy, you are very brave for not letting on that your arm is broken." Dave came closer and crouched next to Sarah. "My goodness Billy, why didn't you tell us?" Sarah gently eased the shirt back on Billy. "I didn't think it was broken Pa, it burned really bad when Daniel pulled on it, but I didn't know what it was." Billy cried some more. His arm really was hurting, and he didn't feel very brave. Dave put his arms around him and Sarah stood up. "You better get Billy up to Doc Harris so he can fix his arm Mister Henderson …Jamie Finch and Daniel Connell have a lot to answer for," she added.

"You won't do anything to those boy's, will you Cole?" Dave asked standing next to Billy. He didn't want Sarah harming the boys on account of hurting their son, he already asked Sheriff Morgan to deal with them.

"It's not up to me to punish them for what they did to your son Mister Henderson, it is up to the sheriff, he is the law here." Sarah folded her arms. Martha went on sobbing. Dave was relieved when Sarah agreed it was the sheriff's job to punish the boys, he wondered though, if it had been Thomas that had his arm broken, would she mete out a just punishment in her own way, regardless of the sheriff? Dave had no doubt she would.

Sarah went to Martha, who was now looking like she was going to faint, and put her arm on Martha's. "Billy will be all right, so long as Doc fixes his arm straight away." Martha dried her eyes then patted Sarah's hand. Knowing their children would be alright, the two women smiled at each other.

Dave and Billy moved to stand beside Martha and Sarah at the firepit. Thomas, feeling he wanted to punish Jamie Finch and Daniel Connell for what they did to Billy, stood beside Sarah, and decided he and Billy were going to be best friends, and he wasn't about to let anyone hurt Billy, not ever.

"Well, I guess we should get going," Dave said not knowing what else to say. It was Sarah who broke the silence that suddenly fell over the group. "You can call me Sarah ...if you like." Sarah smiled at them and Dave smiled back. "And we would like it if you called us Martha and Dave," Dave said to her. Martha smiled too. "Oh!'" she said, remembering. "I almost forgot, these are for you, and Thomas." Martha held the pretty flower-patterned tin toward Sarah.

Sarah took the tin and opening it, saw four small chocolate cakes. Aware Martha was an excellent cook, Sarah smiled. Martha's cakes were well received by anyone who was lucky enough to receive them. "Thomas, find something to put these in please," she said holding the tin out to Thomas. "Oh no!" Martha said. "Please, keep the tin too, you might like to put your own cakes, or cookies in it." Sarah looked at the pretty tin again and then at Martha. "Thank you ...Martha," she smiled. Feeling more at ease now they had become friendlier toward each other Martha breathed a sigh of relief. "Your welcome ...Sarah," she said.

Relieved at this outcome, Dave came up with a suggestion for them to remain on friendly terms. "Thomas is welcome to spend time with Billy anytime he likes Sarah." Dave's arm was around Billy's shoulders. Billy looked pleadingly up at his father. "Pa, can Thomas come visit with us tomorrow, there's no school?" Thomas listened intently for Dave's answer.

"If his Ma says he can, then he is more than welcome to visit," Dave repeated. Thomas looked to Sarah. "Can I Ma?" Considering what happened, Sarah gave her answer considerable thought. The Henderson's were a nice couple. Sarah had always liked them. They kept to themselves and didn't get involved in things that went on around town. "Well, Billy has to get his arm seen to right now, and tomorrow he's not going to be able to play so, I don't know," she said, thinking what else could go wrong, now the two boys were friends. "They don't have to run around …the boys can sit on the back porch to talk and draw." After Martha suggested that, it was agreed by all, Thomas could spend the day with Billy.

"And when Billy is better," Sarah said, deciding there and then to be fair to the Henderson's. "He is welcome to come and stay with us …if it is alright with you of course." Sarah thought it would be good for Billy to play outdoors in the sun, even if the weather was a bit on the chilly side. Billy's smile lit up his face. Dave looked happy with Sarah's approval to let Billy camp with them. Martha, however, looked worried, her precious son would be sleeping in Cole's shelter, out in the open, virtually in the cold. "Woah! can I Pa?" Billy exclaimed, seeming to have forgotten his broken arm for the moment. Dave smiled at his son and then at Sarah. "I think that would be fine." Billy and his parents began to make their way up the trail to Doc Harris's practice. "See you tomorrow Thomas!" Billy called, waving his good arm at Thomas. "See you tomorrow Billy!" Thomas waved and smiled back. Sarah was happy Thomas and Billy were going to be friends, but was convinced she and Christian would no longer be friendly towards each other. Disappointed at herself for her outburst, she wished she had waited before taking her vengeance out on him, but it was too late now, she felt she could never take back what she had done.

Christian watched the Henderson's come out of Doc Harris's Practice. When he saw Billy had his left arm wrapped up tight, and in a sling, he walked quickly across the street before the Henderson's could make their way along the boardwalk. "Just a minute Henderson!" he called. Dave stopped when he heard Christian. Martha and Billy stopped alongside Dave. Christian stepped onto the boardwalk next to them and looked down at Billy. "What happened? Did Cole do this?" Martha sucked in her breath. "Sheriff Morgan! ...how dare you even suggest Sarah would do such a thing to a child!" Dave glared at Christian too. "Sarah didn't do this sheriff, Daniel Connell broke Billy's arm, Sarah was the one who realized Billy's arm was broken and told us to get him straight to Doc's, I suggest you do your job and talk to those boys, they have a lot to answer for ...and maybe you should talk to their parents too!" Anger reflected in Dave's voice when both he and Martha began to walk away. "Come on Dave, let's go home and get supper." Martha held Billy's good hand and all three walked off.

Christian put his hands on his hips, and watching them go, wondered how the Henderson's had gone to Sarah's camp and suddenly came away with calling her Sarah, making him confused by Sarah's attitude. He wanted to call her Sarah too, after all, they had been intimate. But then, he felt sure, he would not have to worry about Sarah anymore. What they experienced in her shelter would never happen again, not now she had hit out at him.

Chapter Twenty

Jamie Finch had been sound asleep when he felt something touch his nose. He didn't wake up completely, instead woke up just enough to brush whatever it was away from his face, then rolled over onto his back and fell into a deep sleep.

Three beds filled the room upstairs in the Finch household. They sat in a row with just enough room between them for the three boys that slept in them to be able to get into bed or for their mother to get around them to pull the blankets in place. Jamie slept in the middle bed between his two younger brothers. This arrangement was so the two younger boys wouldn't fight when they went to bed, keeping the peace in the household.

Harold Finch and his wife Mary slept in the bedroom downstairs directly below their three sons. Their house was designed much the same as others in town. Being built by the same men, the same floor plan had been used for each house. The kitchen, living area, washroom and parent's bedroom were all located on the ground floor. Upstairs consisted of one room and that was where the three boys slept.

The sky was beginning to get lighter, it wouldn't be long now before the sun rose over the mountains casting its rays on the township and bringing people out of doors.

When Jamie Finch began to wake up, he put his arms over his head and stretched, then rolled over onto his side. When his face pressed into his pillow, something wet and sticky covered his face. Jamie frowned when he saw something lying beside him on the pillow. It was furry and its eyes bulging out of its head were staring at him. Jamie lifted his head to get a better look.

The blood curdling scream was unlike anything Harold Finch had ever heard, and it didn't stop, not until Jamie vomited all over himself. Finch flew out of bed, grabbed the plank of wood he used for protection now that his rifle was locked up at the Sheriff's Office, along with everyone else's in town, raced out of the bedroom, and charged up the stairs, stubbing his toes on several as he went tearing into his son's room.

Jamie wasn't in bed when his father entered. He was standing with his two younger brothers whom had woken suddenly when they heard Jamie's blood curdling scream. Both boys let out their own blood curdling scream when they saw the mess in Jamie's bed, and now both boys were sobbing uncontrollably along with Jamie. "What the fucking hell has happened in here? You boy's hurt?" Finch looked at his three sons who appeared to be ok, cowering in the corner.

Jamie couldn't talk, he was frightened speechless, all he could do was point to his bed. Finch could see the sticky, gruesome mess on Jamie's face. There were lumps of what appeared to be meat stuck in his hair. His hair was matted with a red sticky substance and his nightshirt was saturated with the same awful mess.

While the three boys continued to sob, Finch, holding the plank of wood ready to swing it if necessary, approached the bed carefully. Finch reached out gingerly with his free hand and taking hold of the bedsheet with his fingers, lifted the sheet back to see what was causing his sons to be so frightened. The sheet was held up just long enough to take in the bloody mess.

Jamie's bed was soaked with blood. His pillow was covered in it. There were pieces of meat that looked like entrails scattered across the pillow and down inside the bed. The hairy body was further down where Jamie must have pushed it when he tossed and turned during the night, spreading blood and entrails with him. The ugly head, with its bulging eyes, was lying in the middle of a large blood stain next to the pillow where, when Jamie jumped quickly out of bed, it rolled and stayed, its blank eyes staring upwards. Finch pulled the sheets back further, then cursed Sarah. "That fucking bitch Cole!" he yelled before ushering his son's downstairs.

Mary Finch screamed in fear for her sons and grabbed the three of them as they came stumbling down the stairs. Mary was careful not to get any blood or guts that covered Jamie on her hands. Tears streaked her face as she sat Jamie on a chair. The moment he sat down he began to heave. Telling the other two boys to stand back, Mary grabbed the water bucket they carried their drinking water in from the pump outside and held it in front of Jamie. They didn't need telling twice, they cowered near the fire and held each other while they continued to cry.

Finch stayed in the room and had another look at the severed head and the mutilated body of the hairy river rat. Sometime in the night while his family slept, Harold Finch surmised, Sarah Cole broke into their house, mutilated a rat and put it in his eldest son's bed, but why? he wanted to know. He hadn't done anything to Cole to warrant her doing this. It has been a long time since he had a run in with her over her son Thomas. He stayed away from Cole as much as was possible in the small town, and he told his family to do the same.

After checking the bedroom window, Finch went downstairs and checked the front door, then went through to the kitchen and checked the back door. Everything appeared locked up tight. He watched Jamie sitting on a chair crying and heaving into a bucket his mother was holding in front of him. His two younger boys were watching their brother throwing up his stomach.

Finch was furious. "How the fuck did that bitch get in?" he asked his wife as if she had the answer. But he knew very well his wife only knew as much as he did. "The goddamn windows are nailed shut and the front and back fucking doors are locked, Andy! go get Sheriff Morgan!" Andy didn't move, he was petrified. "Andy! go now!" Finch bellowed at his youngest son. Andy came alive when his father yelled. Running out of the house still dressed in his nightshirt, he sprinted to the Sheriff's Office.

Daniel Connell's house was the same layout as the Finch's house. Daniel's room was situated right above his parent's room. Daniel was lucky, he didn't have any brothers, or sisters, he had his room all to himself. His bed was under a window so when the nights were warm, he could open the window to let the breeze cool him.

Now that winter was here the window was kept shut and because the trappers were in town his Pa nailed up all the windows in the house to keep the family safe.

Daniel knew the windows were nailed shut because of one particular trapper. 'That whore bitch' as his Pa called her. 'Cut up a wolf in the church and scared the whole town, just because her spoilt brat son Thomas was taken off her and given to his own grandpa.' Daniel didn't like Thomas Mason, or his Ma Sarah Cole. They were protected by the trappers and everyone in town was scared of them.

When Daniel went to bed, he was thinking about Thomas and Billy. He thought how he fixed Thomas and Billy good and proper, and how he and Jamie had chased them. He thought about how they held them down and how he made Billy tell why Sheriff Morgan gave him five dollars. Daniel was envious. He was already fifteen and he had never in his life been given five dollars to spend on anything he wanted, so he thought, 'why should Billy fucking Henderson be given five whole dollars?'

Daniel's last thought before falling asleep was how he fixed spoilt brat Billy Henderson. He thought about how he twisted Billy's arms behind his back and twisted them until he heard a pop! but he didn't let go, not until stupid spoilt brat Thomas Mason got away from Jamie and pushed him off Billy. Daniel laughed to himself as his eyes grew heavy.

'Thomas Mason punched Billy Henderson in the face and made his nose bleed, that was really funny!' Daniel fell asleep still smiling to himself.

Daniel's father Roy, and his mother Felicity were sound asleep in their bed. The house was nice and quiet, except when the wind blew, a few creaking sounds coming from timber floorboards could be heard. There must have been a breeze that night, because, Daniel swore he could hear the creaking boards while he was sound asleep.

Roy had a tiring day. Working at the lumber yard entailed sorting timber for new buildings. Right now, he was sorting timber for the new Town Hall that was almost complete. Roy was glad it was nearly finished, now he wouldn't have to work so hard. He helped build most of the houses the town folk lived in too, and was proud of the fact he helped build his own house and those of the

Finch and Henderson's. The church and the schoolhouse were two more buildings he helped build. He liked his job, but because he was getting old, hoped one day, Daniel might work at the lumber yard in his place, it was a good job and it paid well. His son was old enough to start work, but Felicity wanted Daniel to get more schooling first, so both parents agreed to wait. Maybe next year, when Daniel turned sixteen, he would apply for work with his Pa. Roy slept soundly all night.

It was coming on daylight when something hit Roy on his cheek. Landing with a plop right near his eye, he flinched but ignored it. He ignored the second plop too, but when the third landed right in his eye, he woke up annoyed. Frowning in confusion, he saw red just as another blob fell from the ceiling, landed with a splat on his face, and sprayed into his now wide-open eyes. Throwing the bedclothes back, he dived out of bed, while at the same time, screaming in terror at the top of his lungs. "Jesus Christ! What the fuck? Daniel!" Felicity woke just as Roy raced out the bedroom door and hurtled up the stairs to Daniels room.

"Daniel! Daniel!" he screamed as he threw himself bodily at his sons' door. The door came open and Roy burst into the room, falling over and skidding across the floor in the process. Daniel woke up when he heard his father screaming and got a fright when his Pa came hurtling toward his bed. "Pa! what the…?" Daniel said sitting bolt upright and looking at his father sprawled on the floor in his long-johns. Daniel looked down when something fell out of his hair and landed in his lap. Whatever it was, was slimy and looked like a worm. As his father got himself up off the floor, Daniel, covered in blood, let out a blood curdling scream. Roy grabbed his son and pulled him off the bed. "Daniel, are you hurt boy?" Roy held Daniel and they both checked to see if he was hurt. "No Pa, I'm …I'm alright!" Although when he looked at the grotesque mess littering his bed, he started to heave.

Felicity came into the room behind Roy and seeing the state of her son and his bed, screamed and proceeded to faint. Roy grabbed his wife to stop her from falling and took her and Daniel downstairs. Leaving them in the kitchen, Roy went back to his son's room where he pulled the bedclothes back to see a huge blood stain covering the pillow and sheets. A mutilated body of a river rat, its head and legs severed from its body lay scattered in the bed. Entrails pulled out of the rat's carcass had been scattered in clumps all through the bedclothes. Daniel had lain in the mess and made it worse when he moved around in the night.

Getting down on his hands and knees, Roy looked under the bed. Blood soaked the floorboards where it had pooled after soaking through Daniel's mattress. It ran between the floorboards and dripped onto Roy as he slept beneath his son's bed downstairs. Standing back up, he stared at the grotesque scene. Daniel had been sleeping in the mess for some time. "How the fucking hell?" Roy said as he stared at the mess. "Did fucking Cole get in? And why the fuck did she get in? And why the fuck did she do this?" He hadn't done anything to Cole for years. Checking the window, he found the nails still in place.

Daniel's whimpering could be heard as Roy came downstairs to the kitchen. "I'll go get Sheriff Morgan, that bitch Cole has done this and I want to know why?" Daniel suddenly stared wide eyed at his father but kept quiet.

Felicity busied herself trying to keep from being sick herself and fainting, she had to be strong for her son, she wet a cloth and started to wipe Daniel's face. "Leave him! I want Sheriff Morgan to see this!" Roy said going to their bedroom. While pulling on his trousers he looked at the blood still dripping through the ceiling and now soaking his pillow. "Fuck that fucking bitch!" Roy cursed out loud. "Sheriff Morgan needs to lock that bitch up once and for all!" Roy said to the empty room.

Angrily pulling open the front door, he stopped and for a moment studied it. "How did she get in?" he asked himself silently "Fuck!" he cursed savagely and slamming the door behind him, half walked half ran all the way across the street, around the corner into the main street and down to the Sheriff's Office.

When Roy rushed in to the Sheriff's Office, there was no sign of Christian. It was Clem's turn to be on duty and he was talking to Andy, Harold Finch's youngest son, who appeared to be in an agitated state. "You got to get Sheriff Morgan now!" Andy was saying. Roy, noticing Andy was still dressed in his nightshirt, interrupted him. "Clem …we got a big problem!" Roy and Andy both started talking at once, confusing Clem. When Roy mentioned they had a dead rat in Daniel's bed, Andy's eyes widened. "You too Mister Connell?" Andy asked in surprise. "Not me Andy, the rats in Daniel's bed, there's a lot of blood too, more blood than what come out of one dead rat."

"Hold on you two!" Clem said, holding up his hands to stop them from talking over each other. "You go back home! I'll go get Sheriff Morgan and we'll be there as soon as we can, don't touch anything!"

Andy didn't wait around to be told a second time to get going, he rushed out the door and sprinted back home as fast as he could, wanting to tell his Pa that Daniel Connell had a dead rat in his bed the same as Jamie.

Thinking maybe he could handle the situation himself, Clem thought it best if he took a look at the Connell house first before he disturbed Christian. There was no need to go to the Finch house, Andy already told him what happened there.

Clem made his way to the Connell house with Roy. After going upstairs to Daniel's room, Clem limped as fast as he could to the lodge to get Christian.

Chapter Twenty-one

$\mathcal{F}$eeling confident in leaving Clem looking after the jailhouse, Christian retired to the lodge for the night. Although after his run in with Sarah, and his mind being on her and her punching him in the face in front of the other men, it took him a while to fall asleep. He felt angry and wasn't going to take being hit by a woman lightly. It wasn't manly to hit a woman, and he wouldn't dare hit Sarah, besides, the trappers would have something to say about that. But she made him feel humiliated in front of everyone that stopped to watch what was happening. He was yet to work out her fines, so made up his mind to fine her bigtime for all the trouble she caused since coming to town. Even if it meant taking all her money she made from her skins, he would take it.

After tossing and turning, he changed his mind about fining Sarah too much, after all, he didn't want her to hate him altogether. He tried instead, to think about the night he spent with her in her shelter. Closing his eyes, he could still feel her soft, silken body pressed against his. As his mind went over her inch by inch, he fell asleep thinking how nice it had been to sleep next to her with her back pressed against his chest and her bottom pressed into his lap.

When he woke the next morning, the sun was just rising, so he washed and got dressed in clean clothes ready for the day. His shin still hurt but the cut on his lip had closed and it didn't feel too bad. While eating breakfast he thought of Sarah again. Thinking how the Henderson's called her Sarah, he made a mental note that he was going to call her Sarah next time he saw her, just to see what she would do about it. He was just finishing breakfast when Clem pounded on his front door. "Sheriff Morgan! Sheriff Morgan! goddamn it! open up!"

Christian opened the door to find Clem standing there in an agitated state.

"What is the matter Clem?" he asked

"You got to come quick sheriff, something's happened at the Finch and Connell homes, there's real trouble!" Not waiting, Clem turned, and rushing back across the porch, hurried down the steps and headed off across the street. Clem never hung about, shooting off at a fast pace whenever he went anywhere, and Christian thought for an old guy with a limp, he didn't move too bad. Christian grabbed his hat, shoved it on his head and adjusted it to make it comfortable. Then grabbing his gun-belt, fastened it around his hips and tried to tie the cord around his leg as he ran along the street after Clem. When he got the cord tied, he worked his gun up and down a few times making sure it came out of its holster freely.

"Come on Clem, tell me, what the hell is going on? What has happened at the Finch's and the Connell's?" Clem was puffing already. "You will see for yourself sheriff! goddamn it! I ain't the one to tell you! you got to see it to believe it!" Both men walked quickly without saying another word.

Taking Christian to the Finch house first, they found the front door standing wide open, so Christian, hearing one of the children crying, and Harold Finch the father, trying to console whoever it was, walked straight in, and heading for the kitchen, saw Jamie, the oldest of the Finch's three children sitting on a chair in the middle of the room, still dressed in his night attire, sobbing. "What happened here Finch?" Christian asked Harold. Mary his wife, stood by the fireplace, her eyes wide open, her face deathly white as she clung to two younger boys who were both sobbing quietly. "Just take a look at this sheriff! look at my boy! that bitch Cole did this and I want you to lock her up where she fucking belongs!" Finch's angry rant about Sarah had Christian baffled, and he furrowed his brow. "Hold on Finch ...what do you think Cole has done?"

"Look for yourself sheriff!" Christian walked around the table, and horrified by what he saw when looking at Jamie, took a step back. Jamie's hair was matted with blood and what looked like bits of meat. The side of his face was smeared with blood and his night shirt was saturated too.

"Are you hurt Jamie?" Christian asked, kneeling down in front of him to get a better look at the mess. Reaching up, he pulled a piece of meat out of Jamie's hair, looked at it closely to see what it was then hastily dropped it on the floor. He just as hastily wiped his hand along the top of his leg to get the slime off his fingers.

"No! this ain't my blood," Jamie sobbed, his face crumpling as he heaved again.

"That's rat blood and guts sheriff, go take a look upstairs!" Harold Finch said as he pointed up the stairs. "Go take a goddamn good look at what that bitch did!" Finch was furious. Clem hadn't been able to stop Sarah from cutting up a wolf in the church and scaring the hell out of them, maybe Christian could stop her, all Finch new was, he wanted him to do something, and do it now.

Every time Finch mentioned Sarah, Christian became more confused. Turning, and without saying another word, he headed up the stairs. Clem wasn't going to hang about in the kitchen with hysterical kids and their parents. He had already seen the gruesome mess at the Connell's house, now he wanted to see what the mess was like in the Finch household. He followed closely behind Christian as he ascended the stairs to the boy's bedroom.

It was obvious from the bloody mess Christian could see spread through the bedclothes which bed was Jamie's. The sight disgusted him and made his breakfast churn in his stomach. A great big ugly hairy river rat lay on the bed clothes near the pillow, its head had been severed and its gut emptied on the bed. Blood, mixed with vomit, soaked the pillow and the bed sheets.

"Jesus!" was all Christian could say as he felt his stomach rise. Going to the window to open it to let fresh air in, Christian pulled but it wouldn't budge. Looking around the frame, he saw the window had been nailed shut and cursed silently. Clem couldn't stand the smell either, his face turned ashen when he tried to stay in the room with Christian. When Christian turned to leave, Clem followed close behind. They both hurried back down stairs to the kitchen to get the full story.

While Harold Finch told them what had occurred, Christian went to the kitchen window and looked out. Noticing this window had been nailed shut the same as the one upstairs he asked, "why are all your windows nailed shut Finch?" and put his hands on his hips in disgust. The house smelt stuffy, and of stale body odours. No fresh air circulated in this house.

"This house is locked up good and tight when those goddamn trappers are in town, especially when that bitch arrives, we don't trust her sheriff, not since she cut up a wolf and threatened us with it, she's crazy, this is just typical of something she would do, goddamn it! you got to do something about her!" Finch finished. Christian didn't ask Finch to elaborate about the wolf. He didn't think cutting up a wolf was too serious a business, after all, Sarah was a trapper, she cut up wolves for a living. 'So what?' he thought, turning his attention back to Jamie. "Did you do something to Cole Jamie? …to make her put a dead rat in your bed!" Christian knew Jamie had done something to get someone's back up. Billy already told him what happened and handed him back his five dollars. Poor Billy was suffering a broken arm all because of Daniel Connell, and Christian needed Jamie and Daniel to confess in front of their parents to what they had done. Still, he didn't think it was any cause for Sarah to take the law into her own hands and do this to either of the boys. Sarah's son Thomas hadn't been hurt, just upset when finding out Billy had been paid to be his friend. Christian remained standing at the window looking out while waiting for Jamie to answer. Except for the outhouse and the back fence, their yard was barren.

"No!" Jamie's voice betrayed him when he answered. Christian didn't believe him. "Well Jamie, why do you think Cole would do this?" When Jamie answered, "I don't know!" with a shrug of his shoulders, a piece of meat fell out of his hair, rolled down the front of his night shirt and landed in his lap. He looked down at the piece of meat and started to heave. Mary Finch quickly grabbed the water bucket again and held it under his chin while he threw up what was left in his stomach.

Christian waited until Jamie stopped heaving before going on. "Come on Jamie, think lad, did you do something to antagonize Cole?" he questioned. "Well, no, not Cole …not exactly." Tears and snot ran down Jamie's face and mixed with the rat's blood that he smeared on himself while he slept. "What did you do Jamie?" Christian asked, keeping his back to Jamie and his voice steady so Jamie wouldn't clamp up. "I …well …I may have done something …to Thomas." As Jamie looked sadly up at Christian's back, Harold Finch pounced on Jamie's words. "What the fuck did you do to Cole's son Jamie? …you goddamn! …stupid boy!" Hitting Jamie hard across his head with his hand, Jamie flinched and tried to duck the blows as more entrails fell out of his hair. "I didn't do anything to him Pa! I just held him off while Daniel held Billy!" he sobbed louder. "I didn't mean anything by it, it was just a bit of fun!"

"Fun! …I'll give you fucking fun boy!" Finch raised his hand toward his son to hit him again. Christian didn't abide violence toward children. Having been on the receiving end of violence as a child himself, he would not tolerate anyone raising their hand to a child. He turned sharply, and grabbing Finch tight by his wrist, gripped his hand in mid-swing. "Stop it Finch, Jamie has had a bad enough scare, he doesn't need you making it worse!" Christian said between clenched teeth. Letting go of Finch's wrist, Finch put down his hand. "You do something about that bitch sheriff!" Finch snarled.

Ignoring Finch, Christian knelt down in front of Jamie. "Tell me Jamie, why did you and Daniel want to hold Thomas and Billy?" Christian knew the answer before Jamie spoke. "We saw you give Billy money, and we wanted to know why you give it to him, we didn't mean to scare them, I didn't know Daniel broke Billy's arm." Christian hadn't mentioned Billy having a broken arm, and was taken aback by his answer.

It had been late in the day when he saw the Henderson's come from Doc Harris's with Billy's arm in a sling, and because it was close to dinner time, there weren't any children in the streets, making him wonder how Jamie knew Billy's arm was broken. Christian looked Jamie in the eye and while Jamie's father stood by, he put the question to Jamie. Jamie looked through tears back at Christian, aware he said something no-one else knew about. Being fifteen, and of an age where boys could be taken to prison, Jamie worried Christian would take him off to spend time in jail once he told him the truth, but he had no choice, he had to tell. "Daniel held Billy's arms behind his back and twisted them real hard, I heard his arm break just before Thomas got loose and punched Billy on the "nose." Jamie waited for his father to belt him across his head again, but it didn't happen.

Satisfied with Jamie's answer, Christian stood up. Feeling grateful, Harold Finch stood quietly by his son's chair. At least it hadn't been his son who broke Billy Henderson's arm.

Chapter Twenty-two

Thomas was already up and dressed when Sarah came out of the shelter at daylight. He even had his boots on. Seeing him coming towards her from the direction of the river, Sarah frowned. "Thomas where have you been?" she asked puzzled

"Nowhere Ma, I got up early cause I couldn't sleep no more, I slept a long time yesterday, and I had to relieve myself, so I figured I'd get dressed." It was true, upset at finding Billy had been paid to be his friend, Thomas had slept most of the afternoon. But Thomas never put his boots on just to relieve himself, and Thomas knew not to lie. Theirs was an honest mother and son relationship, neither found the need to lie to the other, so, with a shrug of her shoulders, Sarah let what Thomas told her go. "Well, help me get breakfast, stoke the fire while I get washed please." Sarah took her towel and headed to the river.

"Ok Ma!" Thomas called, relieved his Ma hadn't twigged to what he had been doing. While Sarah washed her face and hands, and hurried back to the shelter to brush her hair, he got busy putting wood on the fire and getting pans ready to make hotcakes.

While eating their hotcakes, Sarah told Thomas she would spend her day picking blackberries to make them a nice pie, and maybe she said, she would pick enough to make a spread to have on their hotcakes. Thomas was happy for his Ma to go pick berries on her own, he was going to spend the day with Billy. Sarah said she would be back well before dark with as many berries as he could eat and Thomas said he would see her when she got back, and rushed off to Billy's as soon as he finished eating.

Satisfied Thomas was going straight to Billy's, Sarah hooked the bag for the blackberries inside the back of her trousers, then after wrapping the belt for her knife around her waist, she headed up the street to the Livery to get Star. She thought about going to the Sheriff's Office first to get her pistol, but decided she had her knife, she didn't need her pistol just to go pick a few berries, besides, having already decided to wait a few days before apologizing to Christian for her outburst and for hitting him, she didn't want to have a run in with him again today.

As Sarah walked along the main street, she noticed a crowd heading for the Finch's house and wondered what was going on. She didn't want to become involved in something she had nothing to do with, she didn't care at all for Harold Finch or his wife Mary. They along with the Connell's, took Thomas from her when he was a baby, simply because they thought she couldn't look after him and gave him to Major Hardy, who thought he had a right to keep Thomas because he was his grandson. 'Humph' Sarah thought. 'Whatever happened over there at their house, they probably deserved.'

To avoid the commotion, Sarah crossed to the other side of the street, but curiosity got the better of her, and every now and then she glanced at the gathering crowd. It was when she got further up the street she ran into serious trouble. After Christian left the Finch household, he and Clem went to the Connell's and got the same story from Daniel. They came out of the Connell's house into the main street just as Sarah drew level with them. Sarah heard someone shout. "There she is! there's Cole!" and not understanding why they would be calling her, tried ignoring them like she ignored what was happening at the Finch house.

Still feeling hurt because of Sarah punching him in the mouth in front of Joe and the other men and for kicking him in the shins and breaking the skin, Christian came storming across the street toward her. "Cole!" he yelled loudly. Sarah couldn't ignore his yelling at her even if she wanted to, but she made out she didn't hear him and kept going. "I want to talk to you!" he called. Sarah stepped onto the boardwalk but didn't stop. "Damn it, Cole! stop right where you are!" Christian said raising his voice louder. So much for calling her Sarah he thought. Whatever was going on, Sarah wasn't going to be a part of it. Picking up her pace and keeping ahead of Christian, she continued hurrying along the boardwalk. A crowd soon gathered, staring in amazement at what was unfolding as their sheriff rushed up behind Sarah, and grabbed her by her arm. Swinging her around to face him, the crowd, wanting to hear everything that was being said, inched closer.

"What do you want sheriff?" Sarah asked, her face etched with puzzlement. Ignoring Sarah's question and thinking she should know exactly what he wanted, Christian pinned her against the wall, stopping her from reaching her knife. "Goddamn it, Cole! what the hell is it you think you are playing at?"

"I don't know what you mean! what is it you think I am playing at?" Bewildered by what Christian was saying, Sarah tried wriggling her way out of his clutches. Holding her tight so she couldn't get away and thinking she might kick him in the shin again, Christian kept his legs out of reach. Sarah had no right to take the law into her own hands. It was his job to enforce the law, not hers. Feeling anger rising in the pit of his stomach, he spat his words at her. "You know damn well what I mean! ...aren't I the cause of your anger? ...why didn't you just put the dead rats in my bed?" Leaning forward, he held her more forcibly.

Stunned by Christian's revelation, Sarah didn't have to dwell too long on what he said. Knowing full well when he mentioned dead rats who put them there, she wasn't about to tell him who it was. "I don't know what you are talking about!" she said, gritting her teeth and trying again to pull her arms free. But it was no use, Christian's grip was too strong.

"Oh, I think you do know what I am talking about! ...I was told you cut up a wolf ...scared the whole goddamn town, and now because of me, you resort to putting mutilated rats in the Finch and Connell boy's beds! come on Cole! don't play me for a fool! it is not your place to punish those boys for what they did to Billy and Thomas."

Shocked at Christian being told about the wolf in the church, Sarah still managed to snap back. "I didn't do it! ...where is your proof that I did it, huh? ...you got proof it was me?" Then waiting for him to reply, knew full well he couldn't have proof, because she hadn't done it. When he didn't answer, Sarah tried again to get herself free of his grip. "I didn't think so!" she said speaking with a hint of venom.

Thinking about what Sarah said, Christian decided they should go to the jailhouse where they could discuss the situation in private. "You're coming with me Cole," he said, easing his grip on her arms.

Having been taken to jail several times by Clem when Thomas was taken, Sarah swore she would never spend time there again. Trying to break free, Sarah swung her leg to kick Christian, but missed. "You are not taking me to jail!" she snarled, while with some effort, she managed to twist herself free of his hold. Christian's hands though, still gripped her shirt, causing them both to stumble toward the edge of the boardwalk. When Sarah's foot slipped over the edge, Christian couldn't hold her. Falling heavily on the street, landing on her back, her hand instinctively moved to her knife. Christian pounced, and kneeling down hard on her arm, drew his gun and poked it into her chest. Sarah was shocked that he would take this action when they had been together just the night before. While holding her down with his leg, Christian pulled her knife from its sheath, then standing up, left her lying on her back. Onlookers moved back, but lingered to watch the confrontation.

"I'm taking your knife Cole!" Christian said angrily. "You are not going to get a chance to use it on anyone!" The look on Sarah's face was one of unmistakable anger. Picking herself up off the street, she undid her knife-belt and dropped it at Christian's feet, then facing him, replied with her own angry retort. "You get your facts right sheriff! When you figure out who put those rats in those beds, and if you have proof it was me! …you know where to find me!" Turning her back on him and keeping her head high, she walked quickly up the street toward the Livery, where she hurried inside to saddle Star.

Christian picked Sarah's sheath up, and holding it and her knife, watched as she walked quickly to the Livery and disappeared inside. Anger was rising in him, not at Sarah, but at himself. He didn't mean to humiliate her, he just wanted to talk to her, maybe then they could have worked together to figure out who put the rats in Finch and Connell's beds. "You going after her sheriff?" Clem asked, interrupting his thoughts. "No, Cole is right Clem, I don't have proof she did this."

Wanting to see if Sarah's knife matched a fresh cut in the wood he had seen on the front door at the Connell's, Christian started back toward the house, but before going inside, not only Christian, but everyone, heard a yell, and saw Sarah come out of the Livery on Star and spur him toward the bridge. Watching Sarah ride away, Christian felt disappointed that another wedge had been driven between them.

Sarah was angry and upset as she rode out of the Livery. Kicking Star hard, they raced across the bridge, turned south, then rode several miles before turning back to the river and the swimming hole. It was a short ride after leaving the swimming hole to get to where the blackberries grew.

After Christian tackled her in the street, and accused her of putting dead rats in the boy's bed's, Sarah knew straight away Thomas did it. What upset her was not the fact Thomas killed the rat's and put them in the beds, it was the fact Thomas lied to her. He told her this morning, when she caught him already dressed, he had woken early because he couldn't sleep. She should have known that was not the case.

It was understandable Thomas wanted the boys punished for what they did to Billy, but Sarah didn't think he would resort to doing something like she had done when she slaughtered a wolf in front of town folk in their church. The wind stung her eyes as she rode along, and she tried her best to stem her tears. Knowing something was wrong, Star put his head down and carried her away. Once she reached the swimming hole, she stopped.

Sitting in shade cast by tall trees, she pulled her knee's up in front of her and wrapped her arms around her leg's as she always did when plunged deep in thought. Upset Christian had been told about the wolf, and sure he had been told about the threat's she made to town folk, Sarah thought she could see dislike for her on his face when he took her knife, and believed he had good reason to hate her. Finch, she thought, would have told him all about what she had done. However, she was convinced, Finch would never tell Christian the reason why she did what she did, because Finch would never make himself, or Connell, guilty of anything. Sarah became saddened at the lie Thomas told her. They had never lied to each other, not ever. Leaning her head against her knees, she let her tears flow.

After making herself feel more miserable than she already was, Sarah stopped crying, and resolved to have it out with Thomas when she got back to camp. She would talk to Christian too, about how he treated her before he had proof that she had done what he accused her of. She wasn't a child to be scolded, she was a full-grown woman and could stand up for herself. Feeling better about her decision and becoming determined not to let the sheriff of Cedar Creek get the better of her, she rode on to the blackberry patch, and found the brambles had grown thicker and spread out more than when she had been there last winter. The track between the bushes had become narrow, and now she didn't have her knife to cut her way through, she wended Star carefully between them, weaving in and out until they came through to the other side where she tethered him to a tree in the shade. Taking the bag from where it hung inside the back of her trousers, she commenced to pick the plump berries.

The bag was half full when she reached further into the brambles for some really big juicy looking berries. Her right arm was fully extended between thick tangles of branches covered with thorns, and she was being careful not to get hooked up on them when she felt something at her feet.

Keeping her right arm as straight as possible so as not to get snagged, she managed to look down. Becoming alarmed to see a snake had slithered out from under the brambles and coiled itself around her ankles to warm itself in the sun. Angry at not having her knife or pistol with her, all she could do was stand as still as she could and wait for the snake to move on. She only hoped her boots and trousers would give her leg's some protection if the snake chose to strike.

After waiting some time for the snake to do something, Sarah leant back a little, moistened her mouth with spit, and spat at it. The spittle hit the snake on the head causing it to flinch. The snake began to move, but instead of slithering away it tightened itself around Sarah's ankles. Standing as still as she could, Sarah began to sweat. Her arm began to get tired and started to ache. Slowly bringing her arm back, her sleeve snagged thorns. The snake began to move. Sarah stopped and waited. Standing out in the open, she was thankful she was wearing her hat to protect her from the winter sun. Still, she had been standing with her arm extended for some time and now her arm was beginning to go numb.

It seemed an eternity before the snake uncoiled itself from her ankles. When Star began to snort and stomp wildly, Sarah twisted her body around to see the snake slithering toward him. Trying to pull her arm back further to get a better look, thorn's tore her sleeve and scraped along the back of her arm. Feeling a thorn dig in, she screamed in pain, and dropped the bag of berries.

As the snake slithered closer, Star began to shy. Pulling back hard against his tether, trying to free himself, his frenzied bucking gradually worked the tether loose. The snake was in striking distance, Star reared, and bringing his hooves down hard several times, broke free.

Trying to free herself from the brambles and ignoring excruciating pain, Sarah pulled her arm back fast and felt a thorn tear deeper into her flesh. Screaming in agony, she grabbed the bush with her other hand. Ignoring blood oozing between her fingers, she tugged at the bush trying to pull the brambles away. As Sarah watched helplessly, Star whinnied loudly, kicked his legs wildly, and raced straight for the blackberry patch.

Tearing himself on thorn's in his panic to get away, he trampled headlong through the brambles and got himself out the other side. Finding himself free, he galloped away in fright. "Star! come back! ...goddamn it!" Sarah yelled above her pain, but Star, even if he heard her, kept going. Giving her arm one last hard yank, she pulled it free and left pieces of her shirt behind. Blood trickling down her arm soaked into what remained. Using her injured hand, she felt along the back of her arm for what damage had been done. Feeling a gash, she touched something sticking out of it, making her cry out in pain. Sarah didn't think the gash was too bad, it was a thorn, stuck inside the wound causing her the most agony.

Stumbling to the tree where Star had been tethered, she leant back against its trunk and slid to the ground to think what to do. The day was wearing on, it was already well past midday. It was no use trying to make it back to town, she would be caught out in the open in the dark, and not having a weapon to defend herself with, would make her prey for wild animals that hunted at night, so for now all she could do was find shelter.

A short distance from the blackberry patch was a place called 'The Falls' where a few scattered brambles grew around a rocky outcrop consisting of huge boulders that appeared like some powerful being had been in a hurry to stack them together. Teetering precariously on top of each other, they looked like they might fall over at any moment. These boulders could be seen clearly from the patch during daylight hours but disappeared from view at night. Under the boulders was a cavern. When the sun warmed the boulders, the cavern stayed warm for several hours during the night, but became freezing toward morning. Sarah hadn't planned on going as far as 'The Falls,' but being injured, her only choice was to head to the cavern.

Chapter Twenty-three

After going to the Connell's house and looking at the fresh cut on the door, and comparing it with the blade of Sarah's knife, Christian could see Sarah's knife was too big to have made the small cut. Taking Sarah's knife with him, he returned to the jailhouse where he tried to figure out just who would want to punish Jamie Finch and Daniel Connell by putting dead rat's in their bed's and scaring the two boys and their families.

Christian wrote a list of five names on a piece of paper, starting with Billy Henderson. Billy was the least likely to have put the dead rat's in the boy's beds. He had a broken arm and Christian surmised there would be no way he would know how to get in the houses once they were locked up, nor was he ever likely to kill a rat, because Billy told him he hadn't wanted Thomas to kill a rabbit when he snared it. He scrubbed Billy off the list altogether.

Dave and Martha Henderson were next. They were a quiet middle-aged couple who minded their own business. The couple doted over their only son Billy, but would never take the law into their own hand's, even when he was hurt. They insisted on him being the one to talk to Jamie and Daniel. Christian knew for sure it wasn't them and crossed them both off his list.

Next on his list was Sarah. Christian thought deeply about Sarah. He liked her, a whole lot. After giving a great deal of thought to her when he was in bed at night, he was pretty certain he was falling in love with her, and he hated what passed between them at the corrals and again in the street in front of everyone. Getting his thoughts back to the crime in hand, he remembered being told by Finch Sarah cut up a wolf, but he didn't ask Finch to elaborate as to why she had done it. He hadn't thought it necessary, because Sarah cut up wolves for a living. But then, cutting up rats would come easy for someone like Sarah. He agreed she was the most likely to have put the mutilated rat's in the boy's beds. Christian frowned, then asked himself why did Sarah cut up a wolf and threaten the town folk? He thought maybe he should have asked, so now he had something else he needed to find out about. Dave and Martha Henderson said Sarah told them she wouldn't punish the boys for what they did to Billy and that Sarah told them it was his job to punish them. Maybe she did it, maybe she didn't. He felt he would be disappointed if he found out Sarah put the rats in the boy's beds. Christian underlined her name.

Then he came to Thomas. As far as Christian knew, Billy was Thomas's only friend. Thomas sat in the school yard and let Daniel Connell and Jamie Finch kick dirt at him. Daniel Connell held Billy down and broke Billy's arm, forcing Billy to tell them he paid Billy five dollars to be friends with Thomas. Hearing Billy's confession caused Thomas to get angry and punch Billy in the nose. Thomas lost his new friend, then ran to tell his mother. Christian underlined Sarah again. She was still on top of his list. But out of all the suspects, it was Thomas who had the most to lose. Thomas had access to plenty of river rats, but still, Christian thought, how did Thomas get inside the two houses when they were locked up tighter than his jailhouse? He needed to talk to Thomas. Christian drew a circle around Thomas's name.

Leaving the jailhouse, Christian walked down to Sarah's camp to find Thomas wasn't there. He figured, because Sarah had ridden out of town on her own, there was only one other place Thomas might be. The Henderson's seemed to have made friends with Sarah and Thomas after they visited them at their camp, and he couldn't see Thomas up at the corrals with the trapper's, so he went to the Henderson's and was greeted at the door by Martha.

"Why, Sheriff Morgan, is something the matter?" Martha was instantly worried when she saw him standing on her doorstep. Sheriff Morgan didn't usually visit with people unless something was wrong.

"Nothing too serious Martha, can I ask if Thomas Mason is here?"

"Yes, he is, out on the back porch with Billy, they are spending the day together, Billy can't play you know, with him having a broken arm."

"Could I talk to Thomas for a moment please." Martha took Christian through to the back porch where Billy and Thomas were sitting at a table.

"Thomas, Sheriff Morgan would like to talk to you." Martha smiled at Christian. "I'll bring some coffee and lemonade for the boys." Christian turned down the offer of coffee, saying he wouldn't be there long. Martha left Christian with the boys and went to get the lemonade. Dave, busy working in his garden, looked up, and seeing Christian come out onto the porch, leant his hoe against the fence, and came to where Christian was standing. The two men said hello and Christian turned his attention back to Thomas. "Thomas, I need to ask you something son."

Billy was seated at one end of the table and Thomas the other. Both boys had drawing book's and pencils scattered between them on the table. Thomas kept drawing in his book and not looking up replied. "I told you before ...I'm not your son!" Christian ignored Thomas's sharp reply and squatting next to him, looked over Thomas's shoulder at the picture of a rabbit Thomas had drawn and was shading in with his pencil. Thomas was an excellent drawer, the rabbit looked almost life like. "Thomas, sometime last evening Jamie Finch and Daniel Connell had dead rat's put in their bed's." Billy stopped drawing when he heard what Christian said. It was the first time he heard about the rats, and he looked wide eyed at Thomas to see what he would say about it, but Thomas kept shading his drawing. Keeping his voice steady, Christian went on. "I don't suppose you know anything about the rats Thomas, do you?"

"No! why should I know anything about em?" Thomas answered, keeping his head down. Christian noticed Thomas's cheeks beginning to turn pink, perhaps from shame for what he had done, or guilt from being caught out.

"Well, your Ma is in big trouble Thomas, everyone is blaming her for it." Thomas stopped drawing and bent his head further. Christian could see Thomas getting upset at the thought of his

Ma being blamed for the rats. "Do you want to tell me about it, Thomas?"

"I told you, I don't know anything about it!" By this time Thomas's face was red, convincing Christian Thomas wasn't telling the truth.

"Well, I guess your Ma is the person who did it, and she will have to be arrested for what she did." Christian didn't like that he had to threaten Thomas with Sarah's arrest, but he couldn't think of any other way of getting Thomas to talk.

"Ma didn't do it!" Thomas snapped suddenly. When Martha came out carrying a tray with two glasses of lemonade and a plate of cookies on it, Christian stood up to make room for her to put the tray on the table, giving Thomas a chance to jump from his chair and try to run, only to make it as far as Dave's garden before Christian caught him at the back fence. "They deserved it! they broke Billy's arm!" Thomas cried, before checking himself. He was too old to cry like a baby, but he knew he was in big trouble. Christian took him back to the porch where he sat him down. "Tell me from the beginning Thomas, how did you do it?"

Taking a deep breath, Thomas confessed. "I got the rat's out of Ma's snares and bled them into a tin, I went to Jamie's house first and crept upstairs …everyone was asleep, Jamie Finch's Pa snores really loud. I cut the head off a rat and pulled its insides out and put it all over Jamie's pillow, then I poured blood from the tin all around it, then I went to Daniel's house …only I put more blood on his bed because he was the one that hurt Billy." Christian listened intently as Thomas told them all how he did the ghastly deed.

Martha and Dave were horrified, but Billy wasn't. "You did that for me Thomas?" Billy was proud of Thomas for paying Jamie and Daniel back for hurting him. "You are my friend Billy." Thomas looked at Christian. "I would do it again too!" he said sternly.

There was more Christian wanted to know. "Tell me Thomas, how did you get inside their houses?" Both houses Christian remembered, had their windows nailed shut and their doors latched. Thomas shrugged his shoulders. "It was easy …I walked through their front doors!" Dave was horrified. "Walked in! but our doors are locked!" Since the wolf in the church incident everyone in town locked their houses up tight. "Your door is the same as all the others, the wooden latch doesn't clip properly, so the door looks locked, but it isn't!" Thomas said nonchalantly, picking up a pencil.

Christian still wasn't satisfied. "Can you show me Thomas?" Thomas stood up and looking over at Dave standing with Martha, picked up the glass of lemonade Martha sat on the table, and took a big drink. It was nice lemonade, just like his Ma made. After sitting the glass down, he wiped his mouth on his sleeve, then everyone went to the front door. "I watched Billy's Pa lock their door before we went to bed and saw how the latch stayed up, you have to look really close to pick that out, but I saw it, so, I figured Jamie and Daniel's doors were the same." Thomas had keen eyesight. Living where dangerous animals lurked at night, his vision had to be sharp. Dave moved to his front door, closed it, and watching the wooden clip fall onto its latch, found Thomas to be right.

The door appeared locked, but the clip rested on top of the latch. Dave pulled on the door and when it came open in his hand, he felt a shiver run up his spine. Turning to see Christian watching what he did, both men raised their eyebrows in surprise.

Christian was impressed that Thomas had the knowledge to know such a thing. "Finch told me their doors were locked this morning when they got up," Christian said still not satisfied. "Yeah! Well! he would think that, wouldn't he?" Thomas said making his way back to the porch. "I cut the frame on Daniel Connell's wall … by accident," he confessed. "I thought I would have to use my knife to get in so I jabbed at it, but the door came open." Christian found the minute cut no-one else had seen and was now convinced it had been Thomas who broke in to the Finch and Connell's homes. Satisfied Sarah wasn't guilty of the crime at all, Christian wished he hadn't jumped to conclusion's and could take back what he had done to Sarah earlier.

"Are you going to lock me up Sheriff Morgan?" Thomas asked when they had all gone back to the porch. "No Thomas, I'm not going to lock you up, but I will have to punish you, Jamie Finch and Daniel Connell have been punished enough already by what you have done, but I will still talk to them about tormenting you at school." Thomas was relieved he wasn't going to be locked up, Billy was glad too. "Well I never would have thought Thomas would do something like that, but I guess he takes after his Ma," Dave said as he walked Christian out. "Maybe you can enlighten me on something Dave, Finch was saying Cole cut up a wolf, can you tell me the reason she did that?" Christian didn't expect Dave would tell him anything, and he was right. Dave would not discuss Sarah suffice to say. "She had good reason to do what she did." Christian left Thomas at the Henderson's and returned to the jailhouse.

It was getting on toward late afternoon when the Henderson's sent Thomas to his camp so he would be there when his Ma came back from picking berries. Thomas busied himself by lighting the fire in the firepit and putting on a pot of coffee to brew for when she got back. Then sitting and waiting, he began to think. He wasn't sorry he punished Jamie and Daniel, but he was sorry his Ma got blamed for it. She had always been good to him. His Ma taught him how to hunt, and trap, even though he didn't like doing any of it. She taught him how to shoot the rifle she gave him for his eleventh birthday, and she never yelled at him or got cross with him. He loved his Ma and would never deliberately set out to hurt her.

It was starting to get dark, but Sarah hadn't returned. Worried something bad may have happened to her, Thomas ran to the Sheriff's Office to let Christian know. Bursting through the door, he found Christian sitting casually behind his desk. "Ma hasn't come back!" he cried. "Something's not right! Ma said she would be back before dark!" Approaching Christian, he spotted Sarah's knife in its sheath sitting on his desk, and his eyes grew wide. "What are you doing with Ma's knife?" He figured she wouldn't have her pistol, or her rifle with her just to go pick a few berries, but without her knife too, she would be defenseless against anyone or anything that wanted to hurt her. "Ma can't be without her knife! ...she could get hurt!" Not waiting for Christian to answer, Thomas ran out and sprinted back to camp.

In an effort to stop him running off, Christian rushed around his desk after him. "Thomas!" he called, but when Thomas quickly disappeared from view, he stood in the street, looking in the direction Thomas had gone. "Sheriff Morgan!" A man whose voice Christian recognized, came rushing up behind him. "What is it Ham?" he asked keeping his back to Ham. "Cole's horse …he's come back," Ham said sounding worried. "Thomas was just here, worried about his Ma not being back, well, now he doesn't have to worry," Christian said sounding relieved. Ham though was very worried. "No! no! …its Star! he's alone! …got cut's and scratches all over him!" Christian didn't need to be told anything further. He rushed off to the Livery with Ham running along behind him.

Standing in the stall with Star, Christian checked his injuries. Blood covering his body and legs glistened in the dull light cast by lamps. After running his hands over Star's forelegs, he rubbed his hands down his neck and patted him. "Good boy, good boy," Christian soothed, then turned to Ham. "Can you saddle up mine and Thomas's horses, and pack us enough supplies to do us for tonight, I'll also need some torches, Thomas and I are going out to look for Cole." Ham said he would have everything ready for when Christian came back with Thomas.

By the time Thomas got back to camp tears were flowing freely. His Ma could be lying out there somewhere hurt, and feeling cold, and it would be all his fault. Rushing to the shelter, he grabbed his rucksack, threw some food into it, grabbed his small hunting knife, and grabbed Sarah's fur coat. Sheriff Morgan wouldn't help him, he wouldn't ask the trappers to help either, his Ma wouldn't want them to come find her. He was going to find his Ma without anyone's help, and he was taking her coat with him, she would need it when the night grew cold. Thomas felt he couldn't leave his Ma out in the dark on her own. Until he had a sleepover at Billy's, they had never been apart, not ever. Maybe he thought, his Ma was just angry with him and was staying out to teach him a lesson for lying to her, just like when he misplaced his Pa's timepiece. He learnt his lesson then, and never leaves the timepiece lying about.

The quickest way to Sarah's camp was by going along the alley beside the Livery and down the track leading to the river. Christian sprinted along the riverbank, then, when he saw Thomas come out of the shelter carrying Sarah's coat, his face red and tear stained, he stopped in his tracks. "Thomas!" Christian could see Thomas was preparing to go and look for his mother on his own, so had to be careful how he told Thomas about Star. "Do you know where the blackberry patch is?" Sensing something wrong, and keeping a firm grip on Sarah's coat, Thomas's eyes brimmed with tears as Christian came closer.

"Yeah, I've been there with Ma lots of times, why do you want to know that?"

"Can you show me where it is?"

"I can show you, but why?" Thomas held his eyes firmly on Christian.

There was no better way to tell Thomas about Star. "There is something you should know son …and it may seem bad right now …your Ma's horse has come back …without her …but that doesn't mean your Ma is hurt!" he added quickly trying to allay Thomas's fears. A tear ran down Thomas's cheek and he swiped it away. He had to be strong, his Ma's life depended on it. Ignoring the fact Christian called him son he swallowed and replied, "I'm ready sheriff." While feeling sorry for Thomas, Christian saw a determination in him the same as he had seen in Sarah. "Come on then son, let's get going."

Racing up the track together, they passed the Ferguson house, and for a moment Christian thought about telling Joe Sarah was missing, but deciding he didn't need trouble from the trappers on top of what he already had, he ran on until he stopped Thomas outside the jailhouse. "Wait here for me Thomas," he said racing inside. Grabbing his rifle off the rack, and Sarah's knife off his desk, he hurried back outside. Thomas saw what he was carrying but didn't comment, there wasn't time.

Arriving at the Livery, they found their horses saddled and a large bag packed with supplies hanging from Christian's saddle-horn. "Thomas can take the torches," Ham suggested. Six long wooden torches stacked in a bag was handed up to Thomas. After quickly hanging the bag from his saddle-horn, Thomas handed Sarah's coat to Christian. "You can take this for Ma, she might need it if she gets cold." Christian put Sarah's coat on, and found it large enough to go around him, but the sleeves very short for his long arms. Thomas looked like he was about to laugh, but searching for his Ma was serious business so he refrained.

"Take care of Star Ham, we may not be back until tomorrow," Christian said down to Ham. Ham told Christian Star's injuries weren't as bad as he first thought and assured Thomas he would be fine. Christian and Thomas rode out into the dark, crossed the bridge together, and turned their horses toward the swimming hole and the blackberry patch.

The night had grown pitch dark. No moon meant they could no longer see to know where they were going. Bringing their horses to a halt at the swimming hole, both Christian and Thomas called out to Sarah several times but got no answer. As the night wore on the trail became harder to follow. Thomas got one of the torches and when Christian lit it, they rode toward the blackberry patch by torchlight.

As Christian and Thomas rode along, they fell into conversation. Thomas did most of the talking while Christian did the listening, "Why did you take Ma's knife off her?" Thomas asked suddenly. "I took it because your Ma was angry and I thought she might use it to hurt someone." Christian was thinking she might have hurt him with it. "Ma wouldn't hurt anyone with her knife, she cut's animals with it, she doesn't cut people, Ma would never hurt a person sheriff."

"I don't know what your Ma is likely to do Thomas, no-one will tell me anything about her, perhaps you can tell me something." Christian thought now would be a perfect time to find out a few things about Sarah that no-one else would tell him. "What do you want to know?" Thomas asked innocently. Thinking he would get a simple explanation, Christian started with what he believed was a simple question. "That scar on her shoulder …how did she get it?" But he was wrong. Thomas didn't ask how he came to see the scar when it was hidden under his Ma's shirt.

"Ma shot herself," Thomas said looking over at Christian. Christian looked back at Thomas in surprise. "Shot herself! … how?"

"She was going to shoot a wolf when it moved, Ma went to follow it but she fell into some bushes, and her gun went off and it shot her." Thomas went quiet for a moment. Christian was deep in thought about Sarah shooting herself. "Ma nearly drowned too you know!" Christian was even more surprised at Thomas's casual way of saying his Ma nearly drowned. "What? When?"

"When she shot herself."

"Go on Thomas, tell me what happened."

"Ma tried to get to my Pa for help, his camp was on the riverbank, and Ma was on a ledge above the river, she couldn't get to Pa because the wolf was blocking her way ...Ma killed the wolf but they both fell in the river, Ma said the wolf floated but she didn't, so Pa pulled her out, cause he saw her fall in, and he got the bullet out of her ... and then they had me." Thomas thought it important to add the last bit about his Ma and Pa having him. He was an important part of his Ma's life, because his Ma told him so many times that he was a gift from his Pa, and she loved him.

Christian was pleased Thomas told him that part of Sarah's past, but wondered what else Sarah had happen to her. He especially wanted to know about the four trappers and what part they played in Sarah's life, but he didn't get a chance to ask about anything else. "Sheriff look! there's the patch!" Thomas squinted into the dark and pointed out brambles looming ahead of them. Christian could just make them out, and was convinced Thomas had excellent vision to be able to spot the bushes when he could only just see them.

The torch Thomas carried burnt low so he dropped it on the ground where it petered out. Christian lit a fresh torch and taking it off Thomas, rode up and down the edge of the patch looking for a way through. The brambles were growing too close together for Christian's liking. Finding what he thought was the best way to proceed and leading the way, he maneuvered his horse carefully through the twisted brambles. Feeling a thorn tear his trousers and scratch his thigh, he cursed, but was thankful the scratch wasn't deep. Ignoring the stinging the thorn caused, he pushed on until he couldn't feel it anymore. "This must be where Star came through," Christian said over his shoulder to Thomas. "How do you know that sheriff?" Thomas asked, keeping his eyes on the thick spiny branches as his horse followed Christian's. "The bushes are trampled here, Thomas be careful," Christian warned.

After more careful maneuvering they made their way through to the other side. While Thomas stayed on his horse, light from the torch lit up the area directly in front of Christian, allowing him to get down to walk about. Evidence Sarah had been there lay all around. Star's hoofprint's and scuff marks from his shying were obvious. Christian found the bag of blackberries that had been dropped and spilt lying on the ground. When he found a trampled snake, he began to grow more concerned for Sarah.

Had Sarah been bitten by the snake? If she had, where was she? He was wishing he had let her keep her knife, then maybe none of this would have happened. Leaving the bag of blackberries where they were, he walked toward Thomas, and stopped. Staring at a piece of rag hanging from brambles, he gingerly reached in, and taking hold of the rag, unhooked it from the thorn's and held it up to the torchlight. When he recognized the piece of blood-stained material to be a part of Sarah's shirt, his stomach lurched.

"What is it Sheriff Morgan?" Thomas said watching Christian, and seeing him holding something up to look at it. "It's a piece of your Ma's shirt Thomas." Without pausing Christian went on. "Would there be anywhere near here where your Ma could take shelter for the night?" Seeing the piece of shirt made Thomas too worried to think straight. If his Ma's shirt was torn and hanging from the bushes, then she was more than likely hurt, and bleeding. Feeling his stomach tie itself in knots, Thomas forced himself to think about what Christian was asking him. "Not that I know of." Christian looked off into the dark. If Sarah was here, where would she be? "Sarah!" he yelled. "Sarah!" he called again. "Wait!" Thomas said excitedly, suddenly remembering something. "The falls ...Ma could take shelter there!"

"What are the falls?" Christian asked, standing beside Thomas's horse looking up at him, and feeling angry for not knowing much about the area around Cedar Creek, and thinking he really must take the time to get out and explore more. "They are big rocks ...and I remember ...there is a cave!" Thomas thought it was a cave, even though it didn't go under the boulders very far, it looked like a cave. "Ma would go there ...wouldn't she?" he looked down at Christian expectantly. There was no mistaking the worry in Thomas's voice, and Christian didn't want to scare him any more than he already was. "If I needed shelter, and they were close by, then that's where I would go, how far is it to these falls?"

"Not far ...that way," Thomas answered, pointing off into the dark.

"Right!" The Falls were the only place they both agreed where Sarah could be. Christian hoped they were right. He put his foot up in his stirrup and swung his leg over his saddle. "Let's go get your Ma!"

Prodding their horses with their heels, in no time, they were leading them over stones and small boulders on foot. The Falls and its cavern loomed large out of the dark, right in front of them.

Chapter Twenty-four

Sarah was thirsty, but her canteen was hanging on Star's saddle, and the river was too far away for her to walk to. She thought she could manage to go without water for one night, so long as help came in the morning.

The Falls huge boulders never looked better. Shelter wasn't too far away, making her feel a little relieved. Although the bleeding finally stopped, the thorn was causing her no end of pain. Stumbling over stones, and sitting down a couple of times to rest along the way, then clambering up the rocky outcrop and ignoring the stinging pain in her left hand, she gathered up small stones. When she got near the opening to the cavern, she threw the stones as far as she could into the dark cavity and waited to make sure there weren't any animals taking shelter inside. She didn't know what she would do if something came rushing out at her. Waiting for a moment and when nothing happened, Sarah made her way in and sitting down, felt the warmth from the wall against her back. Sarah knew she would be alright until morning when the heat would dissipate leaving the cavern freezing. Knowing the cavern would become cold didn't bother her, she planned to leave at first light and walk back to town. Leaning back, Sarah thought about Thomas, sure he would know something was wrong when she didn't get back before dark and maybe, just maybe, he would bring Joe to find her. She prayed he would bring Joe. It was a long way to ride to town, let alone walk.

It was pitch dark when Sarah woke. Feeling as though she must have slept for a long time, she looked around and was unable to see a thing, but thought she heard Thomas calling her. "Ma! Ma! you in there?" Did she hear him? or was she hallucinating? "Thomas!"

she called. "Thomas is that you?" Trying to get up quickly, she fell back against the wall hurting her arm. "Ma! Ma!" Sarah did hear Thomas calling her, she could see the glow of a flame moving toward her through the dark. "Ma's here!" Sarah heard him call back to someone. 'Thank God,' she thought. 'He has brought Joe.' Thomas came rushing up to Sarah and seeing blood covering her shirt, threw his arms around her and tried to hug her causing her to wince in pain. "It's alright Ma, we are here, are you hurt bad?" Sarah was glad to see Thomas and didn't mind him hugging her. "Thomas, I knew you would come, did Joe come with you?"

"No Ma, I brought Sheriff Morgan," Thomas answered, surprising Sarah. 'Damn! why did he bring him?' she thought. 'Surely he would be the last person Thomas would go to for help.' Christian walked quickly to where Sarah was leaning against the rock wall. "Sarah …are you alright?" he asked, concern evident in his voice as he knelt beside her.

"Do I look alright sheriff?" Sarah snapped angrily. "And why are you wearing my coat? you look ridiculous!" She hadn't meant to sound angry, but she expected to see Joe not Christian and her angry words just popped out. Christian didn't need her insults, so after he and Thomas glanced at each other, he stood up and hurried back to the horses. "Ma, don't be mad, Sheriff Morgan was worried about you, and Ma, he knows it was me who put the rats in the beds, you know too don't you?" Leaning in close to Sarah, Thomas felt sorry for what he did.

"Why did you do it Thomas? why did you lie to me?" Thomas put his head down in shame. "They hurt Billy, I knew you would be mad when you found out, I'm sorry Ma, but they weren't wolves, only rats, you're not in trouble, and Sheriff Morgan isn't going to lock me up …but he said he has to punish me for it." Christian freed the horses of their supplies, and carrying the rucksack and a blanket, came hurrying back before Sarah could ask Thomas what sort of punishment Christian had in mind for him.

"Thomas can you see if you can make a fire, we'll need some hot water so we can get your Ma's arm sorted." Handing a canteen to Thomas, Christian ignored the fact Sarah spoke angrily to him, and knelt back down beside her.

"Yeah, sure sheriff, I'll get the fire going, and then I'll make us some coffee, I'm really sorry for what I did Ma." Thomas put his arm around Sarah not realizing each time he hugged her he hurt her, then hurried away to make a fire. "I think there is a thorn in my arm sheriff, every time I move it hurts." Sarah felt sorry she snapped at Christian. Thomas was right, he had come to help her, still, she felt she should be formal with him, calling him sheriff sounded more appropriate considering the situation she found herself in. He was not here to be friends with her.

Removing Sarah's coat, Christian tried to look at her arm in the dull flame of a torch, but the torn blood-soaked material got in his way. "I can't see anything Cole, either I will have to cut your shirt off you or you are going to have to take it off." Christian felt he couldn't call her Sarah while she was angry with him, at least not yet, he would have to wait for the right moment. Sarah could tell Christian was angry with her, not only because of the way she spoke to him just now, but from their conflict in town earlier. Not wanting her shirt torn any more than it already was, she answered, "I will take it off."

"Right …after you take it off, cover yourself with that blanket." Pulling bandages Ham packed out of the rucksack, he stood up and turned his back. Sarah tried her best to remove her shirt, but the pain in her arm when she moved was unbearable. "I don't think I can get my shirt off …Christian," she said quietly to his back.

Christian felt his stomach flutter when Sarah reverted to using his name. Turning, he looked down to see her holding her injured hand up for him to see. There was no way Sarah could take her shirt off on her own. "What do you want me to do Sarah?" His eyes softened as he looked at her. A lump formed in Sarah's throat and she thought she might burst into tears. "Help me get my shirt off …please." Christian squatted, and holding his hand to the side of Sarah's face, felt sure she was no longer angry with him. "Are we good?" he asked softly. Knowing what he was asking, Sarah answered, "yes."

Leaning forward, Christian pushed his hand through her hair and brought her face toward his. Feeling the softness of her mouth on his, he held their kiss for a long time. "Sarah," he whispered. "I'm sorry for what happened in town." Sarah felt a tear run down her cheek. Christian brushed it away with his fingertip. "I'm sorry too, for the way I spoke just now." Sarah whispered, leaning forward and resting her head against his chest. After accidently shooting herself, she asked Frank to help her, and then pushed him away. Here now she wasn't going to push Christian away, but felt she was going to pass out.

Holding Sarah and not wanting to let her go, Christian looked to where Thomas was busy making a fire. The fire was alight and a strong smell of coffee brewing filled the cavern. "Thomas, I've got to help your Ma get her shirt off." Thomas looked up from the fire to see Christian and his Ma holding each other. "Ok!" he said, studying them. "You mean ...now?" Thomas asked furrowing his brow. "Now son." Sarah noticed Christian call Thomas son and how Thomas didn't seem to mind. "Go ahead sheriff." When Thomas turned his back Christian quickly undid the buttons on Sarah's shirt, letting his fingers slide gently between her breasts to the top of her trousers. Trying not to hurt her, he removed her shirt carefully by gently peeling the sleeve down her arm. A tingle rushed through Sarah at his touch. Her arm hurt, but she persevered with the pain to let Christian help her. When Christian glanced fleetingly at her exposed breasts, Sarah saw him, and was glad when he didn't spend too much time on them. She was hurt and was grateful he was only interested in fixing her arm.

After throwing Sarah's bloodied shirt aside, and wrapping her in the blanket, he got her to lay on her side exposing her arm so he could see her injury. A long moment passed with him not speaking.

"How bad is it Christian?" Sarah asked through her pain. "I won't lie to you Sarah, it looks pretty bad, you have three scratches, the middle one seems to be worse than the other two, I think Doc will need to stitch you up."

"The thorn must be in the middle one ...can you see it?" Sarah stayed on her side while Christian used her knife to cut a piece of cloth from her shirt so he had something to use as a wash cloth. Wetting the cloth in the water Thomas heated up on the fire, he wiped away blood smeared over her body as well as her arm.

"Can you bend your arm?" he asked thinking her injury might not be as bad as first thought. Sarah tried bending her arm, but the pain caused her to moan and tense her body. "Shit!" Christian exclaimed, seeing the thorn causing all the trouble. "I can see the thorn but I don't think I can get it out with my big fingers, Thomas, come here son!" Thomas rushed around the fire and up to where Christian was kneeling next to Sarah. "Can you see that thorn sticking out of your Ma's arm?" He pointed to the deep gash. Thomas bent his head close to take a look and screwed up his nose at the gory sight. "I think so, is that it there?" Thomas pointed to a small bloodied spike just visible in the wound. "That's it, can you grab it and pull it out?" Christian and Thomas looked at each other.

"I don't know! will I hurt Ma?" Thomas sounded worried.

"Thomas! if you don't pull it out it will hurt me more." Sarah tried not to snap at Thomas, but she needed him to get the thorn out quickly, she was trying to hold on, but felt she would pass out at any moment.

"But I will hurt you Ma!" Thomas's eyes filled with tears. "It will only hurt a little, grab it and pull it out quickly, then it will be over, you can do it honey, please …do it for me." Sarah said, keeping her voice low to reassure him. Thomas wiped his face with his sleeve then all of a sudden, pushed his fingers against the back of Sarah's arm. As his fingers dug in, Sarah held her breath, and when the thorn popped up, he grabbed it and pulled it straight out. Sarah groaned as warm blood oozed from the wound. Thomas held the thorn up to show Christian. "Wow! this is a big thorn!" he exclaimed, wanting to show the thorn to Sarah, but her eyes were closed. "Is Ma ok?" he asked Christian. "She will be fine," Christian answered. Thomas leant over and kissed Sarah on her cheek then, taking the thorn with him to study it, went back to the fire.

After bandaging Sarah's arm, and cleaning and bandaging her hand, Christian tucked her under the blanket, then covered her with her oversized fur coat to keep her warm. Leaving her to rest, and taking the remains of Sarah's bloodied shirt with him, he made his way to the fire. Dropping the remnant in the fire, the shirt fizzled, then disintegrated in the flames causing a thick pall of black smoke to rise in the cavern. Thomas handed Christian a mug of coffee and he sat down. "Thank you, Thomas." Christian and Thomas sat quietly by the fire while Sarah slept.

Seeing how his Ma and the sheriff were sometimes nice to each other, Thomas asked. "Do you like Ma Sheriff Morgan?" It didn't go unnoticed how they looked at each other with a look he didn't quite understand yet. He caught them kissing in the Livery the night of the storm and thought they must like each other, because boys and girls don't kiss, not unless they liked each other.

"Sure Thomas, I like your Ma." Christian thought that an easy question to answer, it was true, he did like Sarah, very much, but what Thomas said next was unexpected.

"Do you want to cuddle Ma?" Thomas thought he knew when boys and girls liked each other, they liked to touch each other in certain ways, and they had to cuddle to do it.

"What do you mean Thomas?" Of course, Christian wanted to put his arms around Sarah and hold her, but whenever he did that he wanted more. Christian wasn't sure what a twelve-year old boy knew about men and women. He remembered when he was twelve, he didn't think about cuddling girls at all. He was too busy at the orphanage fighting to protect himself from older boys. Christian was about to find out what Thomas believed cuddling meant.

"You know! …cuddle! …like a man and woman …when they like each other, the man lays on top of the woman …and they cuddle! …you can cuddle Ma if you want …I don't mind!" On his eleventh birthday, Thomas made a wish, not for himself, but for someone to make his Ma happy, and right now he hoped Sheriff Morgan was the man to do just that.

Feeling embarrassed at Thomas's explanation of cuddling, Christian felt his face begin to burn. He had already 'cuddled' Sarah as Thomas put it, and he wanted to cuddle Sarah again, more than anything, but now wasn't the time, or the place, not while Thomas was with them, and certainly not while Sarah was injured as badly as she appeared. It looked as though she lost a lot of blood, and Christian didn't think she would be up for 'cuddling'.

Spreading his bedroll out beside the fire, then with his back to the fire and Christian, Thomas lay down. Pulling his blanket and coat well up over his shoulders he said, "Sheriff Morgan! the sooner we get to sleep, the sooner we can get Ma back to town …you can sleep up there with Ma, and keep her warm …if you want …goodnight." He wriggled around getting comfortable, then lay still.

Thinking Thomas was being pretty forward when he came straight out and told him to sleep with his Ma, Christian sat staring at Thomas's back. Looking over at Sarah, still lying on her side covered by her coat, he smiled then looked back at Thomas. Thomas had gone quiet. "Goodnight Thomas," he said quietly, putting several large pieces of wood on the fire and finishing his coffee.

Having given Sarah his blanket and her coat, Christian didn't have anything else to keep him warm, giving him two choices about where he slept. One, he could lay down beside the fire and try to keep warm, or two, get in under the blanket and fur next to Sarah and be warm. It was one hell of an easy decision to make. He chose number two, Sarah.

Feeling Christian moving about beside her, and before he made himself too comfortable, Sarah stirred. "Christian," she whispered. "Could I have some water?" After helping her with the canteen and both were lying comfortably, Christian felt Sarah hadn't deserved to be humiliated by him taking her knife off her and accusing her of putting the rats in the boy's beds, so he apologized. "I'm sorry Sarah, I shouldn't have jumped to conclusions like I did." Sarah lifted her head to look at him. "I'm sorry too, about Billy and for hitting you …the rats, did you look at the facts like I told you too?" When Christian's arm tightened around her, and his fingers brushed the side of her breast, Sarah leant against him, creating a longing that started deep inside the both of them. "Yes, I figured it to be Thomas." Christian went on to tell her how he figured it out, then asked her how she knew it was Thomas. "I caught him coming back to our camp at daylight and had a feeling he had been up to something, but I didn't know what."

"You should have told me what you knew, it would have saved us both a lot of trouble." Christian wasn't angry, but Sarah thought there was a hint of authority in his voice when he spoke. "I wanted you to work it out for yourself, not to listen to Finch or Connell …those two have been trouble for a long time." After Sarah mentioned Finch and Connell, Christian couldn't mistake the angry tone in Sarah's voice.

"What did Finch tell you about me cutting up a wolf?" Sarah questioned, wanting to know how much Christian knew about her past. "Nothing …he just said you cut one up, and at the time I didn't see any reason to pursue it …you are a trapper after all," he paused. "You want to tell me why you cut up a wolf?" Sarah was relieved Christian didn't know anything. She had moved on and wanted her past to stay in the past. "No …it's nothing you need concern yourself with." Christian pursed his lips, disappointed but not surprised by her evasiveness. "It was Finch who convinced me you must have done it," he went on. "But then why would you, Dave and Martha Henderson are two of the most decent people I know, they said you wouldn't punish the two boys, and I should have believed them."

"I told them it was your job to do the punishing." Even though Sarah thought to punish the boys herself, except for his pride Thomas hadn't been hurt so she let it go. "Thomas is very sorry for what he did Sarah, he's a good boy and knows what he did was wrong." Christian added when she finished.

"Thomas lied to me Christian, he has never lied to me before …he said you are going to punish him?"

"I have to give him some sort of punishment so he learns he can't do what he did and get away with it." Christian gently moved his hand resting under Sarah's armpit.

"How will you punish him?" Sarah worried Thomas's punishment may be time locked in a jail cell.

"I thought I might get him to clean the jail cells, for say, two weeks, he can come in after school and sweep and mop the floors." As Christian felt Sarah's warmth, a feeling of arousal swept over him.

Sarah was pleased with Thomas's punishment. If cleaning out the cells was all Thomas was going to have to do, it wouldn't hurt him to pay for his action's, she hoped he would learn from it. Turning her body in against Christian's, her head lay close to his, her hair brushed his face. Undoing the front of his shirt, she carefully slipped her hand inside and felt the warmth emanating from his body. Christian closed his eyes, then pulling the blanket and coat a little further over them, felt another rush of desire course through him. Both lay holding each other for a long time without speaking.

"Take your shirt off Christian." Sarah whispered breaking the silence. Christian lay still for a moment, giving thought about both of them being unclothed.

"You sure you want me to do that?" He said, hoping she would say yes.

"If you take it off, heat from our bodies will keep us warm." It was no use using warmth as an excuse, they were already warm. Sarah's reason for asking him to remove his shirt was so she could feel his naked body nestled against hers.

"I won't be responsible for what will happen if I take my shirt off," he whispered. Sarah was quiet for a moment. "You want me to be responsible for what happens? because I can be …if you want," she whispered back to him.

"Is your arm hurting you?" he asked softly. "Not so much now the thorn is gone," Sarah smiled up at him. Bending his head, he kissed her, then, before undoing the front of his trousers to loosen his shirt so he could pull it over his head, he glanced over at the fire, hoping Thomas was asleep. Thomas lay with his back to them, sound asleep.

Throwing his shirt aside, he put his arm around Sarah, and lay her against him. It wasn't long before a feeling of desperate wanting coursed through both of them. Lifting himself up a little and carefully wriggling his way out of his boots and trousers, he reached between them and undid the front of Sarah's trousers, then after working them down her legs, he used his foot to push them further. When they were around her ankles, he couldn't get them over her boots, so looking over at Thomas again to make sure he was still asleep, he quickly got out of the blanket, pulled Sarah's boots off her feet and removed her trousers.

Leaving both their boots and trousers at the bottom of the blanket, Christian hurriedly slid in next to Sarah, cupped one of her warm breasts, and gently massaged it.

"I didn't think you noticed," Sarah said quietly. Putting his mouth close to Sarah's ear, he whispered. "I noticed, I wanted you then, but thought you might not want me ...besides, you are hurt ...I'm sorry Sarah, I shouldn't have listened to Finch." Once more Christian felt the need to apologize. Loving the gentle way Christian was touching her, Sarah reciprocated with her own touch. "I want you," she said, before going quiet.

No words passed between them as their fondling heightened their arousal. Christian though, was a little worried about them lying not far from Thomas and completely naked. He didn't think Thomas meant for him to go this far with his mother. But Christian's body was responding to his caressing Sarah. Sarah pressed her body against Christian as his caresses began to take effect. Feeling her trying to move closer, Christian gently lifted her leg over his hip, and made himself comfortable between her legs. The ground beneath them was rough, causing them to make slow, gentle movements until their bodies became so excited, neither could stop.

As Christian reached his orgasm, he whispered "I love you." Thrusting back and forth, against Christian's body, Sarah kept her head against his chest to stifle her moans. Except for gasping when she reached her climax, Sarah didn't answer. With their arms and legs entwined, Sarah and Christian fell asleep, their bodies warm under the blanket and fur.

Waking up, Christian brought his eyes into focus, and looking up at the cavern ceiling, saw the sky had become light already. He thought he must be dreaming when he could smell food cooking and the aroma of coffee. Frowning, he lifted his head and looked toward the fire. Thomas was squatting at the fire. Steam rose out of the coffee pot. Sarah's back and Christian's chest were completely uncovered. Christian quickly reached over Sarah and pulled the fur over them.

Seeing movement where his Ma and Christian were sleeping, Thomas looked up and saw Christian was awake. "Morning sheriff, is Ma awake? I'm making hotcakes, and there's coffee if you are ready." Christian didn't know what to say. Under the blanket both he and Sarah were still naked, and he wondered just how the hell they were going to get dressed with Thomas right there. "Shit!" Christian cursed quietly.

"What's wrong Christian?" Sarah said dreamily, lifting her head and pushing her tangled hair out of her eyes. "Ow! my arm!"

Snuggling up to Christian, Sarah had forgotten she had an injury. Christian stretched over her to take a look at her arm. Blood had seeped through the bandage but not as much as he thought there might be, making him feel relieved that her arm hadn't been damaged too much. But still he had a predicament. "Thomas is awake Sarah, he has food ready," he said keeping his voice low. "Where are our clothes?" Sarah asked, still half asleep. Christian looked to the end of the blanket and his eyes widened. Seeing their legs uncovered, he tried moving his feet to get the blanket back over them but couldn't, not without attracting Thomas's attention. "Shit! they are bunched up at our feet, along with our boot's! …shit! shit! shit!" he said, horrified to think Thomas knew what they had been doing. Sarah smiled, knowing he was worried about what they had done with Thomas being there. But it didn't worry her, she was in love with Christian, and she guessed Thomas knew that.

"Thomas, can you give Sheriff Morgan and me a moment to get dressed?" She said loudly, making Christian mortified. He looked at Sarah and crossed his eyes, making a face that made her giggle. "Sure Ma." Thomas said, turning his back and adding. "Hurry up though, will you? or my hotcakes will burn!" While Thomas had his back turned, Christian grabbed their trousers and throwing Sarah's at her, hurriedly pulled his trousers up his legs and stood up quickly to do up the front.

"Can you help me get dressed Christian, I can't seem to use my arm and my hand is useless." She held up her bandaged hand to remind him of her wounds. Kneeling down, Christian pushed Sarah's feet into the legs of her trousers. Working them up to her knees, he took hold of her around her waist. They both began to stand when Sarah's breasts came in line with his face. Reaching up to take hold of a breast, he baulked. With Thomas so near, he thought better of it, so quickly pulling Sarah's trousers over her hips, he just as quickly did up the front.

"That was quick!" Sarah said, smiling faintly at him, trying to laugh as the colour drained from her face and her knees buckled. Catching her before she could fall, Christian sat her down and wrapped the blanket securely around her to keep her covered while he figured out what she would wear back to town.

"Thomas check your hotcakes now son!" Christian could smell the hotcakes burning. Thomas quickly pulled the pan off the fire and fanned the billowing smoke coming off the hotcakes. "Are they alright?" Christian asked, smiling over at him. "Yeah, a bit brown, but they are good." Thomas was good at cooking hotcakes, they were easy, his Ma taught him how to make them, telling him, if he could cook hotcakes, he would never go hungry.

Even though it would be too big for her, Christian decided Sarah could wear his shirt, saying it would do until she got back to town and got another. "Put it on and we will eat." Helping her get his shirt on, proved him right. The shirt was far too big, hanging loose over her body. When her arms disappeared inside the sleeves, he rolled them up until they were rolled up to her elbows. After tying the front in a knot at Sarah's waist, he smiled, because the loose shirt made her look sexy.

"What shirt are you going to wear Christian?" Sarah asked, beginning to sweat.

"I will wear your coat." He grinned and rolled his eyes as if to say how dashing he would look in her fur coat. Sarah smiled weakly and felt the bile rise in her throat.

"You ok?" Christian asked, concern wiping the smile off his face at seeing how pale Sarah looked, and thinking maybe they shouldn't have done what they did last night when she had already been through so much. "I think so," Sarah said not feeling so good. She didn't think it was her injuries making her feel ill, but not wanting Christian or Thomas worrying about her, kept it to herself.

"We better get you back to town fast, I don't want you getting an infection ...we shouldn't have done what we did last night, you're not well," he whispered near her ear. Stumbling her way to the fire, Sarah didn't comment on what they had done. "Have something to eat first, then we can go."

Christian and Thomas ate the hotcakes, which turned out not to be too bad, while Sarah sat quietly sipping on a mug of coffee that she didn't appear to be enjoying. Christian hurried Thomas along and they packed up quickly. When the horses were ready, Christian helped Sarah get up in front of him where she sat with her backside pressed against his lap. After pulling Sarah's coat across the front of them to keep her warm, he put his arms around her, and she settled back against him.

Finding the trail between the blackberry patch, Thomas led them safely through to the other side. They had to stop well before the swimming hole to let Sarah take a rest. "Are you alright Sarah? Is it your arm that's making you ill?" Christian queried, sitting beside her in the shade of a tree, not sure if three scratches on her arm would make her as ill as she appeared. "What else could it be?" Sarah said, wincing in pain. Christian leant toward her. "But you didn't seem too bad last night," he offered with a smile. Sarah glared at him. "Well I was feeling alright then, but now I'm not?" She snapped angrily. Not wanting to antagonize her, Christian stood up. "If you have had enough of a rest, we should get going." Neither said another word as they set off for town.

Travelling along for quite some time without speaking, they were getting close to town when they spotted four men riding at a gallop toward them. Christian recognized them and so did Thomas. "It's Uncle Joe!" Thomas yelled with a smile. "Damn!" Sarah cursed. Christian frowned when he heard Sarah curse. 'Why wasn't Sarah happy to see the men?' Just like when they helped move the tree off her shelter, she was not happy to see them, leaving Christian feeling confused.

Chapter Twenty-five

The four men slowed their horses when they came alongside Christian and Thomas. "We heard about what happened yesterday and came out to see if we could find you ...how badly hurt are you Sarah?" Joe asked, looking over at her. "I have a couple of scratches on my arm ...nothing to worry about." Christian listened as Sarah told Joe about her injury and how she made light of it. Sarah wasn't feeling at all well, she could feel herself starting to lose her vision. Everything around her started to blur.

"Well, we will ride back with you." Wanting to know the truth, Joe looked suspiciously at Christian. Sarah looked ill, her face was ashen and she appeared to be sweating, he wondered if she was coming down with a fever.

"What happened Sarah?" Will asked riding alongside Christian.

"I got tangled in the bushes, I didn't..." she started to sound far away. "A snake wrapped itself around my feet ...I didn't have my knife to..."

"Where was your knife?" Joe asked, not letting her finish.

"I ...I didn't have it with me, I just went to pick berries ...to ...pie." When Sarah's voice suddenly trailed off, and she went limp, Christian held his arms more securely by her sides to keep her from falling off his horse. "Has she passed out?" he asked Joe.

"Yes! she has! goddamn it! now tell me what happened!" Seeing Sarah pass out, Joe felt his anger rising. Having heard about the rats, the four men went to Sarah's camp looking for her. When neither she nor Thomas were there, they rushed off to the Sheriff's Office, only to be told by Clem Sarah had an argument with Christian, and after leaving the Livery on Star, she turned south, but he didn't know where she was headed.

After Clem confirmed what happened to Jamie Finch and Daniel Connell, the men went to the Finch house and got the full story. Jamie was scared of the trappers, especially Joe, so when Joe pressed him about why rats would be cut up to scare him, he confessed everything. After listening to Jamie, Joe figured out straight away it had been Thomas who did the deed. The four men waited until they got outside the Finch house before laughing at what Thomas had done. All four of them though, were concerned when Sarah hadn't come back. They rushed off to the Livery to find Star covered in scratches, and was told by Ham Thomas went with the sheriff to look for Sarah. The men hastily saddled their horses and rode out to help locate her, only to meet up with the three of them coming back to town.

Christian thought it sounded like Joe was accusing him of something. "It was like Sarah said, she went out to pick berries," he replied walking his horse. "I don't mean that!" Joe snapped. "Why did she go out without her goddamn knife? or her goddamn gun!" The anger in Joe's voice let Christian know exactly how angry he was. "You hear about the rats Joe? word would be spread all over town by now." Christian kept his horse walking steadily along. Thomas rode along quietly, listening to the men talking. "I know all about the rats and you thinking it was Sarah. You accused her of something she didn't do without finding out the facts first, we all know who did it! ...don't we?" Joe said, turning his huge body sideways in his saddle to look at Thomas. "It doesn't take a sharp mind to work out who did it, and why! for Chris' sake!" Joe turned back to Christian.

"I didn't mean to hurt Ma! they hurt Billy, so I made em pay!" Thomas kicked his horse and rode off ahead of the men. Will spurred his horse and racing after him, caught up to him before he could get very far. Taking hold of Thomas's horse by the bridle, Will brought both horses to a stop. Garret rode up to Will and Thomas. "Don't go off like that Thomas, you ain't in any kinda trouble!" Garrett told him. "No! well why did uncle Joe look at me like he did?" Thomas felt like crying, but he wasn't going to let the men see him cry, not like when he ran off to his Ma after Billy was hurt. "Aw!

Thomas, Joe looks at everyone like that …you should know that by now," Garrett said, and both he and Will laughed. The group had to stop once more while Sarah was ill causing all the men to be concerned.

The group crossed the bridge, riding down the main street all bunched together before stopping outside Doc Harris's practice. A crowd gathered quickly when word they were back spread like wildfire through town. Everyone heard Sheriff Morgan had accused Sarah of being the one who did the deed with the rats, and most town folk agreed she had done it, until Joe set them straight. They heard Sarah hadn't come back from picking berries and that the four men rode out looking for her. Now here they were, all of them, along with Sheriff Morgan and Sarah Cole, sitting on his lap, on his horse, looking mighty ill.

The men dismounted and Christian passed Sarah down to Joe. When Joe took Sarah in his arms, Sarah protested, saying she could walk in to Doc's practice. Joe refused to let her walk and carried her inside. Christian and Thomas followed the men in. Doc made Joe lay Sarah on the bed so he could examine her. "You can wait outside Joe …I will take care of her," he said holding the door open. But as Joe went out and stood in the hallway, Christian stepped through the door. Doc glared at him. "You can wait outside too sheriff!" he said, waiting for Christian to go. "Let him stay Doc," Sarah said. Doc closed the door behind Christian, effectively shutting the trappers and Thomas out. The two men moved to the side of the bed. "What happened Sarah?" Doc asked. But before Sarah could answer, the door opened and Gerda came rushing in. Sarah waited until Doc and Gerda stopped fussing over her then told them all what happened. When they looked at Christian wearing Sarah's coat, they looked puzzled. Insisting she would help Sarah, Gerda forced Christian out of the room.

With Christian standing in the hallway with four trappers and Thomas, Doc's practice was overcrowded. Joe was not happy at being shut out nor with Christian. Joe glared at Christian, and just his size was enough to make Christian feel uneasy.

"Come with me Thomas," Christian said, putting his hat on his head, and stepping outside. He wasn't going to stay in the hallway of Doc's practice and have Joe and the other trappers question him about what went on at the cavern. As far as he was concerned, it was none of their business. Joe warned him off from seeing Sarah, but he felt if he wanted to see her, he would, and it had nothing whatsoever to do with Joe, or Garrett, or Will, or damn Fergus. With Thomas following him, he started walking briskly down the street.

"Where are we going Sheriff Morgan?" Thomas walking quickly alongside him asked. "Just follow me," Christian said keeping up his pace. A lot of people were curious as to what happened to Sarah. When they saw the sheriff rushing off down the street, onlookers standing outside Doc's practice scratched their heads, wondering what he was up to.

Going to Crawley's store, Christian hurried around to the clothing section. Following close behind, Thomas still had no idea what Christian was up to. He watched as Christian started going through a pile of blouses labelled 'women's apparel.' Holding different ones up and looking at them, Christian glanced over at Thomas and saw the confused look on his face. "Help me find a shirt for your Ma Thomas," Christian said digging through the pile. When Christian said he was getting his Ma a new shirt, Thomas's face broke out in a huge grin, but he looked like he didn't know what to look for. "Come over here sheriff." Thomas took Christian to the boy's section. "These are what Ma wears." Christian looked at the pile of shirts labelled boys. "Your Ma is not a boy Thomas!" Liking the fact he had first-hand knowledge Sarah was not a boy, Christian smiled then too.

Going back to the first pile he started looking through, he found plain coloured blouses, and blouses with checks and stripes, and most of them were far too big for Sarah, and not something Christian could see her wearing. Digging around in the pile, Thomas held up different ones he thought his Ma might like too. After tossing the pile around, Christian pulled out a long sleeve cream coloured blouse with little blue/grey flowers on it. Holding up the blouse, he could see it would fit Sarah perfectly. He liked how it tapered in at the waist and the lace trim around the edge of the collar and cuffs. "What do you think of this one?" Holding it up high for Thomas to see, Thomas studied it but didn't comment, he didn't have to, his smile told Christian he approved. Christian threw the blouse over his arm and went looking for a pair of trousers. "What about trousers? Your Ma got any more trousers?" There were no trousers labelled women's so he had to settle for boys.

"Ma only has what she is wearing, she has to wash her clothes every week." Thomas answered nonchalantly while rummaging through a pile of trousers on a stand. "What does she do while her clothes are drying?" Christian asked matter-of-factly. Thomas shrugged his shoulders as if what he was going to say was no big deal. "She wears a blanket." Christian raised his eyebrows. Having seen Sarah, the morning after their first night together with just a blanket wrapped around her, she asked him if he had any regrets about staying with her. He had no regrets about staying that night with Sarah. He had no regrets about last night at the cavern either, no regrets at all. They continued rummaging around until they found a light brown pair of trousers.

Feeling ridiculous running around bare chested wearing a fur, even though he had plenty of shirts at the lodge, Christian wanted to get out of Sarah's oversized hooded coat, so he bought himself a new shirt. After putting on the new shirt, he threw Sarah's coat over his arm, then he and Thomas headed for the counter. On the way, they passed a stand holding an assortment of ribbons. Christian grabbed a cream coloured length, paid Crawley for everything, then he and Thomas headed back to Doc's practice.

After Christian and Thomas left his store, Crawley went through to his living quarters where Millicent was sitting doing needlework. Millicent wasn't one for riding or running around, instead she loved to sit and while her time away with embroidery. She had some lovely doilies packed away in her hope chest. Hoping one day she would marry Christian and live in Mountain View Lodge where she could place her work on show.

"Guess who just came in and bought women's clothes?" Crawley didn't wait for Millicent to answer. "The goddamn sheriff! that's who! ...and I can tell you who he bought those clothes for ...none other than that whore, Cole!" Crawley poured himself a cup of coffee from the silver coffee pot they had taken from the lodge. "How do you know they were for her daddy?" Millicent asked putting down her needlework. "Because Thomas Mason was with him when he bought them and they left together ...and another thing ...I heard talk the sheriff and Cole came back to town together. That bitch was hurt while out picking berries and he went out and brought her back. I can imagine what they did while they were there." Crawley was furious to think the man his daughter was interested in had fucked another woman, especially Sarah Cole, the very thought riled him. He hated Sarah with a vengeance for denying Millicent the right to marry Frank Mason and wanted her out of the way so she could marry Christian. Millicent looked innocently at her father.

"Daddy, are you sure he's been with her?" Crawley knew what his daughter was asking "There is no doubt he's been with her, why wouldn't he, she opens her legs for anyone, she's not called a whore for nothing!" Disgusted to know what Sarah and Christian had been doing, the very thought she would one day have to let him touch her that way, Millicent shuddered. When she married Christian, as her father hoped, she would not let him touch her. By then it wouldn't matter, she would be married to the town's sheriff, her station would be one of importance, and they would live in Mountain View Lodge, the grandest house in the county. Frowning, Millicent wondered why her and her father weren't already living in the lodge, after all, her father won it off Coles father fifteen years ago. But Crawley would never divulge the reason why they don't live there, not to his daughter or anyone else. So, for now, Millicent had to be content with living in the attachment behind their store.

"Daddy, we need to get Christian away from that woman …can we invite him for dinner again one night." Before Sarah came off her mountain, Christian had been invited to share many dinners with Millicent and seemed to enjoy her and her father's company. Millicent thought it would be in her best interest if she kept inviting him. "That is a good idea Millie, you ask him when you see him next." Crawley finished his coffee and returned to his store. Smiling, Millicent picked up her needlework and resumed sewing.

When Christian and Thomas entered Doc's practice, they found they were the only one's there. Joe and the other trappers left after Gerda told them Doc would be a while with Sarah and if they wanted to see how she was doing they should come back tomorrow. Gerda met Christian and Thomas in the hall. "Ronald is still in with Sarah, her arm is not good, needing stitches, you can come back later." Christian wanted to see Sarah and tell her he loved her. He told her at the cavern after they finished making love but thought Sarah hadn't heard him, now he would have to wait to tell her again. Christian handed Gerda the new clothes. "Will you give Sarah ...um! ...I mean, will you see Cole gets these?" It didn't escape Gerda how Christian called Sarah by her first name. Narrowing her eyes suspiciously, wondering what was going on between them, she took the clothes off him and took them to the room where Doc was seeing to Sarah.

Satisfied to leave Sarah with Doc, the four trappers returned to the Ferguson House. Sitting in front of the fire, they talked about the rat incident, and Garrett, already having an idea what might be causing Sarah's illness, broached the subject of her being ill. "What do you reckon has made Sarah sick Joe?" Watching Christian and Sarah when they were riding back to town, Garrett glanced at Christian after she passed out, and saw how his eyes softened and how his face held a look of concern. Garrett could see Joe's warning at the corrals hadn't sunk in. Sheriff Morgan was not going to leave Sarah alone.

It was too early to tell what was wrong with Sarah, although Joe had seen it before many years ago when Sarah had been with Frank. Joe didn't speak for a moment, instead leant back and sighed. Will and Fergus watched him expectantly. "I don't think it is a fever, sure, she has injured her arm, but it's not as bad as when she shot herself. She lost some blood, but I don't think that would make her faint or throw up like she did ...maybe she was poisoned by the blackberries ...I don't know," Joe said pensively.

"That is possible Joe, those bushes can harbour disease." Having studied botany some years before joining the cavalry, when he wasn't trapping, Garrett still enjoyed studying native flora and fauna on the mountain. But he wasn't convinced it was the blackberries. Joe didn't think it was that making Sarah sick either. Seeing Christian wearing Sarah's coat, and her his shirt, convinced him Sarah and Christian had been together again. Not only that, the look Christian gave him after Sarah passed out, convinced him Christian was in love with her. They had been together twice now that Joe knew of and Joe knows it doesn't take long for a woman to know she is pregnant, and that was what Joe was afraid of.

When everyone left Doc's practice, Joe found Thomas back at the camp on the riverbank. He argued with Thomas over where he was going to stay while his Ma was recuperating at Doc's. Gerda would take good care of Sarah, but Thomas would be left at their camp on his own. Thomas gave in to Joe's argument and he was taken to the Ferguson House to spend the night with the trappers.

After Thomas had dinner with all nineteen men, Joe showed him Sarah's room. Thomas had never been inside the Ferguson House let alone in the room his Ma used to stay in. Except for a musty smell the room appeared untouched. Fascinated by his Ma having her own room in the house she once shared with the trappers, he ran his hand over the pretty lace quilt covering the big iron bed, then touched the wooden framed mirror standing in the corner next to the tall chest of draws. "Why don't Ma and me stay here with you uncle Joe?" Thomas asked sitting on Sarah's bed. Joe sat down beside him. "We get in her way Thomas, your Ma is very independent, and headstrong, she likes to do things her own way and we respect her for that, that's all." Joe wasn't going to be the one to tell Thomas that after his Pa died his Ma told the trappers to go to hell and that she didn't want anything further to do with them. Even if they were getting along now, Sarah still kept them at a distance. The reason was something Joe thought Sarah should tell Thomas herself when she thought Thomas was old enough to know the truth.

When Thomas went to bed, Joe crept quietly into the room to check on him. Thomas lay curled up asleep with the blankets and quilt pulled well over his shoulders. His curly hair stuck out over the top of the quilt, reminding Joe of when Sarah stayed with the men. It was a long time ago. A time when he watched her sleeping in this very same bed, her long brown hair spread out on the pillow behind her. Sarah hasn't stayed with the trappers since Thomas was born. Now Sarah's son, a boy Joe has watched grow, is asleep in her bed in their house. Joe tiptoed out of the room, and closed the door gently behind him.

Doc Harris stitched Sarah's arm and bandaged it from her shoulder to her elbow. Gerda made up a bed for her in a spare room they used for sick patients, and after eating a hot meal and being told Thomas was staying with the trappers, Sarah fell asleep.

Next morning when she woke and put her feet on the floor, she felt dizzy, her stomach churned and she thought she might throw up. She gagged and swallowed trying not to give in to the nausea. Doc Harris knocked softly on the door and coming in, noticed how Sarah sitting on the side of the bed looked a little pale. "Morning Sarah, how did you sleep?" He asked, putting his hand on her forehead. "I slept fine Doc, but I think I'm going to be sick." Doc grabbed a dish and handed it to Sarah who immediately had to use it. Watching her bent over the dish, made Doc wonder why she was being ill. She didn't have a fever, and her arm hadn't been infected by the blackberry thorns. He waited until she was finished, then took the dish from her. "This has just started Doc." Sarah said, explaining what she meant.

Putting the dish aside, Doc was a little surprised at what Sarah told him. Sarah and Doc remained in the front room of his practice for several hours, only summonsing Gerda in at the end of their discussion. Doc insisted Sarah stay one more night so Gerda could look after her. After informing her Thomas would be taken care of by the trappers, Sarah agreed to stay, just to be sure it wasn't an infection she caught. After resting all day, she had another good night's sleep, and the next morning, promptly threw up.

Dressed in the shirt and trousers she found sitting on a chair beside her bed, she looked at her reflection in the mirror. The shirt was feminine, almost too feminine, it had a tight-fitting shape and emphasized her bust. She ran her hands over her body, then along the sleeves, feeling the soft material. Turning sideways, she looked at her profile, her nausea forgotten for the moment as she felt her face turn pink. She hadn't thought she was pretty, but this shirt made her look and feel pretty, she wondered who had bought it for her.

"Sheriff Morgan bought the clothes." Doc Harris informed her while she sat at their table. Feeling as though she couldn't stomach anything, Gerda gave her some ginger and tea. "You drink this first thing each morning Sarah, you will feel much better," Gerda instructed.

Chapter Twenty-six

fter Christian showed Thomas what he wanted him to do to clean out the jail cells, Thomas left the jailhouse and went back to the camp on the riverbank. Spending one night in his Ma's room at the Ferguson House, while his Ma was resting at Doc Harris's, he decided he was old enough to stay at the camp for the next night. Stoking the already hot coals in the firepit, he threw a larger log of wood into the fire, then set about getting himself something to eat. By the time he got some three-day old bread from the supply box, poked a thin stick through a slice and held it over the hot coals, the coffee pot was simmering on the side of the fire. While he waited for the bread to brown, the four trappers approached the camp, and stopped on the opposite side of the fire. "Hello Thomas." Thomas looked up at Joe and then back at his toasted bread. "Hello uncle Joe."

"Why are you here boy?" Garrett asked. "Why aren't you up at the house with us?"

"Someone has to take care of our camp uncle Garrett, and don't call me boy!" Thomas snapped. Standing up, he pulled the slice of hot bread off the stick, causing him to fumble with it. Almost dropping it, he rushed to the supply box, grabbed a tin plate, dropped the bread quickly on it, then shook his hands vigorously to cool them down. Joe smirked. The men had been to visit Sarah and found her injury wasn't as bad as first thought, but Sarah was worried about Thomas. The men told her they would take him to the Ferguson House again seeing how he spent a night there already.

"You better come stay with us for another night Thomas," Will said, watching him with the bread. Making to go around the firepit and up to the supply box where Thomas was standing, he stopped when Thomas answered. "Nope! I'm staying right here! I can take care of myself!" Thomas didn't look at the men as he spread his toast with thick butter and bit into it. Melted butter ran down his chin and he wiped it off with his hand.

"Your Ma wouldn'a like you to be here on your own now, would she Thomas laddie?" Fergus drawled, smiling and watching Thomas eating the butter-soaked bread.

"Ma ain't here, and besides, I'm old enough to be on my own." Thomas loved his Ma, she was always there protecting him, but sometimes he felt like he just needed to be by himself. He was older now, and the night he spent at Billy's was the first night he had ever been away from her. At first, he felt like crying because she wasn't there, but then he felt he was just being a cry baby, so told himself he had to toughen up. He reckoned he was tough enough now he and Sheriff Morgan had searched for his Ma and they found her because he knew where to look. That made him feel good about himself. He didn't need the men taking care of him.

"I don't need you takin' care of me uncle Joe," Thomas said being firm with his decision. Looking around the camp site, Joe could see everything seemed in order. "Alright Thomas, you stay here, we will see you tomorrow." Joe headed back up the trail. "Good night Thomas," he said over his shoulder as he left.

Will and Garrett both bid him goodnight and followed Joe. "Good night," Thomas called after them. "Any trouble Thomas an' you come get us, you hear me laddie, don't you go takin' it on by yourself now!" Fergus said, remaining at the fire. "There won't be any trouble uncle Fergus, but if there is, I'll be sure and get you!" Thomas smiled at Fergus. "Good on you laddie," Fergus replied, hurrying after the three men who had already disappeared along the track.

When Joe got out of sight of the camp, he stopped the men at the top of the trail. "I want a guard on the top of the ridge tonight, I'll take the first watch, then you Will, then Garrett, you can take the last watch Fergus, we'll keep an eye on the boy tonight." After the trappers left, Thomas made himself another piece of toast and drank a weak mug of coffee. His Ma wouldn't let him drink strong coffee, she reckoned it would make him too excited and he wouldn't be able to sleep.

Thomas sat for a long time at the fire. While watching the flames dancing and the hot coals glowing brightly, he thought of him visiting his Ma up at Doc Harris's and telling her he stayed in her room. When she asked him what he thought of it and he told her it was a girl's room, and that all the frilly things in it weren't for him, she laughed and hugged him. Thinking about the punishment Christian gave him, he reckoned sweeping and mopping floors was woman's work, but he would do it without question because he wanted to spend time with Christian. Remembering back to the wish he made on his eleventh birthday, where he wished for someone to make his Ma happy, he studied Christian when he and his Ma first arrived in town and again when they argued about where their camp was situated. He thought Christian must really like his Ma when he saw him kissing her in the Livery the night of the storm. But there were occasions when he thought he might have made a mistake about him. Like the night his Ma shot the river rats and he shot at her, and when he blamed her for putting dead rats in Jamie and Daniel's beds, he hated him. Thomas's eyelids started to feel heavy, so he let the fire die down until there were only hot coals, then made his way to the shelter and went inside.

Joe took the first watch. After spreading his bedroll out on the ridge, where he had a clear view over all of Sarah's camp, he sat down. Standing on the ridge one morning over a week ago, he watched Christian and Sarah together, now he would sit and watch to make sure Thomas was safe.

Watching Thomas sitting by the fire, Joe remembered back to when he was born. Able to see in his mind's eye the tiny newborn lying against Sarah's chest straight after she gave birth to him on the riverbank not far from her cabin. She was lucky he and the other men came along when they did or Sarah and Thomas may not have survived that cold night. Now here he was, that same tiny babe, twelve years old and acting all grown up. Joe smiled to himself when thinking Thomas was just like Sarah. 'As stubborn as they come.' Thomas was the living image of his father. His thick black hair, his stride when he walked was like Frank's. Joe watched Thomas go into the shelter, then waited for him to come back out, but he didn't, he had gone to bed. The camp became silent. Joe stayed on the ridge and kept watch.

Thomas took off his boots and sat them inside the entrance. Taking off his shirt, he folded it up, then lay it neatly in the small box that held his father's drawing book and silver timepiece. Lifting out his small hunting knife, and while pulling the blanket and fur over himself to keep warm, he gripped the knife in his hand for a moment before laying it next to him where he could get hold of it quickly if he needed it.

While lying quietly waiting to fall asleep, his thoughts returned to his Ma and Christian, convincing him they definitely liked each other. 'Because at the cavern they cuddled, even taking their clothes off so they could touch each other's bodies …yew!' Thomas was thinking. He didn't like girls, and wouldn't like to touch any of them, but then he thought. 'Maybe one day I might like them, and would want to cuddle them.' But he hoped that time would be a long time coming. Visualizing his Ma with Christian, remembering her lying half over him with her back uncovered, with their legs sticking out from under the fur, and their trousers bunched up at their feet, Thomas giggled at why they would sleep unclothed on a freezing cold night. Maybe they would have babies and he would have a brother. He didn't want a sister. They were girls! and he didn't like girls! but he supposed a girl would be alright, if she was his sister.

He felt at ease with Christian, and eager to have a Pa just like Billy Henderson, wanted to get to know more about him. He never had a Pa to talk to or spend time with. Even though he had lots of uncles, like Joe, they weren't really his uncles, and they weren't always there for him when they were off trapping higher up on the mountain. He knew how his Pa died, but he didn't know the reason his Ma never had much to do with the trappers. He just thought his Ma was stubborn and independent like Joe told him she was.

Thomas's last thoughts before falling asleep were of Christian being his Pa. He felt comforted his Ma chose Christian to cuddle over all the other men that asked her to marry them. Some men weren't so bad, like Foley Andrews, he liked him a lot too, but still, he was glad now his Ma had chosen Christian. Thomas couldn't wait for morning to come so he could continue his punishment. It meant he would spend every afternoon for the next two weeks with the man he would like to have as his Pa.

Several uneventful hours passed. Joe saw Christian come to Sarah's camp to check along the riverbank. Looking up at the shelter, he saw everything was as it should be, then turned and disappeared back along the trail. By the time Will came to take over from Joe, Joe had smoked more cheroot's than usual. "How is it Joe?" Will asked. Joe got to his feet. "He's been asleep for a few hours, nothing's happening." Leaving Will with his bedroll, he made his way back to the house.

As the sun began to rise above the distant mountains, Garrett had already finished his turn at keeping watch. Fergus was sitting with one leg bent up, his cheroot flared as he sucked on it. Joe had been to the outhouse beating all the men for its use as usual. Strolling to the edge of the ridge, he stood beside Fergus looking over the camp. "Anything happen?" he asked as he watched the sunrise. "Nope!" Fergus answered, resting his arm across his knee.

"Good," Joe replied. Fergus stood up and stretched. The two men stood side by side and didn't speak. Seeing movement down at the camp, both men's gaze went straight to the shelter.

Thomas stepped outside, and raising his arms above his head, stretched and yawned, then dropped his arms by his side. Joe and Fergus watched Thomas, who hadn't bothered to get dressed, head to the firepit. Still only wearing his trousers he slept in, Joe noticed how solidly built Thomas was. His skin was lightly tanned because Sarah let him run about shirtless, saying the sun was good for him, and Joe believed she was right.

Thomas got the fire going then headed for the trees to relieve himself. Fergus and Joe kept their eyes on him while he peed for a long time, aiming the stream at bushes and waving it about as it hit the leaves. Joe and Fergus almost laughing, had to turn away. When Thomas looked up toward the ridge, Joe stepped back suddenly and pulled Fergus with him. Had he seen or heard them? "Damn, he's just like his mother!" Joe whispered. Sarah would have known they were there watching over her.

Thomas knew they were there. Even though they didn't interfere, they were close by all the time. Knowing the four men would keep him safe like they did his Ma, he put on a show for them. Kneeling at the water's edge he washed his hands and splashed cold water over his face to make him feel more awake. Getting his shirt and boots, he sat at the fire and put them on. Joe and Fergus having seen enough, made their way back to the house for breakfast.

Thomas spent his first night all alone and didn't like it. He missed his Ma terribly.

Chapter Twenty-seven

After spending two nights at Doc's practice, Doc informed Sarah she was to keep her arm dry and covered for the next three weeks. She was to visit him twice a week for him to change the bandage she was wearing under her new shirt. He ordered her to stay off her horse and stay either in town or at her camp. Deciding she would stay at her camp as much as possible, Sarah returned there to resume cooking and taking care of Thomas.

Wanting to keep her pretty floral shirt for special occasions, not that she had any special occasions where she could wear it, but not wanting to ruin it by wearing it every day, an old faded blue shirt that was almost threadbare Sarah used to wrap bread in after baking, was washed and hung out to dry. Coming from school and seeing his Ma wearing the old shirt, Thomas asked where the new shirt was, and was satisfied when she told him she was keeping the new shirt for best.

Each day, when Thomas went off to school, after completing her chores around the camp, and not being able to ride, Sarah went to the corrals to watch the men breaking horses. Raising her arm hurt, so finding she couldn't reach up to climb the fence to sit and watch the men working, she quickly became bored with having to peer through the railings. Because of this she decided now was a good time to visit a few of her friends around town. Patrice Hammond, the first person she called on, welcomed her visit. Patrice's oldest daughter Sissy sat with them while they talked about Christian and what transpired between Sarah and him, posing Sarah some concern. She didn't want anyone knowing intimate details about her and Christian, not until she was absolutely sure of his intentions. When Sissy started asking questions about Will,

Sarah got the impression Sissy was in love with him, and welcoming the distraction, thought if Will was smitten with Sissy and Sissy with him, she would encourage it. She made a mental note to ask Will how he felt about Sissy without giving too much away.

Over the next few days she visited with Esther Morley, the bank managers wife, who was thrilled to see her at last and dismayed at the news about her being injured while out picking blackberries. Esther made lunch and the two women sat in Esther's kitchen while Esther showed Sarah her many embroidered doilies she had made. Sarah came away with a beautiful duchess set for her tallboy that was in her room at her cabin on the mountain.

Sarah didn't see Christian anywhere in town when she went out visiting, and wondered where he might be, but thought it best not to ask anyone, in case they got the impression she was showing too much interest in him.

Martha and Dave Henderson made her welcome when she called on them. Sitting on their back porch in the afternoon sun, they had coffee and cakes while talking about Dave's vegetable and flower garden. Sarah came away with a bunch of flowers, a bag of lemons, and a basket of fresh vegetables. She thanked both Martha and Dave and told Martha she would send Thomas back with her basket. Martha said there was no hurry and the two women hugged before parting company. That was only the first week. Sarah soon ran out of things to do because she couldn't go riding. She felt she could have gone out hunting for rabbits or just ridden out to the ponds to sit on the boulders in the sun. As it were, she obeyed Doc's orders to remain in town and her camp.

Sitting at the firepit having dinner one evening, Sarah and Thomas discussed Thomas's punishment. "I had to sweep out the cells, you should have seen the mess Ma, they were awful dirty, but I swept them and then I got a bucket of water and threw it all over the floors, then I had to mop them dry ...it wasn't too hard, Sheriff Morgan and Clem, they helped me a bit, but I did most of the work, cause, well, it is my punishment." Sarah agreed with Thomas about it being his punishment. She didn't think it too harsh, besides, Thomas looked forward to going to the jailhouse each afternoon.

When their talk eventually came around to school, Thomas got his writing book and showed it to Sarah. "I got the best marks for my writing ...Mister O'Rourke likes my stories." Looking through Thomas's book, although unable to read the words he had written, Sarah could tell how neat his writing was. "Would you read this to me Thomas?" she asked holding the book open and handing it back to him. "Sure Ma." When Thomas began to read, Sarah wrapped her arms around her legs and listened as Thomas narrated his story.

Thomas wrote about trapping the two white wolves. Describing the white of the wolves' coats and the snow-covered mountain in great detail. The story as Thomas told it was beautiful, and vivid. He wrote about Sarah and how she took care of him, and how they were chased by wolves on their way to town. Sarah could see in her mind's eye what Thomas had written. When Thomas finished reading Sarah hugged him. "That was beautiful Thomas, I could see the mountain, and the wolves." Thomas hugged Sarah. "I sure wish you could read it for yourself Ma," he commented, closing his book. "I could never learn to read Thomas ...I am too old," she said looking into the fire and going quiet. "You're not old Ma, I bet Mister O'Rourke could teach you to read, even teach you to write, he is a really good teacher," Thomas yawned. Sarah laughed. "I mean I am too old to sit in a room with young ones such as you." They gave up discussing Sarah learning to read and write when Thomas asked if Billy could come and camp with them on Saturday. "If his folks say he can, then yes, he can come and stay for one night." Thomas hugged her again. "Thanks Ma, I will ask him tomorrow." Sarah decided she would talk to Dave and Martha herself to let them know Thomas would be asking them if Billy could spend the night. Sarah was looking forward to it too. The two boys would help her not think about Christian, and not seeing him.

After Thomas went to bed, Sarah checked him to make sure he was asleep. Thomas lay on his side, his curly hair hanging over the blanket and across his face. Brushing his hair back, Sarah kissed him on the cheek. "Night Ma," Thomas whispered. Sarah thought he had already gone to sleep. "Goodnight Thomas." Going to her side of the shelter, she slipped the flimsy blue shirt carefully over the fresh bandage Doc put on her wound, and removed her trousers. Folding them up along with the shirt and after putting them aside, she lay under the covers waiting to fall asleep, and gave in to thinking about Christian.

The night they made love at the cavern Christian was gentle. Worried he would wake Thomas with his noisy lovemaking, Christian buried his face in her hair to stifle his moans, while she kept her face against Christian's chest when she came, to stifle hers. Even though they were careful not to wake Thomas, Sarah decided she couldn't have Christian come to her camp to be with her, not with Thomas sleeping right alongside her.

Where was Christian now? she wondered. He hadn't been to see her or ask about her wellbeing since leaving Doc Harris's. Maybe he was too busy. Being sheriff was an important role and he no doubt would have a lot to contend with.

Her thoughts eventually came around to what Thomas said after he read his story. Maybe O'Rourke could teach her to read now she had time on her hands, even if it was just a little. Making up her mind to ask O'Rourke if he wouldn't mind teaching her, she went to sleep with a new determination on her mind.

The next morning, Sarah woke early and made herself some ginger tea. She drank the hot liquid, screwing up her nose at the taste, but she had to admit, her stomach felt much better, she even managed to eat a hotcake. Sarah didn't mention to Thomas about her deciding to learn to read and write, she didn't want him to go off to school and blurt it out to O'Rourke before she could talk to O'Rourke herself. Thomas talked incessantly at breakfast about asking Billy to camp with them, and rushed off to school with eagerness. Sarah's day was filled with washing and cleaning inside the shelter and making cookies in readiness to feed Thomas and Billy. Blankets presented her with a real problem when she tried hanging them on the rope line to air. Stretching up hurt her arm, so instead of using the line she had to be content with hanging them over low branches in trees. This turned out better than she expected when the fragrance from the leaves permeated the blankets making them smell clean and fresh.

The afternoon wore on and just before Thomas was due to come out of school Sarah went to the Henderson's. They invited her in to have coffee and while there she asked them if Billy could camp with her and Thomas. Dave said yes to Billy camping with them eagerly. Martha would rather he didn't stay at all, and was a bit more apprehensive when she agreed on one night to see if he liked it, and yes, they both agreed they would not tell Thomas his Ma had already asked. Sarah left the Henderson's feeling happy within herself.

School was still in when Sarah got there, so sitting on a log under a tree outside the schoolhouse waiting, she filled her time by watching people coming and going in the street. Harold Finch headed down the street in the direction of Crawley's store. Sarah still believed Crawley killed her Pa, and Finch, she was absolutely certain, helped steal Thomas away from her, making her despise both men. Roy Connell was another conniving, slimy maggot as far as Sarah was concerned and she would not call any one of the three a man.

She didn't have long to wait before the children came rushing out the door and went running off in all directions. Thomas came out with Billy, jumped off the steps and spotted Sarah sitting on the log. "Ma! what are you doing here?" Billy stood back as Sarah stood up. "I've come to talk to O'Rourke, Thomas why don't you go with Billy, you need to ask Billy's folks if he can camp with us ...hello Billy, you have asked Billy, haven't you?" Sarah smiled over Thomas's head at Billy. "Yeah Ma, I asked him, he wants to camp with us, don't you Billy?" Thomas looked expectantly at Billy. "Yeah, I really do Misses ...um Miss ...um ...Cole!" Billy stammered, not knowing what to call Sarah now he and Thomas were friends. Sarah laughed. "It's Cole Billy, go on you two, and Thomas, don't forget you have to do your punishment, I'll see you back at camp in a while." Thomas said he wouldn't forget and he and Billy ran off. Forgetting what he and his mother discussed the night before, Thomas hoped he wasn't in trouble. "I wonder what Ma wants to talk to Mister O'Rourke about?" Thomas said as they headed to Billy's house.

Sarah entered the schoolhouse cautiously. Jonathon O'Rourke, sitting behind his desk with his head down, looked up as he reached for a piece of paper, and his eyes widened when he saw Sarah at the end of the room. As she approached, he noticed her large hunting knife strapped around her waist and slowly got to his feet. "Cole! ...if it's about Thomas, he's doing fine!" Remembering what happened when they first met, O'Rourke was nervous and it showed in his voice.

Walking right past O'Rourke, and stopping in front of the blackboard Sarah asked. "What are these things on this wall O'Rourke?" Sarah was looking at the letters of the alphabet. "That's the alphabet, and that's a blackboard not a wall." O'Rourke explained nervously. Without looking at O'Rourke Sarah came straight out with her request. "I want to read books and write my name …and I want you to teach me?" Turning from the blackboard, she faced O'Rourke. Hearing Sarah's revelation, O'Rourke swallowed his nervousness. "You don't know how to read …or write?" When Sarah glared at him, he went on. "I would have thought you could, seeing how Thomas does both so well." O'Rourke remained behind his desk. "I wouldn't be asking you O'Rourke, if I could already read and write now, would I?" When Sarah put her hand to her knife, O'Rourke's nervousness returned and he shifted his stance.

"I …I can't teach you Cole!"

"I will pay you."

"It's not the money."

"Then what is it? …you are a teacher …aren't you?"

"Yes, I am a teacher …a very good teacher."

"Then teach me."

"I can't! …not while ever you carry that …that …knife!" O'Rourke said confessing his fear. Sarah dropped her hand down by her side. O'Rourke went on.

"You see …Cole …you get mad at me for something you don't understand, what happens? …you take that knife and …and cut me with it!"

The room was silent for a long time while they stared at each other. "However!" O'Rourke said breaking the silence. "You take your knife off…or …or leave it at your camp …then I could teach you." O'Rourke thought that a reasonable request and waited for Sarah's answer. "I don't take my knife off! …not for no-one O'Rourke!" she said, angry at his suggestion and disappointed at his refusal to teach her.

"Then I am sorry ...I cannot teach you." O'Rourke was worried Sarah might do something now he refused her request. But Sarah turned without saying another word and walked out. Relieved she was gone, O'Rourke sat heavily in his chair. Holding his hands in front of him, he saw how they were shaking. Placing his hand over his chest, he felt how his beating heart had quickened.

Sarah stood outside the schoolhouse trying to think what to do. Neither her father, nor the trappers took the time to teach her to read and write, and when Thomas was just beginning his lessons, she didn't give it a thought, but now she wanted desperately to learn, now the idea had been implanted in her mind and she had the time, she especially wanted to be able to write her name. Coming up with the answer to O'Rourke being afraid of her knife, she turned and hurried back inside.

When Sarah hurried down the aisle towards him and came to a stop directly in front of his desk, O'Rourke stood back up quickly, knocking his chair over in the process and held up his hands to indicate for Sarah to stop whatever she had in mind to do. "Cole ...!" he started, but didn't finish. "If I let you hold my knife while you teach me to read, and write, will you do it? Will you teach me? ...you can give my knife back to me after the lesson." Sarah waited while O'Rourke stared back at her. Had he heard what she said?

Without taking his eyes off Sarah he came up with a solution for the both of them. "I could put your knife here ...in my drawer ... until the lesson is over." O'Rourke pulled out his desk drawer to show Sarah what he meant. "Would that do?" he said, smiling nervously and holding the drawer open while Sarah looked in at all the papers stuffed inside. Sarah didn't smile back. "Yes, O'Rourke ...that would do." O'Rourke closed the drawer. "Then come tomorrow, after class is done ...I will give you an hour each day."

"Another thing," Sarah said, making O'Rourke worry some more. "I don't want you talking about me having lessons with you to anyone! ...understood?" Sarah left O'Rourke looking at her back as she walked out into the afternoon sun. She hadn't smiled or thanked him. Breathing a sigh of relief when she was gone, O'Rourke agreed silently he wouldn't say a word. He didn't want Sarah having an excuse to use her knife on him. When Sarah got outside, she smiled to herself and made her way back to her camp.

Sarah's first lesson commenced the following afternoon. After handing her knife to O'Rourke, O'Rourke put it in his drawer, then started Sarah off with learning the alphabet and making the sounds of each letter. At the end of the lesson he handed her back her knife. Each night after Thomas had gone to sleep Sarah recited the alphabet before going to sleep herself. By the end of the week Sarah could recite the alphabet without looking at the blackboard. Eager to learn now she had started, when the weekend came around Sarah was disappointed.

Billy came to Sarah's camp to spend the night camped on the riverbank. Thomas and Sarah told Billy stories about the mountain and the trappers, leaving Billy in awe of the many stories they told him. Sarah cooked a rabbit she got Martha Henderson to purchase for her from Crawley's store for their dinner. She threaded the rabbit onto a metal rod and hung it over the fire, letting it cook in its own juices. Then just like a real camp out on the prairie, they ate the rabbit with their hands and licked the juices off their fingers when they were done. Sarah made them mugs of hot milk and they ate freshly baked cookies. The boys stayed up late sitting around the fire and talking. When it was time for bed, Sarah slept out at the firepit nearest the river while Billy shared the shelter with Thomas. Sarah listened to the two boys as they talked and laughed for a long time before finally falling silent. When she checked in on them, both were sleeping on their backs side by side, their heads close together. Sarah smiled and went back to the fire. Before Billy went home the next morning, he was excited about having stayed with Thomas and told Sarah he had a good time and asked if he could stay again. Sarah said he could so long as his folks said it was alright. The weekend went by slowly for Sarah, she couldn't wait to get back to her lessons.

Each afternoon for the following week, while Sarah had her lessons, Thomas spent an enjoyable hour after school with Christian at the jailhouse cleaning out the cells, coming back to the camp each afternoon, beaming with happiness. Christian too enjoyed having Thomas there. He learnt a whole lot about the mountain and knew it was a beautiful but dangerous place, and he tried his best to get

Thomas to tell him about Sarah, but Thomas was as evasive as everyone else when it came to talking about her.

Christian wanted to see Sarah, but thought it best to stay away while her arm was healing, besides, he became busy with unruly cowhands and trappers fighting every couple of days in the saloon. One trapper in particular was giving him trouble. Bear was becoming more uncontrollable as the weeks went by, spending most of his time in the jailhouse and getting free meals. Christian was trying to work something out so Bear didn't take up so much of his and Clem's time when Bear himself decided he had better not wear out his welcome.

To stay sober, Bear spent his time out at Major Hardy's with his cowhands, busy rounding up and branding longhorn steers. Meanwhile more steers kept dying out at the dry gulch and neither Christian nor Major Hardy could work out what was killing them.

By the end of the first week of lessons Sarah was enjoying her time with O'Rourke. He was right when he told her he was a good teacher. Sarah told O'Rourke he could call her Sarah if he wished, that it would be alright with her. O'Rourke asked Sarah to call him Jonathon and from then on, their lessons became more relaxed. Jonathon gave Sarah a story book and told her to read it the best she could, she was to draw a circle around the words she didn't know and they would go over the words the next day. When Jonathon gave Sarah her very own pencil, he showed her the proper way to hold it. Frank had given her a small pencil to mark off the days leading up to when they would meet at the shack, but he hadn't cared to show her how to hold it. Thomas had plenty of schooling, and wrote lots of stories, but Sarah never bothered to pick up a pencil and try to write something.

"This is so hard!" Sarah commented while struggling with getting her fingers to hold the pencil. "Pa would never be able to hold one of these," she said, thinking she was talking to herself. Jonathon looked confused. "What do you mean Sarah?" When Sarah realized Jonathon heard what she said, she decided it wouldn't hurt to tell him about her father and the pain he suffered because of his hands. "Pa's hands were bad, he couldn't dress himself ...I had to help him ...with everything," she said sadly, going on to explain her role before her father died. Jonathon was surprised and more than a little confused. Having been privy to talk about the trappers and how Sarah's father signed the deed to the lodge over to Benjamin Crawley because of a card game, this new information made him wonder just how a man with crippled hands could write on a parchment when he could not do up a button to dress himself.

Each night after Thomas went to bed Sarah got her reading book, and sitting at the fire letting the warmth wash over her, opened it and tried reading the words. But some words had too many letters and she didn't know what they meant, so she circled them with the pencil Jonathon had given her for that purpose. By the time Sarah got to the bottom of the first page nearly every word had been circled.

Two weeks after her first lesson, snow began to fall, making it too cold to sit out at the fire. Now was the time the firepit closest to the shelter came into its own. The stone wall at the back of the firepit was high, letting heat from the fire radiate outward, allowing heat to warm the inside of the shelter. While Thomas slept, Sarah, with her lamp burning dully, lay under her blankets and furs with her book. By the end of that second week, the circles grew less and less, until the third week she was half way through the book and the pages had only one or two circles.

Jonathon was proud of Sarah's progress. After handing her a brand-new writing book and starting her on writing, although Sarah's hand was unsteady, she copied letters Jonathon wrote on her first few pages. Most letters were crooked, going outside the lines and filling the page, but each night, Sarah persevered until she got the letters down to a decent size and stayed in the lines. After completing that exercise, Jonathon made her pick letters from the alphabet that spelled her name and write them down. Again, her letters were crooked, but she had written her name for the very first time. When Jonathon looked at her name she wrote, he smiled and congratulated her. Feeling grateful for Jonathon taking the time to teach her when he had children to teach, Sarah showed her gratitude by crying and hugging him. Taken aback by Sarah's way of thanking him, Jonathon gingerly hugged her back. From then on, whenever Sarah and Jonathon saw each other in the street, they greeted each other amicably, giving rise to gossip and inuendo. Only they, and

Jonathon's wife Tilly, whom after hearing the gossip had to be told, were privy to what was really going on.

Sarah practiced writing her name every night until she could write it quickly. Next time when she went to Morley's bank to get money, she told herself, she would sign her full name. In the back of her book, she practiced writing other words and another name.

Sarah's arm was healing well. After her third week of lessons, she visited Doc Harris to get the stitches out. "Ow! Doc that pinched!" she groaned when Doc pulled a stitch from her arm. "Don't be a sook Sarah! you have endured far worse than these few stitches." The door opened and Gerda came in with steaming mugs of coffee and small cakes and the three of them sat around talking.

"I want to go to the ponds to bathe, I haven't been able to wash my hair for weeks," Sarah said biting into a cake. "Yum! Gerda did you make these?" she asked with her mouth full. "No, Martha Henderson made them, isn't it too cold to go bathing in the ponds? it's snowing you know." Gerda watched Sarah lick her fingers. "It hasn't been snowing long enough for the ponds to freeze over yet, besides, they are sheltered." Sarah could handle the cold in an effort to be clean. She hated it when her hair became dull and limp. Gerda glanced at Doc, worried Sarah was putting herself at risk by bathing out in the open, any man out riding could come across her. "You can bathe here Sarah," Gerda offered." No, it's alright ...I would rather go to the ponds, Star hasn't been for a run for weeks, Ham has only run him in the corrals and that isn't good enough ...Star needs to run free." Knowing all about Sarah's stubbornness, Gerda gave up. "Well, if you must, but you be very careful out there." It had been more than a month since Sarah had been with Christian at the cavern. Sarah asked Doc and Gerda again not to say anything until she decided what she was going to do.

Chapter Twenty-eight

Although Sarah's lessons with Jonathon were going well and Doc had taken the stitches out of her arm, Christian hadn't been anywhere near her to find out how she was. So instead of venturing out to bathe, Sarah decided she needed to know why Christian hadn't been to see her. Cedar Creek was a quiet place, most of the time, so he couldn't be that busy, she thought. Desperately wanting to be with him, she formulated a plan. Her plan was simple, she would ask Christian to have dinner with her and Thomas.

Before inviting Christian to dinner though, she needed to borrow crockery and cutlery, she only had two tin plates and two tin mugs, one for herself and one for Thomas, so she headed for Ham's Livery. When she got there, Ham sent her straight through to their residence where she found Patrice busy baking.

"What brings you here Sarah?" Patrice asked, putting a tray of cookies in her oven.

"I need your help," Sarah began awkwardly. "I'm thinking of asking Sheriff Morgan to dinner …and I need to borrow some things." Patrice smiled at Sarah's sudden show of interest in Christian. "Well now, it's about time you did something about the sheriff," Patrice said, pouring coffee into two mugs and handing one to Sarah. "I'm not doing anything about the sheriff, I'm just asking him to dinner …besides, Thomas will be there," Sarah added hastily. The next couple of hours was spent trying to avoid Patrice questioning her about her relationship with Christian. After Patrice agreed to get her a rabbit from Crawley's store, saving her from having to ask Christian to go with her, she left, and made her way back to her camp with a basket of items to help set the scene for her dinner.

Not needing the items in the basket until later that night, Sarah sat the basket inside her shelter and covered it with a blanket. Now she had to get up the courage to ask Christian if he would have dinner with her. Sarah felt her body tingle with excitement, but when she got to the door of the Sheriff's Office, she stopped. Taking a deep breath and feeling nervous, she opened the door.

Stepping inside, a sudden feeling of disappointment started in the pit of her stomach when seeing Clem sitting in the sheriff's chair and not Christian. Clem looked up and leant back in the chair when Sarah came in. "Howdy Cole, you looking for the sheriff?" Clem looked at ease sitting in what used to be his chair. "Yes Clem, I am," Sarah said with obvious disappointment. "You will find him at the corrals with Joe and Fergus, they brought in a mare and he's gone to take a look at it." Sarah didn't wait for Clem to go on, she darted out the door and up the street to the corrals.

Fergus was holding the mare by its tether, while Joe and Christian were looking over the horse, when Fergus spotted Sarah hurrying toward them. "Uh oh! would this be trouble coming Joe?" Fergus remarked, nodding in Sarah's direction. Joe and Christian both turned to see Sarah walking at a brisk pace toward them. Her hips swayed, her arms swung by her sides, her long ponytail swished from side to side as she strode toward the men. The smile Christian had on his face while checking the horse faded. He hadn't had time since bringing Sarah back from the cavern to visit her, things around town had become hectic. Amongst other things, several farmers had trouble with horses going missing. They accused each other of stealing each other's horses and he had to settle the dispute before they came to blows. He spent several days out in the foothills where he located the horses running wild and took them back to the farmers. Two cowhands, out at Major Hardy's ranch, had to be arrested for trying to kill each other over a saloon girl. They had to be brought back to the jailhouse and locked up for a time. "I don't think she has anything to be mad about, do you?" Joe asked, watching the smile fade from Christian's face. "I can't think of anything Joe," Christian replied, not knowing if he should prepare himself for a fight or not. Sarah didn't look angry.

Walking up to the three men, Sarah gave Christian a sideways glance before greeting the two trappers. "Afternoon Joe, Fergus." Joe and Fergus greeted her pleasantly. Christian stood off to one side and Sarah turned to face him. "Can I talk to you Chris ...um sheriff?" Sarah hadn't so much as greeted him and almost slipped up when she went to call him Christian in front of Joe and Fergus. While wondering what she wanted to talk to him about, Christian looked from Joe to Fergus then back to Sarah. "Sure Cole, you can talk to me," he replied, hoping she wasn't going to cause a scene like she had the first time they had been together when she accused him of using her. Putting his hands on his hips, he waited for her to start talking.

Sarah looked into Christian's eyes. Christian looked into hers, and couldn't help thinking, 'wow! her eyes are beautiful.' Taking a deep breath to calm herself, Sarah came straight out with what she wanted to ask him. "Would you have dinner with Thomas and me tonight?" Her heart was racing, there, it was out, the hard part was over, now she hoped Christian would say yes. Sarah couldn't see any reason why he wouldn't say yes to her invitation, surely, he would like to have dinner with her, after all, they had been intimate, twice now. But Christian hadn't expected Sarah's invitation, and was surprised by it. Of course he wanted to see her, but circumstances forced him to keep putting it off. Now here she was asking him to dinner, and he didn't know what to say. Joe was surprised too, but trying to suppress a smile, turned his attention to Fergus and the mare. "Let's take this horse back into the corral," he said, moving away to give Sarah and Christian some privacy.

Sarah's invitation could not have come at a worse time for Christian as well as Sarah. "I'm sorry Cole," Christian started. "But I have been invited elsewhere tonight." Sarah was crestfallen. Christian's refusal was not what she expected. "Oh!" she exclaimed. Thinking she knew whom that someone would be, her face turned pink with embarrassment. "Alright ...um ...sorry ...I should have known better than to have asked." Turning to hide her disappointment, she made her escape. "Maybe another time Cole!" Christian called as she began to get further away. "Yeah ...maybe," she said over her shoulder. Much preferring to have dinner with Sarah, Christian felt sorry for having to say no to her, but he didn't know how to get out of dinner with Millicent and her father. He didn't like to disappoint Millicent either. He watched Sarah walk as far as the Livery and turn down the alley out of sight.

Joe and Fergus, having moved out of earshot, didn't hear the exchange between Sarah and Christian, but they caught a glimpse of disappointment on Sarah's face. The exchange between the two had been brief, and they watched Christian watching Sarah as she walked away. When Christian went back to the men, Joe and Fergus knew what they discussed was none of their business so they didn't ask him what happened. After exchanging looks, Joe and Fergus got back to business with the mare. Fergus took the horse around the corral while Joe, and Christian, both deep in thought, watched him.

Feeling stupid because of Christian's refusal, Sarah hurried back to her camp. Racing into her shelter, she knelt down on the furs to think. Why did she ever think Christian would have dinner with her? Her plans were ruined because he would rather have dinner with Millicent Crawley. Sarah was sure it was Millicent Christian was having dinner with after seeing them talking to each other on several occasions. 'Maybe' she thought. 'Christian preferred Millicent over her.' It was almost time for Thomas to come from school, so holding back tears, she took a deep breath and decided, instead of dinner tonight, tomorrow she would take Thomas out riding. Tomorrow would be Saturday and he didn't have school. They could pack a picnic lunch and ride out to the ponds or the swimming hole, she would let Thomas decide. To make herself feel better, she took a walk in the opposite direction to town. Walking as far as she could along the riverbank before it became too treacherous to go further. Steep cliffs jutted upward and the river ran in torrents over submerged boulders on its way to the waterfall. On her way back, and still feeling like she wasn't over her disappointment, she picked up deadwood for her fire.

Leaving Joe and Fergus with the mare, Christian walked quickly over to Crawley's General Store and went in. With hat in hand he asked Crawley if Millicent was home. "She most certainly is sheriff, come on through." Crawley greeted Christian happily, before leading him through to the back of the store where he opened a door to the living quarters and showed him in. "She's in the dining room, getting things ready for tonight." Christian thanked him and went through to the dining room.

Christian hoped Millicent wasn't going to too much trouble, but when he walked in, the table was already being set for dinner.

There was a very large silver vase of fresh flowers and a huge silver candlestick that looked right out of place sitting in the middle of the table. They looked more like they would be at home in the formal dining room at the lodge. White, gold edged plates and crystal wine glasses sat between silver knives, forks and spoons Millicent was placing in front of three ornate tapestry chairs. Holding a fork in her hand, she looked up and smiled at Christian. "Hello Christian! I hope you have a healthy appetite, because I am baking a huge banquet for tonight." That worried Christian, now he had to let Millicent down as gently as he could. "That is why I am here Millicent …I have …um …bad news." The smile faded from Millicent's face. Stopping what she was doing, she narrowed her eyes and peered across the table at Christian. "What is it Christian? What bad news could you possibly have?" she said through gritted teeth.

Christian didn't quite know how to start. Millicent was going to be disappointed no matter how he said it. He took a deep breath. "I am sorry, but I am unable to come to dinner tonight …I …something urgent has come up and, well, I have to be somewhere else." Fidgeting with the brim of his hat, he waited for Millicent to say something.

Millicent could tell he was lying, she stared at him for what seemed a very long time. "Where do you have to be that is more important than being here? Sheriff!" Christian noticed her tone had changed from one of cheerfulness to one of anger. "I have important things to attend to Millicent, that is all …I'm sorry." Millicent's next words threw him completely. "No doubt, your …important things! are going to see that bitch! Cole!" Christian looked stunned, that was exactly what he intended, but how could Millicent possibly know that? "Go ahead then sheriff! go be with that whore!" Astounded by Millicent's derogatory remarks about Sarah, Christian disliked her right then, thinking her not a very respectable woman to call another woman a whore, he thought a lady would not do that.

Just as Millicent threw the fork she was holding, at him, Christian ducked. The fork, luckily, sailed past and embedded itself in the wall behind him. "Get out!" Millicent screamed. Christian tried apologizing again but it was no use, Millicent would not hear of it. "Get out! …Oh! just …get out!" she screamed again. Deciding it best if he left by the side entrance, Christian walked away quickly. Hearing Millicent screaming for her father, "daddy! ...daddy!" he was glad he wasn't having dinner there tonight.

Hurrying across the street and down the trail, he approached Sarah's camp carefully. After just having a narrow escape with a fork, he wondered what sort of reception he would get there. Sarah carried her large hunting knife everywhere she went, and if she chose to use it on him, he had better be prepared. Seeing Sarah wasn't by her fire, he called out, and when she didn't answer, he looked inside her shelter. Feeling disappointed when it became obvious Sarah wasn't at her camp, he was about to walk away when he saw her walking toward him with her arms loaded with firewood. Having spied Christian standing near her firepit, Sarah slowed but kept walking toward him. "What do you want sheriff?" she asked, dropping the bundle of wood near the pit and brushing snow and dirt off her sleeves.

Christian removed his hat like he had at the Crawley's and held it in front of him. "My plans for this evening have changed ...I ...I find I am free after all ...your invitation to dinner, would it still be open?" His face remained sombre as he watched Sarah drop the wood, but his heart was racing. Sarah felt her heart start to race and tried to keep from smiling. "Yes, my invitation is still open." Christian almost sighed aloud with relief. "What time would you like me to be here?" His heart began to beat faster at wanting to take Sarah in his arms and kiss her right there where they were standing. "I don't know, what time would suit you?" Sarah didn't know time, she knew to get up at dawn, she knew to eat when she was hungry, and she went to bed any time after dark.

"How about seven o'clock?" Christian decided for them. "Seven o'clock," Sarah repeated, locking it in her memory. "That would do." Christian was glad that was settled. "Alright," he said, putting his hat back on. "I will see you at seven ...Sarah." Walking back up the trail with a broad smile on his face, he felt relieved when she hadn't admonished him for calling her Sarah. Sarah waited until he disappeared around the corner of the trail, then smiling, raced inside her shelter to get the basket. She had to move fast to get her cooking organized.

"The rabbit!" she cried, suddenly remembering it. Running along the riverbank, up the track to the Livery, racing past Ham at his forge, she charged inside to Patrice. Patrice wanted to know details but Sarah didn't have time to stop and talk, she had a lot to do. Giving her the rabbit, Sarah raced back along the riverbank. The rabbit thankfully was already skinned and gutted, all she had to do was get it in the pot. Cutting the rabbit into pieces, she seared it in the pot then added onion, herbs and her own spices that made her recipe special. Before adding vegetables, her stew had to cook for several hours for the rabbit to be tender. That done, she set about making a lemon pie. Deciding to leave her bathing until she went to the ponds, she made do with a bucket of warm water instead. Dressed in her new trousers and shirt Christian bought her, she ran her hands over the material, loving the little blue/grey flowers that adorned the shirt, and admiring the lace on the edge of the sleeves and collar.

Benjamin Crawley consoled his daughter, then went back to his store. Standing behind his store window, he watched Christian heading back to the Sheriff's Office with a spring in his step. Christian looked happy and walked with vigour. "That bitch!" Crawley swore out aloud. "She's doing it again!"

There was a time when Frank Mason was being groomed by his father Major Hardy to become Millicent's husband, and he was helping by pushing his daughter toward Frank. If they had married, with Frank's father being a very wealthy man, his daughter would have become a rich woman. Only for Calahan Cole, Sarah Cole's father, Millicent would have been ensconced in Mountain View Lodge too. Cursing silently in anger at the reason why he and Millicent weren't living in the lodge, he kept peering out the window. "That whore stole Frank from Millicent and now she is digging her claws into Sheriff Morgan, Millicent and Sheriff Morgan met months before Cole, so he should be hers, but that whore didn't take long to let the sheriff get between her legs, everyone in town knows what they are up to, well, I will be damned if Cole is going to get away with stealing Millicent's man this time …I will fucking make sure of that!" His cursing stopped when several customers interrupted him when they entered his store.

"Did Cole find you?" Clem asked Christian when he came in. "Yes, she did, can you take over for me tonight, I'm having dinner with her," Christian smiled. "And Thomas" he added. "Sure, happy to oblige." Clem was relieved Christian and Sarah were on friendly terms. Having heard gossip about them, he thought, 'maybe them getting together would be good for everyone.' Thinking of his wife at home alone and how she understood his job kept him away most nights, and how she would go to bed without him …again! Clem was happy to go home much later if it meant the town would be peaceful.

Christian rushed off to the lodge to get ready. After shaving, he heated up a tub of water and climbed in. While soaking, and smiling to himself as he lathered himself all over, he thought about Sarah and him at the cavern and of Thomas sleeping on the other side of the fire, and how they had been as quiet as they could be so as not to wake him when they made love. Remembering Sarah telling him Thomas was going to be there at dinner, he felt sure there wouldn't be any love making. At least, he would endeavour not to put himself in a situation where he and Sarah would be alone together.

Dinner should be interesting, he told himself while getting dressed. Sarah doesn't have a table, so there won't be any fancy dinner plates or candlesticks. He imagined they would sit around the camp fire and balance their plates on their laps. He smiled to himself at the very thought.

After playing at Billy Henderson's house, Thomas came bounding down the trail at a run, and stopped short at seeing his mother wearing her new clothes. "Woah! Ma! you look nice! where you going all dressed up?" Never having had any compliments about the way she looked, Sarah blushed at her son's compliment. "Thank you, Thomas, but I'm not going anywhere," she said stirring the stew. "Well, why are you wearing your new clothes?"

Thomas sat next to Sarah and smelt the stew cooking. "Sheriff Morgan is coming for dinner tonight and I…" she didn't get to finish. "Sheriff Morgan! Why Ma? Why is he coming for dinner?" Thomas was excited at the prospect of Christian coming to dinner. All because of Christian, he and Billy had become best friends.

"Because I invited him, now I have to ask you to wash and do your hair, Sheriff Morgan will be here at seven o'clock." Thomas looked at his mother and frowned. Racing to the shelter to the box where he kept his father's drawing book and timepiece, he took out the timepiece and looked at the time. It was four o'clock, Christian wouldn't be here for another three hours. He went back to the fire where Sarah was busy with her pot.

"Ma, it's a long time until seven o'clock."

"How long is it Thomas?"

"Three hours …Ma …you got ready way too early." They both laughed. "Well, at least the rabbit will be cooked." Sarah blushed and stirred the stew again. After washing and combing his hair, Thomas waited by the fire, wishing the time would go faster so Christian would come. "Where are we going to eat Ma?"

"I guess on our laps as usual, what we need is a table but…" Sarah put her hands on her hips and looked around the camp. There was nothing they could use as a table.

"I can make a table!" Thomas exclaimed excitedly. Before Sarah could ask him how he could make a table, he ran up the track behind the Ferguson House and a few minutes later came back carrying a flat board. Laying it on the ground near the shelter, he built four piles of stones, then sat the board on top of the stones where it balanced perfectly.

"What do you think Ma?" Both studied the makeshift table, then sat down and crossed their legs under it.

"This is perfect Thomas," Sarah said. Thomas was pleased with himself for thinking of it. "But we need something to sit on." Going to the shelter, Sarah carried out pillows, dropped them on the ground, then sitting on them, found them to be comfortable. Thomas could see his Ma was happy. He always tried to make her happy, but sometimes it was hard work, tonight was going to be special.

A tablecloth Patrice leant Sarah was placed over the makeshift table, where it hung over the edge, covering the piles of stones the board sat on. While Sarah saw to dinner, Thomas ran amongst the trees and came back carrying a bunch of ferns and pieces of foliage. Finding an empty tin and filling it with water, he put the ferns and foliage in it and sat it in the middle of the table, then stepped back so both Sarah and he could see his handy-work. "The table looks lovely Thomas." Planning for Thomas to sit between her and Christian, Sarah set wine glasses in front of the plates opposite each other.

"Something is missing Ma," Thomas said studying the table. "I know!" he exclaimed, running to the storage box. Finding more empty tins, and using his knife to punch holes in them, he dropped a candle in one, and sat it on the table next to the tin of shrubbery. "When we light it, it will shine over everything," Thomas smiled. As the sun dropped below the horizon and night fell, candles placed inside other tins he hung from trees as lanterns, let dappled light shine into the tree canopies and onto the shelter, making it look magical. Standing together, they admired their camp.

"It looks like a magic place Ma." Sarah could see what he meant. Putting her arm around his shoulders she turned her gaze to the sky filled with twinkling stars. She couldn't have asked for a better night. Thomas looked at his timepiece. "It's almost time Ma." On hearing what he said, Sarah began to get nervous.

Christian was dressed and ready, but far too early to go to Sarah's camp. To fill in time he went to his office to discuss Clem's retirement again. After leaving Clem, he walked across to the saloon where he got a lot of looks and wisecracks from men standing at the bar. Christian tried ignoring their cajoling. "Where you off to all spruced up like a dandy sheriff?" One of Major Hardy's men drunkenly slurred at him. "She must be extra special!" Another remarked, and they all laughed. Christian didn't answer. Major Hardy's men would drink their hard-earnt cash and go back to the ranch with sore heads. There were no guns, but when the night wears on there would be a few fights. If there was any trouble, Christian felt sure Clem could handle it just for tonight. Foley and Brady, sitting at a table in a far corner having a quiet drink stared at him. Christian nodded in their direction, then bought a bottle of wine to take as a gift to Sarah. They nodded back, swallowed their drinks, then got up and left.

"It's time Ma." After stirring the pot once more, Sarah put the wooden spoon to her mouth and tasted. The stew tasted perfect, she only hoped Christian wouldn't be late so it wouldn't spoil. Thomas kept watching the trail. "Go put your timepiece away," Sarah ordered, not looking up. "Ma!" Thomas tapped her on her shoulder. "What is it, Thomas?" Sarah asked, busy with the fire. "Ma, he's here." Sarah looked up. Christian was coming down the trail carrying a bottle in his hand. Taking him in with her eyes, Sarah thought Christian looked handsome. He had dressed especially for their dinner and her heart raced at the sight of him. "Hello Sarah! Hello Thomas!" Standing on the opposite side of the fire, his eyes on Sarah, he noticed her hair twisted in a long braid, was secured with the cream ribbon he bought when he bought the shirt and trousers she was wearing. She looked lovely, and Christian couldn't help noticing the buttons of her pretty shirt were undone to her bust, allowing him a glimpse of her breasts at the opening.

Smelling the aroma of the stew, Christian looked around and took in what they had done to their camp. "Hello Sheriff Morgan," Thomas said, watching Christian's face as he took in the tins hanging in the trees. Christian liked the glow the lanterns made, and the table with it sparkling centre-piece. "This is really something," he smiled. "Do you like it sheriff?" Thomas asked. "I do Thomas," Christian said, looking across at Sarah. "Very much," he said softly, making Sarah blush. "Thomas did the decorating, it's not too much is it?" she asked, feeling a little embarrassed that they may have made their camp look too fancy.

"Not at all, it looks perfect," Christian said holding out the bottle of wine. "I thought we could have wine with dinner." Thinking the reason Sarah doesn't drink is because she blames herself for giving her father whiskey the night he went to the saloon, the night he died, Thomas snapped, "Ma doesn't drink!" But that wasn't the only reason she didn't drink. Christian pulled the bottle back before Sarah could take it. "It's fine Thomas, Christian can have a drink with dinner." Sarah took the bottle. "I'll just put it in the river to keep it cool for now." Christian watched Sarah tie a piece of twine around the neck of the bottle and sit the bottle in the water at the edge of the river. "Sorry, I didn't know you didn't drink," Christian said, apologizing when she came back to the fire. Sarah hesitated before speaking. "It's just that … I've never tried it." She didn't like to lie, but she tasted wine the night Frank had been whipped and hadn't liked the taste then, and hadn't had a drink since. It didn't matter to Sarah if Christian wanted to have a drink with dinner.

While Sarah served the food, Christian complimented them again on the camp. "It looks like magic, doesn't it, sheriff?" Thomas was back to his happy mood. "It certainly does." Christian smiled as he looked around again. Handing Christian his plate of stew, Sarah was glad the candlelight wasn't bright so Christian couldn't see her blushing. When their eyes met across the table Christian saw her clearly. He liked it when she blushed. It gave her the appearance of innocence.

As they ate, Sarah kept glancing at Christian and he her. The stew was delicious, the meat fell off the bones and Christian and Thomas both ate heartily. "This is yum Ma! what do you think of Ma's cooking sheriff?" Thomas was very talkative and Sarah was glad he was there. "It's really good Thomas." Christian looked across the table. "This is delicious Sarah." Sarah looked down at her plate. "Oh!" she suddenly exclaimed, getting up and heading toward the river. Christian and Thomas both watched her lift the bottle of wine out of the water and bring it to the table where she handed it to Christian. "You can open it Christian and ...I would like to try some, please." Thomas looked from Sarah to Christian and could see by the way his Ma and Christian were looking at each other they definitely liked each other. Thomas ate his stew while Christian poured two glasses of wine.

When Christian handed Sarah her glass, she took it, and Christian lifted his glass. "What shall we toast to?" Christian said keeping his eyes on Sarah. "I want to toast too!" Thomas interrupted loudly. Putting down her glass and going back to the river, Sarah carried a large glass jar to the table, unscrewed the lid and poured some of the cloudy liquid into one of the cups. "What is that you are pouring?" Christian asked curiously. "It's called lemonade, I made it earlier today." A slice of lemon plonked into the cup. "May I try some? ...please," Christian asked politely. When Sarah poured him a taste, he drank the sweet lemony flavoured water, raised his eyebrows and smacked his lips together. "This is nice, very refreshing." He had tasted lemonade once before, when Millicent Crawley made it, and it had tasted bitter. Sarah made good lemonade, and her stew was excellent.

Sarah held up her glass. "To nice lemonade." Christian and Thomas laughed. Sarah laughed too and took a sip of her wine. Christian smiled and drank his wine. Thomas drank his lemonade.

While Sarah was over at the supply box getting the lemon pie, Christian and Thomas chatted about school and hunting, letting their talk gradually come around to fishing. "Do you want to go fishing sometime sheriff? I know a good place for fishing." Thomas was eager to stay friends with Christian now he had finished his punishment. "I would like that Thomas, I will let you know when I have time and we will go." When Sarah came back, he added. "If that is alright with your Ma." Sarah sat the pie on the table. "I'm sure that will be fine," she said. Glad Thomas and Christian were getting along, she headed back to the river to get the pot of cream Patrice had given her.

"I like your table Thomas," Christian said after Sarah left. Thomas blushed and went quiet. "Where did you get it?" Christian didn't have a clue where Thomas would have found a table. "It was just lying about." Thomas hoped Christian wouldn't ask him anything more. "How did you manage to build it?" Christian lifted the tablecloth, and bending down, took a look underneath to see how the table was put together. Satisfied at seeing the stones the table sat on, he bent his head further, and saw red painted letters on the underside of the board. Thomas's heart beat fast. Now he was in big trouble. He swallowed the rest of his lemonade in one gulp. Christian sat back up and putting the tablecloth down, looked toward the river where Sarah was getting the cream, then looked at Thomas, and Thomas looked at him.

Feeling like he had ruined his Ma's special dinner, Thomas watched Christian closely. Christian couldn't believe what he had seen under the cloth. The board was the right size and the red letters were what he had painted. 'No Firearms Permitted in the Town Limits, By Order of The Sheriff' screamed at him from under the table. Thinking it was ingenious of Thomas, Christian began to laugh, quietly at first. They needed a table and Thomas had found a perfect one. Christian laughed louder. "We needed a table," Thomas giggled. Christian put his head back and laughed loudly, Thomas laughed louder too. By the time Sarah came back with the cream, both Christian and Thomas were laughing so hard they had tears in their eyes. Sarah glared at them. "What are you two laughing about?" she asked seriously as she sat down on her pillow.

Both Christian and Thomas stopped laughing and looked at Sarah, then, looking at each other, started laughing again. "Stop it! both of you!" Sarah said, thinking they were laughing at her, and not happy about it. Christian's face still held a huge grin when he sighed. "Sorry Sarah, have a look under the table." Bending sideways, looking at the piles of stones, Sarah could see they looked as they should, but then, red lettering seemed to glare at her. Not knowing what it meant, she straightened up. "I don't see what you are..." she stopped suddenly, her eyes going wide. Bending down again to take another look, she quickly dropped the tablecloth and straightened up. "Goddamn it! Thomas!" she exclaimed looking horrified at Thomas, then at Christian. "I ...I don't know what to say, Christian ...I'm sorry." Christian stopped laughing when he saw how serious Sarah had become. "It's alright," he said. "Just make sure you put my sign back tomorrow Thomas." Then smiling, tousled Thomas's hair. "You're not mad?" Sarah looked incredulously at Christian. "No, I'm not mad," he said, holding up his plate. "May I have a piece of your pie now, please?" Thomas held his plate up too. "Can I have some too Ma?" They all laughed at how funny the situation was, and Sarah cut them all a piece of pie.

The pie was delicious, Thomas had two pieces. "Would you like another glass of wine Sarah." Christian held up the bottle. "No, thank you ...I'm sorry Christian, but I don't like it." Sarah and Thomas watched Christian get up and carry the bottle over to the trees where he tipped the bottle up and poured out its contents. Carrying the empty bottle back to the table he asked, "how about some coffee?"

"You could have finished your wine Christian," Sarah said as he sat down.

"I didn't like it much either," he replied. Seeing their eyes meet across the table, Thomas decided his Ma should spend the rest of the evening alone with Christian. "I'm so full Ma, I'm going to bed." He had a really good time, and because Christian hadn't been mad about the sign, he liked Christian even more. "Good night Sheriff Morgan."

"Good night Thomas, don't forget to take my sign back in the morning," he reminded Thomas with a smile. "I won't, good night

Ma," Thomas said, hugging Sarah and putting his mouth close to her ear. "I love you Ma," he whispered, then kissed her quickly on the cheek. "I love you Thomas ...I will come check on you later." When Sarah kissed Thomas back, Christian watched the exchange between mother and son and envied the love they had for each other. He had never known the kind of love a mother had for her son, or the love a son had for his mother. His childhood had been full of hate and a need to survive. He had been starved of real love all his life, until he met Sarah. He looked at Sarah and felt the love he had for her rising in his chest. Wanting her to love him like only a woman could love a man. "Ok Ma!" Thomas said disappearing into the shelter.

When Sarah and Christian were alone, Sarah suggested they have their coffee in front of the firepit. Sitting beside her, Christian's arm brushed Sarah's, sending a surge of emotion rushing through him. "How is your arm Sarah?" he asked, trying to distract himself from his feelings. When Sarah handed Christian his mug their hands touched, causing a sudden tingle of desire to run through her arm to her chest. "Doc has taken the stitches out, he says it looks good," she answered dreamily, looking into Christian's eyes. Christian took Sarah's mug from her, and sitting it on the edge of the firepit next to his, leant forward and kissed her softly. Sarah returned his kiss, then Christian let her go. Pulling her toward him again, he kissed her passionately. "Sarah," he whispered letting out a groan. "Christian," Sarah whispered. Standing up, Christian took hold of Sarah's hand and pulled her to her feet. "Take a walk with me," he urged. Holding his hand, Sarah replied, "I can't go far Christian ...I don't like to leave Thomas."

"We won't go far," Christian said.

After walking away from the camp and taking Sarah into his arms, Sarah slipped her arms around Christian's neck and opened her mouth to his and kissed him. When their tongues brushed together, Christian pulled Sarah's shirt out of her trousers. Sliding his hands over the smoothness of her back, caused his desire for her to rise in him. Groaning inwardly, he remembered he hadn't come to Sarah's camp to make love to her, so he stopped kissing her, removed his hands, and pulled her shirt down to cover her, then stepped back. "I better go," he said without feeling. Confused, Sarah quickly straightened herself up, and while tucking her shirt back in her trousers, with a feeling of disappointed washing over her, she asked herself what just happened. 'Why did Christian stop? Didn't he want to make love to me? Why did he bring me here if he isn't going to make love to me?'

Christian didn't want to spoil the evening by making love to Sarah on the cold, damp ground amongst trees and bushes, and because Thomas was sleeping in her shelter, he wouldn't risk making love to her like he had at the cavern when he was so close. Taking Sarah's hand, he led her back to her camp and the fire. "It was a lovely dinner Sarah."

"Thank you Christian." Sadness filled Sarah's eyes as she looked up at him. "What are you thanking me for?" Christian frowned. He hadn't done anything that warranted him being thanked. "I'm thanking you for coming to dinner and for not being angry at Thomas for taking your sign." Sarah smiled halfheartedly at him. "What Thomas did was just something I probably would have done when I was his age," Christian smiled.

"What were you doing at his age Christian?" By asking him about himself, Sarah hoped he might stay a little longer, perhaps then he might reconsider making love to her. Christian thought Sarah asked him that question once before, when he told her he had been brought up in an orphanage, obviously she didn't remember, so he didn't remind her. "I better go." Bending his head, he kissed her softly, on her cheek. "Thank you for dinner," he said pushing her away gently and starting to leave. "Be sure and see Thomas takes my sign back, I wouldn't want anyone coming to town thinking they can have their guns!" His words echoed over the river as Sarah watched him disappear along the trail.

The evening hadn't ended at all the way Sarah planned. She wanted Christian to hold her and make love to her, just like he did at the cavern, perhaps then it would prove he loved her and not Millicent Crawley. She went through the same torment thinking Frank was in love with Millicent, and didn't think she could go through that uncertainty again.

When Sarah went to bed, she thought of another reason why Christian suddenly stopped touching her. With Thomas sleeping right next to her, he wouldn't stay. But Sarah couldn't convince herself Thomas was the reason. Thomas would always be where she was, he was her son, and Christian, if he loved her, would have to accept him.

Christian hadn't wanted to leave. His body ached for Sarah but he thought she hadn't invited him to dinner just so he could take her into the bushes and make love to her. He wanted desperately to make love to her, but didn't want to do it out in the open every time they met. He was determined to refrain from temptation until such time as he could get her to sleep with him at the lodge.

Chapter Twenty-nine

It was the end of another busy week. Dinner with Sarah and Thomas had been relegated to Christian's memory, too much had happened since then. He hadn't realized such a small town could have so many problems when he agreed to take on the role of sheriff. Major Hardy's men had been paid and were in a hurry to get to the saloon to get a well-earned drink into them. They had become used to leaving their guns with Christian and he knew which guns belonged to whom now and had no problem tagging each man's weapon. Clem was over at the saloon trying to break up a fight already. After several weeks of staying out of trouble, Bear was at it again. He drank his fill of whiskey and now was hungry for food. Knowing he would get fed if he was locked in the jailhouse for the night, he did what he usually did. He smashed a whole lot of glasses by swiping them all off the bar and started a fight with the barkeeper. Clem didn't have to force Bear to follow him to the jailhouse. Bear happily went along to get his free meal and a quiet cell to sleep in where he could snore as loud as he wanted without the trappers or cowhands telling him to, 'shut the fuck up!' so they could get some sleep.

At the same time Bear was being carted off to the jailhouse, Christian was in his office checking in guns when two strangers rode into town. The men read the sign erected near the Trading Post as they passed it and ignored what the sign said. The two men tethered their horses to the hitching rail outside the saloon, then went inside. The saloon was already full of cowhands, and noisy. The light was dull, smoke from the many cheroots being inhaled, filled the air. The crowd of men at the end of the bar watched the two men come in and saw they still wore their guns. Al, one of

Major Hardy's younger, more daring cowhands already had a few drinks under his belt. These two leather slappers were new in town and Al thought maybe they hadn't understood the sign, so feeling invincible, sidled up to the two men at the bar.

"We got a sign outside town says you got to hand your guns over to the sheriff when you come to town," Al slurred. The two men ordered a whiskey each, then faced off with Al.

"We don't hand our guns over to the likes of no-good sidewinders, and anyone tries taken em, better be good with his gun." The tallest, meanest looking man of the two looked down at Al, sneered at him then turned back to the bar.

"Well, Sheriff Morgan won't be too happy about you wearing those things, he'll take em off you." Al was getting a bit too close for the men's liking when he grinned. The smell of bad breath and whiskey made the tall man closest to him cringe. Flinging his arm out sideways, he grabbed Al by the front of his shirt and pulled him close to his face. "You tell your sheriff he can go to hell, cause he ain't gettin our guns!" Letting Al go with a violent shove, Al stumbled back and bumped into men drinking at the bar. The drinkers, becoming angry at their drinks being spilt, shoved him back toward the two strangers. When Al stumbled against them, the strangers glared at him and put their hands to their guns. Al still had enough sense to take this as his cue to leave. Staggering out of the saloon, Al serpentined all the way to the Sheriff's Office.

Unbeknown to the cowhands, the two men were on the run from the law. Robbing a bank in Moreton, they made their getaway. The posse chasing them lost them in the foothills surrounding the town, and didn't go any further. The outlaws, wanting to lie low, didn't need trouble from Cedar Creek's sheriff, so decided to keep moving. There were plenty of other towns that would welcome them. Swallowing their whiskies, they headed out the door.

Feeling out of breath when he rushed to the Sheriff's Office, Al stammered nervously, while Christian waited patiently for him to tell him what he was trying to say. "Two …two strangers," he puffed. "In the saloon …just come in and are packin," he kept puffing. "I tried tellin em to hand em in …but they didn't take too kindly to me tellin em."

"Ok Al, let's go see what the trouble is." Christian grabbed his hat, and because there was no telling how fast these two strangers were with their guns, and wanting to be ready, he lifted his gun up and down in its holster. Clem was still busy getting Bear in a cell so Christian decided he could handle the two men on his own, after all, he was a pretty good shot and thought himself fast at the draw.

Christian stepped into the street just as another bunch of cowhands from Major Hardy's ranch came riding in, Foley and Brady amongst them. Having no doubt the men would head to the jailhouse first to hand in their guns, Christian nodded to them and then confronted the two outlaws.

Keen to hand in their guns, several cowhands pulled their horses up to the hitching rail outside the Sheriff's Office, but before they could go inside, they watched their sheriff standing in the middle of the street facing off with two leather slappers they saw come out of the saloon.

Foley and Brady pulled their horses up close to Doc's practice. Foley indicated to Brady, and they both stepped over to the opposite side of the street to stand behind Christian where they could keep their eyes on the two men he was facing. The few trappers still in town were busy up at the corrals and didn't know what was taking place outside the saloon.

"I want those guns gentlemen," Christian asked as calmly as he could so as not to cause the men to become agitated and make any sudden moves. The shortest of the two men roared with laughter, while the tall man stood his ground and kept his hand beside his gun.

"Gentlemen! ...you hear that Cord? We ...are ...gentlemen!" The short man continued to laugh uproariously. Cord grinned slyly at Christian, thinking he looked familiar, but he didn't recognize the name the man he shoved aside in the saloon mentioned. "We met someplace before sheriff?" Cord asked Christian.

"I doubt it!" Christian answered, holding his hand away from his gun. "I want those guns, so hand em over now or..."

"Or what sheriff?" The short man heckled. "You want em? Let's see you take em!"

Christian neither wanted or needed trouble. He had enough trouble already, dealing with rowdy trappers and cowhands every time they got drunk. The crowd of onlookers was growing. Women and children were moving about in the street. He had to finish this as carefully as he could so no bystanders got hurt.

Thomas stood with Billy outside the schoolhouse where they had just come from, and watched Christian confronting the men. Thomas worried the two men were nastier than anyone he had ever seen before. Wearing his gun low like Christian, the tall man especially looked bad. The other, shorter man Thomas noticed, had a gun sitting high on his hip. He didn't know why that would make a difference, but he didn't want anything to happen to Christian. He didn't think Christian stood a chance with either of the two strangers.

"I don't want any trouble, how about you two come with me and hand those guns in, you can get them back when you leave town." Christian tried reasoning with the men, but neither man seemed to have any reasoning in them and ignored his request. Tightening his mouth in disgust, Christian flexed his gun-hand.

"We ain't leavin …looks like a real nice town …real, nice lookin people …real, nice lookin women! …we might just stay here forever!" The short man waved his arms about and turned in a circle to take in the crowd. Cord and Christian stared at each other. "I'm sure I know you sheriff …I just can't figure where we met before," Cord said.

Sizing up the situation, Christian figured he could draw on the tall man first, but he would have to be quick. The tall man's gun would come out of its holster fast. The shorter, loud mouthed man would take a few seconds longer to get his gun clear. By that time, Christian reckoned, he would have his hand over his gun and would only take an instant to bring his hand down on the hammer and pull the trigger, taking out both of them, depending on how fast the tall man was, but that was something Christian could not judge.

Christian kept studying Cord, taking in his gruff features. The thick moustache that curled up at the sides. His beard! He never had that before! His hair too! Hanging over his collar was now grey. His hat was battered and well worn. Christian looked at his gun, how it hung low. The gun-belt with its silver studs was different than what Christian remembered. Christian's recollection was a might slow. He hoped his hand wasn't.

The air in the street was becoming tense. Major Hardy's men huddled together in a group and waited. Foley looked around for Clem but unable to see him anywhere, told Brady to stay where he was, while he moved a little further out into the street to stand behind Christian. Other men pushed their women and children out of harm's way. The two strangers and Christian remained facing each other in a stand-off. Christian's gun-hand was steady as he held it level with his gun.

Keeping his right hand poised near his gun, Cord had a sudden recollection of where he met Christian. Lifting his left hand to his face, he clicked his fingers, then ran them over his moustache, twisting the ends as he kept his eyes on Christian. Watching Christian's face change expression at seeing his habit he couldn't shake, told Cord Christian recognized him.

Seven years doesn't seem long enough for a man to forget he has two bullet wounds in his back. Sam 'Wild West' Weston was a man every lawman wanted for robbery and murder, and every bounty hunter wanted for the reward. After forcing the bank manager at Coloured Springs to open the banks safe, netting Weston and his gang one hundred thousand dollars, the banker tried to warn the town their bank was being robbed, but unfortunately for the banker, Weston shot him in the back, and after Weston almost made it to Mexico, he took refuge at the Les Rios and the Brothers of the Holy Father mission near the border. Weston thought it a good place to lay low, after all, who would want to look for him in such a desolate place? He didn't count on one man's persistence.

When Weston and Christian clashed in a vicious gun-fight in the mission's chapel, the Brothers, fearful they would be killed, hid the best they could under pews and in the vestibule. When one of Weston's men suddenly stepped into the open, Christian sent his bullet slamming into the man, but not before he got off several shots at Christian. While some of Weston's bullets flew wide, others hit the seats in front of Christian, sending splinters of wood flying through the air. Christian fired back, missing Weston when his bullets slammed into the alter, shattering candles and sending shards of glass from vases flying in all directions. Being shot at in a crossfire hail of bullets, Christian was made aware someone else besides the first outlaw he killed was there in the chapel with Weston. The first bullet that slammed into Christian's back slowed him down, but didn't stop him.

Convinced if he didn't shoot Weston, he would take a second bullet and that would finish him, Christian took aim. Thinking Christian dead, Weston made a fatal mistake when he stepped out of hiding. Christian's aim was true, his bullet flew straight. Weston, not knowing what hit him died with a look of surprise on his face. When the second bullet hit Christian, all he could think of before he blacked out was, 'I have two bullets in my back, and I am going to die!'

The village doctor, summonsed to get the bullets out of his back, did his job, then left the Brothers to give Christian his last rites. The Brothers vows were such they would not give up on him. Christian woke from his wounds a week later, and was told Weston's partner, a man with a curled moustache, the ends of which he twirled back and forth in a peculiar way, was who shot him, and the man must have known Christian was still alive, because he rode out as fast as he could.

The Brothers took Weston's body, along with the other outlaw Christian shot to the nearest town, and collected the reward. No longer feeling inclined to be a Bounty Hunter, and having given the reward to the Brothers to repair their mission, Christian decided he wouldn't pursue the man that shot him in the back. As far as he was concerned, his days of chasing outlaws was over.

Riding away from the mission in search of a new life, he travelled from town to town in search of what it was he was looking for. Some towns he found better than others, but none were where he wanted to settle, so he kept moving. On one of his many journeys across the country he found himself in Moreton. His time at the mission got drinking to excess out of his system, along with gambling and sleeping with wild women. He no longer drank until he passed out, but he liked to find out about the town he was in and the people in it, and the only way to do that was to spend time in their saloon's. While sitting in the saloon at Moreton, he listened to talk circulating around the room. When men filled their bellies with whiskey, they liked to brag, and that was how he heard about the fur traders. There were men who hunted bear, and men that hunted buffalo, but it was men hunting wolves that interested Christian.

Hearing about a Trading Post and men trapping wolves on a mountain not far from a town called Cedar Creek, he felt he should take a look for himself. Thinking maybe this is where he should be, he rode the two weeks it took to get there. But when he rode in, he was unimpressed. Cedar Creek was a small town consisting of a couple of dirt streets and a dozen or so private houses. Among the businesses were a lumber yard, general store, saloon, bank, and a livery. There was a schoolhouse as well as a church. But what did impress him, was two very large grand houses. Riding past one opposite the Trading Post, he later learnt it once traded as a boarding house, but now the fur trappers themselves owned it.

But there were no trappers. Being told they wouldn't arrive until winter, when the men were forced off the mountain by deep drifts of snow, he planned on not staying long. After making camp on the riverbank, below the trapper's house, he was sitting quietly at a table in the saloon with a whiskey in front of him, when a noisy bunch of cowhands came rushing through the door, stormed up to the bar, and ordered their first drinks. Keeping his eyes on their guns, he sized the men up. Some men wore their guns high. The man with the scar down his face wore his gun low like he did. A younger man standing next to the man with the scar wore his gun the same. The men continuing to drink, slowly got more boisterous as the evening wore on.

When another group of men entered the saloon and joined the first, Christian watched as two men started arguing. Christian knew it was just a matter of time before it happened, it always did. Watching as the pushing and shoving became more violent, it wasn't long before a man Christian reckoned was in his late fifties came limping in to see what all the commotion was about. This man's hair was greying and so was his moustache, and he wore a sheriff's badge pinned to his shirt. Christian watched the old sheriff trying to break up the fight. Threatening to take both men off to the jailhouse, the sheriff managed after a time, to coerce them into taking their fight outside. A large group of drunken men followed the two men and the sheriff into the street. Leaving his unfinished whiskey on the table, Christian followed too, and leaning on a post with his arms folded and his legs crossed, settled down to watch the fight. The sheriff stood in the middle of the street arguing with the two men when the fight suddenly turned ugly. The sheriff, with his back to the crowd didn't see the knife being pulled on him. Seeing the deadly move, Christian leapt off the boardwalk straight at the knife wielder and driving his fist hard across the man's jaw, knocked him out. Seeing their friend attacked by a stranger, an angry crowd of men surrounded Christian and the sheriff. The sheriff hurriedly drew his gun from its holster and Christian did the same. Standing back to back, they faced the circle of men. "I'm taking these two men to the jailhouse to spend the night, why don't you all get back inside and relax." Christian heard the sheriff calmly say. Christian and the sheriff waited for the men to move. "I would do as your sheriff tells you …we can take a couple of you down if you like …it's just a matter of who it will be that we have to decide on." Keeping his eyes on the men in front of him, Christian watched all but two men go back inside, the man with the scar, and the younger man Christian had seen standing at the bar next to the man with the scar. Foley and Brady stayed to see if they could help.

While the sheriff held his gun on the one fighter who remained standing, Christian holstered his gun and hooked his arms under the man's arms that he knocked out. Foley took hold of the man's legs and together they carried him to the jailhouse.

After the sheriff had the two men locked in a cell, he introduced himself to Christian. "Names Clementine, George Clementine, Clem to those that know me, this here is Foley." He pointed to the man with the scar. "And he is Brady." Foley said howdy and Christian and Foley shook hands. Brady stood back a little and just nodded. Christian didn't think anything of him not speaking and nodded back. "We'll see you later Clem, got some drinking to do," Foley said opening the door. He and Brady left Christian and Clem in the Sheriff's Office and went back to the saloon.

"Mighty grateful for your help young fella, how would you like a job?" Clem didn't see any point in wasting time trying to find someone to take over his job. He was tired, his wife was ill, and he was desperate to retire to Moreton so he and his wife could spend time with their grandchildren. Clem grinned at Christian and waited for him to accept the job.

"What kind of job?" Christian asked.

"The sheriff's job of course!" Clem kept grinning. "I'm trying to retire, can't find anyone to take my place, none of them no good cowhands want it, thought maybe because you stepped in and gave me a hand, you might like to take it on."

Christian thought about Clem's request. It was a small enough town. But did he want to stay here? "I don't know what kind of town you have here sheriff."

Clem told Christian to sit down while he poured them both some coffee, then proceeded to tell him all about Cedar Creek. He told him Major Hardy's was the biggest cattle and horse ranch in the county, possibly the state, and that he had twenty men working for him full time. He told Christian about the trappers only coming to town in the winter and that he wouldn't have too much trouble from them, seeing how they worked for Major Hardy while they were here, most of the time. That was when he explained the Ferguson House belonged to the trappers, and was only in use during the winter.

By the time Clem finished talking, Christian had a clear picture of a pretty town on the banks of a picturesque river. He agreed to take on being the town's sheriff, for a time, but only if Clem agreed to stay on as his deputy until he could find a replacement. It meant the pressure would be off Clem, allowing him time with his sick wife. Clem agreed and Christian became sheriff right there and then. Happy now the job was no longer his, Clem showed Christian around town and introduced him to owners of the towns businesses. He met Fess from the Trading Post, Morley at the bank, Ham at the Livery and many others.

He also met Benjamin Crawley, the owner of the General Store, and Mountain View Lodge. Feeling generous, Crawley offered to rent Christian the bottom floor of the lodge. Christian eagerly accepted Crawley's offer. Being camped on the riverbank was not a good place for the new sheriff to be, besides, he couldn't get a decent night's sleep for the marauding river rats, and it wasn't helping his mood.

It was a lot thicker now, and grey, but he should never have forgotten that moustache, or the way Cord clicked his fingers as he twirled the ends. Christian knew one day their paths would cross again and now here he was, facing Cord, the meanest most dangerous man he ever had occasion to meet. Cord wasn't his real name, his name was Jake Roper and he was renowned for using a cord to strangle people, hence the name Cord, or when it was more convenient for him, he just shot them in the back. Christian knew Cord would still have a price on his head. He wasn't sure how much, but figured it must be high after more than seven years of robbing banks and killing.

"We have met before haven't we sheriff?" Paying little attention to his partner clowning about beside him, Cord grinned slyly at Christian. It hadn't taken Cord long to find a replacement after his other partner had been killed at the mission in Les Rios. There were plenty of men who didn't mind thieving and killing innocent people for money. Christian didn't care that Cord recognized him, he was a lawman now, and he was going to take Cord down, right here! right now!

As Christian and Cord faced each other, Clem came out of the Sheriff's Office and stopped dead in his tracks. He had been too busy arguing with Bear over what kind of meal Bear was going to get to be aware of what was going on outside. Christian heard the door slam shut behind Clem. Turning his head slightly to see where Clem was, and while trying to keep one eye on the two men, he saw Bear with Clem, but he didn't have time right then to dwell on why Clem hadn't locked Bear up. Clem's mouth was agape as he watched what was about to unfold. Seeing what was about to happen, Bear stepped aside to get out of the line of fire.

"Christian Morgan! ...Bounty Hunter! ...hell Morgan! I thought you were dead! didn't I shoot you once? No ...make that twice!" As Cord laughed and sneered, he spoke loud enough for everyone to hear, then went for his gun. Christian's gun was in his hand before Cord's left its holster. Pulling the trigger, his bullet slammed into Cord's chest. A look of surprise crossed Cord's face as he fell backwards. At the exact moment Christian fired, another shot rang out. The man with Cord drew his gun, but Christian didn't get to slam his hand on the hammer of his gun to get off a second shot.

The man's gun was pointing toward the ground when his bullet dug into the dirt at his feet before he toppled over dead. Christian spun around to see who shot the second man.

Foley was the only other man that had his gun drawn. Christian and Foley stared at each other for a moment before Foley walked up to Christian. "You can have my gun sheriff," he said, handing his gun grip first to Christian. Holstering his gun, Christian took it. Clem stepped off the boardwalk, and standing in front of the two dead men, scratched his head. The hole in Cord's chest was dead centre. The hole in the other man was almost the same. Foley's bullet hit him from almost standing right behind Christian.

As two dead men were carried off to Phelps the undertaker for burial, Bear made a beeline for his horse and hightailed it out to the dry gulch and Major Hardy's steers.

The crowd, taken by surprise at how fast their sheriff drew his gun, talked about how fast Christian was and how Foley backed him up. Talk soon spread around town and outlying farms and ranches. After overseeing the two men taken to the undertaker, Christian went back to his office to register in the cowhand's guns.

Thomas and Billy saw everything that happened. Billy, wide-eyed, looked at Thomas. "Woah! Sheriff Morgan is fast!" he exclaimed. Thomas, even though he jumped when the guns went off, paid particular attention to Christian as he drew his gun. His gun didn't come out very far before he aimed it and pulled the trigger. Feeling both proud and stunned at seeing how fast Christian was, in reply to Billy, Thomas could only say one word, and that was, "yeah." His friend Sheriff Morgan was a hero. He saved the town from two outlaws, but what was that the man said about him being a Bounty Hunter? What was a Bounty Hunter? Thomas wanted to know. He would just have to ask Mister O'Rourke, because Mister O'Rourke knows everything. He was anxious to tell his Ma what happened in town too, but she told him she was going bathing out at the ponds, so he had to wait for her to come back.

The trappers were busy breaking horses up at the corrals when the outlaws rode into town. They all heard the gunshots and left the corrals to run down the street to see who was doing the shooting. As Joe ran along, he hoped Sarah wasn't involved.

Chapter Thirty

Sarah felt her dinner with Christian had been a success. They laughed about Thomas taking his sign and making it into a table for them to eat off. It was after dinner that hadn't gone to plan. Going for a walk along the riverbank until they were far enough away to be alone, they kissed and held each other, but before they had a chance to go further the evening ended abruptly when Christian walked away. Sarah had been pining for Christian ever since, but she wouldn't be seen chasing after him, if he wanted her, he would have to come to her.

More than a month passed since Sarah had been with Christian in her shelter, and again in the cavern. Now most mornings she woke up well before Thomas to drink the ginger tea Gerda gave her. It was helping, but occasionally she still let go of her stomach contents. Sarah had a pretty good idea what was making her sick, so did Doc Harris. She didn't know what she was going to do about telling Christian. She didn't know where she stood with him, now that he had walked away from her.

The Trappers became busy breaking in another lot of horses. Snow had fallen but wasn't yet deep enough to stop people from getting out and about. Sarah still hadn't washed her hair since hurting herself. Curls hung limply down her back and it had become unruly. Brushing it no longer helped get the shine back into it. The sun was shining and even though the day wasn't warm Sarah decided now was a good time for her to bathe properly. No-one else would venture out to the ponds while it was cold, so she would have the secluded spot all to herself.

Thomas was still in school and Sarah had the afternoon before her lessons to fill in, so after gathering some things together, her cake of soap, a drying towel, her brush, the coffee pot and some coffee, a mug and the tin that Martha Henderson gave her that held freshly baked cookies she made for her and Thomas, everything was placed in her rucksack. Carrying the rucksack on her back, she walked along the riverbank toward the Livery.

Ham was busy working with his hammer at his forge making horseshoes. His constant pounding of metal upon metal could be heard as Sarah came up the track through the trees from the riverbank. "Howdy Sarah," he said giving the hot metal another hit when he saw her come in. "Howdy Ham," Sarah answered going over to where Star was stalled and putting the bit in his mouth. Stretching up to put the bridle over his ears and throwing the saddle over his back hurt her arm a little, but she didn't complain. Reaching under Star, she pulled the girth around him and while Star stomped his hooves anxious to get going, she buckled the saddle tight and hooked her rucksack over the saddle-horn.

Holding his hammer up, ready for another pounding on the hot metal, Ham studied Sarah curiously. "Where are you off to Cole?" Sarah didn't want to tell him where she was going, but thought it best to tell someone else besides Thomas in case something happened like at the blackberry patch and she couldn't get back to town.

"I'm heading out to wash my hair, it has become unruly."

"You going to the ponds then?"

"Yes, and I would appreciate it..." Sarah put her foot in the stirrup and tossed her leg over the saddle. "...If you would keep that to yourself, I don't want anyone coming out there while I am there." Looking down at Ham, she brought Star to the front of the Livery.

"Sure Cole, I won't mention it, you have a nice day now." Ham put his head down and went back to making horseshoes.

Riding out of the Livery, Sarah headed across the bridge, turned toward the river, and rode along the edge of the tree-line. As she drew closer to the ponds, oblivious to what was happening in town, she came across rabbits scurrying to their burrows, and while galloping past, made a mental note to come back and set snares. Rabbit stew always went down well with Thomas.

Coming to the spot where she wanted to bathe, she tethered Star to a tree in dappled shade where there was plenty of grass for him to graze on. Taking her rucksack off the saddle-horn, she walked a little further away from Star to prepare a fire. Gathering stones, she formed a small circle on the ground, then collecting sticks and branches, piled them in the circle. Taking her coffee pot and mug out of the rucksack, she sat them near her fire. She didn't light the fire or make coffee right then. She wouldn't do that until after she bathed. A warm drink, and a cookie when she was done, would warm her before she headed back to town.

Leaving everything ready, she walked down a narrow track, stepping between trees and shrubs on to a grassed area situated in a sheltered gully where small waterfalls trickled over flat rocks that formed shallow ponds along the river. Boulders flanked both sides of the riverbank, protecting the area from strong winds and sheltering it from harsh weather. The sun hadn't taken long to melt the light dusting of snow, and to warm the gully.

To make sure she was alone, Sarah looked around before leaning back against a boulder to remove her boots. Undoing her sheath, she lay it on the ground at her feet, then pushing her trousers over her hips and over her knees, she quickly took them off and folded them. After laying them neatly on top of the boulder beside her boots, she glanced around one more time to make sure she was still alone, then not sensing anyone, quickly unbuttoned her shirt, slid it down her arms and folding it, sat it on top of her trousers. The warm sun and light breeze on her naked body gave her a sense of freedom. Lastly, she removed her hat and sat it on top of her clothes.

Picking up her sheath, she removed her knife, then hastily shoved the sheath in under everything on the boulder. Her drying towel wouldn't be needed until she was done bathing so it was left with her clothes. Stepping into the cold but not yet freezing water, and carrying the bar of soap along with her knife across the flat rocks to a shallow pool near a small waterfall, she submerged her knife in the water, and left it to rest on the flat rocks. Sitting in the pool in front of the waterfall, the water didn't cover her completely, her hips and tops of her legs remained exposed, just the way she liked it. After almost drowning in the river on the mountain, deep water frightened her. Leaning back under the waterfall, the sudden wash of cold water over her head felt refreshing as it ran down her body, making her nipples stand out. While lathering soap through her hair, and even before she spied movement on the riverbank, she sensed someone nearby.

Over the past weeks, when Christian had become busy, dinner with Sarah was the first break he had since bringing her back from the cavern. Since then he hadn't had time to see her, even though he desperately wanted to, each evening he collapsed in bed too tired to wash himself. His days were spent riding around the district checking farms, sorting out trouble with farmhands and cowhands and making sure everything was in order. He returned to Major Hardy's ranch to look at more dead steers, spending several days riding back and forth and still he couldn't work out what was killing them. A lot of ground had been travelled. He hadn't counted on two outlaws coming to town, and was relieved when he and Foley dispatched the two men quickly.

Christian's secret of him being a Bounty Hunter was out. The town was abuzz with talk of him outdrawing Jake 'Cord' Roper. He didn't know what folk would make of him now, so thinking he should take another look at Major Hardy's dead steers, he decided that was a good enough excuse to ride out to the gulch to think about what he was going to do.

After making his way to the Livery to get his horse, Ham greeted him pleasantly. "Howdy sheriff …mighty fine thing you did just now …got good people here …don't need their type spoiling it." Feeling Christian was the type of man Cedar Creek needed as their sheriff, Ham held a knew found respect for him. Ham didn't care when he heard Cord tell everyone Christian had been a Bounty Hunter, as far as Ham was concerned, that only made Christian more suitable for the job.

Agitated by what happened, Christian wasn't in the mood to discuss the shooting with Ham. Ignoring the fact Christian didn't want to talk, Ham watched him saddle his horse. "Where you headed sheriff?" he asked out of curiosity. "Out to the gulch to look at some of the Majors steers?" Christian volunteered. 'And then maybe leave Cedar Creek behind,' he thought to himself.

Having heard about the steers, Ham nodded. "You ought to ride by the ponds, it's a lot quicker than going all the way across the Major's land." Ham gave Christian directions then smiled broadly at him. Climbing into his saddle, Christian looked down at Ham, and wondered why he wasn't treating him differently than he had before he shot the outlaw. Christian thought, 'maybe things aren't as bad as I thought, maybe I'm just imagining my time here is over.' But to Ham said, "I might just do that …thanks Ham." Tipping his hat, he nudged his horse out of the Livery.

Ham went back to making horseshoes. "Now won't that be something?" he said out loud to no-one. "Sheriff Morgan and Cole! …together! …out at the ponds!" He wasn't supposed to tell anyone Sarah was out there, but he couldn't see the harm now Christian and Sarah had been together. Since the incident with the blackberries everyone in town was talking about them. Ham laughed and shook his head from side to side.

'He must have followed me to be here,' Sarah thought, lathering her hair. She watched him come down the track and stand next to the boulder where her clothes were. Closing her eyes to rinse soap out of her hair, and leaning back to steady herself, her breasts rose, her nipples stood firm from the cool touch the water made as it ran over them. Drawing her knees up in front of her, lather washed over her, leaving a soapy trail down her stomach to form a swirl in the water between her legs. Sarah could feel him watching her.

After watching Sarah for a few minutes, Christian turned and started to walk back up the trail. Not wanting him to go, Sarah straightened up and turned her body to face him. "When was the last time you bathed sheriff?" she asked, still feeling it better not to use his first name in case she slipped up when they were in town. Besides, what happened at dinner left her wondering how she should address him. Christian asked her to call him Christian the first night they came together. He wanted to call her Sarah then too but she stopped him. They called each other by their first names when they were alone in the cavern. And out here, at the ponds, they appeared to be alone. So why did she call him sheriff just now? Christian stopped walking away, but kept his back to her.

"Last night Cole," he answered.

'Now see!' Sarah said to herself. 'Why is he calling me Cole?' Sarah needed to know if things between her and Christian had changed since they had dinner together. "I don't mean in a dish, or a tub, I mean in fresh, cool running water." Christian turned to face her. Scooping water up in her hand, Sarah let it run through her fingers. Knowing her nipples were standing up like beacons, she hoped she made him feel aroused. Having only ever seen each other unclothed in shadowed light, Christian couldn't help staring. Here was Sarah, completely naked, and in broad daylight. Keeping his eyes fixed on her, he walked back to where her clothes were.

'He had just killed a man, was he up for this?' he asked himself. 'Hell yes!' he thought. He needed to forget what just happened in town, and Sarah was going to help him forget.

Sarah kept her eyes on Christian as he began to undress. Taking off his coat first, then removing his gun-belt, he sat them on the boulder next to Sarah's clothes. While leaning against the rock to take his boots off, his eyes stayed on Sarah. Unable to resist watching him remove his shirt and fold it, Sarah's body began to react to the sight of his muscled chest and strong arms. The feeling started deep between her legs and rose up through her stomach to her chest, making her heart quicken. She kept watching as he undid his trousers and slowly slid them down his thighs to his knees. Christian looked at Sarah again. Sarah was staring. Christian was aroused. He pushed his trousers all the way down his legs and stepping out of them, folded them up and dropped them on top of everything on the boulder, then started to walk over the flat rocks towards Sarah.

He was standing in ankle deep water when Sarah began to giggle, so he stopped walking, but Sarah kept giggling. Putting his hands on his hips and flexing his muscles made him appear even more manly. "What are you laughing at Cole?" he asked, feeling both embarrassed, and vulnerable. Did he think she was laughing at his body? He was never more wrong. Sarah thought him a very virile, strong, and handsome man, and she liked that he was well endowed. Sarah turned her head away, then turning back, kept smiling. "You still have your hat on sheriff," she said, holding her hand to her mouth to stifle her laugh. Christian raised his eyes upward to see his hat sitting on his head. Smiling when he realized that was what

Sarah was laughing at, he reached up and removed it, but instead of taking it back to the riverbank, he threw it behind him without looking, then continued to walk over the flat rocks toward her. Sarah watched the hat sail through the air and land on the grass not far from the boulder where their clothes were. When Sarah raised her eyebrows, Christian's smile widened. He didn't need to look back to see where his hat landed, judging by Sarah's raised eyebrows it landed pretty close to where he wanted it to go.

As he got closer to Sarah, Sarah stood up and pointed to where she had been sitting. Christian sat down and watched water run down her legs. Sitting in front of the waterfall with both legs stretched out in front of him, his eyes were now level with Sarah's womanhood. As Sarah watched Christian move his eyes slowly upward to her breasts, she lifted each foot and pushed them between his legs, forcing him to move his legs apart. Christian spread his legs wider to accommodate her. Sitting and keeping her legs bent, Sarah moved closer to him. When the space between them narrowed, Sarah straddled him and Christian held her legs. Looking down, Christian's erect manhood sat close to Sarah's body. The mat of hair covering Sarah's womanhood floated like soft reeds in the water between them. Christian removed his hands from Sarah's leg's, and cupped her breasts.

"Uh huh sheriff!" Sarah said shaking her head from side to side and removing his hands. "No touching ...we are bathing," she smiled demurely.

"Stop calling me sheriff Sarah, you can see I'm not wearing my badge, besides, haven't we gone far enough not to be formal with each other?" Christian smiled back at her. Sarah didn't answer, instead put her hand on Christian's chest and pushed him back.

"Put your head under the water," she demanded softly. Christian leant back until water ran over his face and down his chest. Watching his nipples suddenly stand erect from the sudden rush of cold water made Sarah smile to see his nipples were bigger than hers.

To get to the top of his head to lather his hair, Sarah made him bend forward, but still she had to stretch up, which brought her breasts close to his chest. As she washed his hair vigorously, he watched her breasts while his fingertips gently brushed the sides of them, causing him to become aroused further. While she continued lathering, he kept his hands where they were. Leaning back under the waterfall with his eyes closed, he let Sarah rinse the soap off his head, then, after lathering her hands, she rubbed them over his chest, slid them over his now fully erect nipples, and across his abdomen. Sarah's hands moved in a circular motion downward, toward his crotch.

Rubbing ever so gently, she washed the thick mat of hair between his legs. Christian's eyes remained closed while Sarah's hand manipulated his manhood. Opening his eyes, he removed her hand. "Uh! huh! Sarah, we are bathing! ...remember?" While gazing into each other's eyes, Sarah took her hand out of his grasp, and scooping water, washed the soap off his body. When Sarah stood up, Christian wished he hadn't stopped what she had started.

"Move forward Christian," Sarah ordered softly. Moving to sit a little out of the way of the waterfall, Sarah stepped behind him, and sat down. Staring at his back, a frown crossed her face when she saw two scars. Having a similar scar herself, she knew exactly what they were.

When Christian undressed her for the first time, she could tell he had seen her scar, but he hadn't asked her about it. She wouldn't tell him about it anyway. It was something that happened in her past and she wanted it left in her past. Frank had a scar extending from his right shoulder all the way to his left buttock, and when they made love, she put her arms around him and felt it. She hated that she thought of Frank right now. She wanted to concentrate on making Christian love her. Unaware he had already been told how she got her scar, she moved her fingers gently over his, and decided they were none of her business. Perhaps, one day, he would tell her how he got them.

Christian felt Sarah's fingers going over his back, and waiting for the inevitable question, wondered how he would explain his scars. Having seen her scar, the first night they had been together, he hadn't asked her about it, he was too engrossed in wanting to fuck her at the time. It was Thomas, seeming to be proud of how his Ma had been tracking a wolf and had shot herself that told him about it. Now here they were, Sarah was seeing his scars. He hadn't tried to hide them from her when they fucked, her hands just never touched them, that was all. If she wanted to know about them, he would tell her, but he would leave some things out, some things like! 'He once hunted people for a living!' But he needn't have worried. Sarah didn't ask.

Lathering her hands, she soaped his back down to where his buttocks sat in the water, then, after finishing him off by washing the soap away, she stood up and moved around to sit in front of him again. Christian moved his legs apart and let Sarah sit, this time with her back to him. Moving backwards until Christian's manhood touched her buttocks, she reached over her shoulder and handed him the soap.

A rush of excitement ran through Sarah as he soaped her. Christian's fingers gently soaped the sides of her breasts, sending a tingle coursing through him. Rinsing her off and looking at the back of Sarah's arm where three scars were visible, he felt a pang of guilt when remembering she had been hurt because of him. Lathering his hands again, he brought them in front of Sarah and ever so gently, rubbed them over her breasts until the feeling coming over her made her lean back against him. With her head resting beside his, she spread her fingers out on top of his legs. While one hand soaped Sarah's breasts, the other moved slowly downward. Feeling him pushing his body against her, Sarah closed her eyes. Christian's hand circled its way over Sarah's abdomen, and over her stomach, until it found its way to the mound between her legs. Curling his fingers, he gently stroked her as he explored, making Sarah hold his legs tight. They were no longer bathing.

Neither spoke as they moved their bodies in unison. Christian kept his body pressed against Sarah's, letting his fingers work. Sarah could feel her orgasm building, but she didn't want to come there in the water, she wanted Christian to take her to the riverbank where they could lie down and hold each other. Opening her eyes and removing his hand, she turned, and getting on her knees straddled him. Taking Sarah's breast in his mouth, Christian ran his tongue over her nipple, making it stand up hard. Maneuvering her into position, then lowering her onto his lap, Christian groaned with pleasure as the warmth from Sarah's body engulfed him. Wrapping her arms around his neck, Sarah moaned as her feeling of arousal overtook her. Kissing each other passionately, their tongues mingled as their bodies moved together. "Take me to the riverbank Christian," Sarah moaned, feeling she was about to come.

Aware of Sarah's arousal and feeling almost there himself, Christian didn't want to stop, but Sarah's sudden demand made him hold back. Keeping her legs wrapped around him as he stood up, Sarah crossed her ankles, and hung on as he began to walk to the riverbank.

"Wait!" Sarah said unexpectedly, causing Christian to stop. "Put me down ...please." Christian had no choice but to put her down. Unhooking her ankles from around him, she slid to the ground where, when her feet were in the water, she took a few steps back to the waterfall and squatted. Wondering what she was up to, Christian watched and waited. Sarah knew exactly where her hands had to go. Reaching into the water, she lifted her knife into the air, and turned to Christian. When he saw the knife, his eyes widened and his mouth fell open in surprise. "Protection!" Sarah informed him seriously. "Keep that bloody thing away from me Sarah!" For a moment they stared at each other, then laughing, he lifted her into his arms.

Nearing the boulders where their clothes were, Christian kept walking. Snow had melted from around the boulders making the grass feel warm underfoot. Holding her knife away from them, blade down, she let it go. The knife dropped, stuck in the ground, and stayed upright.

Carrying Sarah past the boulders and their clothes, he lay her gently on her back in the shelter of the rocks and moved his body over the top of hers. Pushing her fingers through Christian's hair, Sarah brought his mouth down to cover hers. Their tongues played as their kisses became urgent. 'So much for waiting until I get Sarah into my bed!' Christian thought. He wanted to fuck her, and right then he didn't care where they were. Pressing his body against Sarah, he pushed against her. Locking their bodies together, neither wanting to stop the urges overtaking them they pushed harder, trying to get their bodies to give more. The moment he felt his body giving in, Christian whispered, "I love you Sarah." Sarah let the warmth flowing from Christian overtake her and didn't answer.

As Sarah's womanhood erupted in uncontrollable spasms, and her legs pressed tight against Christian, he slid his hand under Sarah's buttocks, and lifted her against him. Lying in each other's arms, they continued breathing heavily, waiting for both orgasms to ease.

Gently removing himself, Christian lay on his back, gazing up at the sky as dappled sunlight shone through the trees and cold air rose from snow still lying in patches on the ground. "What do you call this place Sarah?" A look of confusion crossed Sarah's face. "The Ponds, you don't know this place Christian?" she asked sounding surprised, while thinking he should be aware of this wonderful secluded spot.

"No, no-one has told me about it." That wasn't quite true, Ham told him to ride past the ponds to get to Major Hardy's, but he didn't elaborate that to Sarah. "It's beautiful, like an oasis in the desert," he whispered. Sarah didn't know about oasis's, or deserts, but she knew this place was special, even if it was winter, she always came here to bathe. Waiting until her breathing eased then sitting up, she studied Christian. Neither felt shy about their bodies or shy about looking at each other. Smiling at seeing his manhood lying limp in front of him, Sarah got up, and brushing grass off her bottom, went to where her knife was. As she headed away from Christian, he watched her brush grass off her behind and smiled. Sarah's butt was beautiful, perfectly proportioned, and her skin smooth. Walking toward the water's edge, she pulled her knife out of the ground as she passed it, and carrying it with her to the river, stepped into the water where she squatted. While washing dirt off her knife, and scooping water into her hand to wash between her legs, Christian squatted in the water beside her. When Sarah stood up in front of him, and he looked at where he had just been, he realized he had truly fallen in love with her. She made him forget he had just killed someone.

His feeling of contentment left him when he remembered what happened in town. Standing up, and not wanting to spoil what just happened between them, he decided he wouldn't tell Sarah, she would hear about it soon enough.

Walking side by side back to the boulder where their clothes were, Sarah put her knife back in its sheath, picked up her towel and began drying herself. Christian stood next to her, and taking the towel off her, knelt down and rubbed the towel between her legs and over her hips and bottom. When he finished, he stood up and kissed her softly. Sarah let him dry himself while she began to get dressed. Leaning forward, she put one leg inside her trousers then the other. Seeing Christian watching her, Sarah took her time. After pulling her trousers over her hips, she bent forward to push her feet into her boots. Mesmerized by the fullness of Sarah's breasts as they bumped together, Christian couldn't help staring. Lifting her arms to twist her hair into a braid and fasten it made her breasts rise further. Sarah flicked her braid over her shoulder then put her shirt on. After doing up each button, she tucked it into her trousers then watched Christian getting dressed. When he put his shirt on, Sarah saw the sheriffs badge pinned to it, making her realize the enormity of what they had just done.

After tucking his shirt in, and putting his coat on to keep warm, Christian was reaching for his holster when Sarah's nose caught the aroma of coffee. "Son-of-a-bitch!" she cursed, sniffing the air. Shoving her hat on her head, and grabbing her sheath, and not waiting for Christian, she hurried along the track, back to where Star was tethered.

"What the hell Sarah! ...what is it?" Christian questioned, buckling his gun-belt and hurrying along behind her. Bursting out from the track, Sarah saw her fire alight and her coffee pot sitting in the middle of a fire. Two tin mugs sat side by side on the ground beside the stones. "Son-of-a-bitch!" Sarah cursed again, and rushing over to the fire, walked around it to study the scene. Hurrying over to Star, Sarah grabbed a jacket tied to her bedroll, and whilst unable to see or sense anyone about, she shoved her arms inside the cowhide coat. Christian's horse tethered next to Star, seemed fine.

"What is it Sarah? What is wrong?" Christian asked, holding his hands out in confusion. Sarah pulled her coat closed around her, and pacing back and forth, glared at him. "Damn it, sheriff!" she replied in anger. Christian wasn't happy when Sarah resorted to calling him sheriff. But his badge shone in the sun, reminding her of what he represented, and them coming together out of wedlock, was as serious as things could get, because someone had been spying on them and Sarah, not knowing everyone knew about them already, thought now the whole town would know. She silently cursed herself for letting her guard down.

"Look around you sheriff, what do you see?" Sarah put her hands on her hips and waited. Christian was a lawman, he was supposed to be able to figure things out, he should be able to see things that weren't visible to others, couldn't he see what she saw?

"Bloody hell Cole! ...what?" he exclaimed. Christian wasn't stupid, nor concerned. He studied the fire when he came walking out from the track, and knew someone had lit it and put Sarah's coffee pot on to heat up. No-one was lurking about, so he couldn't see what the problem was. Sarah didn't say anything, instead, threw her hands up in frustration and let them fall by her sides. Christian thought he better say what he knew. "The fire wasn't lit and the pot was sitting beside the stones when I came along, and there was only one tin mug, someone besides us has been here!" 'So?' He questioned silently. 'They probably watched us fucking ...good for them!'

'Thank goodness' Sarah thought. 'He is smart after all.'

"That's right, someone else has been here, I only brought one mug with me, someone had to have been watching what we were doing to know to leave another mug, damn son-of-a-bitch!" Sarah cursed again, angry with herself because usually she could tell when someone was near, but she had been so engrossed in what Christian and she were doing, she let her ability slip.

Christian had all but forgotten about the outlaw he killed. What he let Sarah do to him and what he did to her, helped him feel at ease. He didn't need this to remind him about bad people, he just wanted to forget and move on. "Don't get upset Sarah, so we gave whoever it was something to look at!" When Christian smiled, Sarah glared at him. "You might like it sheriff, but I don't! I don't want someone watching what I do! what I do is my business, not anyone else's!" Christian walked over to her. "Come on Sarah!" he soothed.

Studying the ground trying to find hoofprints from the other horse, Sarah could see where the snow had been disturbed. Stars hoofprints were visible where he was tethered and she picked them out straight away. "Don't be so mad Sarah, I understand what you are saying, but we were out in the open, anyone could have come along and seen what we were doing, we can't change that." Christian studied the patches of snow. Ignoring what he said Sarah concentrated on finding other hoofprints. "Has your horse got any markings on its hooves?" she asked without looking up. "No!" Christian snapped. "Sarah ...come on! there's nothing we can do about this! let's enjoy a cup of coffee that, whoever it was made for us." Going back to the fire, Christian picked up one of the mugs, and when he reached for the coffee pot, Sarah stopped looking at the ground and straightened up. "You are not going to drink that! are you?" she exclaimed, looking incredulous. "Sure ...why not?" Christian said nonchalantly. "Because you don't know what is in it! It could be poisoned for all you know!" Sarah's eyes widened as she watched Christian pour coffee into the mug and take a mouthful. "Mmm ...tastes good ...and it's hot!" he said smirking before sitting on a log by the fire. Throwing her hands up in surrender, Sarah sat beside him. "Don't worry Sarah, whoever it was may not have stayed long, but they obviously thought we would need this when we were finished doing what we were doing." He held the mug to his lips and trying to suppress a smile, took another mouthful. Sarah couldn't help it. She smiled at his insinuation that they wore themselves out and needed replenishing.

But Sarah worried who the person might be that spied on them. She could track a trapper's horse better than anyone. If it had been a trapper, things wouldn't be so bad, but if it was one of Major Hardy's men, or someone from town, word would spread like wildfire that, 'the sheriff and Cole are fucking,' and that would be exactly how it would spread. Sarah didn't understand why Christian wasn't worried about that. Did he want people to know what they were doing? Sarah let Christian pour her some coffee while she opened her tin of cookies and passed them to him.

Suddenly reaching over Christian, she took the mug he was drinking from off him, looked at it, then handed it back. "Well, who was it?" Christian asked. Sarah didn't know if she should tell him. When she didn't answer he asked. "You want to know who I think it was?" After a moment more of silence Sarah asked, "who do you think it was?" Christian said only one word. "Joe!" A sadness crept into Sarah's voice when she agreed who it was. "That's right ...it was

Joe!" Christian on hearing her sadness put down his mug and held her in his arms. "You do know Joe spies on you from up on the ridge behind your camp?"

"He does not spy Christian …he keeps a watchful eye."

"It's the same thing Sarah …watching, spying …there's no difference."

"He's only making sure I'm safe …Joe has always made sure I'm safe."

Joe had been at the corrals when the two outlaws came riding in, and the shooting started. By the time he and the other trappers got to the saloon, the two dead men were already at the undertakers and Christian had gone for his horse. Joe didn't mean to pry, he just wanted to know where he was headed, so riding out of town, he watched Christian riding ahead of him in the direction of the mountains. When Christian suddenly changed direction and headed for the river, he doubled back too, and riding toward the ponds, came upon the two horses tethered under the tree, where he saw Sarah had prepared her fire.

After walking down the track between thick undergrowth, and standing behind trees out of sight, Joe peered into the gully where small waterfalls flowed. It was bloody cold, but knowing Sarah liked to bathe here every winter he would never impose on her, leaving her to have her privacy, but today she wasn't alone. He wouldn't stay to spy on her. He would just check to see she was alright.

Joe was watching the two of them bathing each other when Sarah sat on Christian's lap and started doing something Joe felt he shouldn't have been watching, and worse still, when Christian suddenly stood up and carried Sarah back to the riverbank, he saw just how big Christian was, causing him to raise his eyebrows in wonderment. And watching the two of them on the grass, made him feel like a pervert. Turning abruptly to leave Sarah and Christian alone, he bumped into bushes, causing the bushes to rustle. Hoping Sarah and Christian hadn't heard him, he stopped and waited. Sarah's hearing was keen, she could hear a mouse moving through the undergrowth if she wanted too. Joe listened to Sarah and Christian's loud grunts as they made love to each other. Neither stopped to draw breath and Joe felt the colour rise in his cheeks.

'Shit' he thought. 'Those two will kill each other with their fucking.' Thinking it best to leave them alone to get on with what they were doing, and thinking if Sarah wanted to fuck the sheriff it was no business of his, they seemed to be getting along pretty darn good, he crept quietly back to the horses and lit Sarah's fire.

Getting his tin mug from his saddlebag, he sat it next to Sarah's mug, filled her coffee pot with water from his own canteen, spooned coffee into the pot, and placed the pot into the fire, all the while thinking, Christian will definitely need a strong drink when he is done, right now though, coffee will have to do. Sarah and Christian will know he had been watching them. But they had to expect someone would see them fucking out in the open, they were just lucky it had been him. He wouldn't share what he saw with anyone. Sarah wasn't a little girl anymore, and if she wanted to fuck a man, she was entitled to it. But 'hell' Joe thought. 'Did she have to do it out in the bloody open? Why didn't they fuck in a bed like everyone else?' Joe shook his head, smiled broadly, then laughing, rode back to town.

Chapter Thirty-one

Christian knew well before Sarah who the person was that had been spying on them. When he rode out of town, he turned in his saddle to see if anyone was following him and saw the man riding a good distance behind, but then lost sight of him when he turned his horse toward the river. Continuing to follow the river north, he came to the ponds and found Sarah's horse tethered to a tree.

He hadn't gone out to the ponds deliberately to meet up with Sarah, he was simply following Ham's advice and taking the shorter trail to Major Hardy's land. It just happened he came across Sarah, the same as the man had done. Christian was pretty sure at the time it was Joe. When he and Sarah agreed it was him, and Sarah said he would keep what they had been doing to himself, they sat and drank their coffee peacefully. The cookies were a treat too, Sarah was a good cook, that being evident from the dinner he shared with her and Thomas. He walked away from her that night and wished he hadn't. He just now had the best fuck he could ever have right there at the ponds. Christian felt fulfilled. His body had relaxed.

"Just what were you doing out here anyway Christian?" Sarah asked as they sat beside each other drinking their second mug of coffee.

"I was on my way to Major Hardy's, some of his steers have died mysteriously, and he wants me to figure out what killed them." Christian didn't mention the fact he had just been involved in a shootout and killed a man, and just wanted to get out of town. Sarah stopped her mug nearly to her mouth when Christian told her about Major Hardy's steers. "Ha! …good luck with that!" she said with sarcasm.

"Don't tell me Sarah! …you don't like the Major!" Christian said bending down, and picking up a small piece of wood. After dropping it on the fire, he held his hand out to warm it. "If I asked you why you don't like the Major, you're not going to tell me are you?"

"Nope!" Sarah wasn't one for mincing her words, and Christian didn't want to fight with her, not right after being together, she made him feel good, and he wanted more of what she had just given him, but he was aware things weren't going to be that easy between the two of them, so tried to make light of his questions. "So, you don't like Crawley, and now the Major, care to tell me who else you don't like, and why?" he said with a smile.

"You don't need to know the reason why I don't like someone Christian," Sarah answered, staring off across the prairie. Usually about now Foley Andrews would ride up and she would share her coffee with him, then he would propose to her and she would turn him down. Sarah wondered what Foley would think if he were to find her sharing coffee with Christian. Sarah looked down at the wood burning fiercely on the fire.

"Come for a ride with me Sarah? I could use that knife of yours to…" Immediately becoming defensive, Sarah glared at Christian, interrupting him before letting him finish speaking. "My knife! what do you mean? …you could use my knife!"

"If you let me finish, what I meant was …I need to open up some of the Major's steers so I can find out what killed them, and that knife of yours would go through their hides a whole lot easier than my axe, I don't want to mess them up too much." Christian put his hand on Sarah's arm, pleading with her. "Why not come with me and see for yourself?" Sarah pulled her arm out of his grasp. "I am not going to Major Hardy's!" She replied, keeping her eyes on the fire. "Well then, let me borrow your knife, I will bring it …" Standing up, Sarah walked around the other side of the fire. "You are not borrowing my knife Christian! no-one borrows my knife! you took it once before, remember, you are not taking it again, not ever!" Folding her arms in front of her in defiance, she turned away from him. Circling the fire, Christian took her in his arms and tried to look at her. "Come on Sarah, please, come with me, just take a look at the steers with me."

"No! Christian I…" Sarah baulked then looked up at him. "I … can't." She didn't see any reason to tell Christian why she couldn't go with him. "Why not Sarah? Why won't you come with me? What are you afraid of?" he queried, holding her in his embrace. Sarah looked sadly into his eyes. "I can't Christian, …please, don't ask me why, I just can't." Holding her away from him, Christian looked despondent. "So that's it, you don't want to help me …thanks Sarah, I thought after what we just did you might like to spend some time with me…I don't know what's going on, if you don't want to tell me, fine …I promise I won't let anything happen to you." Christian wasn't aware, promises should not be made lightly.

Exploding with anger, Sarah pushed Christian forcibly away from her. "Don't you go making me a promise you cannot possibly keep! …sheriff!" Pouring the left-over coffee over the fire and throwing the pot and mugs angrily into her rucksack, Sarah rushed to her horse while Christian, watching on in disbelief, hurriedly kicked snow and dirt on the fire to make sure it was out and raced after her. "Sarah! …you forgot something!" he called, holding up the floral-patterned tin. About to put her foot in the stirrup, she turned, and snatching the tin off him, shoved it in the sack. "Alright …you don't have to help me … just …don't be mad at me." Christian could confront men with guns but was at a loss when saying or doing the wrong thing where Sarah was concerned. Sarah lifted herself up into her saddle, then after a moment of contemplation, looked down at Christian. "If you make it just for a little while …I will go with you." Breathing a sigh of relief, Christian made for his horse. "Just for a little while … I prom …thanks Sarah," he replied.

Nudging her horse with her heel, she gave a quick glance back along the tree line looking for Foley. He hadn't come along as he usually did, making her wonder why.

As Star leapt forward, making for the trail leading toward the dry gulch and the dead steers, Christian jumped on his horse and followed closely behind. His eyes were on Sarah's backside as it swayed from side to side in her saddle. Her back was straight, her long hair she tied back in a tail bounced against the back of her coat. Sarah's refusal to help him baffled him. After killing the outlaw in town, he needed her to comfort him, which she had done successfully, but then confused him with her sudden outburst at his simple request to use her knife. Sarah was a beautiful but determined woman, and a complete mystery to Christian.

Wending their way between trees along the river's edge in silence, they listened to the sound the river made as it meandered along under thin layers of ice and over small pebbles. Bringing their horses into a clearing where the river flowed around a bend, they crossed through shallow water to the other side. Riding up a small grade where trees grew thickest, the snow-covered trail almost disappeared. Knowing exactly where she was going, Sarah wound her way through the trees and came to a nook where a small dilapidated shack stood close to a rocky outcrop. Sarah stopped her horse ahead of Christian and looked at the building.

The shack has been here a long time, the timber is old and worn. Two broken steps and a small stoop lead straight to the front door. The windows are boarded up with the same weathered timber boards nailed across the front door. Long grass growing amongst low growing shrubs thick with red berries, now covered in snow, covers the ground right up to the steps at the front of the small stoop. To Christian the shack appears to have been abandoned a very long time ago. To Sarah, this place holds good memories as well as bad.

While watching Sarah, and wondering what it was about the shack that brought back a memory, Star suddenly became agitated, stomping his hooves in the snow and snorting. Sarah pulled him around, and stroking his neck to calm him, nudged him forward and rode off.

Following on behind, Christian looked back at the shack, and made up his mind he was going to come back to look around.

Coming out of the trees into the gulch, they stumbled across the dead steers. High cliffs covered in snow, jutting off to one side, and low-lying hills could be seen in the distance. The river runs shallow alongside the cliffs, but the gulch lays barren. The only greenery are bushes covered in red berries growing abundantly amongst tall trees lining the riverbank. Dead steers dotting the area lay frozen, already covered by snow. Some steers covered with dry brush, had been burnt to stop wolves feeding on their carcasses and endangering town folk, but there were still other steers to be dealt with. The stench from rotting flesh was overpowering. Sarah and Christian were now on Major Hardy's land.

As Sarah rode between several steers, she looked about cautiously, checking the hills and ridges in the distance, on the lookout for Major Hardy and his men. If Foley happened to be out here, he would be with Brady and Major Hardy. Sarah covered her nose and mouth with her hand as she guided her horse between the steers. Christian wound his way through behind her, picking out some of the steers that appeared to have died just that day. Hearing a sudden yell, Christian looked up. Sarah kicked Star hard and raced off at a gallop toward the foothills. "Goddamn it, Sarah! …where are you going?" Christian called, only she was already too far away from him to hear. Kicking his horse, he gave chase. Coming to the top of the rise, he pulled his horse to a standstill alongside Star. "Sarah, what the hell?" he asked looking at her, but she was staring into a gully on the other side of the rise and didn't speak.

Keeping her eyes fixed on the gully below and ignoring his question, she asked, "what do you see, sheriff?" Christian followed her gaze to the gully below. "I see a lot of steers …and men … why?" he answered. It was true, there were a lot of steers milling about, foraging for what little grass there was. Some were standing in the river, others stood grouped about under trees along the edge. Sarah didn't answer, she was concentrating on the cowhands and trappers, hired to keep watch over the steers, that were gathered in a circle instead.

Two men, one, a giant of a man, the other half his size, were standing in the middle of the circle, naked to their waists, exchanging blow for blow. But it was the bigger man of the two that was winning. Parker, Major Hardy's cowhand, didn't stand a chance against Bears more powerful blows. Bears size and weight stood in his favour. As cowhands and trappers cheered both men on, steers wandered unnoticed around the gulch. Sarah and Christian sat silently watching the men fight as several steers made their way through the shallow river and disappeared behind a low hill. Having seen enough, Sarah turned Star and rode at a gallop back down the rise. Not knowing what Sarah was going to do, Christian turned his horse and followed.

Riding at a gallop past dead steers, Sarah waved her arm in the air and yelling, rode fast toward a steer that had made its way around the hill to the dry gulch. The steer, becoming startled as Sarah's horse came along-side, weaving sharply and digging its hooves in, turned and ran back through the shallows. Christian saw what Sarah was doing and taking off his hat, waved it in the air, and together they drove the steers back to the herd.

Riding toward the circle of men, Sarah and Christian watched as blows from Bears fists connected with Parkers head, sending him reeling backward, with blood pouring from a cut above his already swollen black eyes. Having not been locked up for fighting in the saloon, Bear missed out on a free home cooked meal and so itching for a fight, made his way back to the herd, and picked a fight with the first man that looked at him the wrong way, and that happened to be Major Hardy's cowhand, Parker.

Reeling from Bears blow, Parker slammed headlong into the crowd of men. Lifting Parker to his feet, they shoved him back toward Bear. Bear stepped aside, and clenching both hands together, hit Parker on his back as he went stumbling past, sending him careening into men standing on the opposite side of the circle. Falling heavily amongst the men, Parker hit the ground and stayed down. A loud cheer went up from the trappers. The cowhands weren't happy about losing the fight and jeered at their loss, but their noise stopped when they saw Sarah and Christian approaching.

"So, this is what you get up to when the Major isn't watching!" Sarah smirked, bringing Star to a stop near the men. "It's just a bit of fun, Cole," Bear replied wiping blood off his face. "Doesn't look much like fun for Parker," Sarah answered turning sullen. "What are you doing here Cole? You shouldn't be here! ...if the Major comes along..." Wilkes, one of the cowhands started to say. "Seems I'm doing your job Wilkes!" Sarah interrupted before he could say too much. "You men are paid to look out for the Majors steers, and all you can think about is the easy dollar you make from fighting." Christian was familiar with this type of fighting, having been involved in them himself over the years. His ears pricked however, when Wilkes mentioned Sarah shouldn't be here. Sarah hadn't wanted to come with him, and again this made him wonder why. "We been watchin em Cole ...you know how borin it is? ...all day ...all night, just watchin steers eat grass!" One of the cowhands moaned. Sarah thought about that and had to agree it would be boring. "You better git Cole, before we put some lead in you!" Another added, putting his hand to his gun. Christian frowned at his threat and expecting trouble, moved his hand to his. Wilkes suddenly made a grab for Sarah trying to pull her off Star. Star became startled causing Sarah to hang on to stop her falling off. Bear dived at Wilkes and tossed him aside like a rag doll. When a scuffle broke out, cowhands and trappers drew their guns on each other but no-one fired a shot. Christian drew his gun but didn't speak. "You better not try!" Bear warned. "Or I will break you in half with my bare hands!" Taking stock of Bears threat, the cowhands holstered their guns and backed off. "You going to tell the Major about this Cole?" A cowhand asked, worried what it meant now they had been caught lazing off. "It won't be me that will tell him," Sarah said turning Star. Christian looked puzzled, because Sarah seemed unaffected by what just happened. Sarah though was agitated, because she had not stepped foot on Major Hardy's land for more than twelve years and being caught here could bring trouble. Leaving the men to sort each other out she and Christian rode back to the dry gulch.

Tethering their horses so they couldn't run off, Sarah began to help Christian investigate why the steers had died. Glancing around at the surrounding area, she thought solving that mystery might be easier than she first thought. "Let's cut this one open and see what's inside," Christian said indicating one of the recently dead steers. Standing beside the steer with her knife gripped in both hands, Sarah plunged it high up in the hide. Amazed at seeing how sharp her knife was, Christian stood back and watched her work. Sarah cut what appeared to be a flap, then working together to peel the hide back enabled them to look inside the carcass. Then using his axe, Christian cut through sinew and bone letting the beasts stomach and intestines fall to the ground. When Christian knelt near the stomach, Sarah held her hand over her face and every now and then cursed. Christian thought she could handle the sight of the insides of animals, after-all she was a trapper, she should be used to it. When he looked at Sarah though her face had turned pale.

"Goddamn it that stinks!" she gasped, holding her nose and heaving.

"Yeah it does a bit, cut the stomach open for me so I can see what's in it." Sarah quickly swiping her knife across the pouch and split it open, letting its contents ooze onto the ground, staining the snow. "Ugh!" she gagged. Inside the stomach was a sticky, thick, pink goo, with streaks of green and yellow through it, and it smelt atrocious.

"What the fuck is that?" Christian said, standing up quickly to get away from the mess. Sarah didn't say anything. She ran behind one of the steers and Christian followed to see if she was alright. "You alright?" he asked as she threw up. Sitting her down, he made her lean back against the steer's carcass, then feeling her forehead, found her to be sweating. Running to his horse, he grabbed his canteen, then hurrying back, poured water over his hand and wiped it across Sarah's forehead. Handing her the canteen she poured water into the palm of her hand, then slurping some into her mouth, swilled it around and spat it out, then putting the canteen to her mouth, drank deeply. "I thought you could handle this sort of thing," Christian said frowning. "I can usually, but what I skin is a lot smaller, and not so smelly," Sarah said drinking more water.

"Well, sit here for a while …let me have your knife and I will carry on." When Christian held out his hand, Sarah looked up at him, and screwing up her face as if to say 'you are not getting my knife' stood up. "I'm alright …I can do it," she offered, going to another steer and cutting it open like the first. When its stomach split, along with its intestines, they found the same thick sticky goo as before. Seeing Sarah walk quickly between decomposing steers to the trees and shrubs near the riverbank, Christian thought she was going to the trees to be ill, but having surveyed the area, she came straight back.

Standing next to the mess they made of the steer, Sarah was about to tell Christian what she found, when she saw movement on the ridge. "Goddamn, son-of-a-bitch!" she cursed shoving her bloodied knife back in its sheath while looking around frantically for a way to escape. Christian watched three riders appear over the hill coming towards them fast. Panicking, Sarah tried to make a run for Star, but Christian stopped her by grabbing her by her arms. "Let go of me!" Sarah cried frantically. Christian frowned at seeing fear in her eyes.

Gritting her teeth, Sarah appealed to him to let her go. "Let me go! Christian, please!" she begged, looking at the three men. "Goddamn it, Sarah, it's too late!" Christian warned seeing them almost on them. "Let me handle this, stay behind me, they won't do anything while I'm here." Pushing Sarah behind him, he silently prayed they wouldn't do anything.

The two men flanking Major Hardy, with their rifles at the ready, were well known to Christian. Brady, the younger man, always had a sombre, almost fearful look on his face. Christian wondered what bothered him so much that he never found the need to speak. If a man couldn't talk to you, then he was to be treated suspiciously. Foley was known for visiting his housekeeper Maria, but after seeing Foley and Sarah appearing almost too friendly outside the saloon, he wondered what their relationship was. After his confrontation with the two outlaws, he appreciated Foley's help backing him by outdrawing one of them, and at the time, reckoned Foley would be a good man to have as his deputy, but here now, he brushed the thought off after noticing the way Foley was looking at Sarah, and because he wanted to find out what was happening between Sarah and the Major, he had to push all thought of their friendship to the back of his mind.

Major Hardy could not mistake seeing Sarah but ignored her presence. "It is about time you came back sheriff, I have been losing cattle every day since you were last here, why didn't you come back when I asked you to?" he said sternly, letting his eyes focus on Christian. Christian's eyes darted between the three men. "I have been out here several times already Major, you may think I sit around all day waiting for things to happen, but it just so happens I am a very busy man," Christian said abruptly, feeling sure the Major knew about the shootout. Foley and Brady would have told him when they got back to the ranch, and if they didn't tell him, then one of his other cowhands would have. Christian didn't think the Major's steers were important enough for him to warrant spending all his time figuring out what or who had killed them.

"I heard there was trouble in town, lucky for you my men were there to help you out, now perhaps you might repay the favour ... you have found out what killed my steers, haven't you?" Christian ignored the Major's reference to the shootout. Sarah frowned when wondering what the Major meant by trouble in town.

"Not yet, we are still working on it." Saying 'we' was a mistake Christian was unaware he should not have made. Major Hardy wanted to wait until he found out about his steers, before confronting Sarah, but now he couldn't wait any longer. His eyes grew dark with menace. His hand moved to where his whip hung as he glared angrily at Sarah. Seeing the change in the Major's demeanor, Christian, expecting trouble, moved his arm behind him and tried to keep Sarah hidden from view.

"You know I don't like trespassers Cole! ...I warned you never to set foot on my land! ...you know my men have orders to shoot you ...on sight! ...I could shoot you myself and be within my rights! ...trespassing is against the law! ...isn't that right sheriff?" Major Hardy sat tall in his saddle, like he owned the world, and expected everyone to bow to him. So now Christian knew Sarah had been warned off the Major's land. But why was she warned off? The Major clearly had something against Sarah, and clearly, Sarah was afraid of the Major. Still, he tried to defend her. "Now wait a minute Major, Cole's here because I asked her here, your men told me I needed a knife that would cut through these tough hides and that I should get a trapper's knife." Christian watched the Major move his hand to his whip then back, as if he had second thoughts about using it.

"Cole is not the only goddamn trapper sheriff! you could have asked any one of those men for the use of their knife! She knows she shouldn't be here!" Major Hardy stopped talking to Christian and addressed Sarah. "I will give you one-hour Cole! ...then I want you off my land! or I will have my men deal with you!" Taking a firm hold of his horse's reins, Major Hardy looked down at Christian. "You don't go bringing that...!" He stopped himself calling Sarah a whore. "Woman! ...out here again sheriff! ...I expect you to come by the ranch on your own to let me know what you have, or have not found!" With that he pulled his horse savagely around and rode off. Foley and Brady took another look at Sarah and Christian before following the Major up the rise.

Christian watched the men ride to the top of the rise and stop. "Sarah?" he questioned without turning to face her. After a moment of speaking together, Major Hardy and Brady continued out of sight, leaving Foley with his rifle resting across his legs, in full view.

"I told you I couldn't be here!" Sarah said, ducking out from behind Christian and running toward the trees. Grabbing her before she got to Star, Christian pushed her against the trunk of a tree to prevent her from escaping. "Sarah, damn it! …tell me what the Major meant! what did you do that was so bad he had to warn you off?"

"It has nothing to do with you!" Sarah replied savagely. "No! well, I happen to think it does …what did you do?" Christian demanded. Sarah's eyes burned with fire as she tried to escape Christian's grip. "Let! …me! …go!" she cried through gritted teeth. But Christian wasn't going to let her go, not this time, not before he got answers.

"Goddamn it, Sarah! I am not letting you go, not until you tell me what you did!" Sarah didn't answer. "What did you do?" Christian begged, shaking her. "Tell me!" he insisted. Resting his cheek against the side of Sarah's face, he quietened his voice. "Tell me Sarah, please …tell me …what was so bad Major Hardy had to warn you to stay off his land?" Tears Sarah tried to hold back ran down her face, leaving her no choice, she had to tell him about Frank.

"I …I …killed his son!" she whispered, drawing back a sob. Christian's eyes widened in disbelief, and stepping back, he let her go. "Satisfied sheriff?" Sarah said, wiping away a tear and going back to the steers.

"What do you mean? …you killed his son?" Christian's mind was in turmoil as he followed her. 'So that was why no-one would tell me about her and why she didn't want to come here!' While Sarah kept walking away, he thought it inconceivable that she could kill someone.

"Major Hardy blames me for Frank's death…and he is right! …oh, I didn't pull the trigger! …but I was the cause of Frank dying." Christian's stomach lurched at her admission. Frank could only be Frank Mason, the man whose name he found inside Thomas's drawing book and Sarah's bible.

Christian was shocked to learn Frank was Major Hardy's son, and that Thomas being Frank's son, was Major Hardy's grandson.

But what shocked him more than that was the fact Sarah had been blamed for killing Frank. How had she killed him? She said she didn't pull the trigger, but the Major blamed her. Why? All Christian could do was stare after Sarah as she walked over to a small shrub covered in red berries and pull it out of the ground. Walking back to where Christian stood, she shoved the shrub into his hand. "You tell the Major this is what is killing his steers, the bushes are not poisonous when they don't have berries on them, they can eat as much as they like …when there are no berries." Sarah looked up at Christian with tear filled eyes. "Tell him to burn them out, don't tell him it was me who told you, you tell him you figured it out, and tell him about his men not watching his steers." She hadn't wanted Christian to know about Frank. Her face was crestfallen, her eyes had taken on the same sad look Christian had seen the night she shot the river rats. They were dull, and lifeless. He didn't try to stop her leaving, but didn't know what to think of Sarah right then.

Riding back to town the way they came to the gulch, by going by the shack then crossing the river and heading back past the ponds, no longer caring what Christian thought of her, Sarah stopped crying. Sarah thought she saw judgement in his eyes, and if he was going to judge her, then so be it, the relationship she had with him, as far as she was concerned, was over.

Christian was numb, he held the berry bush in his hand and remained where he was. There were so many questions going over in his head. 'If she killed Frank, why had she killed him? What had Frank done for her to kill him?' Frank's message in Sarah's bible he remembered, read. 'Forgive me for what I am about to do.' Did Frank do something to Sarah? The scar on her shoulder! did he shoot her? Is that the reason she killed him? But then he remembered Thomas saying she shot herself. Did she tell Thomas she shot herself to cover the fact Frank shot her and she him? but then Sarah said she didn't pull the trigger. Christian stood where he was for a long time, not knowing what to make of what Sarah told him.

Foley waited on the ridge looking back at Sarah and Christian. When the three of them came riding over the ridge and found Christian inspecting the dead steers, he got a shock to see Sarah with him. Sarah had been warned more than twelve years ago never to set foot on the Majors land or she would be shot, and he and Brady had been the men the Major ordered to shoot her. He would never shoot Sarah. He could never shoot the woman he was in love with. Seeing her with Christian just now made his stomach churn. He heard talk they were together, but tried not to believe the gossip. Now after seeing how Christian tried to protect her, he was convinced the stories were true. Sarah turned every one of his proposals to marry her down, when all he ever wanted was to be her husband. He felt disappointed she had found love with a stranger.

Foley kept watching as Christian and Sarah, appeared to be arguing. When Sarah suddenly mounted her horse and rode off, going back across the river the way she came, he had no doubt Sarah would have been bathing in the ponds before they came along, figuring Christian had been there with her. When Sarah disappeared through the trees, Foley turned his horse and rode toward the Majors ranch in disgust.

Christian carried the bush with the red berries to his horse and shoved the plant in his saddle-bag. Before getting on his horse he looked to the hill where Foley was waiting and found him gone. Christian didn't head for Major Hardy's ranch right away. He had something else he wanted to do first. He headed back to the shack.

Chapter Thirty-two

Tethering his horse to the stoop rail at the shack, Christian took his axe out of the bag he had hanging off his saddle-horn and walked up to the front door. The boards nailed across the door looked worn, like they had been there a very long time. Finding the nails holding the boards across the doorway rusty, he hooked his axe-head over one of the boards and pulled. The board being worn broke away easily. Christian continued pulling boards away until he had enough space to enable him to kick the door in with his foot. When the door crashed open with an almighty clatter, Christian climbed in under the few remaining boards.

It was dark inside, daylight streaming in from the doorway wasn't enough to see by so he went back outside and removed boards from the windows. When he went back inside to look around the light streaming in was much better. The shack consisted of one room, an open stone fireplace graced one wall and there was no furniture of any kind. A crumpled, dirty jacket lay just inside the door. Spread out on the floor in front of the fireplace was an equally dirty blanket. Dust covered candles lined the hearth in front of the fireplace and more candles sat along the mantle above it. A pile of what looked like old rags lay next to the blanket. Christian picked up one of the rags and saw it was a shirt that looked like it would fit a young boy. The other rag turned out to be a much larger shirt. There were two pair of trousers, and two pairs of boots. An old broken wicker picnic basket and broken shards of glass lay scattered on the floor near the blanket and clothes. Christian stood up and surveying the scene, wondered what went on in the shack for a pile of clothes to be there along with a picnic basket.

'Why did Sarah seem to be remembering something about this shack?' Christian asked himself. Walking around the room trying to find something to tie Sarah to it, he stood back against the far wall directly opposite the fireplace. 'The blanket, the clothes, the broken glass, the candles, two people had been here and they had undressed, but one a boy and the other ...a man?' Christian wasn't naive, being aware there were men who liked men and women who liked women, he brought his thoughts back to figuring out what happened for the clothes to be there. 'Why didn't they get dressed when they were done? Maybe they brought a change of clothes with them! but who brings a change of clothes to a secret rendezvous?' To Christian that was what this appeared to be. But something obviously happened here, because whoever they were, they didn't get a chance to put their clothes back on.

Squatting back down, Christian looked at the broken glass. Some of it appeared to be from a wine bottle. He picked up a broken stem from a wine glass, then put it back down. 'Whatever happened here happened a long time ago, and whatever happened here,' Christian thought, 'Sarah was involved,' he was almost sure of it. Studying the fireplace while walking along the front and running his hand along the dust covered mantle, he came to the end and his heart skipped a beat. Proof that Sarah had been here lay hidden in the shadows near the hearth that made up the fireplace. A declaration of love had been carved in the wall. Now he had found them, the words stood out clearly, as if they had just been carved. While reading 'Frank Mason Loves Sarah Cole' over and over, Christian gripped the handle of his axe until his knuckles turned white. He didn't know how long he stood there staring at those names, but he knew the pile of clothes had been theirs. They weren't the clothes from a boy and a man at all, they were from Sarah and Frank. Sarah wore boys clothing. Christian knew that from when he and Thomas went to Crawley's store to get Sarah her knew shirt and trousers. Thomas had taken him to the boy's section, but he hadn't wanted Sarah to wear boy's clothes, he wanted her to look feminine, and she had. When he went to her camp for dinner, she looked beautiful, and very feminine dressed in the clothes he bought her.

'What happened to Sarah and Frank here? What had it been that Sarah was remembering when they rode past? Was she remembering that day long ago when she and Frank had undressed and made love and Frank declared his love for her by carving their names in this wall? When Major Hardy sets fire to the berry bushes, this shack will go up in smoke.' These were the thoughts going through Christian's head as he lifted his axe above his shoulder. With a violent swing, he drove his axe into the wall. He kept swinging, time and time again, until finally the section of board with the names carved on it came free. Then stepping around the blanket and pile of clothes, and carrying the board, he went to his horse. The board was too long to put in his saddle-bag so he shoved it inside the bag his axe was carried in. Leaving the shack behind, Christian rode back along the trail to the dead steers. Following the trail over the hill the way Major Hardy had ridden, he headed for his ranch.

Riding towards the ranch, he let his thoughts about Sarah consume him. He knew very little about Sarah and Frank. He knew Frank was Thomas's father. So why did it bother him about finding they had been together in the shack? Frank had carved their names in that wall for posterity, an everlasting memory to their love. They had undressed and made love, but why were their clothes still there on the floor? Just like him and Sarah at her shelter, and when they made love at the cavern, and again today at the ponds, they stripped off, but they dressed when they finished. Christian began to wonder just how many men Sarah had been with before him.

Was she a whore? Was that why Crawley called her that? She certainly knew how to make a man feel good when they fucked. And she didn't seem to care where they did it. By the time Christian arrived at Major Hardy's ranch he was questioning his relationship with Sarah. Did they even have a relationship? They fucked, but was it a relationship? Never once did Sarah say she loved him. He told her he loved her that night at the cavern. He told her again earlier today at the ponds, but Sarah never said those words back to him.

Riding through the gate at the ranch confused and angry, he wanted answers and hoped Major Hardy would be the person to give them to him. The cowhand standing guard outside the ranch-house took his horse. Christian had been expected and was shown straight in. Major Hardy, sitting in his study, didn't bother getting up, instead indicated with his hand for Christian to sit on the couch opposite him.

"Well, Sheriff Morgan, what did you find?" Major Hardy acted as if nothing happened out at the gulch. Before telling the Major anything, Christian wanted to know why he blamed Sarah for killing his son. "I may have found something Major, but first I have some questions for you." Any questions the sheriff had about his steers he was happy to answer. "Go ahead sheriff, ask me anything," Major Hardy smiled. "Why did you threaten Cole with trespass just now?" Taken aback by Christian's question and thinking it none of his business why he threatened Sarah, Major Hardy's whole demeanour changed. Forcing himself to keep a smile on his face he answered. "I just don't like stinking trappers on my land, that's all." But his answer didn't satisfy Christian. "I don't believe that for a moment Major, you have trappers working for you."

"Well …some trappers are better than others," Major Hardy was quick to answer. "I don't want that whore traipsing around my land in front of my men, distracting them from their work!" Christian didn't like that the Major called Sarah a whore.

"Who is Frank Mason?" he asked knowing the answer. Major Hardy's expression changed from one of satisfaction to one of shock, and standing up, thought Christian had no right to question him about his son. "If you haven't found out what is killing my steers sheriff, you had better leave."

It seemed Christian hit a nerve, but Major Hardy was just as elusive as everyone else when it came to Sarah. Christian stood up and reaching for his saddle-bag, pulled out the shrub Sarah had given him. The bush was crushed but still thick with berries. "This is what has been poisoning your steers Major, the berries are poisonous and the gulch is littered with them, they grow especially thick around a small shack at the back of the gulch." Eyeballing the Major, Christian tried to gauge his reaction when he mentioned the shack. A faint hint of surprise crossed the Major's face but nothing more. "You may need to burn it and the bushes out!" Christian said before moving to the door. "Oh! and another thing, your men have been spending their time gambling and fighting rather than keeping your herd from the gulch." His hand was on the doorknob when he saw a framed photograph of a young boy sitting on top of a bureau near the door. Frowning, Christian picked the photograph up and studied it. This could only be Frank. His eyes, his smile, the curly hair was the same, but this boy appeared much older, his similarity to Thomas was uncanny. "This is a nice picture of Thomas Mason Major?" Christian asked not knowing the Major didn't recognize Thomas as his grandson. "You are mistaken sheriff, that is a picture of my son Frank!" Realizing his mistake, Major Hardy tried covering it up. "Cole's son belongs to one of those trappers!" Christian was taken aback by his reply. Sitting the picture down and before going out the door, Christian turned back. "I get a feeling there is bad blood between you and Cole …the reason why is none of my business …but if this picture is of your son …then Cole's son is the living image of his father!" Christian slammed the door behind him and walking out, left the Major looking more closely at a picture of his son that was the image of a boy that carried his sons name. Except for stealing Thomas away from Sarah that one time, Sarah kept his grandson from him. Thomas was either in school or off with his mother somewhere, rabbit snaring or picking berries, either way, she managed to keep Thomas from him for twelve years. He was sure she wouldn't have told Thomas he was his grandfather. Cole always claimed her son was Frank's, and he tried his best not to acknowledge it, until now. It took a stranger to make him see what he tried all these years to deny.

Snow began to fall more heavily as Christian rode away from the Major 's ranch with more questions than answers on his mind. He wanted to confront Sarah with them, and wanted to know if she loved him and if so, did she intend staying in Cedar Creek come spring. He made up his mind as he rode back to town that what the Major said about Sarah didn't change his feelings for her, and what Sarah and Frank had been doing at the shack didn't matter to him. He knew Frank saved Sarah from drowning. Even though Thomas hadn't mentioned Franks name, Thomas told him who he was. Sarah and Frank had been in love and they had Thomas, so be it. He refused to believe Sarah had been the cause of Frank's death.

Although Christian had been surprised to learn Thomas was the Major's grandson, he could no longer deny his feelings for Sarah. Why should he care if the Major hated Sarah? The Major was an arrogant, overbearing man and as far as Christian was concerned that was no great tragedy on his part. He decided he wanted Sarah to move into the lodge to be with him, and the sooner the better, he didn't want her and Thomas camping on the riverbank amongst marauding river rats any longer. All he had to do though, was convince Sarah to move in with him. That wasn't the only problem he had. He was afraid she would tell him to go to hell after pressing her into confessing about Frank.

Leaving his horse at the Livery, he went back to his office where, closing himself in the back room, he sat on the bunk, and tried to figure out just what to say to Sarah. After racking his brain over what to say, he thought maybe he should just come straight out with it and ask her to marry him. Taking the board out of the sack and holding it up, he read again, 'Frank Mason Loves Sarah Cole.' Staring at the words, he thought maybe she would like him more if he gave her the board as a keepsake. He quickly shoved the board back in the sack when he heard a commotion in the office.

Thomas was excited when Sarah got back to their camp and blurted out what happened in town while she was out bathing at the ponds. Sarah was furious with what Thomas told her. After having a fight with Christian about what she had done to warrant being warned off the Major's land and confessing to him she was to blame for Frank's death, Sarah felt Christian had been too quick to judge her. Yet here she was, hearing that Christian Morgan, Sheriff of Cedar Creek, the man whom she had been intimate with, had once been a Bounty Hunter, the worst kind of hunter there was. She hunted wolves and got paid for their skins, but Sheriff Morgan! he hunted men and claimed the reward. Sarah had no doubt he would have killed some of those men and she wasn't going to take it. How dare he judge her for believing she killed Frank when she hadn't. Frank ended his life when wolves attacked him so he wouldn't be eaten alive. It didn't matter to Sarah that Christian didn't know this fact. She stormed up the street to the Sheriff's Office to give him a piece of her mind. As she walked along her knife swung at her side, her arms stretched in front of her as she swung them back and forth, and her boots crunched in patches of snow on the ground. People walking about recognized that walk and knew that look on her face. They knew someone was in trouble, and they hurriedly got out of Sarah's way.

Storming through the door at the Sheriff's Office, she found Clem sitting behind the desk. "Where is he? Where the hell is the goddamn sheriff?" Not waiting for Clem to tell her where Christian was, she hurried around the desk and into the back room where she found Christian sitting on the bunk. Christian heard Sarah's raised voice, but still, was surprised when she barged in unexpectedly, causing him to stand up quickly. "What do you want Cole?" All thought of saying what he wanted to say to Sarah disappeared when he saw the look of anger on her face.

"I want to know what you think you are doing sheriff! ...how dare you! ...to think you can judge me! ...you! ...you goddamn! ...bounty hunter!" she exclaimed in disgust, and going on before Christian could say a word. "You are the worst kind of man there is! ...I hunt wolves, but you! ...you hunt ...people!" Sarah's eyes suddenly brimmed with tears. Glad he was getting somewhere at last, Christian let her go on. "I didn't kill Frank! ...he killed himself! ...he had to ...because of the wolves ...up there ...on the mountain ...goddamn it! ...Major Hardy blames me because Frank loved me! and Major Hardy didn't want him to ...and you ...you killed those two men ...you came out to the ponds afterwards and we...!" she stopped, then. "How could you even think about...!" she stopped again. "You acted like nothing happened!" she yelled, her eyes overflowing.

Even though Christian hadn't killed both outlaws as Sarah said, he didn't correct her. It didn't matter, Sarah was riled enough about him taking advantage of her at the ponds. "I'm not judging you Sarah, but aren't you doing the same thing? You are standing here now ...judging me ...yes ...I 'was' a bounty hunter ...but that was a long time ago, don't you think some things should remain in the past?, what happened between you and Frank, out at the shack ... don't you think that should remain in the past?" Sarah glared at him, 'Did he know what happened at the shack? Had he been to the Major's ranch and asked him about her and Frank? Had the Major told him everything?' She tried to look at him through her tears. "Oh hell!" she cried, before running from the room.

This was not how Christian wanted him and Sarah to end up. Even though he was glad to find out she hadn't killed Frank, and his feelings for her hadn't changed, he made up his mind he was going to leave her alone for now, and didn't speak to her when he saw her in town. He decided he would wait until Sarah wasn't so angry with him, then he would ask her to come to the lodge where they could be together without worrying if anyone were spying on them.

It was this winter, Thomas had turned twelve, and the town had a new sheriff, that Foley, for the first time, didn't ask Sarah to marry him.

One week after Sarah and Christian had been out at the dry gulch investigating why the Majors steers had died and their clash at the Sheriff's Office, Foley was out riding the boundaries when he came across from the Major's land and met up with Sarah out snaring rabbits.

After the Major found out his men were holding fights instead of watching his steers, instead of firing them, because he needed every man to help with his herd, he withheld a month's pay from each man. Knowing full well where Foley wanted to go and whom he wanted to see, Brady stayed with the men to make sure they were doing what they were paid to do, and let his brother ride off alone. Brady knew Foley was in love with Sarah. He also knew it was a waste of Foley's time, him trying to get her to marry him, especially now she had been with the sheriff.

Crossing the river and riding back along the edge of the trees, Foley came across Sarah sitting on a log with a fire burning and her coffee pot steaming. Staying on his horse, he leant on his saddle-horn and looked down at her. Sarah looked up at him. "You want some coffee Foley?" she asked, squinting into the sun. "There's enough in the pot for two." Foley didn't answer, instead threw his leg over his saddle and got down, then rummaging around in his saddle-bag found his mug. Carrying his mug over to where Sarah stood with her pot, he watched her face as she concentrated on pouring the hot brew. He wasn't put off by the fact Sarah had given herself freely to Christian, his heart was racing. Feelings he had for Sarah were more than he would ever have for Maria. Squatting in front of a tree, he reached inside his coat and pulled out a cheroot. Sarah watched as he struck a match on the side of his boot and lit the smoke.

"Why do you smoke those awful things Foley? They stink, you can smell you all the way from across the river!" Sarah exaggerated a little on how far she could smell the odour. Foley took the cheroot out of his mouth and looked at it. "I don't know, started smoking on cattle drives, something to fill the time I suppose." He spoke softly, took a drink of his coffee and sat the mug on the ground at his feet. Foley knew about Sarah's keen sense of smell and made up his mind, if she didn't like him smoking, he would give it up. Looking over at Sarah sitting in the shade from under his hat, he thought her so darn pretty it hurt his chest to look at her.

They talked about general things, like the last cattle drive Foley went on and how many skins Sarah got. Foley could tell Sarah was especially pleased when she talked about the two white skins. They didn't mention the town having a new sheriff, nor that Sarah had been with him. Sarah didn't want to talk about Christian, she hadn't spoken to him since confronting him in the back room at the Sheriff's Office. Neither Foley nor Sarah mentioned what happened out at the gulch. They talked about Thomas putting the rats in Jamie Finch and Daniel Connell's beds, they even laughed about it. "How is your arm Cole?" Foley asked. Everyone knew she had been hurt berry picking. "It's good Foley, Doc took the stitches out weeks ago." Sarah thought about her and Christian making love at the ponds not long after the stitches were removed. Foley stood up when he finished his coffee and smoke. He could see Sarah was deep in thought about something, and figured she was probably thinking about Sheriff Morgan.

Right about now was when he would ask Sarah to marry him. Walking over to his horse he shoved his mug into his saddle-bag. Expecting him to come back to her to propose, Sarah stood up and waited. Even though she had feelings for him and had almost said yes last winter when he proposed, she would have to turn him down again, she was in love with Christian and hoped she and Christian could sort out their differences. Foley put his foot in his stirrup and swung up into his saddle. "Thanks for the coffee Cole," he said tipping his hat. Giving his horse a nudge with his heels he rode off, leaving Sarah staring after him. Sarah was surprised when he rode away. He asked her to marry him every year since Thomas was a baby, so what was different about this year? After watching him disappear along the trail, and thinking maybe him not asking her was a good thing, Sarah shrugged her shoulders, packed up her things and went to check her snares.

When Foley rode away, he thought it no use asking Sarah to marry him, she would only say no like she did every year. Now she was seeing Sheriff Morgan, just like the time she got with Frank Mason, he knew he didn't stand a chance at winning her affection. Her refusals only served to make him upset that he had been rejected again. He would end up going to the saloon and getting so drunk he couldn't stand up. He would get into a drunken brawl, and cowhands from Major Hardy's ranch would have to cart him back to the ranch with him feeling sorry for himself, and he would end up with a sore head the next day. Then he would be mad at everyone for the rest of winter. Even though he didn't love Maria, he made up his mind he would keep on seeing her, only to have his needs attended to.

Chapter Thirty-three

The very moment Sarah and Frank started making love, Sarah's body reacted to Frank's lovemaking. Sarah thought that was because she had never had a man make love to her before Frank made her his. Now here she was, her body was reacting again, and Christian Morgan only the second man she had ever been with. Having rejected plenty of offers of marriage from trappers and cowhands alike, it took a man she knew very little about to win her heart.

After the fight with Christian at the dry gulch, then confronting him in the Sheriff's Office, and having him say what happened at the shack should remain at the shack, Sarah decided she needed to think what to do with regard to him. Instead of riding north to the ponds where she risked running into Foley and Brady or Major Hardy, or perhaps Christian, she decided to ride south to the swimming hole. She wasn't going to swim, she didn't know how to swim, she just wanted to sit on her blanket, look at the waterfall, and think. Thomas was at school, her lesson with Jonathon wouldn't take place until she got back later that afternoon.

Spreading her blanket out on the grass not far from the swimming hole, she sat down, and pulling her knees up in front of her, wrapped her arms around her legs like she did as a young girl. It wasn't long before she was deep in thought.

Her arguments with Christian made her question herself. They shared wonderful moments where they loved each other so much they couldn't get enough of each other, but they fought, just as hard as they made love. Christian was stubborn and liked to get his own way, and she was the same, so undoubtedly, they clashed. Sarah didn't want them to fight, but she wouldn't give in to him easily either. She wasn't going to be a pushover and there were things from her past she didn't want Christian to know about. She wasn't ashamed of what she did when it came to protecting her family, but she wasn't sure if Christian, having been brought up in an orphanage would understand. The fact the man she loves has never known the love of a family, upsets her. She has a family, a very large family which includes the trappers. She adored her father, and when he died, she had been devastated. She had known her first love with Frank, even though it had been for such a short time, and she has Thomas, her wonderful gift from him.

Sarah thought about the first day she met Christian, how they fought when she knocked him off his feet outside the schoolhouse, and fought over her guns. She thought at the time, he didn't like her at all, but the very next night in the Livery he kissed her and they touched each other intimately, both satisfied to take what they started further. Kicking him in the shins when mistakenly thinking he paid Billy to get Thomas out of the way so he could have his way with her, and punching him in the face, was unladylike to say the least. Feeling disgusted with herself, she held her hand up and made a fist. She had been so wrong about Christian then.

While thinking about them making love quietly under the blanket at the cavern, she watched the trees swaying gently in the breeze. The sound of the waterfall cascading into the swimming hole lulled her into a relaxed mood, and so she continued thinking about Christian.

When Christian came to dinner, she was disappointed after he walked away leaving her feeling in doubt about their relationship. But then out at the ponds she was pleased when he came along. Becoming aroused while bathing each other, Christian pushed her to the brink of complete satisfaction, knowing exactly how to make her give all of herself to him.

Going to the dry gulch was a stupid thing to do. She knew she could be in danger if she was found on the Major's land, but she went anyway, because she didn't want to fight with Christian. When the Major came along and just warned her about being there, she thought it was because Christian, being the sheriff, the Major would not welcome trouble from the law. The day had not ended well though, when Christian forced her to tell him why she wasn't allowed on the Major's land, and now, they weren't speaking to each other.

Sarah didn't think Christian knew much of anything about her. He wouldn't be able to get anyone to talk, not even Joe, who was always around where she was. Joe would never tell tales about her. Christian knew she cut up a wolf and frightened the town folk, but did he know where she cut it up, and why? Sarah didn't think he did. He knew she didn't like Benjamin Crawley, but did he know the reason? She hadn't told him the reason. She has no doubt Crawley killed her father and still firmly believes he stole her house. Crawley claimed he won it fair and square, but Sarah knows differently. She knows her father would never sign away their house, not to that murdering, thieving, maggot! not to anyone. Everyone in town, including the trappers, thinks her father fell while drunk and bumped his head by accident. Sarah knows what really happened. Crawley has told her many times how he killed her father, but she can't prove it. No-one, not Joe or Fergus, nor Garrett or Will, believed her when she tried telling them the truth.

'Damn' Sarah thought. She has little information about Christian. She hadn't even asked him if he had ever been married. This fact made her wonder how many women he had been with before her. He certainly had experience in how to make a woman respond when he made love to her. He hadn't told her he had been a Bounty Hunter, she had to find that out from Thomas. Why couldn't he have told her about his past? After a lot of thought, Sarah decided, because she hadn't volunteered anything about herself, it was only fair Christian didn't offer up anything about himself. Taking a deep breath, and because her brain hurt, she stopped thinking about Christian for a while.

The swimming hole looked inviting. A cool breeze blew across the water. The sun was shining, the snow was melting and the waterfall was making a roaring sound as ice water from the mountain cascaded over boulders and into the deep pool. A pretty rainbow glistened in the spray. Sarah felt like taking her boots off and paddling. She wouldn't go in far, just paddle along the edge.

The sound of a horse's hooves echoing on the trail as it came closer, made Sarah look around to see Christian approaching from the direction of town. Sarah's stomach fluttered, her face became flushed, she wasn't expecting him and was surprised to see him ride up. Turning back to face the swimming hole, she waited for him to walk over to her.

Christian needed to take a ride somewhere to be alone to think, and when he went to get his horse, Ham told him Sarah was at the swimming hole. Knowing she would be alone, he decided now would be a good time to tell her how he felt about her. After striding over to where Sarah was sitting, he stood facing her. "Hello Cole," he said down to her. "What are you doing all the way out here?"

"I came here to be alone Christian, what about you?" Christian ignored Sarah saying she wanted to be alone but liked that she called him by his name. "I was out riding, so I thought it was time to take a look at the swimming hole," he lied.

"So, what do you think?" Sarah tried to stay calm, he was entitled to ride wherever he wished, she just wished he had ridden somewhere else so she didn't have to be near him, her heart was racing already.

"I haven't had a chance to look at it." Christian put his hands on his hips and turned to look at the waterfall, then turned back to Sarah. "Mind if I sit down?" he asked.

"No, go ahead." Sarah kept her arms around her legs. Christian sat right next to her, letting his arm brush against hers. When he pulled his legs up in front of him and put his arms across his knees, Sarah remembered sitting like this a long time ago, with Frank, only they were sitting on boulders at the ponds. She remembered it was Christmas and Frank gave her Star. On the way back to town, Frank kissed her. That was the first time she had ever been kissed. They had spent other days sitting on boulders at the ponds, but that day was the most memorable.

"What are you thinking about Cole?" Christian asked looking over at the pool of water.

"I was thinking how nice a day it is, that's all." Sarah's voice was quiet, she wasn't about to tell him she was thinking of Frank.

"Have you ever swam in the hole Cole?" Christian laughed suddenly at what he said. When Sarah laughed at how silly it sounded, the wall of ice they had between them fell away.

"Why are you calling me Cole? There's no one else here Christian." They looked sideways at each other, then, both turned back to look at the waterfall.

"Have you Sarah? ...swam in there I mean," Christian repeated.

"No ...I can't swim." Sarah thought it wouldn't hurt if Christian knew that small fact. She was sure he knew she hadn't been able to read when they first met. She felt embarrassed that he could tell, and felt ignorant when he looked at her with his deep blue eyes, thinking he could see right into her soul. Now she was having reading and writing lessons, she didn't feel so ignorant, and thought what harm could it possibly do if she told him she couldn't swim. Maybe if she gave in a little, he would tell her something about himself.

"You can't swim?" he said sounding incredulous.

"No ...I can't swim," Sarah repeated quietly.

"Well, it's about time you learnt!" Christian reached down and pulling his boots off, dropped them beside him on the blanket. Standing in front of Sarah, he undid his gun-belt and sat it next to his boots, then smiling down at her, took hold of his shirt by the back of its collar and pulled it over his head. Quickly pulling his arms out of the sleeves, he dropped it on top of his boots and holster. Watching what he was doing, Sarah stared at his smooth, muscled chest that flexed when he moved, while thinking some men had hair on their chests, but besides hair under his arms, the only hair Christian had on him was on his legs ...and his crotch. "What are you doing?" she asked when she saw him start to undo his trousers.

"I'm going to teach you to swim." Bending down, he took both of Sarah's hands in his and pulled her to her feet. When he reached for the front of her shirt, she slapped his hands away with a gentle swipe of her hand.

"What are you doing Christian?" Sarah repeated more sternly.

"I am going for a swim and you are coming with me," he smiled. What transpired between them out at the gulch and later at the Sheriff's Office was pushed to the back of his mind. When he came along and saw her sitting on her blanket looking all alone, his heart went out to her, and he didn't want to start anything that would cause her to cry and him to get angry.

"No, I am not!" Sarah said folding her arms across the front of her in defiance. When Christian flexed his muscles, Sarah felt a thrill course through her and forgot for the moment about their argument at the gulch and their confrontation at the Sheriff's Office.

"Come on Sarah, let me teach you to swim," he urged, going back to undoing his trousers. "Come on," he repeated. Slowly pushing his trousers over his hips, the dark growth of hair between his legs came into view and he stopped just before exposing himself completely.

"That water is freezing!" Sarah exclaimed. Christian kept smiling. "We won't feel the cold." Christian knew he would grow warm as soon as he saw Sarah's naked body. He warmed up when he felt her lying against him at the cavern, and he warmed up straight away at the ponds when he saw her sitting naked in the shallow pool. Taking hold of his trousers he pushed them over his knees. Stepping back a little and becoming enthralled at the size of him, Sarah's face became flushed at the sight standing before her. Frank had been big, but Christian made Frank look quite small. Christian lifted his legs out of his trousers and throwing them aside, stood naked and vulnerable in front of Sarah and held out his hand. "I will make sure you are safe Sarah …I won't let you go."

When he kept his hand outstretched toward her, a memory of Frank came to her. They were at the cemetery. It was pouring with rain and Frank, sitting opposite her, let her hit him until she drew blood, then he held her while she cried. When she was done crying, he stood up and held his hand out to her. Placing her hand in Frank's made her feel safe. Reaching out now and taking Christian's hand made her feel equally safe. Christian walked backwards toward the water taking Sarah with him. When he stepped into the swimming hole, he let go of her hand. "Come on Sarah, you are not going to swim in your clothes, take them off!" Standing in ankle deep water, Christian kept his eyes on Sarah while she looked him up and down. His body was firm, his arms and legs hard and muscled. Feeling that familiar ache of wanting surging through her, Sarah looked around at where they were, and not seeing or sensing anyone nearby, looked back at Christian, undid her sheath from around her waist and dropped it on the ground. After quickly undoing the front of her shirt, she took it off. Christian's eyes focused on her breasts. Undoing her trousers, she slipped them down her legs, bent forward to take off her boots and pulled her feet free of her trousers. When she straightened up, she looked straight at Christian's crotch and saw his reaction to seeing her unclothed. Sarah couldn't help smiling and turned her head away. Christian smiled too when he saw Sarah watching what was happening to him.

Putting his hand out again, Sarah reached out and took it. Walking backwards, getting further away from the edge, letting the water slowly rise above his knees, Sarah walked a little way then stopped. Standing in water up to her thighs, feeling afraid, she pulled her hand out of his grasp. "I can't go in deep water Christian," she said, clasping her hands in front of her. "It's alright Sarah, watch me." Christian pushed himself backwards until only his head was out of the water. Keeping his eyes on Sarah, he swam a little way out, then paddled back toward her. It was true, the water was freezing, Sarah could feel her nipples hardening. When the water covered the mat of hair between her legs, she took one more step and stopped.

Taking hold of both of Sarah's hands, Christian started to take her out further, but Sarah baulked and pulled back. "Trust me Sarah, I won't let you go." While Christian kept his eyes on Sarah, she wondered should she trust him?

Stepping away from the edge, until the water lapped the bottom of Sarah's breasts, making them appear to float on top of the water, Christian smiled and took another step until the water was up to his chin. When the water touched Sarah's nipples, she took another step. Too late! she stepped out of her depth. The water rose over her head, and she began to panic. Christian tried to hang on to her hands, but she fought to free them, and because they were wet, he couldn't hold her. With her head under water, Sarah couldn't breathe. Keeping her eyes clamped shut, she lashed out wildly and kept thrashing. Christian tried grabbing her, but she continued to fight against him, forcing him to wrap his arms around her in a vice like grip. When he managed to bring their bodies crashing together, Sarah came up coughing and sprayed water all over him.

"It's alright Sarah, I've got you," he assured her, taking her back to shallow water.

"I trusted you!" Sarah screamed, wiping water and hair out of her eyes. "You let me go in deep water …goddamn it!" she cursed, turning her back on him. "I didn't know it would go over your head!" he said honestly, putting his arms around her. "I trusted you Christian," Sarah said more softly. "I'm sorry," Christian apologized, pressing his slippery body against her. Turning to face him she let him kiss her wet face. "Come on …let me teach you how to paddle, we'll stay in shallow water." Underwater, feeling Sarah's body against his, along with everything else, his desire for her was growing. Kissing her passionately, he thought. 'So much for wanting to wait until I can get her into my bed at the lodge.'

After calming down, Sarah let him show her how to paddle. At first, he got her to turn her arms like wheels by making them go around in circles in the air, then she tried it in the water. Sarah felt ridiculous, but when Christian praised her, she kept going. Lying in the water with her body stretched across his arms, he got her to keep her legs straight and kick her feet. Sarah splashed wildly. "Now, I want you to paddle and pull the water towards you," he advised. Turning her arms like crazy, Sarah felt her backside rise out of the water. "Are you looking at my bottom Christian?" Sarah joked as she kept paddling.

"It's a beautiful bottom Sarah," Christian laughed.

"Are you laughing at me?" Sarah laughed too.

"No!" he said laughing harder as her bottom rose higher in the water. When Sarah stopped paddling and stood up, they hugged and laughed some more.

"We have got to be serious Sarah, if you happen to fall in the river again, being able to paddle could save your life." Christian's words stopped Sarah laughing. She was under the impression Christian didn't know she had once gone into the river and almost drowned. But he did know, Thomas told him when they were on their way to find her at the cavern. Sarah had been lucky Frank was there that day. He pulled her from the river, dug the bullet out of her shoulder and made her warm in his shelter. It was only during a violent storm when Frank went to her cabin and she let him stay that she fell pregnant with Thomas. The memory made Sarah pensive and she went quiet.

"Sarah? …are you ready to learn some more?" Christian was saying when Sarah brought her mind back to the present. "Yes Christian, I'm ready." Sarah became serious, Christian was right, it could save her life, hunting wolves on the mountain was often carried out along the river.

While Christian pulled her along, he made her kick her legs. Then he got her to paddle her arms and kick her legs on her own. At first, she couldn't get them to work together, but as she persevered, all of a sudden, her arms and legs were going in tandem, moving her along ever so slowly in the shallow water. Sarah paddled toward Christian until he moved into deeper water. "Paddle to me Sarah," he urged, moving further back until all that was out of the water was his head and shoulders. "I can't!" Sarah said standing in water waist deep. "Yes, you can, paddle to me and I will hold you, then we will paddle back together …trust me!" Christian added. Sarah didn't move. "Trust me Sarah," he said again.

Sarah wanted to trust him, but he let her head go underwater when she first got in. "Paddle to me Sarah," Christian demanded softly, holding both hands out to her. Deciding she had to trust him, because her life depended on it, she stretched her body lengthwise and started to paddle. "Kick your feet!" Christian urged loudly. Sarah kicked and started to move. "That's it, keep going!" Paddling madly, pulling at the water, getting her hands to go around in front of her, she could see herself getting closer to Christian. Kicking her feet furiously, she made the water splash violently behind her. When Christian smiled, she tried to smile back, causing her to stop paddling. Her mouth went under, she swallowed water and while coughing because of it, she began paddling again. "Keep going Sarah!" Christian said. "Come on, come to me," he encouraged. Almost there, Christian grabbed her hands, and pulled her to him. When Sarah suddenly stopped kicking, her body sank and bumped against him. "Put your legs around me," Christian said, letting his body press against hers. Wrapping her legs around him, she felt his body between her legs. Christian moved Sarah's arms around his neck. "Now!" he said smiling. "I've got you."

"Are you standing on the bottom Christian?" Sarah asked after feeling something happening below water. "No, I'm treading water." Sarah shivered and said, "treading water! …you can't tread in water Christian," and he laughed at her innocent comment.

"Come on, lets paddle back to the edge." Paddling side by side, Christian was full of praise and told Sarah what else she should do when she hunted by the river. "Remember, if you ever fall in, keep paddling and kicking, and swim to the closest riverbank and you will be alright." He was happy with what Sarah had achieved and Sarah was happy that he was happy for her. Holding each other, they kissed some more.

As Christian pushed himself between Sarah's legs, a moan of desire escaped him. Suddenly standing up, and lifting Sarah out of the water, she wrapped her legs around him, and let him carry her all the way up to her blanket. Once there, he lay her down, and wrapped the blanket around them. When their wet bodies slipped against each other easily, Christian worked at pushing against Sarah and Sarah pushed back, letting herself come when he came. With their bodies spent, they lay quietly, each deep in their own thoughts. Sarah could feel the air getting colder as the sun dipped behind a cloud. More snow would be coming to Cedar Creek. It was barely two weeks until Christmas and two months before the trappers would leave town for the mountain.

Christian brought Sarah out of her thoughts. "Sarah?" he said rolling over and holding his body against her. "I don't want you staying on the riverbank any longer, I want you and Thomas to move in to my place with me." He thought once he asked her to move in with him, she would be thrilled to stop camping on the riverbank. "I want to make love to you in my bed," he whispered, waiting for her answer.

"Your place?" Sarah said, sounding incredulous. She knew Christian lived in the lodge, but she didn't know he referred to it as his place.

"Yes, my place …you know what I mean, we have only ever been together outside, on the ground, I want to make love to you in a warm bed." Christian kissed her, then keeping his face above Sarah's, looked seriously down at her.

"You want me to go to the lodge?" Sarah looked just as seriously into Christian's eyes.

"Yes," he said, smiling innocently down at her. "That is where my bed is." He went to kiss Sarah again, but she turned her head away. Christian frowned and let go of her. Sarah stood up and gathered her clothes. "I can't!" she said, starting to get dressed. This was not what Christian expected Sarah to say, just like out at the gulch, he was confused and angry.

"You mean you won't! don't you Sarah?" He waited for a reply that did not come. "So, it's ok for us to fuck out in the open! but don't get in a bed with me! is that what you mean?" Both knowing they were about to fight, Christian stood up too and began to get into his clothes. Sarah looked incredulously at him and tried to ignore what he said. "I won't go to the lodge Christian."

"Why not? That is where I live! don't you want to be with me? Inside, out of the cold! in a house! ...god ...damn ...it!" Christian pulled his shirt on angrily. "Yes ...just not in the lodge!" Sarah pulled her trousers on. "What is it with you Sarah? what is wrong with coming to the lodge and getting in my bed? we fuck on the ground ...out in the cold! for Christ sake!" As Christian's voice grew louder, he yanked his boots on in anger.

"Don't you yell at me Sheriff Morgan!" Sarah let slip. Realizing what she said she opened her mouth to apologize. She didn't want to be angry with him, not after him teaching her to swim, and not after their frantic lovemaking just now, still, she was adamant she wasn't going to go to the lodge.

"Oh! here we go! you are fucking mad at me! ...all I want is for you to fuck me in my bed and not on the goddamn ground! ... you refuse ...and you! ...are fucking mad! ...at me!" he said, angrily pointing his finger at himself.

"I am not mad at you Christian! just don't ask me to go to the lodge! I won't step foot inside a house that maggot Crawley owns! I won't ever step foot inside the lodge!" Sarah sat down and pulled on her boots. She wasn't mad at Christian objecting about them coming together on the cold hard ground out in the open for anyone passing to see, she wasn't too pleased about it herself. She would love to go somewhere where they could be in a bed together, but where? She couldn't go to Joe and say. 'Hey Joe! Christian and I want to fuck! can we borrow my old room?' There was nowhere in Cedar Creek they could go. Christian should not have suggested she go to the lodge, a place she vowed she would never step foot in.

"Who cares if Crawley owns the fucking lodge! that is where I live!" Christian tried lowering his voice so he wouldn't sound so angry, but it didn't work, he still sounded angry.

"I care Christian!" Sarah snapped. "I won't go there! …not ever! and don't you go cursing at me!" Looking at him, with her eyes misty, she tied her sheath around her waist.

"You care! …you fucking care!" he repeated savagely. "You won't make love to me in my bed, but hey! …it is ok for us to fuck on the ground, or …or in a cavern, or the fucking ponds, or anywhere else though, isn't it?" He did up his gun-belt by angrily pulling the belt through the buckle and pulling it tight. Then bending down, he savagely picked up his hat and jammed it on his head.

Sarah tried to make Christian see reason. "What difference does it make where we do it? so long as we are together! …but I will not make love in that maggot's house!" Trying to make her voice sound softer, less angry in the hope it would placate him, Sarah thought Christian would give in.

"Why don't you say fuck Cole? Why don't you just come out and say the word fuck? Because that is what we are doing, isn't it? Fucking! we are not making love, we are fucking! When two people love each other they make allowances, but you don't make allowances, do you? You just love to fuck, and fuck the consequences!" Christian spat the words angrily as he made for his horse. Turning back, he stormed toward Sarah. "You just let me fuck you out here in the open for anyone passing by to see …well you know what? a goddamn whore can be fucked anywhere!" He stormed back to his horse. "I am done!" he called over his shoulder. Sarah was stunned by what Christian called her, so stunned she could feel a tightness stretching across her chest as tears stung her eyes. "Christian!" she called after him.

Getting up in his saddle, Christian pulled his horse around to face her. "Another thing I want to ask you Cole! …just supposing we spend all winter fucking …are you going back to the mountain in the spring like nothing happened?”

The mountain was her home, that was where her cabin was, here in Cedar Creek she and Thomas lived on the riverbank, on the mountain, they had a roof over their heads. Sarah knew her answer would make Christian angrier than he already was. Looking at the ground she answered. “The mountain is my home Christian.” Keeping his horse steady, Christian snapped. “That is not what I asked you! …are you going back to the mountain?”

Sarah thought what difference would it make if she were to go home now Christian said he was done with her. “Yes.” Was all she could bring herself to say through the choking lump in her throat. Christian’s shoulders slumped with disappointment. If Sarah had said no, she wasn’t going back to the mountain, that she wanted to stay in Cedar Creek to be with him, he would have made one hell of an apology to her right there, but she didn’t give him the answer he wanted.

“I don’t want to see you Cole … not ever …we are finished!” he said looking down at her before kicking his horse savagely and riding away.

Remaining where she was, her mind raging in a fog of thoughts and emotions, Sarah tried to grasp what Christian said. ‘He called me a whore! Is that what he thinks of me after all the time we spent together? I thought he loved me …he said he loved me …I heard him say it!’ It didn’t make sense, they had just made love, Christian had been a little rougher than usual, but she put that down to their bodies being against each other in the water. Sarah knew Christian had been excited when he slipped between her legs, she had become excited too. But had Christian’s attitude changed when they were lying wrapped in her blanket? Had he been thinking about asking her to go to the lodge while he made love to her? Afterwards, when he said he was fucking her, not making love to her, she knew they were one and the same, but it didn’t cheapen her when she said she was making love to him. Did he hate her that much? Was he treating her like a whore? She had been called a whore before. Major Hardy called her that, and so did Crawley. She didn’t expect Christian would ever call her names? She loved him! didn’t he love her?’ She felt hurt and confused. Of course, it stood to reason she would be going back to the mountain, he should have known that before asking her. It suddenly dawned on Sarah what Christian was saying. They were having casual sex because she would be leaving in the spring, leaving him behind like he didn't matter. If they had a place other than the lodge to live, perhaps she would stay, but once he said he was done with her, it was too late. Sarah sat on her wet blanket and cried uncontrollably.

After crying for some time Sarah rode back to town in a daze. How did they end up fighting? Christian wanted her in a bed, a bed in the lodge, her lodge, the one place she would never step foot in. She had never minded that Christian lived there, he didn't own it, it wasn't him that had taken it from her. Sarah couldn't for the life of her think what difference being in a bed made, if Christian loved her it should make no difference where they made love. But according to him they weren't making love, they were fucking. He made their love sound dirty. Sarah's day at the swimming hole had turned ugly. What happened between her and Christian was the worst possible thing that could happen, and now it was over between them.

When Sarah took Star to the Livery, Christian's horse was in its stall. Ham tried to talk to her but she ignored him and went straight to her camp. Relieved Thomas wasn't back from school, she went to the shelter to lie down, then wept some more as her mind began working. 'What can I do? I have to go back to the mountain, I can't stay here on the riverbank, this is just temporary until the pass is clear and the snow is gone. Damn the pass! why couldn't I have stayed on the mountain? Then I would never have met Christian, and I would not be in such a predicament!' When Thomas came from school, Sarah was sitting in front of the firepit preparing dinner like nothing happened.

Chapter Thirty-four

Christian hated himself for his angry outburst when he mistakenly thought Sarah would gladly go to the lodge to be with him. When she refused, he rode back to town in an agitated state.

They had been having fun together, laughing and frolicking around like two silly children, when all he really wanted was to make love to her. Sarah didn't have to do anything to get him worked up. The moment she undressed his body reacted instantly, and Sarah, unable to miss what was happening to him, stared right back. Knowing what would happen when their bodies came together wrapped in her blanket, he pushed Sarah to the limit, and by the time they both came they were sweating.

Not wanting to keep sneaking off to places to have sex with her like a wild animal, he thought it time for them to be together properly so hadn't seen any reason for Sarah not to join with him in his bed. As far as he was concerned, saying she wouldn't step foot in a house Crawley owns was a pretty poor excuse not to agree to live with him. The lodge is a nice house, where Sarah and Thomas would be safe out of extreme weather. Doesn't she love him? Doesn't she want to be with him? Why would she want to have sex on the cold, hard ground? Christian's thoughts became dark when thinking maybe that was what she did on the mountain. Maybe she slept with some of the trappers. Maybe that's why Crawley call her a whore. Maybe she doesn't love him, but he loves her. His wanderings had taken him to a lot of places, and he had his fair share of women, but none when he thought about it, ever came close to being like Sarah.

Her answer when he asked her if she was going back to the mountain devastated him. On the way back to town, he realized how stupid he had been for deciding he wasn't going to keep seeing her if at the end of it all she was going to leave. Becoming angry for ruining everything between them, he stopped riding, got off his horse, and walking away so as not to frighten the animal, opened his mouth and vented his anger as loud as he could. Sarah didn't deserve being called names, not after coaxing her into the water and teaching her to paddle, and certainly not after they made love. He wanted to keep seeing her. They still had another two months before Sarah and the trappers would head back to the mountain. 'Maybe,' he thought, 'I still have time to work something out to get her to stay.'

Still feeling rotten when he made it back to town, Christian left his horse with Ham, and not stopping to talk with anyone, went straight to the lodge. Relieved when Clem didn't come looking for him, he sat at the small dining table, and after giving a great deal of thought to what happened between him and Sarah, and feeling disgusted for the cruel words that came from his mouth, it didn't surprise him at all if Sarah hated him, and so making up his mind he would go to her camp, and tell her he was sorry, he ate the meal Maria left for him and decided to tell Sarah all about his past and get it off his chest.

It was getting late. Christian expected Thomas to be in the shelter asleep and Sarah to be sitting at the firepit where she could usually be found. As he walked past the Ferguson House, he wondered what the trappers would say if they found out what happened at the swimming hole. Thinking Sarah was right when she said what difference did it make where they made love, so long as they were together, he wondered whether she would accept his apology.

When he got to the clearing, he saw the camp was bathed in darkness. The fire had almost gone out. Sarah wasn't sitting where she usually sat. If Sarah and Thomas were in their shelter, they were both asleep. Christian stood in the dark for a moment wondering what to do. Finally deciding he couldn't do anything, he walked away.

The events of the next few days kept Christian so busy he had no chance to say he was sorry. While doing the rounds of farms and visiting several outlying ranches, checking things were alright with the owners, making sure no horses had got loose and there were no disagreements with neighbouring farmers and ranchers over land rights, he had to break up a fight between two ranch hands that got into a fight and threatened to kill each other, by bringing one of the men back to the jailhouse for a few days to cool off. He went back to the gulch several times to check Major Hardy's longhorn steers. Major Hardy had his men set fire to the brush along the riverbank. After the whole area along the river burnt out, the only thing remaining of the shack were charred timbers and the stone chimney. Christian wasn't trying to avoid Sarah, but it seemed, that was what was happening.

Millicent stepped out of her father's store just as Christian came strolling along the boardwalk and stopped him. Having forgiven him for turning down their dinner weeks before, she smiled broadly. "Hello Sheriff Morgan, how are you?" If she was trying to impress Christian with her smile it wasn't working. "Hello Millicent?" Christian responded while looking around for a way to escape. "Sheriff …Christian, you do know the Town Hall has been finished and the first dance is on this Saturday?"

Christian had completely forgotten about the dance, if he had remembered, before his and Sarah's fight, he would have asked Sarah to attend the dance with him. "Yes Millicent, I know about the dance," he said, sensing something coming. "Do you remember making me a promise you would take me to the first dance? You do remember, don't you?" Millicent said still smiling. Christian had a sudden recollection of him and Millicent at a picnic.

It was just after he arrived in town and he was feeling lonely. He kissed Millicent and realized afterward he had made a mistake, then promised her, when the Town Hall was finished, he would take her to the first dance. 'Damn!' he thought. "Yes, I remember making you that promise," he was saying when Sarah came walking up from the trail on the opposite side of the street. Seeing Christian talking to Millicent, for an instant, their eyes met. Hoping to get away from Millicent as fast as he could so he could talk to Sarah, Christian quickly averted his eyes back to Millicent. The dance was only four days away, and he had no hope of getting out of his promise, and no hope of asking Sarah to accompany him, but maybe he could ask her to see him tonight and he could at least apologize for his outburst at the swimming hole. "It would be my pleasure to take you to the dance Millicent, what time would you like me to call for you?" he said rather too quickly, starting to move away. "Oh! Christian, thank you, thank you!" Millicent cried bobbing up and down and clapping her hands with glee. Then, without warning, she took hold of Christian's face in both hands and kissed him, leaving Christian stunned. "Come for me around six Christian," she said, keeping her hands either side of his face so he couldn't escape. Fully aware Sarah had seen Millicent kiss him, Christian forcibly removed Millicent's hands. "I look forward to it ...bye Millicent," he said, hurrying across the street in the hope of catching up to Sarah. But unable to see her anywhere, he had no choice but to return to his office.

The letter came all the way from Washington. It arrived on the supply wagon, and Joe was anxious to read it for himself first before showing it to the other three men. Sitting on his bed in his room at the Ferguson House, he eagerly tore open the envelope, and was glad to see it was from his friend Senator Watson, written on official looking paper with the Senators name and his official capacity printed on the top.

'My Dearest Friend Joseph' it began

My God! fancy hearing from you after all these years! I had no idea you were still breathing. You know, I had to look at a map to see if I could find Cedar Creek, but the only place so far away I could find, seeing how it was stamped on your letter, was a place called Moreton. I gather you are not far from there. Nonetheless, it is good to hear from you after all this time, and by god to think you are still trapping.

I must apologize for taking so long in providing information about the man you call Christian Morgan. My search proved information was scant, however, a lad by that name was recorded being raised in an orphanage in Philadelphia. He and another boy, Maxwell Best, absconded from there and it was assumed they became drifters. There was no further information as to the pair's whereabouts for quite some time. The name Christian Morgan became synonymous with bounties. Instead of handing outlaws over to the law, he dispatched them for the reward on offer. The reason he became a Bounty Hunter is unclear, I think, from what I can gather, it may have been in retaliation for his friend being murdered.

Morgan was last heard of hunting an outlaw by the name of Sam Weston and be damned if the man wasn't tarnished with the name "Wild West'

Recalling what he knew about an outlaw called Sam Weston, Joe continued reading.

'The information I gleaned, tells of Morgan following Weston and his gang to a mission somewhere near the Mexican border where a gunfight saw Weston killed. One of the men with Weston was reportedly killed in the gunfight and the other supposedly got away, but not before Morgan was wounded by one or both men. Morgan apparently stayed at the mission for some time. I was told, and if my information is correct, he took up studying law, then gave up hunting outlaws. I guess staying at a mission would do that to a man, he probably found religion, and that may have helped him change his ways. There was no further information on Morgan at the time I received your letter, which again, by the grace of god, I was happy to receive. If Christian Morgan is the same man you have as your sheriff, I feel you have no real concern, except in that the outlaws themselves put a price on his head.'

The letter ended on a friendly note

'These days I am feeling a little infirm, so I invite you to Washington before too much more time passes between us so we may relive our glory days serving the country. But for now, my dear friend, I do not bid you farewell, for someday, we shall meet again.

Senator Aiden Watson, Retired.'

Thinking about what his friend wrote, Joe was satisfied Christian was the best man to have as the town's sheriff, and now he knew the reason why Christian wore his gun low. He had to know how to handle a gun and be fast on the draw, to take on men like 'Wild West'. Joe dug deep into the recess of his mind for what he knew about Weston. Weston was a vicious killer, a bank robber who didn't mind killing anyone that stood in his way. He heard too about Weston being killed, but hadn't heard by whom. Nor had he known before he received his friends letter that Christian had a price on his head. Even if it was the outlaws who put the price on him, it made Christian a marked man. There were a lot of men in and around town, trappers, cowhands and the like, who wouldn't hesitate to kill a man for money.

Joe resolved to keep this information to himself, deciding not to show his letter to Fergus, or Garrett and Will. But what did it mean now he knew who the man was Sarah was showing a lot of interest in? Joe took the letter out to the fireplace where he lifted the heavy steel lid from the stove and shoved the letter down into the fire.

352

Chapter Thirty-five

The building of the Town Hall was complete, and the first dance to celebrate the opening was underway. Lamps were lit and hung indoors and out, bunting was swinging in the breeze, making the hall and the night look festive. Everyone was there, all except Sarah, she hadn't been invited to take part in the celebration. Sarah pretended it didn't matter, but deep down she felt hurt. If only she hadn't fought with Christian, she was sure they would be dancing in each other's arms right now. Standing in the dark amongst a stand of trees near the corner of the Ferguson House, she could see light shining from the doorway of the hall. Loud music was playing, a fiddle and a piano belted out a tune, laughter and talking could be heard, everyone seemed to be enjoying the festivity.

In the days leading up to the dance, Sarah told herself she couldn't care less who Christian took to the dance, she didn't own a dress anyway, but she felt if she had been asked, she may have been able to find one. Sarah never worried about such trivial things as dresses. Even though as a young girl she wore the frilly dresses she owned, she liked wearing trousers more. Her father liked her to wear dresses when they came from the mountain, he said she looked like a lady when she wore them, but it wasn't the dress that bothered her. It was the fact Christian had taken Millicent to the dance instead of her that was really hurting.

After Christian became angry when she told him she would be going back to the mountain, and he said, 'he could fuck a whore anywhere at any time,' they haven't spoken to each other since. Still waking up ill, she wasn't about to let Christian know why. He didn't love her, so he didn't deserve to know. Sarah felt bad about it, but she was hurt by his change of attitude toward her.

The day Sarah saw Christian and Millicent standing outside the General Store and saw them kiss, she was on her way to have a reading lesson with Jonathon. Seeing them together, took her back to a time when Frank was seeing Millicent, even though he told her there was nothing between them she had been upset by it. Millicent was always impeccably dressed, and Sarah thought her worthy of any man's affection. Even so, seeing Christian with Millicent made her feel her world had ended. Instead of going for her lesson she turned down the alley beside the Livery and rushed back to her camp where she hid inside her shelter. Not since Thomas was taken had she cried so much, she hadn't let anything bring her to tears in a long time, but that seemed to be all she did lately.

Over the following days, Sarah managed to pull herself together and continue with her lessons. Jonathon said her reading and writing was coming along really well. The day before the dance she was sitting in the classroom with him when he innocently asked if she was going to the dance with Christian. Becoming upset and grabbing her knife, she ran out, leaving her book behind, and now she had nothing with which to fill her nights.

Creeping closer to the edge of the Ferguson House, keeping herself hidden behind the trees, she admired the women's pretty dresses as she watched everyone arriving. The men looked handsome too, dressed in their Sunday best. Sarah didn't see Christian and Millicent arrive, so made up her mind to stand outside all night if she had to, just to get a glimpse of Christian.

Music was playing and Sarah could hear people stomping their feet as they danced. The night wore on and Sarah kept waiting. When there was a lull in the music, she saw a man come out of the hall and walk down the steps to stand under one of the lamps. Her heart skipped a beat, then started to beat faster when she recognized Christian, looking handsome in his dark jacket and trousers teamed with a white shirt and satin embroidered vest. Sarah couldn't miss seeing his gun strapped low at his side.

Christian remained standing under the lamp for some time, and Sarah, watching, thought maybe she should go and talk to him, but what could she say? She still wouldn't go to the lodge, and she was definitely going back to the mountain in the spring. All Sarah thought she could say was she was sorry, and wish him well. Stepping out from behind the trees, Sarah quickly stepped back again when a woman came down the steps and approached Christian. When the woman walked up behind him and put her hands over his eyes, Sarah moved further back into the shadows and watched Christian take the woman's hands away and turn to face her. The woman laughed shrilly, then kissed Christian. Sarah's heart almost stopped beating. Millicent Crawley kissed Christian fully on his mouth, and Christian, laughing loudly while holding both her hands, looked like he enjoyed it.

Sarah's eyes widened as she focused on how Millicent was dressed. Millicent's dark hair, fastened to one side, had several loose curls falling over her bare shoulder. Around her neck she wore a gold chain that held a gold heart. The heart touched the white lace around the top of the loosely fitting blue velvet dress Millicent was wearing. Matching white lace trimmed the three-quarter length sleeves. Recognizing the dress as being one that once belonged to her mother Elizabeth, Sarah kept staring. Hardly believing what she was looking at, she grew angry. Not because Millicent was wearing one of her mother's dresses. Not because Christian held Millicent's hands, nor at the kiss, but because Millicent was wearing the locket Sarah's father had given her for her tenth birthday. It had belonged to her mother, and her father gave it to her when he thought she was old enough to look after it. Sarah only ever wore it when she was in Cedar Creek. It was no secret, because Benjamin Crawley owned the lodge, that over the years Elizabeth's elegant dresses were slowly disappearing one by one. But Sarah didn't care about the dresses. Millicent could keep all of them for all she cared, but to take her locket, something her Pa had given her, that was beyond what Sarah could tolerate.

After watching Christian lead Millicent back inside, Sarah paced back and forth in the shadows. Then without thinking of the consequences, she stormed toward the Town Hall. Climbing the front steps, she pushed her way through the throng of people standing just inside. Music played, men and women were dancing. Those that weren't dancing were either standing around or sitting, clapping their hands and stomping their feet in time with the music. When they saw Sarah, the clapping and feet stomping slowly died away. The music stopped and the dancers stopped dancing.

Everyone turned to stare. Walking slowly down the centre of the hall between rows of tables and chairs, Sarah scanned the room and spotted Joe. Fergus and Garrett were sitting at the back of the hall near the music players. Will was on the dance floor dancing with Sissy Hammond. Christian stood on the dance floor with his arms around Millicent, so Sarah made straight for them.

"What are you doing here Cole?" Christian asked, almost sounding sad when she approached. Sarah didn't answer straight away, instead stared at the locket hanging around Millicent's neck. "I'm not here to dance sheriff!" she replied sarcastically while moving her hand closer to her knife. Christian saw her hand poised and moved his hand within easy reach of his gun. "Then what do you mean by coming here and disturbing tonight's proceedings?" Unaware of the circumstances of Christian's and Sarah's last meeting, Jonathon informed Christian she wasn't coming. Christian would have asked Sarah to the dance, but once they fought and he had spoken vehemently to her it was too late, besides, he had to keep his promise to Millicent. Now here they were, facing each other, with Sarah standing her ground, looking mighty angry at Millicent. Ignoring those around her, Sarah kept her eyes firmly on Millicent. "I want that locket Millicent is wearing!" Millicent's hand went to her throat. "That is my locket Millicent and you know it! ...your thieving, murdering father stole it! and I want it back!"

Joe, Fergus and Garrett moved away from the tables and out onto the dance floor, bringing themselves close to where Sarah was confronting Millicent. Will said something to Sissy, she nodded and when she moved away, Will pushed his way through the couples that had been dancing to stand near Joe.

"You are wrong Cole, this is my necklace, daddy bought it for me, didn't you daddy?" Keeping her hand covering the locket, Millicent looked around for her father to support her. Feeling bold because Christian was with his daughter, Crawley stepped forward to stand next to them. "That's right Cole, we all know about you and your crazy accusations! ...you are not welcome here! so why don't you just ...disappear!" he said, making his hands imitate a puff of smoke.

"You are a liar! and a murdering thief! and your daughter is no better than you! ...you son-of-a-bitch!" Sarah's eyes never strayed from Millicent as she cursed both of them. "Well at least my daughter isn't a whore like you!" Loud gasps reverberated around the hall when everyone heard Crawley's smear. Sarah didn't let his disparaging remark faze her, she was used to being called a whore by Crawley, and now it seemed, Christian. Christian's hair stood up on the back of his neck when Crawley called Sarah the same as he had. "You had better leave …now Cole," he said in dismay, stepping between Sarah and Millicent. "Not until I get my locket! I don't care about my dress, she can keep that, along with all the other dresses she has been stealing! …but I want my locket!" Frowning at Sarah's accusation that Millicent was stealing dresses from her, Christian could see clearly this dress, and others he had seen her wearing, would fit someone with Sarah's curves better than they would Millicent.

The hall became silent as everyone watched the two women face each other. "How dare you accuse daddy of stealing! …my daddy bought my dress, and my necklace from his catalogue! …it is true what they say about you Cole! …you are as crazy as those wolves you trap! …you are nothing but a stinking troublemaker! so why don't you go back to your mountain and stay where you belong!" As Millicent's voice rose to fever pitch, Sarah, along with others glared at her. Christian watched both women carefully. The four trappers stood together and listened to Millicent's shrill child-like voice as she went on putting Sarah down.

"Daddy is right, you are a whore! …I hear talk you are sleeping with anyone that wants a fuck!" There were loud gasps of astonishment when Millicent cursed. No-one thought Millicent knew such a word, let alone would ever utter it. Disliking what Millicent was saying about Sarah, Christian dropped his guard by turning away from Sarah to look at Millicent, giving Sarah the opportunity to lunge at her.

Reaching out far enough to touch the chain around Millicent's neck, but before her fingers could close around it, Christian pushed Millicent out of reach. Crawley grabbed his daughter as she stumbled back, holding her so she wouldn't fall. Sarah wasn't so lucky. As Christian lunged, his hand caught the side of her face sending her reeling sideways, crashing into a table and sending chairs skidding across the room. When chairs and tables began to be thrown about, men grabbed women, and moved them quickly out of the way. Joe moved quickly, stooping down while Garret, Will and Fergus, keeping everyone back, formed a circle around Sarah lying on the floor. "Don't Sarah," Joe whispered before lifting her to her feet. "Leave this to us ...go! ...now!"

Feeling the stinging pain from Christian's hand catching her face, she looked up at him, and was unable to read the look he was giving her. Although disappointed by what happened, Christian had to keep the peace. He stood in the middle of the dance floor, one hand on the grip of his gun, the other clenched in a fist. "Get out Cole!" he ordered. Trying to fathom what just happened Sarah glared at him, then, pushing her way through the crowd and keeping her head up, hurried down the steps and into the dark. Once out of sight of the hall, with the slap still hurting and tears stinging her eyes, she ran as fast as she could back to her camp.

Christian swallowed the lump in his throat, then told the musicians to play some music and get the celebration going again. "There is no need for what happened here to spoil the evening, everyone, dance ...enjoy the rest of the night." Turning his attention to Millicent, he looked again at the necklace and frowned. "Sorry Millicent, you best get your father to escort you home." Figuring he was going to follow Sarah to her camp, Millicent's eyes narrowed. "But Christian! you promised we would dance all night!" Christian didn't feel much like dancing. "I'm sorry," he repeated. "Take your daughter home Crawley." Upset by his hand catching Sarah on her cheek, Christian wasn't happy by his action, nor was anyone else. Christian looked around the room, everyone was staring at him, and not one person was smiling.

"Of course! ...come on Millie." Crawley took Millicent by the arm, but Millicent, not finished belittling Sarah, brushed her father's hand away. "Cole is just an ignorant, mountain crawling, filthy stinking trapper! I don't know where she gets these crazy notions of hers, daddy bought this necklace and dress for me especially for this occasion." Millicent took hold of the locket. "Anyway!" she went on, not knowing it took a certain way of pressing the locket for it to open. "This is not a locket, it is a solid gold heart, Cole is nothing but a trouble making stupid, cheap…!" Christian had had enough of Millicent putting Sarah down. Leaving her still talking, he pushed his way through the crowd, and walking out, hadn't noticed the four trappers had already left.

Outside, the torches had burnt out. Stepping down the steps, Christian found himself standing in the dark. He hadn't meant for his hand to strike Sarah. Knowing he had made things worse, he wanted to apologize for what happened between them here, as well as at the swimming hole. Did he believe Sarah about the necklace? He didn't know. Millicent was adamant her father bought the dress and necklace from one of his catalogues. Having seen the many catalogues Crawley had in his store, Christian thought it possible Millicent was telling the truth. But then, Sarah seemed sure the necklace was hers.

He began to walk across the street toward the trail leading to Sarah's camp when three men stepped out of the shadows. Fergus stood in front of him while Will and Garrett stepped up to stand either side. "Where are you going sheriff?" Fergus asked in disgust, stepping closer so his face was level with Christian's. Christian's hand went to his gun, but before he could pull it free, Garrett grabbed his hand and pulled it away. Reaching down, Fergus took Christian's gun out of its holster. Christian kept his eyes leveled at Fergus and didn't try to stop him. "You won't be needing this where you are going sheriff …I will hold onto it …just in case you have a mind to shoot one of us!" Fergus grinned.

"I need to talk to Sarah." Christian and Fergus stared at each other. "Sarah now is it! …not tonight you don't …let's take a walk!" Fergus's voice was stern, his demeanor changed from the friendly man Christian had come to know to someone he wouldn't like to cross. The first couple of days the trappers were in town, they each appeared to have a friendly nature, but this being his second encounter with them, he was finding out they had another side to them. "I'm not going anywhere with you men …and where is Jones?" Christian looked around to see if he could see where Joe was. "He will be along! …but you! …you are coming with us!" Fergus's voice remained stern. "Where are you taking me?" Christian asked as they started walking. "We are going to the lodge." Garrett's voice answered from out of the dark.

Chapter Thirty-six

Furious about what he witnessed at the dance, and leaving the other three men to take care of Christian, Joe stormed down the trail to Sarah's camp. Joe recognized Sarah's locket around Millicent's neck as soon as Millicent came to the hall wearing it. In fact, he had drawn it to the other three men's attention. Fergus said he recognized it too, and the dress. The four men all agreed Sarah shouldn't have burst in the way she had. If she had stayed out of it, Joe would have dealt with Crawley for giving Sarah's locket to Millicent. Joe was cursing to himself as he made his way down the trail. Now he had another fine mess to deal with.

Approaching Sarah's camp and seeing the fire burning but Sarah not sitting at it, he hurried past the pit and up to the shelter. "Sarah …you in there?" He needn't have asked. Hearing her crying, he pulled back the canvas flap, and saw her lying on her furs, her face hidden by her long hair. "Sarah," he said softly, feeling saddened at hearing her sobs. When he put his hand on her shoulder, Sarah suddenly sprang up, and putting her arms around him, buried her face against his chest. Sensing something very wrong, because Sarah hadn't done this, not for a long time, not since losing her father, Joe put his arms around her.

"It is my locket Joe," she sobbed. "You know Pa gave it to me …it has Ma and Pa's pictures in it." Joe knew there was no way he could get her locket back, except maybe offer Crawley a sum of money for it. Crawley being the greedy man he is, surely would accept his offer to buy the locket. At least Joe would have tried, but right now, he wanted to find out what was really upsetting Sarah. She had never gotten over her father's death, but he wondered if the locket was the only thing troubling her! "Is the locket all that you are upset about Sarah?" he asked.

Pushing herself away from Joe and wiping her eyes, she looked up at the big man sitting in her shelter. She missed his arms around her. Joe held her when her father died and comforted her after Frank's death, only to have her push him away when she blamed him for not taking care of Frank, telling him to go to hell along with the other three men. She has always regretted having spoken those words to him.

"No! ...Christian is seeing Millicent!" she said almost angrily. "He doesn't want to see me anymore."

"Why doesn't he want to see you anymore? What did you do Sarah?" Joe thought he may be getting somewhere.

"I didn't do anything Joe! ...why is it always assumed it is me that's done something? ...we had an argument because I won't go to the lodge ...to sleep in his bed ...with him! ...that's all!" Sarah stopped talking for a moment and wiped her eyes before continuing. "You know how I feel about the lodge! I will never step foot in that house! not ever! ...I told Christian that and he didn't understand!" she said, stepping outside and going to the fire. "Did you tell him why you wouldn't step foot in that house?" Joe knew she wouldn't have. "He doesn't need to know the reason! he should have accepted what I told him," she said, sitting down. Joe shook his head from side to side and pursed his lips in a tight scowl.

"Sarah, we have to talk!" he said following her to the fire.

"What is there to talk about Joe?" she asked looking up at him.

"Goddamn it! what you are doing has gone on long enough! ...you love the man, don't you?" Joe looked across the fire, taking in how dark circles surrounded her eyes.

"No! ...I ...I do not!" Sarah turned her face away from Joe as more tears threatened to fall. It wasn't the first time she ever lied to Joe. She lied when she told him she didn't love Frank, but Joe knew that wasn't true. "He is with Millicent, and I won't love a man that sleeps with another woman."

Joe knew Sarah was lying. She was in love with Christian, if she wasn't, she wouldn't be so upset. She said the same thing about Frank and look what happened, the two of them ended up having Thomas. He reasoned when Christian didn't stand up for her, knocking her over in front of everyone, she felt humiliated. If Christian loved her, he should have looked into Sarah's accusation about Millicent stealing her locket, but he didn't, he defended Millicent instead. Joe watched Sarah with Christian the morning after the night they were together in her shelter and again at the ponds, figuring if they weren't in love with each other, then something was seriously wrong. No two people could be together the way they were and not love each other. But then, Joe wondered, Christian and Millicent seemed awful friendly toward each other too. Maybe Sarah is right, maybe he is sleeping with Millicent. If Christian is sleeping with her after being with Sarah, he and his three friends are going to put a stop to him ever seeing Sarah again, but right now, he had a bigger issue to deal with. Studying Sarah's face, he knew there was a whole lot more going on with her. There was no other way. Taking a deep breath, he came straight out and asked her what was on his mind. "Sarah ...are you pregnant?" When Joe asked Sarah his question, Sarah stared into the fire, and thinking it was none of Joe's business, folded her arms across the front of her. Besides, why should he care? He didn't do anything when she fell pregnant with Thomas. Raising her eyes, she met Joe's gaze. Sarah didn't have to answer him. Joe already had the answer.

"Goddamn it, Sarah! are we going to go through this again?" Joe rubbed his hand across his forehead, Sarah was pregnant! He knew Sarah like he knew the back of his hand, and because she loved Christian like she loved Frank, it stood to reason she would get herself pregnant. "Don't you go telling him Joe ...please!" Sarah begged, standing up and going around the fire. "Please Joe, don't tell him!" Sarah's eyes filled with tears. Joe reached out and pulling her to him, hugged her tight. Resting her head against his chest, she let her tears wet his shirt. This was the first time they hugged each other since Frank died.

"Goddamn it, Sarah!" he repeated, then while pushing her to stand away from him, he made her an offer. "You don't have to go back to the mountain ...if you want to stay here to be with the sheriff, you don't have to go to the lodge, you can stay in the Ferguson House, you still have a room there remember, we won't need the

house until next winter, you could have the house all to yourself …
and Thomas could continue to go to school, he loves school you
know." Joe thought about offering the Ferguson House to Sarah
after he had seen her and Christian out at the ponds, he reckoned
then Sarah and Christian's relationship was going further than they
both realized. "Go back inside and think about what I said, get some
sleep …and don't go near the Crawley's! …and don't whatever you
do, go near Sheriff Morgan!" Sarah looked sadly into Joe's face. She
loved him, since her father died Joe had become a father to her, and
he always knew best at what to do. "What are you going to do Joe?"

"I don't know yet! …I'll think of something! …I'll see you
tomorrow …where is Thomas by the way?" Joe's mind was already
working out how to fix things between Sarah and Christian.

"You know you can't interfere Joe, you can't break your promise
to Pa …Thomas is staying at Billy's tonight, being a big boy, they
have the house to themselves while Martha and Dave are at the
dance …Oh! Joe! everyone was there! …I make a terrible mess of
things, don't I?" When Sarah looked like she would cry again, Joe
shook his head from side to side.

"Sometimes Sarah, I don't know what to do with you."

"Only sometimes Joe?" Sarah asked. Joe never forgot the words
Sarah said to him on the mountain when Frank died. Every one of
the trappers she said were to blame for Frank being alone when the
wolves attacked him, she especially blamed him. Sarah told him she
never wanted to speak to him again and that she didn't hold him to
his promise, but he yelled back, saying it wasn't her promise, and
she couldn't be the one to break it. He walked away from her that
day but never left her, he wouldn't, he couldn't. He made another
far more important promise, one that will never be broken. One he
will one day tell Sarah about, but now isn't the right time.

"Get some rest Sarah, I will see you tomorrow." Joe made to
go. "Joe!" Sarah stopped him leaving. "I am sorry for all the terrible
things I said to you …I know it must have hurt the four of you
…especially you …you have always been there for me, and I love you
for that …are we good Joe?" Knowing Sarah was asking if he had
forgiven her and having forgiven Sarah a long time ago, he kissed
her on the forehead. "We are good Sarah." But right now, Joe was

about to break his promise he made to Sarah's father. Sarah was going to have another baby, and he wouldn't let her go through the same thing she had gone through after Frank died. Sarah needed Christian now more than ever.

Leaving Sarah at her camp, Joe walked back up the trail, happy he and Sarah had finally sorted out their differences. Sarah retired to her shelter and stayed there as Joe asked. Joe made his way quickly to the lodge to sort Sheriff Christian Morgan out.

Chapter Thirty-seven

Three trappers led Christian along the street in front of the Ferguson House then up the street where the lodge was situated. Christian walked slowly, trying to delay the men for as long as he could while thinking of some way to get away from them, but it was no use, Fergus and Garrett walked either side of him and Will walked behind until they made their way up the steps to the porch. Surrounding him while opening the front door to let them in, the three men shoved him inside, then stepped through the door themselves. All three were shocked at the dilapidated condition they found the lodge to be in.

"What the hell!" Will exclaimed looking around. Garrett was more than a little shocked. "What the fuck has happened to all the furniture?" he cursed. Fergus though, grinned and stepped over to the green winged chair. "Well, at least this is still here!" Although he wasn't laughing when he sat down in it.

"Will, can you get this fire going? You got any coffee sheriff?" Fergus asked, pursing his lips. Christian didn't answer. Going to a cupboard, he got a bag of coffee, and sitting it on the table said, "help yourself!" Grabbing the bag and the coffee pot, Will went through to the kitchen, where a second later his shocked voice called back to the men. "Hey Fergus! take a goddamn fucking look in here! Where in hell is the fucking water pump? …god …damn!" It was becoming obvious to Christian these men knew this house. Bewildered by why the men brought him to the lodge, he wondered just what they intended doing with him.

"Why don't you tell me what's going on Fergus?"

"We best wait for Joe, he can tell you!" Joe was their leader. These men wouldn't scratch themselves unless Joe told them to.

Before Fergus could go to the kitchen to look at the water pump, Garrett walked over to the room that served as Christian's bedroom and opening the door, cursed in disgust. "Fucking hell, Fergus! take a look at the study!" Fergus got out of the ugly green winged chair and took a look in the room, then both men went to the kitchen. With their faces reflecting their disgust, Fergus and Garrett came back to the fire.

"How long has the place been like this sheriff?" Fergus wanted to know. Christian shrugged his shoulders and sat on a chair at the old timber table. "It was like this when I rented it from Crawley." Christian didn't want to be here with these obviously angry men, he wanted to go to Sarah, to make what happened between them right. Fergus thought the house probably became like this soon after Sarah was thrown out of it.

The three men made themselves at home. The fire was lit, coffee brewed and drank. The pot was filled again. The smell of fresh coffee filled the air as footsteps were heard approaching the front door. Jumping up, Garrett pulled the door open and let Joe in. Joe didn't look happy, his face told everyone he had been to see Sarah.

Ignoring Christian, Joe walked around the house looking in each room just as the other men had done. "Christ!" he muttered, coming back to the fire. While staring into the flames, he warmed his hands and didn't speak for a few minutes. "What is it like upstairs Morgan?" he asked, keeping his back to Christian. "I don't know, the doors are locked up tighter than the jailhouse up there."

"Come with me!" Joe said, wheeling around suddenly, and going to the stairs. Taking them two at a time, he raced up to the landing. Christian and the four men stood in a bunch outside the first door. Joe got out his hunting knife, and forcing it behind the steel bolt attached to the wall, pulled down hard and cut through the timber. When the steel bar came crashing away from the wall, Joe kicked the door and it flung open, smashing back against the wall. Filing into the room, the four men gasped at what they saw and cursed out loud.

"Here are all Elizabeth's things!" Will said in amazement. Not knowing who Elizabeth was, Christian frowned. The room was packed to the brim with furniture. There was a leather sofa pushed against a small four poster bed, the covers of which were tossed aside and crumpled like they hadn't been disturbed for many years. A huge dining table with high backed tapestry chairs stacked on top, sat in the middle of the room. The table was so big, Christian wondered how it came to get upstairs into this room. The room was full of boxes and books stacked haphazardly in piles everywhere. Empty bookshelves that had been removed from the downstairs study lined the walls. Pots and pans sat piled on the dresser along with crystal lamps and silver candlesticks. A dozen or so floor rugs stood rolled up and leaning against a wall, leaving not much room to move around in, but Joe pushed his way through and opened a closet door. "This room used to be Sarah's before Crawley forced her down those stairs and threw her out!" He lifted a small dress that looked like something a young girl would wear out of the closet and held it up. "Sarah wore these when she came here for the winter, she hated it, but she wore them to please her Pa." Joe put the dress back in the closet. "Goddamn son-of-a-bitch threw her out of her own goddamn house and we couldn't do a damn thing about it!" He said angrily slamming the door closed.

Christian was shocked at Joe's revelation about the house being Sarah's. All of a sudden it became clear. Now he knew why Sarah wouldn't come here to be with him. But why couldn't she tell him she once owned the lodge? and why did Crawley throw her out? Christian had more questions he needed answers to. "Tell me about this house Joe!"

"That is what I intend Morgan, but first, you have to see something …if I can find it!" Joe was searching for something, but whatever it was, it wasn't in this room. Charging into the hall, with all four men following, their faces still very much sombre, he rushed to the next room. Breaking the lock on the door, they entered the master bedroom.

A mahogany desk stood against a huge four poster bed. The canopy over the bed matched the deep red velvet drapes covering a huge bay window that looked across the river and out to the mountain range in the distance. The bed had linen and blankets stacked all over it. Like the smaller room, the room was cluttered. More rows of empty book shelves stood along the back wall near a three-mirrored dresser. A huge cast iron bath on legs stood next to two black leather couches that were pushed together. The bath was full of books, the two couches were littered with more books, and crystal lamps were stacked on top of them. Christian took all of it in, but didn't know what to think. Sarah had once owned the lodge as well as all of these things? Christian watched Joe make his way through the packed room to another closet, where he pushed armchairs aside so he could open the doors. "Son-of-a-bitch!" Joe swore as he flung the doors wide open and reached in. The closet was almost empty, save for a single silk evening dress hanging on a hanger. A train of silk fell from the back, its heart shaped bodice adorned with crystal droplets set the dress apart from others Elizabeth brought from the city. "This closet was full of dresses like this ...goddamn it!" Joe put the dress back and closed the door.

In a corner of the room, next to a huge dresser that would have had fine china displayed on its glass enclosed shelves, Joe found paintings and framed pictures stacked against each other. Some were covered, while others stood in their gilded frames. Joe pushed his way through the armchairs until he came to the paintings. Pulling them forward one by one, he studied each carefully. Christian stayed where he was and took the time to look around the room. An open fireplace that would be lit to keep the room warm during the winter months was almost hidden behind more books and boxes of items that would have been in the rooms downstairs but were now stacked haphazardly around this room.

Holding several paintings away from the others, Joe waved his hand behind him and clicked his fingers. "Will, come here!" Will pushed his way through the pile of furnishings and made his way to Joe. "Grab that chair!" Joe ordered, indicating a tapestry upholstered armchair. While Christian watched, Will pulled the chair over to where Joe was, then stayed opposite. "Ok Will, help me lift this out." Lifting the heavy felt covered picture together, they sat it on the arms of the chair. Christian wondered what Joe was doing when Joe looked over at him. "I want you to look at this Morgan and tell me what you see." Christian waited. Joe looked at

Will. "Ready Will?" Will nodded, and together they flung the cover over the back of the painting.

Christian's heart leapt in his chest. Blinking back tears, while trying to swallow the lump forming in his throat, his eyes took in the portrait in front of him. He stared at the painting for a long time, taking in her deep blue eyes that were smiling out at him. Her nose was perfect, her full, pink lips, appeared soft and beckoned to be kissed. Her long brown hair, pinned to one side, lay in curls over her bare shoulder where they sat in soft wisps, the tip of one, touching her breast. A gold chain about her slender neck held a gold heart shaped locket nestled against her cleavage. Christian had seen the very same necklace earlier tonight. It had been worn at the dance, along with the blue dress the woman in the painting was wearing, by none other than Millicent Crawley. Millicent had tried to emulate this same portrait but had failed miserably. All this convinced Christian Sarah told him the truth about the locket and the dresses.

Watching Christian closely for his reaction, Joe walked away from the painting and stood alongside him. Will, Garrett and Fergus stood beside the two of them, and the five men stared at the woman in the portrait.

"Well Morgan?" Joe said after a time.

"Sarah!" Christian whispered, the lump in his throat, causing his voice to break.

"Elizabeth," Joe said simply. Christian tore his eyes from the painting and looked at Joe. "What!" he exclaimed. "Elizabeth …Sarah's mother!" Joe repeated softly, without taking his eyes off the painting. He wanted to cry at the memory of her. Elizabeth was a beautiful woman who was delicate and kind hearted and never had a harsh word to say about anyone. Elizabeth brought an air of sophistication with her when she came to Cedar Creek as Calahan Cole's wife. Because they respected Calahan, every man respected her. Every man on the mountain fell in love with Elizabeth. Joe fell deeply in love with her.

"But Joe, it could be Sarah, she is beautiful!" Christian said, keeping his voice low. Will, Garrett, and Fergus, remembering Elizabeth too, wiped their eyes and snorted, and yes, they agreed with Christian, she could be Sarah. Sarah was very much like her mother to look at, but not in her ways. After spending so much of her life with the trappers, and if they had to choose someone for Sarah to be like, she was more like Joe.

Not wanting to waste any more time, Joe coughed and cleared his throat. "Will, Garrett, bring that painting, we'll put it back where it belongs!" Joe rushed out of the room and back down the stairs to the fireplace where he stood with his hands out getting them warm while waiting for the men to bring the portrait. Will and Garrett carried the painting down the stairs, and Fergus got two old wooden chairs for them to stand on. After hanging the picture above the mantle over the fireplace, all five men stood across the room and looked at the painting again. No-one moved or dared breathe while they took in the delicate features of the woman that was Sarah Cole's mother.

"Make more coffee!" Joe suddenly ordered. While Will made the coffee, Christian went to the cupboard, and finding a bottle of whiskey, got five glasses and poured each man a drink. "You were going to tell me about this house, and Sarah Joe," Christian asked again. Eager to hear what Joe had to say, he swallowed his whiskey in one gulp.

Joe nodded. "This house belonged to Calahan Cole, Sarah's father, and Elizabeth." He glanced back up at the painting and raised his glass in salute. "Sarah was born not long after the house was built …we helped build this house!" Sweeping his hand around at Will, Fergus and Garrett, the men nodded in agreement. Of course! Christian nodded, now he knew how the men came to know the house so well. He listened intently as Joe continued to speak.

"But Sarah was born in the cabin up on the mountain, because it was to be her home. Calahan wanted her to be part of the mountain. This was just the place they came to for the winter. Sarah was two years old when Elizabeth passed from fever." The four men bowed their heads in memory of Elizabeth's passing. After a moment of reflection, Joe went on. "Sarah was asleep upstairs when Crawley came in the middle of the night and threw her out." The men going quiet, pulled their chairs around in front of the fire, and sitting with their glasses of whiskey in their hands, listened as Joe recounted the years they spent with Sarah. Beginning with telling Christian the promise they made, explaining Calahan was Joe's best friend and how they promised they would take care of Sarah if anything should happen to him, Joe told Christian, although they didn't take responsibility for Sarah until she turned fifteen and Calahan had died, their promise took effect when Sarah was barely three years old.

Joe told of how they helped Calahan teach Sarah how to use a rifle, and how she took to it, never missing what she aimed at. They taught her to ride and dismount while still in motion, skills they themselves learnt whilst in the cavalry. Trapping he explained, came easy for Sarah, that was something she took to because she was born to it, all they did was hone her skills. They each agreed, Sarah could skin a wolf with her eyes closed, and she was fast at it. Joe told Christian about Sarah's ability to sense when the trappers were near and who it was by their scent. Christian had seen her ability in action and admired her for it. She had known he was watching her that day out at the ponds, she also smelt the coffee long before he had, and she knew someone had been watching them make love in the water and again on the riverbank. Sarah knew it had been Joe, Christian was pretty sure of it too, and they both agreed it was him. Joe went on talking while the four men sat silently by listening to him tell of Sarah's life after her father died.

He talked about the night Calahan gambled away all his money, and how he handed the deed to Mountain View Lodge over to Crawley before he died. Telling Christian Sarah blamed Crawley for killing her father and how she vowed never to step foot back in this house gave Christian the answer to why Sarah refused to come to the lodge. Now he knew the reason Sarah and Crawley hated each other, and that was why she would rather make love anywhere other than here. He also wondered why Sarah couldn't trust him enough to tell him about any of these things, and he asked Joe.

"Sarah will never talk about her past, what someone knows about Sarah is what they hear, most of it is just gossip …and that is why I am telling you Morgan, so you will know the truth …it is up to you when I am finished how you judge her." Joe paused. It was important for him to know how Christian felt about Sarah. Looking at Christian sitting beside him, he could see the anguish on Christian's face as he talked about her. Shifting in his chair, he asked. "You are in love with Sarah! ...aren't you?" Looking Joe squarely in the eye Christian didn't hesitate before he answered. "Yes, Joe ...I am in love with her."

Will suddenly came to life. "Then tell me this, Morgan! ...just why did you stop seeing her? Why did you get with Millicent Crawley? And why the fuck! were you with her at the dance and not Sarah?" There was anger in Will's voice. When Sarah came into their care, he wanted her to love him. When he confessed to her, he loved her, she said she loved him like a brother, he was family, just like all the trappers were family. Sarah told him that was the reason she couldn't love him as a woman loved a man. He had been heartbroken at the time, but accepted what Sarah said. His promise meant he would never see Sarah hurt by any man, and if Christian Morgan was going to hurt her, he swore he was going to put a bullet in him.

Christian wasn't surprised by what Will was asking him. "I asked Sarah to come to the lodge to be with me and she refused, I didn't know she owned this house and I was angry with her for refusing me ...she told me she will be going back to the mountain in the spring and there is no way I can stop her! I won't follow her to the mountain! ...I'm not Frank, and I won't be compared to him! ...I like being sheriff ...I like this town and the people in it! If Sarah doesn't love me enough to stay ...then I will let her go! ...and another thing Will! ...I resent what you just said! ...I am not 'with' Millicent Crawley as you imply! ...and as for taking her to the dance! ...I made Millicent a promise I would take her when the hall was finished! ...I made that promise before I met Sarah, and just like you men made your promise and have kept it, I had to keep my promise! ...I regret making that promise! ...it was fucking stupid!" Christian stood up, poured himself another whiskey and drank it in one gulp. Leaning on the mantle, he looked up at the picture of Sarah's mother. He loved Sarah, how she must hate him for what he said to her. He hated himself straight after he said those horrible words, and right now, he hated himself even more.

The four men exchanged looks. "It took Frank two years to get Sarah to fall in love with him," Garrett said behind Christian's back. "That's not true, Sarah was in love with Frank long before that, hell, she was in love with Frank the day he gave her that goddamn horse!" Fergus broke in. "Maybe it was when Frank sat with her in the pouring rain at her father's burial and she belted the shit out of him ...remember?" Fergus and Garrett started comparing memories about Sarah and Frank to each other, pointing out how they avoided each other but were obviously in love. "Shut the fuck up, both of you!" Joe snapped, remembering what they were saying. "We are not here to talk about Frank!" The two men quietened, letting Joe continue to tell Christian about Sarah.

"Calahan made us promise we wouldn't make Sarah our own. There have been a lot of men fall in love with Sarah, she has been proposed to more than once over the years, and I think she probably would have been proposed to a lot more only for me beating Logan within an inch of his life," Joe added. "I nearly killed that man for what he tried to do to Sarah." Joe looked at Christian, guessing he wanted an answer as to why Joe belted one of the other trappers nearly to death. "We caught him going into her shelter one night ...son-of-a-bitch!" Christian remembered Joe saw him coming out of Sarah's shelter. Peering over at Christian, Joe knew what he was thinking. "It happened a long time ago Morgan." Joe continued on. "Sarah hasn't chosen any of the men from the mountain, or from town, and we haven't pushed anyone toward her, Sarah decides who she falls in love with, not us ...we don't interfere, Sarah has to decide what she does and who she wants to share her life with, that's all part of our promise ...we have kept our promise as best as we know how ...we let her find out for herself what life is about ...sure, we taught her to shoot and how to ride, even taught her how to fight to defend herself." Christian remembered the day Sarah arrived in town. She certainly defended herself. After knocking him off his feet, he promptly fell in love with her.

Joe went on talking. "Everything else Sarah has found out for herself ...when she fell down, she picked herself up and kept going." Joe lowered his voice. "Sarah has only ever loved one man. We all thought Frank would be the man Sarah would spend the rest of her life with." Joe continued by telling Christian about the time Sarah shot herself, when she got attacked by a wolf and Frank saved her from drowning all in the same day. That, Joe was certain, was when Sarah knew she was in love with Frank. Thomas told Christian of that day, but now as Joe explained it, he had the full story and it didn't surprise him at all that Sarah and Frank had become lovers.

Christian listened to Joe talk about when Sarah found out she was pregnant with Thomas and the night at the shack and how Frank got whipped saving her. Hearing about the role Foley and Brady played in saving Sarah, Christian had a new respect for the two men, especially Foley for suffering a whiplash to his face, simply because Major Hardy didn't want Sarah to have anything to do with his son. Having come away from looking at the shack, he questioned himself about whether she had been with any of the trappers. Christian didn't need Joe telling him more. He was convinced Sarah had never been with anyone except Frank, and himself. Christian remained silent while Joe continued telling him of how Frank had been attacked by wolves up in the High Country, and how he had to shoot himself to save himself from being eaten alive and never got to see his son. Christian thought how ironic it was that Frank had to kill himself to save himself, he thought Frank a very brave man.

As Joe talked about the time Sarah gave birth to Thomas on her own on the riverbank and telling the trappers to leave her alone, Christian came to know Sarah as an incredible woman, one who has endured so much in her life. It made him want to go to Sarah and tell her how much he loves her, and that it doesn't matter where they are, that he would love her anywhere she wanted them to be. But he couldn't, not right then, Joe had a lot more to say.

While Christian listened to the men talk well into the night, it became obvious the men loved Sarah. They might have made a promise not to make her their own, but Sarah was theirs, they were her family.

They made Christian realize, Sarah is what is missing from his life. Seven years ago, Brother Abraham from the mission in Les Rios, told him he would find what he had been searching all his life for. Back then, Christian hadn't believed him. But having found Sarah, he believed. Now all Christian wants is to hold her in his arms and tell her how much he loves her. But there is yet another piece to Brother Abraham's prediction that has still to come to pass. 'Three will become Four.' Christian still doesn't understand what that means.

It was Christian's turn to tell the men about himself. Joe leant back in his chair as Christian told the four men about his past.

Not leaving anything out, they listened without interruption until he finished, then Joe, satisfied Christian was the man he said he was, told the men about the letter he received from his friend in Washington. Christian and Joe laughed at the irony of it. Christian said he hoped the information he got was right. Leaving out the part about outlaws having put a price on his head, Joe said it matched what Christian told him. Sarah was important to these men, and having nothing to hide, Christian wanted them to know how he felt about her. The men listened intently as he let his emotions flow. When telling them about their argument at the swimming hole they pursed their lips in anger but remained silent. When he said he wanted to go to Sarah's camp to try and make things right between them, Joe stopped him

"Wait until morning Morgan, Sarah was treated unfairly tonight and she's feeling hurt and angry, it won't do you any good trying to talk to her tonight." Christian agreed to wait.

"Tell me about the wolf Joe, the one Sarah cut up!" The men looked at each other. Joe took a deep breath. "Thomas was just a couple of months old ...it was winter, like now, and we had all come off the mountain ...Sarah carried him tied to her chest to keep him warm ...and safe ...we stick together because wolves wait for us at the bottom of the mountain ...every year we have to run for our fucking lives!" Joe explained before going on. "That year Sarah refused to come with us, I argued with her as we always did since Frank died ...I thought she had a better chance of making it to town when the wolves attacked if she was with us ...and they did! ...goddamn it! we spent two nights at the wells waiting for her before we gave up and made it to town ...I remember Sarah saying she went out wide when she came down the mountain ...took her longer to get here, but by Christ she made it. We expected her to stay with us ...she has a room at the house ...but because she blamed us for Frank, she made camp on the fucking riverbank, I was so fucking furious! but she made her choice ...there was nothing we could do." Joe stopped talking, rubbed his forehead and looked at his empty glass. "I sure could use another drink!" The whiskey bottle was empty. Christian got up and going to the cupboard, rummaged around until he found another bottle and brought it back to the fire. The men held out their glasses for a refill.

"Go on Joe." Christian sat back down next to the men and Joe picked up where he left off. "Sarah was only in town a couple of days when she was invited to some sort of gathering to show off Thomas." Joe remembered the day like it just happened and went on. Christian listened as the story unfolded. "They took him to Major Hardy's ranch," he ended.

"Why Major Hardy's?" Christian knew Thomas was Frank's son, but he didn't know for what reason they would take Thomas off Sarah and give him to his grandfather. Joe told Christian Major Hardy held Sarah to blame for what happened to Frank, and still does, so he retaliated by taking Thomas from her. The story included the night they slaughtered Major Hardy's prize bull. Joe was certain Christian wouldn't do anything about them killing the bull now he knew what Sarah had endured. By the end of Joe telling Christian about Sarah and Thomas, all the men were almost in tears.

It was well after midnight when the five men, still crowded around the fire, heard a knock on the front door. Having finished the second bottle of whiskey, more coffee was being brewed. "It's O'Rourke!" Will said as he opened the door to let Jonathon in. Stepping gingerly inside, Jonathon saw the men getting warm by the fire. "Hey Joe!" he said, looking from one man to the other. Seeing their faces appearing gloomy in the glow from the fire, he settled his gaze on Christian. "I saw what happened at the dance, and well, sheriff, I have something I want to show you." Jonathon was nervous as he gripped what appeared to be a book in his hands. "I wanted to show you this." Holding out the book to Christian, Christian took it, and staring at it, saw Sarah's name written in crooked letters on the front. "I've been teaching Sarah to read and write." That came as a complete surprise to Joe, he knew Sarah had never been taught to read, no-one had taken the time to teach her, not even her own father who read to her every night before she went to sleep and here in the lodge were enough books to fill a library. Will looked at Jonathon. Fergus and Garrett looked at each other, then at Joe and Christian. They all knew Sarah couldn't read or write, they were trappers not teachers, teaching Sarah these things, was not part of their promise. They crowded around Christian to look over his shoulder as Jonathon went on to explain. "For the last month or so, Sarah has been having lessons with me. She has learnt how to write her name and she can read a little, she has surprised me with how fast she has picked it up." Jonathon looked from one man to the other as he spoke proudly of Sarah.

"What has all this got to do with anything O'Rourke?" Christian asked even though he already knew Sarah couldn't do either. He watched her holding the map of the town he drew upside down while trying to read it, convincing him straight away she had no schooling. "Sarah has been writing her name in that book!" Jonathon said, tapping the book with his finger. Christian flicked the pages. Holding the book open several pages in, he could see how bad the writing and misspelt words looked, but gradually, over the next few pages, mistakes became correct and the writing neater. "Get to the point O'Rourke!" Christian snarled, closing the book and trying to hand it back.

"Turn the book over to the back." Christian looked impatiently at Jonathon, then turning the book over, opened it. Just like in the front, the spelling was all wrong, and the writing terrible. Christian turned a page and his heart skipped a beat. Turning another, and yet another, he found the spelling correct, the writing much neater, and the words 'SARAH COLE LOVES CHRISTIAN MORGAN' written over and over in bold letters, filling the page. As Christian read, his eyes misted. Quickly wiping his eyes with the palm of his hand, he handed the book to Joe. Joe took it and read it. "Do you need more proof Morgan?" Joe asked him. "What do I do Joe, she's not going to stay with me," Christian sniffled. "How do you know?" Joe said quietly. "Wait just a minute!" Jonathon interrupted. "I have something else that may be of interest to you, and you Joe …and you lot!" Jonathon looked around at the men, then stepped between Joe and Christian. "Go on O'Rourke, say your piece!" Christian snapped, feeling overwhelmed by everything. He wasn't about to take Joe's advice and stay away from Sarah. He wanted to see her, even if it meant they would argue, he would make her listen to him.

Jonathon sat in front of the fire and the men pulled their chairs in closer and gathered around. "When Sarah and I finally got talking, she opened up about her father, and about the time her father lost this house!" Jonathon was excited and waved his hand around the room.

"We all know how he lost this fucking house O'Rourke!" Joe stood back up, leant over Jonathon and placing his hands firmly on his hips, towered over him. Joe was a big man and his fur coat made him bigger still, making Jonathon cower in his chair. Holding up both hands to ward off any aggression that might come his way, he begged them to listen. "No! ...no look! ...Sarah told me her father couldn't do up his clothes! ...that her Pa couldn't dress himself ...right?"

"Yeah ...so? ...Sarah did mostly everything because his hands hurt him...so what?" Joe was becoming impatient with Jonathon.

"What if I tell you, Sarah's father couldn't have signed the deed to this house over to Crawley!" The room fell silent while the men tried to grasp what Jonathon was saying. But Joe wasn't going to take any shit from Jonathon. "What the fucking hell do you fucking mean O'Rourke?" Grabbing Jonathon by his coat, Joe lifted him out of his chair. Not wanting Joe to hurt him, Jonathon talked fast. "Sarah told me she did everything from skinning wolves, setting traps, cooking, cleaning, undressing her Pa, and dressing him! Her Pa's hands were crippled with what I believe is something called arthritis, I asked Doc about it, and he agreed Calahan could have been suffering from this ...arthritis!" Joe let Jonathon go. Jonathon took a deep breath and sitting back down, went on. "I gave Sarah a pencil to write in her book and the first thing she said was 'Pa would never be able to hold one of these.' I was confused and asked her what she meant, that's when she told me about doing everything ...his hands were especially bad in cold weather and this arthritis, Doc and I think is like that!" The men stared at Jonathon, trying to understand what arthritis was.

"Sarah told me her father signed over the deed to this house to Crawley the night he died?" Jonathon looked at Joe. "Yeah, he went to the bar and someone, I can't remember who, got him something to write with and he signed the deed, we all saw him sign it." The men nodded in unison. "But did you actually see him write on the deed?" Jonathon said becoming more excited. "Well ...no ...not exactly, but Calahan read out what he wrote, he said he signed it over to Crawley." Sitting down Joe hung his head, and leaning forward, rested his arms on the top of his legs while recalling Calahan's last words. Could it be possible his friend hadn't signed the deed over to Crawley? The room fell silent.

After what seemed like an eternity it was Christian who broke the silence. "I want to look at that deed!" Jonathon smiled widely at him. "Me too!" he said excitedly.

"Yeah! ...maybe we should all take a look at that deed!" Garrett said.

"No-one really saw it ...did they?" Fergus asked no-one in particular.

"Fuck!" Joe cursed and stood up. "Where would the deed be, do you suppose?"

"The bank! ...Morley would have it at the bank ...in one of those…!" Will clicked his fingers trying to figure out what the boxes in the bank were called. "Private boxes ...where people keep their important stuff," he said giving up. "Can we get a look inside the box?" Joe asked urgently. While everyone was thinking, Christian suddenly announced, "I can!" and everyone looked expectantly at him. "I am a lawman! ...I can demand to look at it!"

The men were all talking at once. Jonathon put his hands up, and stopping them, continued to tell them how he came to figure his notion out. "I didn't put two and two together, not at first, when Sarah told me about losing this house and telling me about her Pa's hands, I discussed it with Matilda …Tilly, she's my wife!" He said for those he didn't think knew. "That's when we both figured it out." Jonathon was happy to give some of the credit for finding out about the deed to his wife. Tilly was trained to be a teacher too and Jonathon always reckoned she was smarter than him.

"Why are you doing this O'Rourke? after what Sarah did to you the day she came to town." Christian asked him. Jonathon nodded in agreement. "Since spending time with Sarah I've gotten to know her, and what I witnessed at the dance tonight convinced me Crawley is crooked, when Sarah said Millicent was wearing her locket, and her mother's dress, I believed her." Christian hadn't believed Sarah, but O'Rourke had! Christian felt disgusted with himself. He pointed to the picture hanging above the fireplace. "Take a look at that O'Rourke, and tell me what you think." Jonathon hadn't seen the picture when he came in. Looking up at the painting, then walking backwards to get a better look, his back bumped against the wall on the far side of the room and his mouth fell open. "My god! it's

Sarah! she's beautiful!" he exclaimed. The men grinned at Jonathon from where they were sitting.

"That is not Sarah, O'Rourke, that is her mother Elizabeth!" Christian informed him, sounding proud that the men thought Sarah as beautiful as her mother. He already knew she was beautiful, long before he ever set eyes on the picture. "Wow!" was all Jonathon could say, coming back and standing in front of the fire. "When Sarah shot the rope off my bell, she scared the hell out of me, but now I've gotten to know her, I like her! …Sarah is not the person I've heard people say she is, and Thomas, no one can say she hasn't raised him well, he is my best student, smart and very well mannered." When Joe again explained why Sarah cut a wolf up in the church, Christian felt Sarah was justified in doing what she did, she had no choice but to do the only thing she knew how to do to get her son back. They talked about Frank's death and how it affected her. The more Christian heard the more he knew he loved her. And Jonathon? well, he was in awe of her.

All six men agreed, that in the morning, they would meet at the bank to look at the deed. Wanting to get the locket off Millicent and give it back to Sarah, Christian had to be warned again by Joe to stay away from her, at least until they had a chance to see what was written on the deed. It was only a few hours before sunrise that the men parted company. Jonathon let Christian keep Sarah's book, and taking it to bed with him, he read over again written proof Sarah loved him. She had never so much as said the words, but there they were, written on paper for him to see. Before falling asleep, he hoped and prayed the deed had not been signed. Even so, he vowed to make Crawley pay for the cruelty he bestowed on Sarah. Then there was Thomas, he would try to be the best father he could possibly be to Thomas. Christian surprised himself with this revelation. Could he be a father to Thomas? That would mean marrying Sarah. He wanted very much to marry her. He wanted her to be his wife and Thomas his son. He couldn't wait for morning to come.

Chapter Thirty-eight

Sarah was being chased by wolves. Time and time again, he saw her falling into a dark abyss. He tried to save her, but the trappers surrounded him, stopping him from getting to her. He saw her mutilating wolves with axes and knives and running blindly between trees. Hearing gunshots and seeing her falling in the snow, caused him to toss and turn through the night. She stood in the river unclothed beckoning him to come to her. He called her, but she kept getting further away and didn't answer. Waking in a sweat, and while getting dressed, Christian made up his mind no matter what they found at the bank, he would get down on his knees and beg Sarah to forgive him and ask her to marry him.

Making his way eagerly to the Ferguson House, he knocked vigorously on the door. "Come on in sheriff," Fergus said opening the door and stepping aside. With all nineteen trappers crowded around their table talking loudly and eating, it was a noisy household. A herd of cattle were needing to be branded, so the men were busy getting their gear ready to leave for Major Hardy's ranch. "What time do you want to go to the bank Morgan?" Joe asked chewing on a piece of bread and drinking coffee. "Now Joe!" Christian smiled nervously at him. "The sooner the better."

"Right then, let's go!" Joe ate his bread quickly and swallowed the rest of his coffee.

"Do you suppose Morley will be there yet Morgan?" Garrett asked. "He will be there, if he isn't, we will get him." Anxious to get going, the four men stood up as one and Christian led them out the door. Early that morning Joe informed the rest of the trappers as to what was happening, making them swear not to say anything, warning them if word got out, he would not only have the wolves' skins, but their skins as well. All were glad something was finally being done about Crawley.

Christian and the four trappers walked quickly up the street to the bank and found Jonathon standing outside waiting for them. "Look, there's O'Rourke!" Will said pointing to Jonathon standing on the boardwalk. Christian was glad Jonathon talked to them last night, and relieved to see he had joined them this morning. "O'Rourke is Morley inside?" Will asked as they drew closer. "I think so, but I only just got here myself." Jonathon was both excited and nervous as he smiled up at the men. He wasn't a tall man and these men towered over him, causing him to worry that they would think him a dumb shit, and that they would take his skin if what he told them happened to be wrong.

Christian stepped up to the door of the bank and opening it, led the men inside. Lewis Morley's teller Michael, was behind the counter fidgeting in a draw getting ready for the day, and only stopped when he saw the men enter. Morley, standing beside Michael telling him what he wanted done, turned when he heard the door open. Although it was not unusual to see so many men in the bank at any given time, when he saw the six men, Morley raised his eyebrows. "Gentlemen, what are all of you doing here so early this morning?" Morley smiled and looked from Christian to Joe and back again. "Morning Morley, we are here on official business." Christian informed him. Morley laughed. "Anything to do with this bank is official sheriff, what official business can I do for you?" Not wanting to waste time, Christian came straight out and asked about Crawley. "Has Benjamin Crawley got one of those official looking boxes?" The other men stood in a group behind Christian and watched Morley intently.

Not too sure where telling the men about Crawley's personal bank box was leading, Morley frowned when asked about it. "Yes, he has one."

"Get it for me! ...I want to see what he has inside it!" Christian kept his voice firm.

"But sheriff, bank boxes are private, you can't just..." Morley didn't finish what he was going to say before Christian cut him off.

"I can Morley!" he said, speaking a little too loudly. "I am the law, and I demand to see Crawley's bank box!" Christian's hand rested on his gun.

Morley didn't want trouble inside his bank. He swung around and without saying another word hurried to a back room. After a few minutes, he came back carrying what looked like a strongbox. Sitting the box on the table in front of Christian, all the men crowded around, including Morley.

"Open it," Christian said lowering his voice, becoming nervous about what they might find. The best thing would be the unsigned deed, the worst, would be finding the deed had been signed, or wasn't in the box at all. Christian began to feel sick to his stomach. Morley got the master key and unlocking the box, lifted the lid. All seven men leant in to see what was inside. Reaching in, Joe lifted out a small decorative box, which, when he opened it, a melody played 'green sleeves.' The men listened to it while Joe picked out a crystal necklace. "Elizabeth's goddamn jewel box, and jewellery!" he snarled while holding the necklace up for the men to see.

"Are you sure Joe?" Christian looked at the necklace sparkling in the light.

"Positive." Joe put the necklace back in the box and picking up a string of pearls, showed them around to the men. All four men remembered seeing Elizabeth wearing them at one of her many dinner parties. Joe put the pearls back and sat the jewel box back in the box.

Jonathon reached in and lifted out a yellowing parchment. "I think this might be the deed," he said, swallowing and holding it towards Christian. Christian didn't want to take it.

"You read it O'Rourke." Christian was too afraid to look at the paper and felt his heart thumping wildly in his chest.

"You sure you want me to read it sheriff?" Jonathon looked at Christian, his eyes questioning.

"Read it O'Rourke," Christian repeated trying not to show any feelings. When Jonathon unfolded the parchment, the men waited while he scanned the document.

"Read it out aloud, goddamn it!" Christian snapped impatiently.

"I think you had better read it," Jonathon said holding the parchment out for Christian to take. Without taking his eyes off Jonathon, Christian took it, and with shaky hands held it up in front of him, then casting his eyes on the deed, began to read.

'Let it be known, on this, the twenty-third day of June, eighteen forty-four, the said property, known as 'Mountain View Lodge' being claim number fourteen of said deed, its structure and all its chattels, wholly owned by the undersigned, Calahan Cole and Elizabeth Cole, is hereby registered in Cedar Creek, in that land known as Wyoming.'

Calahan and Elizabeth's signatures were visible under the declaration. Morley's bank handled land sales and held deeds to properties in the county. Lewis Morley's signature along with those of the four trappers was written under an official looking stamp. 'Nothing unusual about that,' Christian thought. Joe shook his head up and down, acknowledging the fact he was there the day they signed it, as was the other three men. Christian stopped reading out aloud as he looked at the bottom of the deed. A look of surprise spread across his face as he looked up at Jonathon. Jonathon smiled back at him. "Read it Christian …read it out aloud so everyone can hear," Jonathon said. "He wrote on it, Joe, Calahan wrote on the deed," Christian said, as he and Joe looked at each other.

"Goddamn son-of-a-bitch!" Joe said feeling gutted. He had prayed Calahan, with his hands as bad as they were, hadn't been able to write anything. Now he felt he had let Sarah down.

"Fuck!" Clearly disappointed at hearing what Christian said, Will, Garrett and Fergus all cursed together. They hoped Calahan hadn't been able to write anything either. They were feeling their hopes for Sarah still owning the lodge had been dashed when Christian looked at Jonathon and a hint of a smile crossed his face.

"The deed also says, 'I, Calahan Cole, on this day, first of December eighteen fifty-nine, do sign over everything pertaining to the property known as Mountain View Lodge to…" Christian hesitated as his eyes misted. He could hardly read the next few words. "…Mountain View Lodge to…" he repeated and then hesitated again while swallowing the lump rising in his throat. "To my daughter …Sarah Elizabeth Cole."

There was a moment of stunned silence as the men digested what Christian read. Suddenly, the room erupted. Cheering and hugging each other, they patted each other on the back and laughed, they wiped their eyes and cursed, Jonathon laughed and whooped, Morley joined in the cheering, Michael, although smiling, stood back and wondered what all the fuss was about. "Calahan did it, he signed it over to Sarah!" Joe couldn't believe it, he grabbed the parchment and read what had been written. "Son-of-a-bitch!" he laughed, then, handing the parchment back to Christian, hugged him.

"You know what this means Morgan? It means Sarah owns Mountain View Lodge, she always has, that maggot Crawley knew this parchment had been signed over to Sarah and hid it from everyone so he could keep the lodge for himself. Sarah camped on that riverbank all these years, raising Thomas the best way she could." Joe crossed the room to a chair and finally realizing the injustice Sarah had suffered, sat down heavily. "He's been stealing from Sarah all these years …that fucking snake!" Now Joe understood why Sarah had for many years called Crawley those vile names, she had good reason. Sarah knew all along what Crawley had done. Joe kept his head bowed for a time while going over the years Sarah spent out in the cold raising a small boy on her own. Feeling as mad as a diseased wolf, but at the same time happy for Sarah, he knew there was no way of making up for the years Sarah lost. If only they had believed Sarah when she told them Crawley was a thief. If only they had seen the parchment earlier. If only! Joe had another more sinister thought. Could Crawley be a murderer? Did he somehow kill Calahan? Sarah believed he had, she told them time and time again Crawley killed her Pa, but they hadn't believed her. Joe's eyes watered as he shed a tear, then standing with the other men, discussed what they were going to do to get the lodge back to Sarah.

"Well he won't be stealing from her anymore Joe, I want everything Crawley has ever taken from Sarah given back to her." Christian adamantly told them. "He's going to go to jail for a very long time for what he's done." The gunshot was heard inside the bank.

Chapter Thirty-nine

"What the hell! Who has a gun in town!" No-one was more surprised than Christian when he heard the shot, as far as he was aware, no-one had a gun. He quickly turned to Morley.

"Morley, has Sarah got a bank box?"

"No, but I can give her one," Morley said excitedly.

"Good, put these in it and keep them safe." Christian handed the parchment and the jewel box to him.

"I most certainly will!" Morley said, happy to find out Sarah still owned the lodge, and pleased the men let him stay to see what was in the box. He would put Sarah's bank book in the box for safe keeping too. Nineteen trappers over the past fifteen years made Sarah a very wealthy woman, and her book needed to be kept safe.

When the men came out of the bank, Clem came running down the street towards them, his face red from exertion. "Sheriff!" he puffed. "Sounds like that shot came from the riverbank." Clem felt he couldn't keep running around fast for much longer. "Sarah's camp? Where did she get a gun this time?" Christian asked as the men gathered in a group. "Not Cole, she hasn't got a gun, I checked, her guns are still locked up back in the jailhouse." Doubling over, Clem put his hands on his knees and tried to catch his breath. Leaving Clem to walk behind, the group of men ran down the trail.

As they approached Sarah's camp, they could see the fire was out, but not seeing Sarah, Christian looked inside her shelter. "Look at this!" Will said, picking up Sarah's knife still inside its sheath. "What the hell, Sarah doesn't go anywhere without her knife, how did you find it Will?" Joe asked. "It was here, on the ground, pointing this way." Will pointed the sheath toward the trail leading up behind the Ferguson House. Joe nodded. "Something's not right ...Sarah's leaving a trail ...come on!" As Joe took the sheath and ran off, the men followed. Pushing through thick brush, they ran up the trail and came out behind the Ferguson House.

Millicent crept into Sarah's shelter while Sarah was still asleep. Sarah woke when she smelt an unusual sweet-smelling fragrance. It wasn't anything she smelt before and it surprised her. When her eyes focused in the early morning light, she saw Millicent standing over her with a gun in her hand and tried to keep her voice steady. "Millicent ...what are you doing? Why are you here?"

"What I should have done a long time ago, get up! ...get up now! you stinking whore!" Sarah looked Millicent up and down and got quickly to her feet.

Millicent noticed how Sarah was looking at her. "You think you are the only one who can wear trousers!" Millicent smirked. "Daddy's store is full of trousers, and I can wear anything I want, now get out here!" Keeping her gun pointed at Sarah, Millicent stepped backward as Sarah came out of the shelter and faced her. "What are you going to do Millicent?" She asked, moving further into the open.

"I'm going to rid this town of you once and for all, then Christian and I can be together! ...daddy should have rid us of you when he got rid of your father, but never mind, I will do it for him ...now get moving!" Millicent waved her gun in the direction of the trail behind Sarah's camp. Sarah wasn't shocked at Millicent's revelation about her father killing her Pa, she knew all along Crawley killed him, but now she had further proof.

Poking the gun in Sarah's back, Millicent forced her to head toward the ridge. Sarah's mind worked on how to get Millicent to fire the gun to let someone know she was in trouble before they got out of the town boundary. "Wait!" Millicent exclaimed. "Take your knife off! ...you won't be needing that where you are going!" Figuring now was her only chance to attract attention, Sarah made a task of taking her knife off slow. Slowly undoing the belt from around her waist, she just as slowly bent down and sat it on the ground. Standing up quickly, she startled Millicent by grabbing hold of her gun-hand. The two women wrestled, both falling heavily to the ground as Sarah's hand covered Millicent's, forcing Millicent to pull the trigger. The gun went off with a loud report, echoing along the river and over the town. Sarah tried wrestling the gun from Millicent's grasp, but Millicent, grabbing a hand-full of her hair, pulled hard, making Sarah let go. Breaking free, Millicent pointed the gun at Sarah. "Try that again and I will shoot you! you bitch! ...now get up!" she screamed. As Sarah got to her feet, Millicent struck out with her free hand and slapped her hard across her face. Sarah's face stung, her eyes watered, but she stopped herself from lashing out. "Get going!" Millicent sneered, shoving the gun in Sarah's back and making her walk faster. As they pushed their way up the trail, unbeknown to Millicent, Sarah snapped branches from shrubs before shoving them out of her way. 'Maybe,' she prayed, 'someone will follow my trail.'

Christian and Joe took the lead. With the other men bringing up the rear, they ran south along the ridge high above the river. Ice water flowing from the mountains, roared over submerged boulders and deep holes, making the river a swirling torrent. As the men hurried between trees and low growing shrubs, Joe stopped to look at foliage where branches had been broken. 'Good girl,' he thought. 'Sarah had been paying attention when they taught her how to keep herself safe.' The men ran on. "Look!" Christian yelled, and all five men stopped and looked to where he was pointing.

Two figures, appearing almost identical could be seen heading through the trees close to the edge of the cliff. Both were dressed alike, wearing light coloured shirts and brown trousers. One with black hair, the other much lighter brown hair. Both had their hair braided with a single braid down their back, but one was tall and thin, the other smaller, more feminine. Christian recognized Sarah straight away. Running faster, the men came up on the two figures near a clearing. "Sarah!" Christian called. On hearing her name, Sarah turned and saw Christian with Joe. 'Thank goodness they heard the shot,' she thought feeling relieved. Hearing Christian call Sarah too, Millicent swung her arm around Sarah's shoulders, pulling it tight across Sarah's throat in a strangle hold, cutting off Sarah's airway. Seeing the gun in Millicent's hand, Christian's stomach lurched. Millicent pointed the gun at Sarah's head and forced Sarah backwards.

"Don't come any closer Christian!" Millicent called. "I should have got rid of this whore a long time ago! ...she spoils everything for everyone! ...well not anymore!"

Christian studied the shirt Millicent was wearing. The little blue/grey flowers and lace around the collar and cuffs, made it identical to the one he bought Sarah when he brought her back from the cavern. Christian tightened his mouth in anger when he saw Millicent wearing Sarah's gold locket about her neck. Christian and Joe stood side by side. Will and Garrett suddenly appeared and stood off to one side of the men.

"Don't any of you move! ...I won't hesitate to shoot this bitch!" Millicent screamed. To keep Millicent from choking her and cutting off her windpipe, Sarah gripped Millicent's arm, and at the same time, tried to keep her stomach calm, but she wasn't calm, not at all. Feeling like she was going to be sick she swallowed, and stepping back, forced Millicent to move toward the edge of the cliff.

Christian could see the two women getting close to the edge. "Millicent, please, you don't want to hurt Sarah," he begged, hoping Millicent would let Sarah go.

"She's nothing but a stinking trapper whore! ...I met you first Christian ...then this bitch comes to town and spoils everything! ...everyone is talking about her ...everyone knows you and she have been fucking! ...she needs to go ...then you and I can be together!" Millicent suddenly laughed and snorted. "Did you know she stole Frank from me? I was supposed to marry Frank ...it was all arranged ...daddy and Major Hardy had it all figured out ...Frank and I would get married and live in the lodge ...imagine that ...Frank and me ...living in Cole's house!" Millicent laughed shrilly and went on. "Then this no-good whore spoilt it by having Frank's baby! ...well she's not going to have you ...I will get rid of her ...then we can be together ...it will just be you and me ...like it should be!" Millicent's voice was becoming more child-like and shrill as she babbled. The night Sarah tried to take back her locket, Millicent's mind snapped. She hated that Sarah had come to the dance and accused her of stealing. Millicent knew all along the locket belonged to Sarah. But according to Millicent's distorted way of thinking, her daddy won the lodge, and everything in it was theirs for the taking, including Cole's jewellery.

"Millicent please, you don't want to do this!" Christian begged. Able to tell Millicent had lost her mind, Joe took a furtive step sideways, bringing him closer to Christian. "Tell Millicent something she wants to hear …tell her you love her," he whispered barely loud enough for Christian to hear.

"What!" Christian didn't think he heard Joe right.

"She's crazy Morgan! …she will hurt Sarah if you don't do something, goddamn it! tell her you love her! maybe then she'll let Sarah go!" Joe repeated more sternly while keeping his voice just above a whisper. Christian couldn't believe what Joe was asking, but agreed he had to try something to save Sarah. He went quiet for a moment while thinking about what he should say.

"You come closer and I will shoot her!" Seeing Fergus and Jonathon come from behind the trees to stand near Will and Garrett, Millicent moved her gun closer to Sarah.

"Millicent," Christian started. The two women were standing precariously close to the edge of the cliff. Afraid they would fall, he had to try what Joe asked of him. "Millicent …darling!" His throat went dry. "Please …you don't want to hurt Cole …she isn't worth it …you hurt her and you will be locked up for a very long time …and we won't be able to be together …you don't want that …do you?" Christian almost choked on his words and struggled to keep his voice steady while trying to sound convincing.

"You want us to be together Christian?" Hearing what she wanted to hear from what Christian was saying, Millicent lowered her gun but kept it pointed at Sarah. "You …you love me?" Millicent asked in her child-like voice. Christian knew if Millicent pulled the trigger the bullet would hit Sarah in the stomach and Sarah would die. He couldn't risk having her shoot the woman he loved.

"Yes Millicent, I knew when we went on our picnic …you remember? …when I first came to Cedar Creek …I kissed you …I knew then I loved you." Unable to forget that kiss, he felt sick that he had to lie and sound like he meant what he was saying.

"But you are fucking this whore! …everyone in town knows the two of you have been fucking! …she is nothing but a dirty whore! …when we marry you won't touch me like you touch her …I won't let you touch me in that filthy way! ...we will marry though ... won't we?" Joe and the group were men who thought nothing of using foul language in conversation with each other, but hearing Millicent's words didn't make it sound better. Christian tried to ignore Millicent's reference to Sarah and his lovemaking, but having said the same things to Sarah, he felt ashamed, but had to go on with his charade. "It didn't mean anything Millicent, darling ...you told me, if you remember, you wouldn't let me touch you until we were married ...but I am a man ...what harm could it do to let a ...a ...whore ...like ...Cole ...take care of my needs?" Christian stammered over his disparaging words.

Listening to what Christian was saying, only helped confirm for Sarah what Christian thought of her, and that he used her, that he never loved her. The horrible nasty words he said to her at the swimming hole were still fresh in her mind. Christian went on. "After we are married Millicent ...I will be true to you." Joe glared at Christian. He hadn't meant for him to say as much as he did, or sound so convincing. Frowning, even he was having doubts whether Christian really loved Sarah.

"You mean that Christian?" Millicent believed everything Christian was telling her. Sarah believed every word he was saying too. Her eyes welled, and overflowed, tears ran down her cheeks wetting Millicent's shirt sleeve.

Moving her feet ever so slightly, Sarah made Millicent take another step back. Standing at the highest point of the cliff above the river, Christian and the other men watched Sarah and Millicent stepping closer to the edge. The sound of rushing water below was almost deafening. "I mean it Millicent ...Cole doesn't mean anything to me ...just let her go ...then you and I can be together." Christian's voice broke as he lied.

"Christian!" Sarah managed to say through her tears. Not knowing what Christian was saying was simply for Millicent's benefit, Sarah's voice strained against the hold Millicent had on her throat as she spoke. "I'm ...I'm going to have a baby!" Hearing clearly what Sarah said, Christian's eyes darted from Millicent straight to Sarah. "Oh Sarah!" he said, his heart swelling with love for her. Knowing straight away Sarah's situation had gone from bad to worse, Joe cursed Sarah's sudden declaration.

Hearing the soft, loving tone of Christian's voice when he said Sarah's name, Millicent knew every word he spoke to her was a lie. Christian Morgan loved Sarah Cole, and not her. "No!" Millicent screamed, swinging her gun-hand towards Christian. In an instant Millicent decided, if she couldn't have Christian, Sarah wasn't going to have him either.

When Millicent moved the gun away from her, Sarah seized the moment. Flinging her arm out wide, she knocked Millicent's arm sideways. The gun went off. Christian and the men dived for cover. Using her body as leverage, and not giving a thought to what could happen, Sarah quickly pushed Millicent backwards. A look of terror crossed Millicent's face as she screamed and flung her arms out wide letting Sarah go. As the two women disappeared over the edge, Sarah twisted her body, and grabbing Millicent's gun-hand, pulled it towards Millicent's chest. The river came up fast as both women plummeted toward it. With just enough time, Sarah straightened up, and while holding her breath, hit the river feet first. Plunging beneath the surface, her toes touched the riverbed. Pushing herself off the bottom, her body began rising, but something was wrong. Instead of going straight to the surface, she found herself being pulled along by the swift current.

When Millicent fired her gun, Christian flung himself out of the way and watched as both Sarah and Millicent dropped over the edge of the ridge. What he didn't see, was Sarah grabbing Millicent's gun-hand and pulling it toward Millicent. The sound of a report echoed all around, followed by a terrifying scream, and Christian knew it came from his own throat. He rushed to the edge in time to see one woman hit the river on her back, the other feet first.

"Oh God! Sarah!" Christian cried. It seemed his nightmare had come true. Five men stood beside him and looked down into the torrent of swirling water. Snapping out of his moment of disbelief, Joe yelled, "come on Morgan! we've got to get down to the river!" and hit Christian hard on his arm to get him going.

"Ow! fuck! damn it!" Christian cursed, grabbing his arm. Joe stopped and looked at him. "Christ Morgan! ...you've been shot!" Looking down, Christian saw blood had soaked his sleeve, but he had no time to dwell on himself. "It's only a scratch ...come on Joe, let's get down there! ...Will ...you stay here so we know where they went in!" Will nodded, and while the rest of the men took off back along the trail toward town, he stayed behind.

While running along, Christian's mind was racing. 'Why did Sarah do that? ...why would she push her and Millicent over the edge? ...no-one could survive such a fall!' Both Joe and Thomas told him Sarah had fallen into a river once before, but that time Frank saved her. Christian didn't think that fall could have been nearly as high as this one. Then he remembered what Sarah said just before she went over the edge. It had to be his baby. She wouldn't tell him she was pregnant if it wasn't. Sarah was going to have his child.

Making it to Sarah's camp in quick time, he saw Clem holding back a large crowd gathered on the riverbank. Racing down to the river's edge, passing everyone, he hoped to get across, but where he stood the river was too wild, so running back up the trail and grabbing the first horse he saw, he swung himself up into the saddle, kicked the horse furiously, and racing up the street, sent the horse galloping across the wooden bridge, then turning it sharply down the bank, passing the pier, brought the horse to a standstill. Jumping from the horse, and without waiting for anyone, he ran along the stony riverbank. After getting hold of one of the trapper's horses, Joe followed Christian across the bridge.

Stopping at Sarah's camp, Fergus and Garrett, figured if Sarah were to survive the river, the town would soon know about her being pregnant again, so to get the gossip over with, they let it be known. "Sarah and Millicent have gone into the river and we are looking for them ...and another thing ...Sarah is expecting Sheriff Morgan's baby." Then both men raced after Christian and Joe.

News of what happened travelled through town quickly. Thomas was at Billy Henderson's helping Billy and his Pa Dave in their garden when they heard his Ma had fallen into the river. Putting Thomas and Billy in their buckboard, Dave took it across the bridge, and turning it down the other side, steered it precariously along the bank past the pier, then pulled it to a stop just before the bank became too steep. Jumping out, Thomas raced down the steep incline and along the riverbank while Dave and Billy waited at their buckboard for him to come back.

Getting to the spot where Will was standing on the cliff, Christian scanned the river and found, caught amongst boulders, a woman's body floating face down. With his heart in his mouth, he waded into the river to retrieve the body. Brown pants, cream coloured floral shirt, and a long braid floated in the swirling water. Christian felt his heart would stop beating as he pulled the body to the edge where Joe helped him lift it onto the riverbank. Hearing Thomas screaming for his mother as he ran toward them, Christian and Joe quickly turned the body over. A moment of relief passed between both men when Millicent's cold dead eyes stared up at them. Seeing the bullet hole in her chest, Christian tore the gold chain and locket from around her neck and shoved it in his shirt pocket just as Thomas came running up, his face crumpling. "Ma!" he screamed as loud as he could. Putting his arms around Thomas, Christian stopped him seeing the body. "It's not Sarah Thomas! ...it's not your Ma!" Christian assured him. Thomas buried his head against Christian and clung to him. "Ma! ...where is she sheriff?"

"I don't know son," Christian said looking up to where Will was waving his arms wildly and pointing down river. "Come on Thomas! ...you too Joe! ...let's go find Sarah!" Christian wasn't going to give up, not until he found Sarah alive, or dead.

Sarah's head bobbed out of the water. Her body was being tossed about in the turbulence. Gasping and taking a deep breath, before suddenly tumbling over and over, then unable to tell if she was up or down, she swallowed water, came up again and gagging, remembered what Christian taught her. As her arms and legs smashed against things hidden beneath the surface, she swung her arms like paddles, and kicked her feet, trying to make them work. When her hip smashed into a boulder, she tried grabbing hold of it, but her hands slid over the slippery rock and she kept going. The roar of the river grew louder as she swept toward the waterfall.

Afraid if she went over the edge, she would never survive the fall, she made her arms work faster, and paddled furiously. 'I have to swim to the nearest bank like Christian told me!' but she was tiring. When her head came clear of the river, she got a glimpse of a body of still water she was coming up on rapidly. Sweeping past a dead tree hanging in the water, snagging her shirt, she tried desperately to grab its branches. Her shirt tore, her hands slipped over a slime covered branch, and she kept going. 'I have to get to that pool' she urged herself, swinging her arms, and stretching her legs as she kicked harder. But the pool seemed so far away. *'I can't do this, I can't keep going, it would be so easy to give up, stop paddling, stop kicking, just let the river carry me off, just float away, be with my Pa, be with Frank.'* Sarah's thoughts as she swept along were becoming erratic. 'No!' a voice screamed inside her head. *'What about Thomas? What about Christian? Don't you love them? What about your unborn baby? Swim, damn you, swim!'* The voice shouted. She could never leave Thomas, and she loved Christian. Even if he didn't love her, their baby had to have a chance at life.

Joe was of the belief Sarah was dead. "Sarah can't swim Morgan ...she hasn't got a hope of surviving this torrent." By letting Sarah die in the river, Joe was convinced he had broken the promise Calahan, and Elizabeth had asked him to keep. Entrusting their beloved daughter to his care, he had failed his best friend, and the woman he once loved.

While Christian and Thomas clung to each other, Christian was deep in thought. "Yes, Joe! she can! ...I taught her! ...she can swim, damn it! ...she can! ...come on!" Christian let Thomas go and began to run in the direction of the waterfall. He hoped in his heart Sarah remembered what he taught her, even so, the river was wild, Sarah would have to fight hard to survive against the rapids.

Joe walked as fast as he could while Christian and Thomas ran quickly ahead of him. Watching Thomas running along with Christian, he suddenly felt old. He had failed Thomas, and he had failed Sarah. How he wished, just like he had with Frank, that Sarah and Christian could have been together. They would have been happy. Christian would have made a good father for Thomas, but now it seemed, it was all too late.

Sarah's arms and legs worked harder against the swift current sweeping her along. Almost exhausted, the river itself flung her into the pool. Suddenly, the roaring turbulence sounded far away. She stopped paddling, stopped kicking, and straight away began to sink. Still submerged she gagged, and swallowing a mouthful of water, struck out again. Stretching her legs and kicking furiously once more, her head rose to the surface. Coughing and spitting she sucked in air and felt her fingers dig in to the soft grit along the side of the pool. Grabbing a fist full of grit with each hand, she pulled herself to the edge where she pushed her feet into pebbles lining the riverbank. Dragging herself onto the stones, she lay on her stomach and shivered. Her chest heaved as she filled her lungs with air. Her arms and legs hurt from being battered against rocks. They ached, from paddling and kicking. 'Goddamn it, I'm alive ...now what? ...Christian said he loves Millicent ...he confessed that in front of me, Joe heard him ...Jonathon must have heard him, and the other men too!' No longer having the strength to cry, Sarah lay with her head on her arms.

The sound of the waterfall was deafening. Christian and Thomas slowed down and looking at the churning white water, scanned the river. The rocky ground, made the going slow, giving Joe time to catch up to them. "Morgan!" Joe stopped, and grabbing hold of Christian's arm, pointed at something ahead of them. Joe may have become old but there was nothing wrong with his eyesight. Christian looked to where Joe was pointing. Something was there, a long way off, he could just make it out. A cream coloured shirt, brown trousers and light brown hair, and it was kneeling on the riverbank. Christian's heart lurched as he started to run. Thomas ran after him while Joe came hurrying along behind.

Sarah was on her knees when Christian called out. Thomas yelled too. She didn't have the strength to get up, so staying where she was, cried at seeing the two of them together. Falling to his knees in front of Sarah, Christian threw his arms around her. Thomas fell to his knees and embraced the two of them. "Sarah," Christian's voice broke. "I love you so much," he declared, kissing her on her face, her eyes, her nose, and then her mouth.

Clinging to each other, thoughts of Christian not loving her faded. "Christian ...I swam ...oh I love you both so much!" Sarah tried to hug Thomas and Christian, but her arms hurt and she struggled to lift them. Coming up behind them, Joe looked like he was going to cry. "Thank God Sarah, you are safe ...are you alright?" Seeing the three people in front of him were going to be alright, Joe pushed all thought of having broken his promise to the back of his mind.

"Don't thank God Joe, thank Christian, he taught me to swim, and yes, I'm alright ...now." Noticing Christian's blood-soaked sleeve, Sarah became concerned. "You're bleeding ...when Millicent aimed her gun at you, I tried to push it away." Sarah leant heavily against him. Christian felt his injury was minor compared to what Sarah had endured. "It's nothing ...can you stand?" he asked, helping her to her feet. Standing slowly, Sarah's legs felt like they would give way and she would fall. "I don't think my legs will work for a very long time after kicking so hard." She didn't mention she had been smashed against rocks.

Scooping Sarah into his arms, and with Thomas and Joe walking beside them, Christian carried her back along the riverbank. When they got to where Millicent's body was, Fergus and Garrett were putting her on a blanket ready to take her back to town. "I killed her Christian ...what will happen to me now?" Expecting him to say she would be locked up for a very long time, she closed her eyes and waited for the inevitable. "Nothing is going to happen Sarah ...everyone knows Millicent tried to kill you." Relieved with his answer, Sarah felt she had to ask him one more thing. "Those things you said to her ...up on the cliff ...did you mean them?" She prayed Christian would say he didn't mean any of the things he said.

"Not a word ...I love you Sarah ...I have loved you from the moment you knocked me off my feet that first day you arrived in town ...we have so much to talk about."

Having thought about what Joe said about staying at the Ferguson House when the men go back to the mountain, and having him say Thomas could continue to go to school and spend time with his new friends, and that would allow her to see Christian every day, she liked the idea, and so having made peace with Joe, she made up her mind. "I'm not leaving Christian." Hoping she was going to stay to be with him, Christian asked. "And just what do you mean by that?"

"I mean, I have decided to stay, Joe suggested Thomas and I could live at the Ferguson House while they are trapping ...we would have the house to ourselves ...and Christian ...I have a bed there ...if you are interested," Sarah smiled at him. "I am very interested Sarah, but we best get married first," Christian said softly, looking into Sarah's eyes. "Are you asking me to marry you, Sheriff Morgan?" Sarah said, her voice barely a whisper. Christian stopped walking and putting her down, held her in his arms. "Yes, I am … Sarah …will you marry me?" He thought about proposing to Sarah in a better place, and under better circumstances, but right now, he wanted her to know how he felt about her.

Figuring she had fallen in love with Christian that day outside the schoolhouse, Sarah didn't hesitate before answering. "Yes, Christian …I will marry you." Standing together they held their kiss for a long time. Joe and Thomas smiled as they watched on. But Sarah experienced a terrible trauma, falling from a great height, and her body had been pummeled in the river. Joe worried Sarah might lose her baby, so wanting to get her to Doc Harris, he hurried them up.

Reaching Dave and Billy waiting at their buckboard, Christian sat holding Sarah in the back, and after Thomas and Joe climbed in, Dave steered the buckboard back across the bridge. Meanwhile, Fergus and Garrett carried Millicent's body back to town. Dave stopped his buckboard outside Doc Harris's practice where a crowd was waiting, and ignoring everyone, Christian carried Sarah inside where Doc ordered her out of her wet clothes and into bed. Finding it difficult to undress herself she asked Christian to help her. After kissing her on her forehead, and wrapping a sheet around her he swallowed in dismay at noticing amongst bruises covering her arms and legs, a large bruise stretching across her hip. Feeling the pain in her hip as she moved, Sarah began shaking uncontrollably.

Christian rushed into the hallway. "Doc!" he yelled. "Sarah's shaking, do something quick!" Doc hurried into the room carrying a blanket he warmed in front of his fire. "Get Sarah on the bed quickly!" he demanded. Christian lifted Sarah onto the bed just as Gerda came in carrying a bucket of warm stones she heated in her oven. Doc covered Sarah with the warm blanket while Gerda placed the stones she covered under the blanket around Sarah's body. "We need to keep her warm, her body is going into shock," Doc explained. "Will she lose the baby?" Christian asked, sounding worried. He wanted to be a father to Thomas, but having his own child would be more than he could ever wish for, convincing him, the four of them would be a happy family.

It was at that precise moment Christian understood Brother Abrahams prediction. When he was recuperating at the Les Rios Mission, he hadn't understood what 'three would become four' meant, but now he did. They would become four when their baby was born. Putting all his faith in Brother Abraham, Christian prayed Sarah and his baby would be alright. Sarah stopped shivering, but closing her eyes, gave in to her ordeal. "I don't know Christian," Doc was saying. "Sarah is a strong woman …we just have to wait and see …the next couple of weeks will be the hardest for her …she needs rest …we will keep her here with us for now."

"I will visit every day Doc …no matter what happens …I am going to marry Sarah." Christian put his mouth gently on Sarah's and kissed her once more, then left the room.

Chapter Forty

Doc cleaned Christian's bullet wound and told him he was lucky. When he flexed his arm to see what damage the wound had done, Christian was satisfied. His arm was a little stiff, his hand though, was still working fine. Asking Sarah to marry him and having her say yes before she passed out, made him happy. Sarah had accepted him, but he still had a lot of apologizing to do. Gerda ushered him outside so Sarah could begin her recovery. Stepping onto the boardwalk, he was confronted by a large crowd gathered outside. A woman asked how Sarah was. "Sarah is very ill …she needs a lot of rest …hopefully then she will be fine." That was all Christian was going to tell them. As far as he was aware, they didn't know Sarah was pregnant.

"Sheriff Morgan!" When Christian heard someone call him from the back of the crowd, he pushed his way through the throng of people and came face to face with Benjamin Crawley standing in the middle of the street outside his store. Having heard Sarah shot Millicent and her body was being recovered from the river, Crawley rushed to the undertakers just as the men carrying Millicent's body got there. Staring down at the bullet hole in his beloved daughter's chest, he seethed with hatred for Sarah. Because of her, Frank Mason and his daughter were dead. Determined to take from her what she had taken from him, he left Phelps the undertaker measuring Millicent for her coffin, and hurried back to his store. Everyone moved aside when they saw Crawley, and let the two men face each other.

Christian understood Crawley would not be happy about what happened to his daughter, he had a right to be upset, but it was Millicent's own fault, not Sarah's.

"What do you want Crawley?" Christian demanded.

"What do you want Crawley!" Crawley mocked with a sneer. "I want that bitch dead! that's what I want! but if I can't have her, then I will settle for you!" Shocked murmurs emanated from the crowd as they moved to get out of harm's way. Christian hadn't been prepared for a confrontation with Crawley. He hadn't tried moving his gun up and down in its holster as he always did so it would slide free when he thought there might be trouble. Christian's arm hurt. The injury Millicent inflicted on him had been close to him wearing a bullet. The bullet shaved skin and muscle off as it tore past his arm. When Doc bandaged him up, he said he would be fine, but warned he was going to be left with another scar to add to the two he had on his back. ""Don't be stupid Crawley! you don't want to end up like your daughter," Christian said trying to threaten him into surrendering.

"Don't be stupid Crawley!" Crawley mimicked angrily. Christian held his hand away from his gun in readiness, and sized up the situation when Crawley opened his coat to show he was wearing a gun-belt. The gun in its holster sat high. Crawley would have to bend his arm for his hand to grab hold of the grip to pull the gun up and out of its holster, then he would have to aim the gun straight before he could pull the trigger. It meant Crawley would need time for his draw to be true, but there was no telling how fast Crawley was.

"You don't want to do this Crawley!" Christian tried once more to talk him out of doing something stupid. "Don't I? That bitch killed my daughter because of you!" he bellowed. "Millicent should be marrying you, not that whore you are fucking! ...that bitch can't keep her legs closed, and now I hear she's filled with your bastard kid!" Christian was taken aback when he heard what Crawley said. No-one except him, the four trappers, Jonathon, or Doc and his wife should have known Sarah was pregnant. Someone had let Crawley know, and now it seemed, the whole town knew, but he was going to marry Sarah anyway, so whoever it was, he didn't hold it against them. Christian wasn't appreciating any of Crawley's bad-mouthing his wife to be. "I never loved Millicent, I love Sarah and I am going to marry her ...I won't have you! or anyone else calling her filthy names!"

But Crawley wouldn't let up and Christian was tiring of him, he just wanted to end Crawley's ranting when Crawley went on. "Millicent was supposed to marry Frank and live in the lodge, then that bitch put her legs up for him ...who knows who else she puts her legs up for ...there's a whole lot of men in this town that propose to her ...maybe you just want to fuck her like they want to!"

There was no way Christian could stop Crawley's rant, except with his gun. He flexed his gun-hand. "You stole Sarah's house Crawley ...Sarah's father never signed the lodge over to you, he signed it over to Sarah, you've been pretending all these years you owned that house ...I often wondered why you didn't live there, and now I know ...you can't live there because Calahan's deed, proves you don't own it!" Voices became raised in amazement from the crowd at hearing the truth about the lodge. Christian felt pleased the town at last knew about Crawley.

When news filtered around town that Sheriff Morgan and Benjamin Crawley were going to have a shootout the crowd grew larger. People standing on boardwalks and in the street listened intently as Christian continued to out Crawley's thieving ways. "You've been stealing from inside Sarah's house for years while Sarah raised her son on that goddamn riverbank!" Joe stood with Garrett and Fergus on the boardwalk. A little further away, Will stood behind Thomas, with his hands resting on Thomas's shoulders, holding him firmly in his grasp. Billy stood beside Thomas. "Is Mister Crawley going to shoot Sheriff Morgan?" Thomas asked Will. "I don't think so Thomas, Sheriff Morgan is a good shot," Will answered, giving Thomas's shoulders a squeeze. Thomas hoped Sheriff Morgan wouldn't get himself shot. He couldn't stand it if his soon to be new Pa was going to get himself killed. Right now, Mister Crawley looks meaner than the outlaw Sheriff Morgan beat to a draw, and no-one knows if Crawley is a good shot or not, everyone has to wait to find out.

"I won the lodge fair and square! Cole cheated me out of it, so I took what was mine!" Crawley yelled in anger. Everything Calahan owned Crawley envied. He wanted to beat Calahan for a very long time, and saw his chance the night Calahan came to the saloon looking like he already had a belly full of whiskey, making it easy to draw him into the game. He knew a losing hand had been dealt to Calahan, because he was the one who marked the card.

While listening to Crawley, Joe's mind began to work. "I checked those cards that night …couldn't find one …what did you do with it, Crawley?" His memory of that night was becoming clearer. "What happened to the …ah …nine …nine of …club's? …you take it with you?" Crawley didn't answer as he and Christian stood staring at each other.

Sitting in a box in Billy's room at his house holding his most treasured possessions is an old faded, worn-out nine of club's card. "I've got that card!" Billy suddenly exclaimed, looking up at Will. Then without waiting for Will to say something, he raced to his house, flew up the stairs and tipped everything out of his treasure box onto his bed. Picking up the card, he raced back downstairs and into the street. Glad to see when he got back nothing had happened. "Here!" he said running up to Joe and holding up the card. "Take a look, Mister Jones!" Joe looked at the worn-out card Billy was holding. "Look Mister Jones! look at the corner!" Billy pressed.

Taking the card from Billy, Joe decided, wouldn't hurt, so taking it and holding it up to the light, he could see in one of the corners, a group of small holes. Rubbing his finger over the back of the card, he could feel indentations the holes made. "Jesus …he did cheat Calahan! Billy has proof!" Joe said loud enough for everyone to hear. "That card, don't prove nothin!" Crawley yelled. "That kid could've got that card anywhere and put holes in it himself!" he sneered in anger. "No-one mentioned holes Crawley, only someone who put them there would know about these holes!" Joe said, convincing everyone of Crawley's guilt.

While he couldn't ignore Crawley being guilty of cheating either, Christian was satisfied to let it go until he found out what happened to Sarah's father. "Tell me Crawley …did you kill Calahan Cole?" The crowd fell silent as they waited in anticipation for Crawley's answer. "Ah hell!" Crawley said knowing he was caught out, but it didn't matter, he was going to kill Christian anyway. "It was so goddamn easy …the drunken fool!" Wanting everyone to hear Crawley confess to how he was able to get away with killing Sarah's father, Christian asked him how he did it.

"I stood on his foot!" Crawley laughed at how incredulous he sounded. "All I did, was stand on the damn fool's foot and he lost his balance and fell over!" Not satisfied, Christian wanted details. "Explain to me how you mean you stood on his foot." Crawley laughed as he went on to explain how he killed Sarah's father. "Cole signed his deed then stuck the goddamn thing in my pocket before I could get a look at it. He had a nerve asking me if he and his whore girl could have time to get out of the lodge ...well I told him to get alright! ...get that whore bitch of yours I said, and get out now! ...Cole didn't like that ...he took a swipe at me ...only I saw it coming ...so ... I stomped on his foot, and ducked! ...that fool's fist went sailing right on by me and he toppled over ...like a dead drunk!" Crawley laughed some more. "Dead! ...he was dead all right! ...I took that deed home and when I saw what Cole wrote, I put it in my bank box and left it there ...I won the lodge fair and square! and I was keeping it!" Christian recalled what he knew of the law. "No court anywhere in this country would agree with you Crawley, it can be proven you cheated, Calahan wrote Sarah's name on that deed, and that is as good a will as you can get, she is the rightful owner of Mountain View Lodge."

"My daughter is dead because of that bitch! ...and you!" Crawley screamed at Christian. Christian ignored Crawley's outburst. "Both you and Millicent welcomed me to this town and I appreciated your kindness ...your daughter died because she had a misguided idea that I loved her ...I never gave her that impression ...I fell in love with Sarah the first day I met her ...and we *are* going to have a baby and I *am* going to marry her." Christian no longer cared what the town folk thought about what him and Sarah had been doing.

After hearing what Christian said, Joe felt a whole lot more respect for Christian. To stand in front of the town and confess his love for Sarah was proof enough for him. He thought if Christian doesn't get himself shot, he will make a good father to Thomas and a good husband to Sarah.

Fergus swore under his breath, glad Christian said what he said, but he was afraid for him, even if Crawley wasn't a quick draw, Christian was wounded and his arm looked stiff. Garrett moved to one side, he didn't have a gun, but he thought he might be able to distract Crawley so Christian could get Crawley's gun off him. Feeling sure Christian could outdraw Crawley, Will kept hold of Thomas.

Right then, as well as despising Sarah, Crawley despised the whole town. The large crowd standing either side of Christian looked to be siding with him. Crawley wasn't going to let Sarah be happy when his loving daughter was lying in a wooden box at the undertakers.

Christian could see Crawley starting to move. "Don't do something you may regret for the rest of your life Crawley!" he barked. Crawley didn't heed Christian's words. When he went for his gun, the crowd stepped back simultaneously.

Christian's hand pulled his gun from its holster. At the same time, Crawley bent his arm and reached for the grip of his. Christian baulked. Crawley's hand lifted his gun clear. Christian levelled his gun at Crawley. Crawley tried levelling his gun at Christian. Both Christian and Crawley fired. Christian's bullet slammed into Crawley's chest lifting him off the ground. Crawley's gun was pointing at Christian when it went off. Christian felt the impact of Crawley's bullet as it hit him. Christian staggered backwards but stayed on his feet. Joe, Garrett and Fergus saw him stagger and ran quickly to him. Will stayed with Thomas, gripping his shoulders tighter to hold him back. Thomas gasped when he saw Christian stagger. Doc Harris rushed to where Crawley lay sprawled on his back on the street. Several women standing in the crowd screamed when the two men drew their guns. Then the whole crowd fell silent.

Christian looked down at his chest, and reaching into his shirt pocket, lifted out the gold locket and chain. He had forgotten he had taken it off Millicent's body and put it in his pocket to give to Sarah. Joe stood next to him while Christian stared at the locket. Christian turned the locket over to see a small dent in the back, then poked his finger through the hole the bullet made in his pocket. "I'll be damned!" Joe said. "Sarah's locket saved your life Chris," Joe said smiling at him.

"Sarah saved my life the first day I met her Joe." Christian put the locket back in his pocket. Garrett pushed his hat back on his head. "Well goddamn, who would have thought?" He smiled at Christian as Christian holstered his gun. Doc Harris checked Crawley for signs of life, but everyone knew there wouldn't be any. Two men lifted Crawley's lifeless body off the street and carried him to the undertaker's where he was laid in a wooden box next to his daughter. Thomas broke free of Will's grasp and running to Christian, slipped his hand into Christian's as they stood beside each other. Christian looked down at Thomas and squeezed his hand. Joe stepped closer to Christian. "You were a bit slow back there, what made you hesitate?" Shaken by the experience, and giving some thought about his inaction, Christian didn't answer Joe's question right away. He could have taken Crawley easy, if he hadn't hesitated. He flexed his hand and his arm hurt. "You heard what Crawley said about how easy it was for him to kill Calahan?" Christian rubbed his arm.

"Yeah ...he stood on his foot ...you know, Sarah always claimed Crawley told her that was how he did it ...we didn't believe her because it sounded too incredible to believe a simple thing like that would have the result it did." Joe recalled every past winter, when Sarah had an argument with Crawley, she always left the store wild with rage. "She tried telling everyone that would listen Crawley killed her Pa, but no-one believed her." Joe looked up the street at the crowd now mingling about in groups and gossiping amongst themselves.

"Tell me Joe, have you ever known Sarah to lie about anything?" Christian asked him. Joe never knew Sarah to lie, but believed accusing Crawley of murder was different and he said so. Christian answered Joe's earlier question. "I hesitated because I thought maybe I should just shoot him in the arm, or leg, but then he confessed to killing Sarah's father and tormented her about it for years ...and all those things he said about Sarah ...I didn't like it ...and another thing ...he pulled a gun on me, and I am the sheriff ...no-one pulls a gun on the sheriff and gets away with it."

Christian had one more thing he wanted to ask Joe. "Will you help me Joe?" Joe was confused with Christian suddenly asking him for help. Surely Christian didn't need any help, he was handling everything just fine. "What do you mean ...help you?" he asked. "I want to put Sarah's house back in order." Still not sure what Christian meant, Joe asked him to explain. "Before I marry Sarah, I want to put Mountain View Lodge back the way it was when Sarah lived there." Joe's face broke out in the widest smile he could muster.

"Well we can certainly help you with that Chris," he said patting Christian on the back. Joe had shortened Christian's name to Chris, and Christian, feeling he had found his niche, liked it.

While Sarah slept, Benjamin Crawley died. Crawley's store was kept operating by Crawley's hired help Henry. Lewis Morley searched through Crawley's personal papers held at the bank and found Crawley had a will. The reading of the will took place in the Town Hall. All of the town folk gathered to witness the reading simply out of curiosity. When Morley read the will, it came as no surprise to anyone that the store was left to Henry, except to Henry himself. The Fur Trading Company set up the Trading Post when trapping first started on the mountain. Not long after, Henry, a young boy of nine at the time, started working for Crawley in his storeroom. Crawley only had Millicent as family and she had never been interested in being a lowly shopkeeper.

Over the next two weeks while Sarah recuperated, the sign above the store was changed from 'Crawley's General Store' to 'Henry's Emporium.' The Lodge had been put back the way it always should have been. Elizabeth's dresses were cleaned and hung back in the closet in the master bedroom. All the crockery and silverware, was back in the kitchen and all of Elizabeth's jewellery was returned and safely stored in Sarah's bank box in Morley's bank. All except the gold locket.

Christian visited Sarah in the days after shooting Crawley and the burials for Millicent and her father had taken place. Sarah wasn't to be told about Crawley's demise, not until she was on her feet. Christian sat by Sarah's bed while she slept. He kissed her lovingly and put her locket around her neck, letting it sit near her heart where it belonged. Sarah's bruises were bad, her arms were black and blue, as was her body. When Christian lifted the sheet to look at them, Sarah opened her eyes to find him sitting on the side of the bed with a worried look on his face. "Are you looking at me, Sheriff Morgan?" Sarah said weakly. "Yes, I am, you are too beautiful not to look at." Sarah smiled faintly and closed her eyes. "Did I tell you I love you?" she whispered. Christian put his mouth close to Sarah's ear. "Yes, you did, but I never tire of hearing it ...I love you." He knelt down beside the bed. "Marry me Sarah." As a tear rolled down the side of Sarah's face, she turned her head toward him. "Have I lost our baby?" she asked, her voice breaking in a sob. "No … no …you're still carrying *our* baby!" Christian emphasized lovingly. "Marry me Sarah?" he asked again. He had asked her while on the riverbank, but she passed out and he didn't know if she remembered saying yes, so he resolved he was going to ask her every day until she was his wife. "Yes," Sarah answered barely above a whisper. Christian kissed her fully and let their happy tears mingle while he held her gently.

Chapter Forty-one

While Sarah spent two weeks being taken care of by Doc Harris and Gerda, Thomas stayed with the trappers. They made sure he attended school and were happy to have him with them. Thomas visited with Sarah in the afternoons before going to the Ferguson House to stay in her room. The trappers and Christian moved all the furniture that was packed into four rooms upstairs in the lodge back downstairs where it belonged.

Thomas and Billy helped stack books back on the bookshelves in the study. Amazed at the number of different books there were, they vowed they would read all of them. The mahogany desk and leather chair along with a leather couch had been returned to the same room. The very large cedar dining table and twelve high backed tapestry chairs were carried back to the formal dining room. A dresser was filled with blue floral, gold edged crockery and crystal glasses. Silver cutlery was set back in drawers. Candlesticks with candles sat along the mantle over the open fireplace. A black leather couch was put back in its place in front of the open fire in the informal living area beside the ugly green winged chair. A small cedar dining table and four wooden backed tapestry chairs were placed behind the couch. The hand pump for drawing water was reinstalled over the sink in the kitchen. The wooden board with the words 'Frank Mason loves Sarah Cole' was placed on the mantle under the portrait of Sarah's mother Elizabeth. These words Christian said, played an important part in Sarah's life, and he wanted Sarah to see the board he saved before Major Hardy burnt down the shack. Christian swore everyone to secrecy, Sarah wasn't to be told about Mountain View Lodge, not until she was feeling better.

As Sarah gradually regained strength, her arms and legs still hurt when she tried moving them. The bruises covering her body came out worse, making her body black and blue. Doc Harris told Christian he wasn't allowed to touch Sarah while she was ill. Sarah and Christian had other ideas about Doc's orders. They held each other intimately in the privacy of Sarah's room. Both Doc and Gerda knew to stay out when Sheriff Morgan was visiting.

Christian lay naked beside Sarah under the blankets. Seeing him holding his hand clenched shut, Sarah wanted to know what he was hiding. When he opened his hand, a gold ring, its emerald stone surrounded by a circle of small diamonds sat in the middle of his palm. He asked Sarah to marry him for the dozenth time and Sarah said yes for the dozenth time. Christian slipped the ring on Sarah's finger, then made slow, gentle love to her.

Sarah had regular visitors each day. All the trappers visited in small groups. Joe, Will, Garrett and Fergus visited together. The Henderson's and the Hammonds visited, so did Jonathon and Tilly O'Rourke. Doc Harris was continually worried Sarah was overdoing it. He felt sure she wasn't getting the rest she needed to allow her body to recuperate. Sarah felt she was getting far too much rest and wanted to get out of bed and get back to her camp. Doc Harris and Christian argued with her, saying she wasn't to go back to camping on the riverbank. They told her when she was better, she would be going to stay in the Ferguson House, in her old room, but Sarah was stubborn and wouldn't give in to their demands.

The day before Sarah was to go back to her camp, she asked Christian to bring certain people to visit her. He rode out to Major Hardy's ranch to get the two men Sarah asked him to get. Confused by Sarah's request, Foley and Brady rode to town with him simply out of curiosity. Morley from the bank was summonsed as a matter of urgency, and he hurried over to Doc Harris's Practice. Christian brought Deputy Clementine, only saying to him Sarah wanted him to visit with her. The five men gathered around Sarah's bed.

Sarah sat in bed wearing a lace bed-jacket over the nightgown Gerda bought for her from Henry's Emporium with her hair brushed and sitting curled over her shoulders. "I guess you are all wondering why I have asked you here?" All four men mumbled their confusion at Sarah's request to see them. Sarah looked at each man and smiling, took a deep breath. "Being here has given me time to think, and I have a proposal to make," she said causing the room to fall silent. "Christian needs a deputy, and Clem needs to retire so he can take his wife to see their grandchildren." Clem nodded in agreement. "I propose," Sarah paused while taking another breath. "Foley, you be Christian's deputy so Clem can retire!" then waited for Foley to agree. But Foley didn't seem overly excited about Sarah's proposal. If this was why she asked him and Brady to come visit her, he thought it no big deal. When Christian was confronted by two outlaws he willingly stepped in and helped outdraw one of the men. After which he gave some consideration to becoming Christian's deputy, only he didn't think Christian would hire him when on more than one occasion, Christian treated him with suspicion. Foley figured being Major Hardy's gun-hand was reason enough for Christian not to trust him, so he let the idea slide.

"I already have a job Sarah," he said eyeing Christian. Sarah went on regardless. "You have always told me Foley that you would leave Major Hardy if something better came along." Foley nodded in agreement. "Yes, but is being deputy better than what I already am? Besides, I have a place to live, with Brady and the other men, I don't ...hell, where would I live? and what about Brady?" He gave Sarah a fleeting look. "You don't '*live*' at Major Hardy's Foley, that is not living when you have to live with a whole lot of other men!" Sarah said almost too sternly while looking down at her hands.

"Well, you used to live with a whole lot of men ...and don't tell me you didn't like it!" Foley laughed half-heartedly. "It just so happens I like being in the company of a whole lot of other men," he lied. He hated his living conditions and so did Brady. Foley folded his arms in defense of his seemingly perfect living arrangements.

"I was a child then Foley, the trappers took care of me." Sarah lowered her voice and kept looking at her hands. "Sorry Sarah, I didn't mean anything by it." Foley never liked saying something that would hurt Sarah. They had been friends for a long time, and being a shy, serious man, he would never allow his feelings for Sarah to show, but he feels they should be more than just friends. Sarah continued. "Oh! and what about Maria, have you asked her to marry you yet? she won't wait forever you know!"

After listening to Sarah and Foley's discussion, Christian fell into deep thought, then didn't let Foley answer Sarah about Maria. "I think Sarah is right, after backing me against those outlaws I could use you, and Clem would be free to retire." Sarah smiled up at Foley. "There, you see, even Christian agrees with me."

"I don't want to live in the jailhouse Sarah, that would be no better than living at the Major's ...with a whole bunch of men," he added, going quiet and glancing at Brady. Besides he argued, he didn't want to leave Major Hardy in the lurch, nor would he leave his brother at Major Hardy's on his own. Brady hasn't spoken since their family perished in their burning farmhouse.

Just a small boy at the time, Brady stole one of his Pa's cheroots and tried smoking it. It tasted disgusting so he put it out on a tin plate on the kitchen table. Only after the fire, did he think he must not have put the smoke out properly and it caught papers left scattered on the table. Foley tried telling him it was a piece of wood that fell from the fireplace that caused the fire, but Brady wouldn't hear of it, it was his fault and nothing Foley said would make him believe any different. The kitchen went up first, engulfing the rest of the house quickly. Brady and Foley sleeping in the front room were the only ones able to escape without injury.

Trying his best to put out the fire, Foley didn't notice his little sister, with her clothes burning, running toward Brady, screaming for him to save her. Brady tried putting out the fire that was consuming her by rolling her on the ground and hitting her with wet feed-sacks, but he had been too late. Devastated by the horror he witnessed, Brady never spoke of it, and has not spoken since.

Christian pursed his lips in frustration at not knowing Brady was Foley's brother until that moment. No-one, not even Joe when he told him about Foley and Brady helping Sarah the night Frank and Foley were whipped had thought to mention they were brothers.

"Will you be selling up when you retire Clem?" Sarah said turning her attention to Clem. Leaning quietly back on his chair listening to the talk around him, Clem liked the idea of Foley taking his place. It would be the chance he needed to take his wife to see their grandchildren. "I will be selling Sarah ...when I leave here, I won't be coming back." Sarah smiled. "Will you sell your farm to me?" she asked. Everyone except Morley stared open mouthed at Sarah's request. Even though he didn't know what Sarah intended, Christian held her hand tight. "I would sell it to you Sarah but what do you need it for?" Having almost given Christian's surprise away, Clem's eyes widened when Christian glared at him. Shaking his head from side to side Christian hoped Sarah didn't notice. Sarah had no idea she owned Mountain View Lodge and that Christian was planning on surprising her by moving her back in there after they were married. Luckily, Clem realized what he said and covered his mistake. "I mean ...um ...I mean ...it would be ...um ...a good place I suppose ...for you and Thomas to live out each winter." Sarah let go of Christian's hands and clasped her hands together. "I don't want it for me Clem, I want it for Foley and Brady."

On hearing this, Foley straightened up and stepped back in shock. When Brady heard Sarah say she wanted Clem's farm for them, he immediately thought now they would be able to get out from under Major Hardy's rule. He hated the way Major Hardy controlled everyone, and especially hated the way he treated Sarah. Throwing his arms around Foley's shoulders, he tried his best to mouth the words he wanted to say, but Foley pushed him away saying, "we can't take it Brady!" When Brady looked disappointed at Foley, Sarah held up her hand and stopped Foley saying more. "Foley ...you remember the night you brought me back to town from the shack? I was there with Frank ...you remember?" Sarah's eyes became distant as she recalled that night. "I remember ...I will never forget it ...how could I!" he said angrily. "You and Brady saved my life that night, I would not have Thomas only for you ...I owe you for that, please ...let me do this for you, I want you to be Christian's deputy, Brady can take care of your farm." Brady's eyes welled, and rushing over to Sarah, bent down and hugged her. Sarah wept too and hugged him back. "Th ...thank ...you so m ...much ...S ...Sarah," he said, finding his voice. When Brady uttered his thanks, everyone in the room went quiet, especially Foley. He knows Brady has always wanted to follow in their father's footsteps and be a farmer. It would never replace the farm or family he lost, but it would go a long way to making him whole.

While the two men hugged, Sarah looked at Morley sitting quietly by while all of this was taking place. "Morley, do I have enough money to cover what Clem wants for his farm?" The men stopped hugging and stared at Sarah, then Morley. Christian was thinking maybe Sarah would not have enough money to buy the farm, and that Foley and Brady would be let down, and maybe she should have asked that question first.

"That depends on how much Clem wants Sarah," Morley said, looking at Clem. Everyone's eyes turned to Clem, making him nervous at all the attention focused on him. Christian knew the farm would be worth a lot. He had been out to the farm several times and was aware Clem would sell one day. At one time he even thought about buying it for himself.

"It's a good farm, rich soil, good for growing crops, there's a good sturdy farmhouse, and a big barn," Clem was saying, but what would be a fair price? He didn't want to sell himself short. Thinking if Major Hardy's once prized bull cost five thousand dollars, then his farm was worth equally as much if not more. Coming up with a figure he thought could be negotiated, Clem rubbed his sweating palms along the top of his legs.

"Would five thousand be too much to ask?" The men sucked in their breath at hearing Clem's exorbitant price. Sarah didn't question the price Clem wanted. "Morley?" she said turning to Morley. Christian thought it far too much, a thousand would have been enough. While Sarah studied Morley, Christian, Foley and Brady as well as Clem, stared at Morley in expectation.

Morley laughed at the look on everyone's faces. "Sarah you have enough money to buy Clem's farm a dozen times over if you so wished." When hearing, Sarah had so much money she could buy a dozen of Clem's farms, the men, in amazement, turned their attention to Sarah. "I only want to buy it once Morley," she said, not knowing how wealthy she had become because of nineteen trappers banking part of their own earnings into her account to help her raise Thomas.

Having fallen in love with Sarah two years before Frank at her father's burial, Foley vowed back then he would one day marry her, but watching her now, he would gladly step aside, even if it hurt him to do so, because it was obvious, she loved Christian, not him. Approaching Sarah's bed, Foley looked over the top of Sarah to

Christian. "I would like to be your deputy," he said holding out his hand. Christian stood up and reaching out, took Foley's hand in his and sealed the deal. "I still have to swear you in, but as of today you are my deputy, Clem you want to hand him your badge?" Clem took off his badge and pinned it on Foley's shirt. Clem just found himself retired.

Gerda came in carrying a tray with a stack of glasses on it and Doc followed with a bottle of wine. "Is it too early for this? Has the deal been made?" Doc asked. To have the five men visit her all at once, Sarah had to let Doc and Gerda know what she planned. Gerda found a bible and while everyone watched, Christian swore Foley in. Foley then turned to Sarah. "You have never owed me anything for that night Sarah …I could never repay you for what you are doing for Brady and me." He looked down at Sarah sitting in bed and wanted to kiss her. He wanted to kiss her every time they met out near the ponds, but they had never been physical. He knew if he kissed Sarah, he would want more, and he wouldn't touch her, not unless they were married, and now that was unlikely to ever happen. "You are a good man Foley Andrews …I expect to visit your farm from time to time." Knowing he had been in love with her all those years ago, Sarah smiled up at him, but she didn't know he still loved her when she pushed him toward Maria. "Ask Maria to marry you, you have kept her waiting long enough …I have a feeling she may give in." Sarah knew for sure Maria would say yes.

Having visited Sarah at Doc's, the women's talk turned to Foley. Maria, like everyone, was aware Foley asked Sarah to marry him every winter, and like everyone, was aware Sarah turned him down. Still, Maria asked Sarah how she felt about Foley, and Sarah informed Maria that she liked Foley, but only as a dear friend, and that she, Maria, need not worry she would come between them. Sarah informed Maria she loved Christian, and would never be unfaithful to him. Maria was happy with Sarah's answer and told Sarah if Foley were to ask her to marry him, she would say yes.

Maria however, was tired of running back and forth to farms and ranches to do housework. Even though she obliged most of them, she was tired of the men propositioning her for sex. Unbeknown to everyone, Maria wasn't in love with Foley. Being Major Hardy's foreman, and hired gun, Foley was considered a decent man, well respected in and around Cedar Creek, but for Maria, he was just a means to an end. If she married him, she would not return to Mexico. Maria had been thinking about what it meant to be married to Foley for some time, and would do anything for that to happen.

Foley, now wearing the deputy's badge, and Brady, rode back to Major Hardy's ranch and informed the Major they were quitting. Major Hardy said he would make a good deputy and wished him well. Foley thanked him and they shook hands. He and Brady collected what pay was owed them, but before leaving, Foley had to get something that was bothering him off his chest. "I appreciated my job here Major, but I never appreciated the way you treated Sarah and your son Frank, they were in love and they deserved to be happy …I would never have followed your orders to shoot Sarah for being on your land." Brady stood beside his brother giving him support, and watched the Major for his reaction to what Foley said, but there was none. Foley continued to say his piece. "You have a grandson that you have missed seeing grow up …all because of your hatred for Sarah's father …Sarah never deserved your hatred …I pity you for your loss Major." Foley put on his hat. "Goodbye Major!" Brady uttered with his newly found voice. Foley and Brady left the Major's ranch for the last time.

Clem rode home to his ranch and told his wife to start packing, they were going to Moreton to be with their children and their grandchildren. As soon as he told his wife he sold the farm and was no longer deputy, she started to feel better. They would leave Cedar Creek as soon as the papers were signed and the money exchanged hands. Clem felt happier than he had for a long time.

Morley went back to his bank and started work on getting the deeds to Clem's farm drawn up, ready for Clem and Foley to sign. In a few days Sarah would be five thousand dollars poorer, and Clem would be five thousand dollars richer. Foley and Brady would own a farm.

Christian and Sarah set a date for their wedding. It would take place the first week of spring before the trappers returned to the mountain, when Sarah would be four months pregnant.

Sarah was pleased with the way things turned out. Foley and Brady had a place to call their own. Christian had a deputy, one that was fast with a gun and would back him up in any situation that arose. Clem and his wife would spend their retirement with their grandchildren, and she had a wedding to prepare for. There was one more thing Sarah had to do.

Joe visited Sarah the following day. While sitting on a chair beside her bed, Gerda brought them coffee and a plate of cookies for them to enjoy while they talked. Sarah told Joe what she had done with regard to Foley and Clem. Joe listened and was pleased Sarah had taken that initiative. "I want to ask you something Joe." Joe put down his mug. "What do you want to ask?" he said leaning forward and facing her. Sarah looked into Joe's eyes. "We have sorted out our differences …haven't we?" Joe thought about Sarah's question. "Our differences being?" he said matter-of-factly. "About what I said, to you and Garrett, and Fergus and Will." Sarah's voice grew softer. "When Frank died …you remember, I told you all to go to hell." Sarah burst into tears. "Will you ever forgive me?" Joe got off his chair, sat on the edge of the bed and held Sarah in his arms. "There is nothing to forgive you for Sarah …you were heartbroken at losing Frank and we understood that." A tear ran down Sarah's face. "But Joe …I've been so awful …I've held it against all of you all this time," she sobbed against his shoulder, "I'm so sorry." Joe held her away from him. "We forgave you a long time ago Sarah, all we want now is for you to be happy, get married, have your baby and let Christian take care of you, that way …I will get some rest." He made a face and Sarah laughed at him through her tears.

"Now …didn't you say there was something you wanted to ask me?" Joe watched her dry her face with the edge of the sheet. She stopped sobbing and drawing back through her nose, looked Joe squarely in his eyes. "Will you give me away at my wedding?" Joe was surprised by Sarah's request but didn't hesitate to answer. "I will never give you away, but as I said, I will be more than happy to walk you down the aisle so Christian can take care of you for me." Sarah put her arms around Joe and they held each other. Returning to the Ferguson House, Joe told the trappers Sarah had asked him to give her away and that the rift between them was over. The men were happy to hear the news, agreeing there had never been a rift, Sarah was merely growing up.

Two weeks later Sarah went back to her camp. Christian argued with her over her staying on the riverbank. He didn't want her living rough when she was carrying his child. Sarah argued she was feeling fine and simply going back to live on the riverbank would not hurt her or their baby. They stopped talking to each other. Sarah cried herself to sleep each night when Christian didn't come to see her. Thomas worried his Ma and Christian wouldn't marry and he wouldn't get the father he wanted. Joe tried pacifying the two of them but neither would give in. Christian refused to see Sarah while she insisted on staying on the riverbank. He would be more than happy for her to stay at Doc Harris's or with the trappers, but not on the riverbank. Doc and Gerda both said they would be happy to have her stay with them until they married.

A week passed slowly for Sarah and Christian. Both were hurting from their seemingly petty argument. Feeling rotten for making Sarah upset, when Christian saw her walking along the street heading for Henry's Emporium, he rushed up to her and taking her by her arm, tried to apologize to her, but they got into another heated argument instead. Sarah argued about where they would stay after they were married, never mind before they were married. Christian argued she should have thought of that before she bought Clem's farm and gave it away, they could have stayed there.

Town folk gathering around to listen could only shake their heads at the pair of them. "There goes Cole again!" one of the onlookers commented. "Poor Sheriff Morgan, he doesn't know what he is in for!" someone else was heard saying.

Not wanting her finding out about the lodge, Christian skirted around the fact Sarah owned it. Only Sarah brought the lodge up herself. "Oh, well, then! ...sheriff! I suppose you expect me to move in with you ...at the lodge!"

"Well, would that be such a bad thing ...Cole?" Christian said in retaliation. "Yes! it would!" she snapped. "You know the reason I won't go there, and don't say you don't! ...I know Joe told you!" As Sarah looked into Christian's eyes, her eyes brimmed with tears because they were fighting again. Standing over Sarah with his hands on his hips, seeing her about to cry, Christian decided he had to give up keeping his secret until their wedding. "Now I suppose you will be mad at me for suggesting you move back in ...to your own goddamn house!" He emphasized loudly so not only Sarah, but everyone in the street could hear, then waited to see what impact his words had on her.

Trying to make sense of what Christian said, Sarah furrowed her brow, and studied his face. "What? ...what do you mean? ...my own house!" she said staring at him.

"You own Mountain View Lodge Sarah, you always have, Benjamin Crawley cheated you out of it that night at the saloon just like you always said he had ...your father never signed the lodge over to him ...he signed it over to you." As Sarah started to sway, Christian quickly put his arms around her. "Why? ...but! ...how long have you known Christian?" She managed to say. "I've known since the day after that damn dance ...I wanted to surprise you at our wedding, but I guess I should have told you right away, I'm sorry ...will you move in with me so we can be together ...I can't live without you," he whispered. When Sarah and Christian kissed, everyone cheered and clapped. "Thank the lord for that!" someone said speaking for every-one.

So there they were, Christian, Thomas, and the four trappers, all gathered together to take Sarah to the lodge. It felt strange to Sarah to be walking up the steps after so long. Christian and Joe held her hands as she looked around nervously to see the men smiling at her. Facing the door, she squeezed Christian's and Joe's hands tight for reassurance. Not having stepped inside her home for a very long time, she wondered if she could stand it or if she might faint dead away. Guessing how she was feeling, Thomas looked up at her. "It's alright Ma." Sarah looked down at him. "You knew about this too Thomas?" Sarah was surprised that Thomas knew. "Yeah Ma, Sheriff Morgan swore at me to keep it a secret!" Everyone laughed when knowing what Thomas meant. When Christian opened the door, Sarah let go of their hands, and taking a deep breath, stepped inside.

Standing just inside the doorway, she could see candles placed along the mantle lighting up the room, and a fire burning in the open fireplace making the house warm. The cedar dining table shone from the reflection of the fire. The low backed tapestry chairs were all there like they had been when she was a little girl. The leather couch she remembered spending many nights sitting on, sat facing the fire. Sarah spotted the green high-backed wing chair and walked quickly towards it. Picturing her Pa sitting in it, brought tears to her eyes. "Pa" she whispered, putting her hand on its back and walking around it. Sarah looked back at everyone watching her. "Pa used to sit here and read to me." A tear rolled down her cheek. "It's such an ugly chair," she said rubbing her hand over the smooth velvet material. "But Pa loved to sit here." Christian went to Sarah and taking her in his arms, whispered, "welcome home."

Feeling a hot tear run down his cheek, Joe swiped his sleeve across his face and snorted. Fergus and the other two men turned their backs and did the same. Thomas just stared at everyone, happy his Ma was finally home, and because this house was going to be his, and his new brother or sisters. Joe ushered the men out of the house. "You too Thomas," he said waiting for him to leave with them. "But Uncle Joe!" Thomas began in protest. "Let your Ma and Christian be alone, come on, you come and stay with us." Joe held out his hand for Thomas to go. Thomas looked back at his mother and the man who was going to be his father as they clung to each other. As the four trappers and Thomas walked away Thomas was happy, and told them so. "I bet I would have liked my Pa if I had known him, but if I had to choose a Pa, I would choose Sheriff Morgan." Joe put his arm around Thomas's shoulders and they walked together to the Ferguson House.

Sarah and Christian spent their first night together in the lodge. While Sarah went from room to room telling Christian about the house, Christian listened patiently. She noticed several things out of place, but it didn't matter, Christian told her Joe and the other men tried their best to remember how the house was before Crawley got his hands on it, and that they put everything back where they thought they belonged. Sarah was happy everything was mostly as it should be.

After eating dinner together at the small dining table, Christian carried Sarah upstairs to the master bedroom. Sitting on the side of the bed with Sarah standing in front of him, and holding her hands, he again declared his love for her. "I love you Sarah Cole, but if you don't want to sleep with me before our wedding night, I will understand." Sarah pushed his legs apart, and stepping between them, hooked her hands around his neck and pulled him to her. "I will not be sleeping in any other bed than the one you are in Christian, I want to sleep with you, every night," she whispered. Christian smiled. "You don't care if people talk about us sleeping together before we are married?" The whole town already knew about them sleeping together, and knew Sarah was expecting his baby, Christian was just toying with her.

Undoing her buttons, he pushed her shirt over her shoulders, brought his mouth over her breast, and covering her nipple, rubbed his tongue across it. Sarah moaned as her nipple began to swell. Letting her nipple slide out of his mouth, Christian studied it and felt himself becoming aroused. "How about we give them something to really talk about." Sarah said seductively, undoing the buttons on his shirt and helping him remove it. Letting Sarah do, to his breast what he did to hers, brought his nipple up hard. Standing up, he quickly slid his trousers down his legs and began undoing Sarah's trousers. Sliding them over her hips, and kneeling in front of her, he pulled them down to her feet. When Sarah stepped out of them, Christian pushed his face between her legs, causing Sarah to moan as his warm breath made the excitement of what was to come, rise in her body. Christian and Sarah made love for the first time in the big red velvet canopied bed. When they were done, they sunk down in the pillows and slept in each other's arms.

Chapter Forty-two

There was something Christian needed to do before he and Sarah married. As he headed out to Major Hardy's ranch, the only thing on his mind, was to sort out the differences between Major Hardy and Sarah.

When Christian arrived at the ranch, Major Hardy welcomed him in. Christian had only been in the ranch-house once before, and that was the day Major Hardy threatened Sarah when they were out at the dry gulch gutting his steers. The two men sat in the large expanse of Major Hardy's living room, facing each other in front of a fire burning in the ornate fireplace. It was spring, although it was warm outside, the house was large and it took some effort to warm it. This room they were sitting in felt comfortable. The two men drank coffee the housekeeper brought them and talked about the men Major Hardy fired after they let his cattle die, until Christian changed the topic. "You have no doubt heard Sarah and I are getting married?" Word travelled to the ranch pretty quickly after his confrontation with Crawley.

"Yes, I have heard, I don't know whether I should congratulate you or give you commiserations about that, you are going to need all the luck you can muster marrying that woman." Christian ignored Major Hardy's remark and went on. "I would like for you and Thomas to get to know each other, after all, Thomas is your grandson? That picture of Frank…" Christian pointed to the framed photograph of Frank sitting on the sideboard. "You can't deny that picture could be Thomas …can you Major?" Major Hardy didn't need to look at the picture Christian was referring to. He cast his eyes down at his hands instead. "No, there is no denying it, Thomas is Frank's son." He went on. "But I don't have anything to do with Thomas

...too many things have happened between Cole and me for that." Major Hardy stood up, and going over to the sideboard, picked the picture up and studied it. "Cole and I are equally to blame for Frank dying ...I hurt my son badly that night ...but I will not forgive Cole for him following her up that godforsaken mountain ...and I know she will never forgive me for what I did." Aware of the night the Major was referring to, Christian got up from where he was sitting, and stood next to him. "There is something you can do about that Major, you can forgive Sarah! the only reason for your dislike for her is because she is like her mother ...I know you loved Elizabeth, but that is no reason to hate Sarah, she is not to blame for what her father and Elizabeth did to you ...let it go Major and spend time with your grandson."

Major Hardy was taken aback by Christian's knowledge of him and Elizabeth, it could only have been Joe Jones that told him. "You are crazy sheriff if you think I would ever forgive Cole for my son! I won't forgive her, not for that! ...and I don't need you telling me what I have missed out on! ...I know damn well what I have missed out on!" Major Hardy became furious at Christian having the nerve to come to his home and ask him to forgive Sarah. Her father was to blame for his hate, and even though he is gone, he believes Sarah inherited that blame. Ignoring Major Hardy's outburst, Christian kept pushing. "Don't you want to spend time with Thomas? He is a very bright boy ...you would like him." Of course, Major Hardy wanted to get to know his grandson, but still he refused to give in. "You think if I say sorry for what happened in the past, everything will be alright? Cole denied me my son! and she has denied me my grandson! ...I will never forgive that woman! ...not ever!"

Not ready to give up, Christian remained firm. "I know what happened between you and Sarah, and Frank ...Joe told me everything."

"Jones! He's nothing but a trouble-making pain in the ass! ... him and his three friends slaughtered my bull! ...Jones cost me a lot of money on account of what he did!" Major Hardy could not forget when his bull had been slaughtered. Believing it was Joe that did it, back then he couldn't prove it, and still couldn't. For all the gossip or perhaps in fear of reprisal, no-one has ever talked about that night. "Forget it sheriff! …I will not forgive that woman …or those men!"

"Then it is your loss Major …think of Thomas in all of this, he hasn't done anything to deserve what is going on between you and Sarah, he deserves to have a grandfather who loves him, you are his family!" Major Hardy let Christian finish saying his piece without interruption, then moved to the door. "I think you had better leave sheriff! get out of my house! …and stop interfering in things you know nothing about!"

Christian however, hadn't finished. "I am truly sorry Major, life must be very lonely and bitter for you …Thomas, and certainly Sarah, deserve better." As Christian walked through the marble foyer and out into the sun, Major Hardy remembered Foley saying a similar thing before he left. When the door slammed behind Christian, he left the ranch feeling disgusted with Major Hardy and disappointed with himself for failing to get him to agree to forgive Sarah. All he could do now was talk to Sarah. If she truly loved him, she would do what he asked. Christian firmly believed Sarah could not be happy, not while ever she had hatred for Major Hardy in her heart.

One week before the wedding, spring came to Cedar Creek in all its glory. The trappers got busy getting ready to head back to the mountain. Joe was staying behind until he walked Sarah down the aisle and handed her over to Christian. Will, Garrett and Fergus were staying too. Christian looked forward to Thomas becoming his stepson. Thomas was excited, there would soon be a man in his family he could call Pa.

It was then Christian made a terrible mistake, one that threatened to tear his and Sarah's relationship apart. He asked Sarah to forgive Major Hardy for the terrible things he inflicted on her and Frank.

"Never!" Sarah screamed. "I will never forgive that man as long as I live!"

"Sarah please, it was a long time ago …don't you think Thomas deserves a grandfather? …his real grandfather," Christian begged. "I know you Sarah …I know you will never be happy while your heart is filled with hatred."

It was while recuperating from being wounded at the mission in Les Rios, that the Brothers taught Christian how to let go of his hatred, and he learnt how to forgive, and from that moment his life had taken on new meaning. Now he hoped he could convince Sarah to let go of her hatred so they could both be happy.

"You think you know me, sheriff? …well you don't!" Sarah bellowed. She would never forgive Major Hardy, it was wrong of Christian to even suggest it.

"I do know Sarah, I know what it is like to hate and I know what it means to forgive, the men told me what passed between you and Frank, and his father." Christian pleaded. "Oh! just what do you think you know? Huh! …tell me!" Sarah demanded, folding her arms and insisting he tell her everything he thought he knew.

Putting his hands on his hips, Christian took a deep breath. "I know you lost your Pa and your house to Crawley." That much Sarah knew he knew. "I know you shot yourself, I know you got attacked by a wolf, I know you almost drowned …twice, goddamn it! …you killed a wolf and skinned it in the goddamn church when Thomas was taken…" Sarah interrupted him. "It was the Major who took Thomas! …I should forgive him for that!" Ignoring her, Christian went on. "I know you loved Frank, I know how he died on the mountain leaving you carrying Thomas, and I know you had Thomas beside the river …on your goddamn own!" He took a breath. "I know you can be a pain in the goddamn ass Sarah …and most of all, I know I love you." There were so many things he knew about Sarah, he couldn't go on. Sarah didn't speak while thinking about what he said. "Do you know Franks father … Major Hardy… whipped him?" She said after a time, ignoring him telling her he loved her.

"Yes" Christian answered sadly.

"Do you know the whip was meant for me?" Sarah gasped back a sob. "Frank threw himself across me to protect me so I wouldn't be hurt!" When Sarah's eyes flooded with tears, even though what happened to Frank happened a long time ago, Christian could see how raw the memory was for her. He wanted to hold her and comfort her, but "yes," was all he could muster through the lump forming in his throat. "Do you know what he went through? …the pain he suffered because of that whipping?" Sarah wiped her hand across her face to brush away a tear. Dropping his hands by his side at seeing her dismay, Christian replied. "No, I can only imagine … but this isn't about Frank, it is about you …and me." Sarah ignored him saying it was about them. "You can only imagine," she said mocking him. "I love Frank! …I feel his suffering! …his own father caused his suffering!" Tears she couldn't hold back, ran down her cheeks and dripped off her chin.

When Sarah said she loves Frank, Christian was taken aback. "You can't still be in love with Frank Sarah, he's been gone a long time!" He said frowning. "Are you Sarah? …still in love with Frank?" He questioned. "Every time we make love, is it Frank you think of when I touch you?" Sarah didn't realize what she said until Christian asked her if she was still in love with Frank. It wasn't what she meant to say. She was in love with Christian, Frank was her first love, and it stood to reason she would still hold a place for him in her heart. Didn't Christian know that? Hesitating before answering, Sarah hoped Christian would understand when she tried to explain what she meant. "I will always love Frank but…" But Christian didn't give her a chance to explain.

"You didn't answer my question Sarah! …is it Frank you think of when I make love to you?" Putting his hands back on his hips, he demanded she answer him. But instead of answering, Sarah held up her shaking hands, and removed the ring Christian had lovingly placed on her finger. "Perhaps you shouldn't be marrying me after all …I will be going back to the mountain …with Joe!" Holding the ring out to him, Christian stared at it but didn't take it. Dropping the ring on the ground at his feet, Sarah turned and ran blindly passed the Livery and down the track to the river. Stooping down Christian picked up the ring, and ran after her.

Trappers busily gathered around their horses lining the front of the Livery and the corrals getting ready to leave. The four trappers were helping load the men's packhorses when they saw Christian and Sarah having a heated discussion. Stopping what they were doing, they became aware trouble with Sarah was brewing again as they watched her take off her ring and drop it on the ground, then burst into tears and run off. When Christian picked up the ring and ran after her, the four men followed him to the riverbank. Thomas, sitting on the corral fence watching the men loading their horses, saw the commotion.

"What's with your Ma now Thomas?" Logan asked seeing what happened. "Sheriff Morgan going to belt some sense into her?" he sniggered nastily at Thomas.

"Aw! Ma is just being stubborn, Sheriff Morgan isn't going to do anything, he isn't the beltin' type." Thomas hoped his Ma wasn't doing something stupid to jeopardize his chances of having a Pa.

Christian caught up to Sarah, and taking her by her arm, spun her around to face him. Sarah never felt so bad in all her life, she loved Christian and wanted him to know that, but once upon a time she loved Frank, and would always hold him close to her heart. Frank was alone on the mountain when he died, and because she had never said goodbye to him, he remained a part of her life. Sarah didn't know how to convey this to Christian without making things worse. "Let me go!" she cried trying to pull away from him.

Coming to the riverbank, Joe put his hand up indicating to the men to slow down.

"I don't want you to go Sarah, please …I love you!" Christian begged, suddenly afraid he was going to lose both Sarah and his unborn child. "I am leaving Sheriff Morgan! …I will have my baby on the mountain!" She replied defiantly. "It is my baby too Sarah! don't I have any say where our baby is born?" But it didn't matter what he said, he couldn't convince Sarah to stay. "If you cared about me you wouldn't have asked me to forgive the Major …I can never forgive him for what he did! " It wasn't entirely what Sarah wanted to say, but it was too late, she had given Christian back his ring, the wedding was off, she was going back to her cabin where she belonged. Feeling he couldn't force her to stay, Christian let her go. Finding herself free, Sarah raced back up the track, passing the four men who were all there as usual listening to her and Christian argue.

When Sarah disappeared up the track, Joe turned to Christian. "Sorry Chris, once she makes up her mind to do something there is no changing it." Now there was no reason for them to stay, they would all go back to the mountain. Not knowing what else to say, Joe followed Sarah up the track to their horses.

Christian stood in the main street watching Sarah load up her supplies. When the trappers became confused with the four trappers hastily getting supplies for themselves, Joe informed them the wedding was off and they were leaving too. Two hours later with their horses loaded, Sarah climbed up on Star. Christian was back in his office sitting at his desk while Foley, standing outside on the boardwalk, watched the trappers packing up. Oblivious to the argument that had taken place earlier, he wondered why Sarah would suddenly decide to leave Christian and Cedar Creek. 'Didn't she love Christian after all?' he wondered.

Foley didn't have the courage to ask Maria to marry him. Now he was deputy, he figured one day he might, but in the meantime, he would keep seeing her when he needed his passion attended to. He didn't have any regrets having asked Sarah to marry him each winter before she met Christian, but he hated that he had to put his feelings aside when she fell in love with him. He felt he would have been happy as Sarah's husband if she had said yes. He may even have gone with her to her mountain, Sarah's mountain didn't frighten him. But Sarah was stubborn, quarrelsome, and hard to please, she had a mind of her own and stood firm by anything she said. Christian soon found that out after asking her to stay in town. She said she loved him, even said she would marry him, but stay in Cedar Creek, never! Foley figured he would never understand women for as long as he drew breath, figuring they were all fickle.

If Foley had known Christian wanted Sarah to forgive Major Hardy for what he did in the past, Foley would have told Christian he was a fool to even suggest she forgive the man. Foley could never forgive him for what he did that awful night out at the shack either.

Christian was in his office when the trappers mounted their horses. As Sarah and Thomas took the reins of their packhorses, Foley stuck his head inside the Sheriff's Office. "They are leaving!" he informed Christian. Grabbing his hat and going outside, Christian could see the corrals from where he stood. This was his last chance to get Sarah to stay, so stepping off the boardwalk he walked quickly toward the corrals, then looked up at Sarah as he stood next to her horse. "Sarah please don't do this, you can't ride in your condition, stay here with me!" he begged. "I am leaving!" Sarah said, looking over his head to the street where people were gathering. Doc Harris and Gerda were standing outside his practice. Ham and Patrice were watching from outside the Livery. A handful of Major Hardy's men were standing to one side watching what was happening too. Christian had no doubt they would tell Major Hardy Sarah had thrown him over and gone back to the mountain, as Major Hardy would expect she would. "You are having my baby Sarah!" Christian pleaded holding tight to Star's bridle. "Don't I have any say in our future?"

"I won't be staying!" Sarah said before pulling Star around. As Star swung away, Christian let go of the bridle. "I won't be here next winter Sarah! I am leaving! I will not stay to see you come here each winter with our child like you do with Thomas!" As Joe led the trappers toward the bridge, Sarah pulled her packhorse in behind her. "You are only leaving because I want you and the Major to forgive each other! you are both so goddamn stubborn and mule-headed neither of you will give in! ...doesn't it matter that I love you?" Christian called to Sarah's back as she brought her horses in line behind Fergus and Garrett. Thomas went next, then Will. The rest of the trappers fell in line behind them.

Thomas didn't want to go, he wanted his Ma to marry Sheriff Morgan, but now everything was ruined. Why was his Ma being so stubborn? She and Sheriff Morgan liked cuddling each other, he saw that when they were at the cavern the night his Ma had been hurt berry picking, now they slept in the same room together, even in the same bed. Thomas could tell something was seriously wrong between them for his Ma not to want to stay. He liked school, and had lots of friends, even Jamie Finch and Daniel Connell made friends with him after he put dead rats in their beds and scared them. "Damn it all Ma!" he said to himself. But he loved his Ma and would do anything she asked of him so he had to go with her. Maybe they would be alright once they got back to their cabin. Looking back at Christian standing at the end of the bridge watching them ride out, he wanted to cry, but vowed instead never to forget him.

Feeling at a loss as to why Sarah would do this to them, Christian stood alone, watching the last of the trappers make their way out of town. His heart was breaking seeing Sarah disappearing along the trail. Having fallen heavily for her, he wanted desperately to be a father to their child. How could Brother Abraham have been so wrong? His foretelling 'three would become four' was not true. Sarah was taking his child that would have made his family four away with her.

Doc Harris approached the bridge and stood beside Christian. "I'm so sorry Christian, Sarah will never give up her mountain." Christian didn't answer, instead, turned on his heel and headed back to his office. Walking past the crowd standing on the boardwalk, he opened the door and went inside. Closing the door quietly behind him, he sat behind his desk with his head in his hands, and went over in his mind the last four months he spent with Sarah, ending with feeling devastated at her going, and at a loss as what to do next.

Foley leant on a post outside the Sheriff's Office. "Well there they go!" he said to no-one in particular. It was the same every year. He knew what it was like to wait for Sarah to come to town. First, he would ask her to marry him, she would say no, he would be in a shitty mood all winter, she would cause a whole lot of trouble, then she would go back to her mountain. He looked toward the bridge where the trappers had gone. Nothing had changed.

Joe always led the trappers off the mountain, and back again. This year, because he was going to walk Sarah down the aisle to marry Christian, he handed the lead over to Samuels. Samuels would have made as good a leader as any one of the four trappers, but because Sarah's wedding was off, he handed the lead back to Joe. Looking over his shoulder, Joe could see Fergus and Garrett riding behind him, then, a little further back, Sarah. He questioned as to what Sarah was doing, and why she was doing it. But it was her decision, and her life. He had to stay out of it.

Sarah rode along seemingly in a daze. Knowing she had given up her chance to be happy, erratic thoughts spun in her head. Deep within her heart, she loved Christian, maybe she loved him too much. She loved his touch, his smile, when he made love to her, she couldn't get enough of him. Frank was dead and Major Hardy was right, it was all because of her. Christian wanted her to forgive him for keeping her away from Frank and whipping him. She would never forgive him, not for that. Now she was pregnant again, but she wasn't going to stay so Christian could see his child grow up. 'Why am I being so selfish?' she asked herself. 'It isn't selfish to want to go home …is it?' Sarah's mind was in turmoil as she rode along behind the men.

After riding back to the ranch, Parker saw Major Hardy waiting for him outside the ranch-house. Major Hardy wasn't happy to see him. "Parker you disgust me! look at you! why are you so goddamn late getting back here? You no good lay-about! get to the barn and get that horse looked after! …then get to the corral and see to those steers!"

"Sorry Major, I've been watchin what was happenin between Cole and the sheriff, seems they parted company, Cole's goin back to her mountain!" Parker didn't draw breath. Major Hardy wasn't quite sure if what he heard was right when Parker was talking so fast. "What do you mean Parker? goddamn it, man! slow down and tell me what you mean!"

"Well, something about forgiveness came up, and Sheriff Morgan, he accused Cole of still being in love with Mason! sorry, Frank! she tossed his ring back at him and said she was going back up the mountain!" Major Hardy looked shocked at Parker's revelation.

"When?" Major Hardy asked.

"When what?" Parker said, scratching his head at not understanding the question.

"When the hell is Cole going back to the mountain?" Major Hardy pursed his lips in frustration when thinking he would need to have a good talk to Parker.

"The trappers rode out just before I came back, I think Cole is on the trail as we speak!" Parker started to lead his horse off to the barn when Major Hardy yelled at him.

"Parker! goddamn it, man! …get my buckboard …*now!*" Major Hardy raced back inside. By the time he came out with his hat and coat, his buckboard was waiting for him.

Steering the buckboard out to the dry gulch as fast as he could, hoping to run into the trappers on the trail, he bumped the buckboard through the trees and along the track. Racing past where the shack once stood, he steered it quickly across the river and along the other side to the ponds. Relieved when he saw the trappers making their way slowly toward him, he pulled his buckboard to a stop and waited.

"What are you doing here Major?" Joe asked coming alongside the buckboard and thinking it strange Major Hardy should be sitting here when he had never done it before. Fergus and Garrett stopped along with their packhorses. Bringing her horses to a stop next to Joe, Sarah stared down at Major Hardy and wondered what he was up to. By the time Thomas came behind her, Major Hardy's buckboard was surrounded. Will stopped his horses behind Thomas. Curious as to what was going on, the other trappers slowed down. "Keep going!" Joe ordered. "We will catch up!" Obeying Joe, the trappers kept moving along the trail.

Ignoring Joe asking what he wanted, Major Hardy looked around at the circle of men before letting his eyes settle on Sarah. "I have something I want to say to you Cole," he replied. "Well I don't want to talk to you Major," Sarah said down to him. "You don't have to talk …just listen!" he said. Sarah pursed her lips to show her displeasure for his disruption. "Well then! …go on …I'm listening!"

"Major!" Joe said sternly, eyeing him with suspicion.

"Shut up Jones! this is between Cole and me! she is old enough to hear the truth!" When Major Hardy snapped at Joe Sarah glanced over at Joe, then brought her eyes back to rest on Major Hardy.

"I was engaged to your mother!" Major Hardy stated for all to hear. Although he was already aware of the Major's history with Calahan and Elizabeth, his declaration came as no surprise to Joe. Sarah however, was stunned. "My mother!" she exclaimed feeling bewildered. Major Hardy glanced quickly at Joe then continued.

"Before your father stole Elizabeth from me, we were to be married …it was I who introduced your father to her …stupidest thing I ever did, introducing them to each other …Elizabeth broke off our engagement as soon as they met. I was devastated when Elizabeth told me she was marrying Calahan, and at having to watch the two of them together here …Oh, it was obvious they were in love …even I could see it, but you see, I …I never stopped loving her …even after she died …I couldn't let her go …I couldn't …and I hated your father for stealing her away from me for a very long time."

While listening to him, Sarah's mind was racing. "But you had a son! ...Frank must have been ...three years old when I came along? ...my parents were only married a year when I was born!" If the Major had a son when her father and mother met, then the Major had to have known another woman when he was supposed to be in love with her mother. "How do you explain that Major?" Major Hardy thought Sarah smarter than anyone gave her credit for. "Yes ...I knew Frank's mother a long time before I met Elizabeth. Victoria's family and mine were close ...we were childhood friends ...Victoria and I had an on again off again relationship for many years. When Victoria became pregnant, it was expected I would marry her ...but I fell in love with Elizabeth and planned to marry her ...so I refused to marry Victoria. Frank was two when I brought him and his mother out to the ranch, the same time Elizabeth married your father. Knowing I was still in love with Elizabeth, was why Victoria left me and took Frank back with her to her parents. I tried for a long time to get her to return, but she knew I would never give up my love for Elizabeth."

Sarah couldn't understand why he remained in love with a woman who had been dead for many years, then realized this was what Christian accused her of? He thought she could not love him if she were in love with another man, even if that man was just a memory.

"What about Frank? and me? you hated me having anything to do with him." Sarah needed to know why the Major hated her for her relationship with Frank. Was it because he wanted Frank to have power and wealth? He had once thought that. But that wasn't the reason. Looking at Sarah, he could see Elizabeth. "I thought you would be like your mother ...and that you would never be faithful to Frank ...how could you? Like Elizabeth, you are far too beautiful for men not to want you ...I was mistaken Sarah, I know now you would have been good for Frank ...if he had lived you would still be together and ...and I would know my grandson." Sarah looked away for a moment. "You would have had more grandchildren Major, that's how much I loved Frank." Major Hardy looked at Thomas. "I want you and Thomas to be welcome at my ranch ...anytime ...I want Thomas to know all about his Pa."

Sarah's hand went to her chest. "Thomas knows everything he needs to know about his Pa!" she snapped angrily, then, having had enough of listening to his talk, pulled her horse around. "I never wanted any of what happened to you and Frank to happen Sarah! I was just trying to scare you ...you must believe me ...if I could take what happened back, I would!" Sounding like he was begging for forgiveness, Major Hardy's voice cracked. But Sarah wasn't about to forgive him. "It is too late Major ...I'm going back to the mountain." Sarah's voice was distant when she spoke. Suddenly feeling dizzy, she gripped Stars reins tight. Joe, seeing perspiration break out on her forehead and seeing her begin to topple, pushed his horse next to Sarah's, and grabbing hold of her shirt, stopped her from falling off her horse.

Sarah felt Joe grab her, and making herself fall toward him, forced him to hang on tight as she collapsed forward, causing the trappers and Thomas' horses to become agitated at the sudden jostling around them. Major Hardy climbed quickly out of his buckboard. "Put her in the back here, the canopy will give her some shade." Fergus helped Joe get Sarah off her horse and to the buckboard. After getting her in the back, Joe climbed in. "You alright Sarah?" he asked, holding her. "I'm always doing this Joe, it's the baby." Feeling concern for Sarah's welfare, Major Hardy climbed in and sat alongside her. "You shouldn't be riding Sarah, get some water Fergus," Joe said taking control as always. "Here Joe!" Fergus said handing Joe his canteen. Offering to help, Will and Garrett got down from their horses and crowded around the buckboard. Joe wet one of the men's bandana's and handed it to Sarah.

"Why did you cut my hair?" Sarah asked Major Hardy as she took a drink from the canteen and wiped her face with the cloth. "I don't know Sarah, I guess I thought, if you weren't so darn pretty, maybe Frank wouldn't be interested in you ...I admit I was angry with you for stealing Frank's affection away from me ...I never had a chance to get to know my son when he was a boy, I didn't know what a father and son relationship was like, I guess I wanted to punish you for that ...I am sorry if I hurt you." Apologizing, Major Hardy didn't think cutting her hair was a big issue, but to Sarah, it obviously had been.

"Frank said it was only hair, that it would grow back, but it took a long time to grow back the way he loved it." Sarah looked at him again, this time her eyes full of tears. "Frank hated the scar on his back, he never wanted me to see it ...he hated what you did to him …he was your son …he loved you." When Sarah said Frank loved him, Major Hardy's eyes welled. He never once gave Frank the opportunity to tell him how he felt about him. "I am so sorry," Major Hardy repeated softly. Looking sadly at Sarah, he could see why Frank fell in love with her.

"I am an awful, horrible man!" Major Hardy said seriously to her.

"I could think of some better words to describe you!" Sarah said, looking into his eyes. Major Hardy laughed, "I bet you could." They studied each other for a moment, then laughed together. Joe watched Sarah and the Major talking amicably for the first time in almost fifteen years. There was no yelling or venom in their words. Joe was hoping now things might be better between them.

"Why are you leaving Sarah? You love him, don't you?" Major Hardy was confused at why Sarah would want to leave the father of her child. "He thinks I still love Frank." She didn't tell him it was also because of him. Major Hardy looked quizzically at her. "Do you?" Major Hardy thought she did, just like he still loved her mother, she would never let Frank go. At that moment, it became clear as to what he had done, by loving a woman he had long ago lost, he had denied himself the happiness he could have had with his son. If Frank had married Sarah, they would have been happy and he would have a grandson to be proud of. But Sarah was doing exactly what he had done by leaving Christian because of her love for a man long dead.

Sarah remembered Christian asked her the very same thing. "I have Frank …here," she said placing her hand over her heart. "In a corner of my heart …I will always have him here …I love Christian with all of my heart …but now it is too late."

"It is never too late Sarah, we cannot change what happened in the past, but we have our future …we have Thomas, and you and Christian will have your baby …he loves you Sarah." Major Hardy watched Sarah slide off the back of the buckboard. Feeling much better for having rested, and having listened to Major Hardy, she wanted to get going. "We have wasted enough time here …let's go!" Sarah climbed into her saddle and pulling on Stars reins, made him turn along the trail.

"What about Thomas?" Major Hardy questioned, hoping to do something to stop Sarah from leaving. "What does he want?"

"Thomas is coming home! ...with me ...where he belongs!" Sarah snapped. Joe thought the moment had passed where Sarah and the Major would ever speak to each other amicably again.

"I don't want to go Ma!" Thomas held his horse steady as he spoke to Sarah's back. She was already moving off and he had to say what he wanted to say before it was too late.

"Thomas!" Sarah questioned, looking over her shoulder at her son. Joe began moving away and the men followed. "I want to stay in Cedar Creek!" Thomas dared to say, not wanting to hurt his Ma this way, but he had to do something to get her to go back to Cedar Creek and Christian.

"You can't Thomas ...you have to come with me!" Sarah wanted to get going, Thomas was holding them up, Joe had begun to get further away.

"Ma, when Billy asked me if I wanted to be his friend and I asked you what I should decide, you told me it was my decision to make, not yours."

"Yes, well that has nothing to do with now Thomas ...come on!" Sarah kicked Star and he took a few quick steps further away from Thomas and the Major.

"Yes, it does Ma, I've decided ...I want to stay here."

Sarah stopped her horse. Major Hardy was thinking maybe Thomas himself would be the one to decide whether he would get to know his grandson. He sat quietly in his buckboard as Thomas told his mother his reason for wanting to stay.

"I have made a lot of friends, and I like school, I like Sheriff Morgan too and I thought he would be my Pa, I don't want to go back to the mountain Ma...you want me to be like Joe and the other men, but I don't want to be a trapper ...it scares me." Aware the mountain is a dangerous place, Sarah didn't question why trapping scared Thomas.

"What do you want to be Thomas?" she asked instead.

"I don't know Ma, but I know I can't be what I want to be if I'm up there on the mountain. The world is a big place, I don't want to just see it in books, and Ma!" he stopped, unsure if he should hurt his Ma by saying more. "I want to get to know my grandpa." He waited for Sarah to say something, or yell at him, but she didn't.

"Fine!" she said, waiting to see if Thomas would change his mind. When he didn't move, she pulled her horses around sharply. "You can stay!" she mumbled, prodding Star. Getting a little way along the trail she looked back at Thomas's horse still standing next to the Major's buckboard and blinked back tears. Thomas was forcing her hand. Stopping where she was, she pulled her horses around to face him and the Major.

Glancing back at Sarah, Will gave his horse a prod, and pulling his packhorse along behind him, yelled, "hey Joe!" but Joe was getting further away, forcing Will to gallop after him. "What is it Will?" Joe asked as he came alongside. "It's Cole! …she's stopped again! …back there!" Indicating back the way they came, Joe turned to take a look.

Sitting on her horse with her head down, Sarah questioned herself as to why she was leaving. 'What am I doing? When I get back to the mountain, I will have our baby alone, just like I did with Thomas, but then the mountain has always been my home, I love its beauty, and the freedom it gives me, I am my own person when I am up there …but am I truly happy? Is that what I want? What about Thomas? He wants to stay in town, he loves school and has friends, and what about Christian? He said he is leaving Cedar Creek for good …I won't see him ever again …If I marry Christian, Thomas could go to school all year instead of just in the winter. Our baby would grow up in town and go to school all the time too. This is our baby, Christian's and mine,' she thought resting her hand on her stomach

Sarah wasn't moving. Star shook his head from side to side while he waited. Joe rode back and stopped beside her. "What's wrong Sarah?" Sarah kept her eyes on Thomas. "I am making a terrible mistake, aren't I?"

Joe glanced down the trail to where Sarah was looking. "Depends!" he said.

"Depends Joe?" Sarah frowned. That wasn't what she wanted to hear, she wanted Joe to help her decide.

"Yep! depends on what you are saying your mistake is." Joe leant on his saddle-horn.

Sarah sat thinking for a moment. Star stomped his hooves, anxious to get going. "If I leave, I lose him, don't I?" Joe knew who she meant she would lose. "He isn't staying …that's what he said." Joe put his head down trying not to appear too impatient. "What about the mountain Joe? If I go back to town, I will never see it again." Joe lowered his voice. "The mountain will always be there Sarah."

"What if I go back and I am too late? What if he has already gone?"

"Then you come back to the mountain! Sarah, if you love Christian enough to have his child, then you can love him enough to stay in Cedar Creek …with him!" Joe shifted in his saddle. "But it has to be your decision," he said, looking back along the trail to where three trappers were waiting. "You and Christian have been through a lot together …you know we can't decide for you." Thomas waited while Sarah and Joe sat talking. After a time, Sarah decided what she must do.

"I am going back Joe!" she said, her eyes still on Thomas. Joe didn't smile, he didn't want Sarah to see how glad he was with her decision. "Go on then, what are you waiting for?" Thomas and Major Hardy watched Sarah reach over and hug Joe, then after prodding Star with her heels, watched her ride toward them.

"We are going back Thomas!" Sarah smiled, bringing her horse to a stop beside the buckboard. "Alright Ma! …*see you Uncle Joe!*" Thomas yelled as loud as he could to Joe's receding back. When Joe heard Thomas, he put his arm up in a salute and kept riding toward the trappers.

"You can visit with each other if you want …I won't stop you," Sarah said to Thomas and Major Hardy. She hadn't forgiven him, but she would make allowances for Thomas's sake. "Thank you, Sarah." Major Hardy and Thomas smiled at each other. As Sarah and Thomas turned their horses toward town, Thomas called. "See you …grandpa!"

Satisfied he would see Thomas again, Major Hardy turned his buckboard back the way he came and headed for his ranch, all the while, hoping one day he and Sarah would be able to forgive each other, although he was convinced it wouldn't happen too soon. When he got back to his ranch he strode inside with purpose. Taking the whip off the wall where it hung, he stepped up to the open fireplace, and tossing the whip into the fire, stood back and watched the whip burst into flames and disintegrate.

Christian sat in his office, trying his best not to cry. Far worse things had happened to him than this. He was tough, and tough men don't cry. Only he loved Sarah so much it hurt inside his chest and now he had lost her. The Brothers from the mission must have been wrong. He found what he had been searching all his life for, but now he had lost it. Three, was going to become four, but he wasn't going to be a part of it. He felt despair and covered his eyes with his hands. He didn't know what else he could have done to convince Sarah to stay. He told her he loved her, he said he would be a good father to Thomas. He wanted to be a father to his own child, a child he was never going to see. Even though he liked the people of Cedar Creek and made many friends, he didn't want to be sheriff anymore. Moving on would be hard, but he had to do it, he couldn't stay here waiting each winter for Sarah. He would hand in his badge, ride out and never return. Maybe he should have followed her, but he didn't want to know the mountain, he wasn't a trapper, and would never become one.

Christian wiped the palm of his hands across his eyes just as Foley stuck his head through the door. "You better get out here sheriff! riders coming!"

"You are my deputy Foley! you deal with it!" Christian said angrily. He was far too upset and didn't feel like doing much of anything.

"I can't deal with this kind of trouble sheriff, you better get out here, they are coming fast!" Foley pulled the door closed behind him and stood on the boardwalk where he could watch the riders. Grabbing his hat, Christian shoved it on his head hard, then taking hold of his gun, slid it up and down in its holster making sure it would slide out free so he could draw fast. This was going to be his last job before he rode out forever.

Foley watched the four horses as they came down the street and stopped in the middle of town. A crowd gathered and stared open mouthed at the riders sitting, waiting. Coming out of the Sheriff's Office, Christian stared too. Stepping off the boardwalk into the street, he started to walk toward the horses. A rider took its feet out of the stirrups, threw a leg over the saddle-horn and slid to the ground, where it landed on both feet before striding toward the sheriff.

Holding his hand level with his gun, Christian walked briskly toward the rider. Doc Harris and Gerda stood on the boardwalk outside his practice and watched. Foley watched as the gap between Christian and the rider got smaller.

When they were an arms-length apart, Christian's hands shot out, and grabbed Sarah around her waist, pulling her against him. At the same time, Sarah flung her arms around Christian's neck. Oblivious to loud cheers and clapping from the crowd, their mouths came together in a passionate kiss. "I love you so much," Christian said when they stopped kissing. "I love you with all of my heart Christian," Sarah whispered. "Don't ever leave me Sarah …I won't be able to go on if you leave me." Christian kissed her once more. "I won't ever leave you," Sarah said returning his kiss.

Thomas was finally going to get the father he always wanted, and his Ma was going to be happy. Jumping off his horse, he ran to Christian and Sarah, who pulled him into their embrace. Doc Harris and Gerda watched Christian and Sarah holding each other. "Looks like there's going to be a wedding after all!" Doc said smiling, and putting his arm around Gerda, gave her a gentle squeeze.

Epiloque

A rider was sent out to the prairie to catch up with the trappers before they got too far away from town to enable them to come back. Four trappers in particular turned their horses. They had a wedding to go to and didn't want to miss a thing. Joe reckoned Christian wouldn't have left because he was too much in love with Sarah to have ridden out straight away. The four men moved back in to the Ferguson House where they planned to stay until the day after the wedding when they would finally head back to the mountain.

The day of the wedding came around quickly. Spring had well and truly arrived and the weather was getting a lot warmer. Preparations for the celebrations were made. Tables were lined up end to end, stretching from one end of the street to the other. Colourful lanterns and bunting were hung, and a dance floor was built where music would be played and dancing would be held. The marriage ceremony was to be on the riverbank at the very spot where Sarah's camp had been. Long seats from the church were placed in the clearing. Men carried the organ out of the church, much to the horror of Preacher Barnes. He was frightened his precious organ would be dropped and ruined. The men struggled to carry it, but managed to get it to the riverbank where they stood it near an archway of flowers set up in front of the ridge below the Ferguson House.

Christian, the four trappers and Thomas got dressed at the Ferguson House. Sarah dressed upstairs in the main bedroom of the lodge, where she and Christian spent the past week living and making love to each other. When Sarah was ready, she felt nervous and unsure of herself. The three women, Patrice, Martha and Gerda, helping her get ready assured her she looked beautiful, but Sarah didn't believe them, she felt awkward, her stomach felt swollen, even if it wasn't yet showing she worried Christian wouldn't like the way she looked.

Joe left the Ferguson House to walk across to the lodge to get Sarah. Christian, along with Thomas, Will, Garrett, and Fergus made their way down the track to the grassed area opposite the pier. Seeing a large crowd had already gathered, Christian felt nervous all of a sudden. His life had changed the day he met Sarah, now he was anxious to be a husband to her, a father to Thomas and soon his new child, whom he couldn't wait to meet.

The trappers, having come back when word got to them that Cole and the sheriff had sorted out their differences and were finally getting married, were there to the last man. They decided they could wait to go to the mountain, after all, the wolves and the mountain would always be there, it wasn't every day they got to attend a wedding as well as a feast. All the men Christian noticed, had cleaned themselves up as best as they could. He smiled and shook hands with most of them.

"Hey sheriff!" One of the men laughed. "I wonder what colour trousers Cole will be wearing!" Another called, "we are taking bets on that!" And every man guffawed. Christian shook his head and laughed with them, but silently prayed Sarah wouldn't be wearing trousers. He didn't care if she wore trousers every other day, just not today.

Preacher Barnes stood under the archway waiting patiently. After telling Sarah she would have to come to church to pray for forgiveness for what she had done twelve years ago in his church if she wanted to be married by him, Sarah said she would never step foot inside his church, and told him he could go to hell. Joe stepped in and made things right, telling Preacher Barnes they would get the preacher from Moreton to come and officiate if he felt he couldn't do it. Preacher Barnes soon changed his mind, saying he would not have another preacher coming to his town to attend his flock. Waiting nervously for Sarah to arrive, Christian, Fergus, Will and Garrett all stood together. Thomas stood in front of Christian.

Thinking this day would never come, Joe walked up the front steps of Mountain View Lodge. There was a special bond between himself and Elizabeth before Sarah was born. Having loved Elizabeth too, he was devastated when she passed just two years after giving birth to Sarah. Fifteen years ago, Sarah lost her father and was thrown out of her winter home. Now, thanks to Christian, here he was collecting Elizabeth's daughter from her beloved home, and walking her down the aisle. At least, Joe thought, the aisle on the riverbank, to marry a man that he and every trapper had come to respect.

Joe knocked on the front door and Patrice let him in. Stepping inside, Joe felt nervous as he wondered how Sarah would look. Waiting at the bottom of the stairs, he fidgeted with his coat, wanting to get out of the fancy duds he was wearing as quick as he could so he could get back into his old worn out trapping gear and oversized fur coat.

Holding the dress up a little at the front so as not to trip and fall with the dress touching the ground at her feet, Sarah took the stairs slowly down to Joe. She looked radiant, her cream silk dress with crystal droplets adorning the bodice accentuated her bust. The long bell-shaped sleeves she wore off her shoulders. The dress draped full from under her bust and a train stretched along the floor behind it. Her gold locket hanging about her neck sat nestled on the rise of her breasts. Sarah's long hair pinned to one side, curled and fell over her bare shoulder. A halo of small flowers from Martha Henderson's garden sat on her head and she carried a bouquet of the same flowers in one hand.

With a lump in his throat, and the thought he might cry at the sight of her, Joe watched Sarah coming toward him and remembered back to another time when he watched Elizabeth coming down these stairs wearing the very same dress. Elizabeth was hosting a dinner party that evening, something she often did during the winter months while staying at the lodge. Joe attended many of her parties along with Doc and Gerda, and Ham and Patrice. His friends Fergus, Garrett and Will attended too. They had all seen the many beautiful dresses Elizabeth brought with her from the city. Sarah stood in front of him now, looking as her mother had. "Joe," Sarah whispered as she met him with a smile at the bottom of the stairs. Joe brushed a tear from his eye and could hardly speak. "You look beautiful Sarah."

Hooking her arm in Joe's, they made their way along the street toward the track leading to the grassed area where her camp had been. "Is everyone there, Joe?" Sarah asked. "Everyone is there," he replied. The three women walking on ahead of Sarah and Joe stopped when they got to the top of the trail leading to the riverbank.

A buckboard sat baring their way. Major Hardy looked from Sarah to Joe. "Get out of our way Major!" Joe barked. Any other day Joe would welcome trouble, but not today. "You are not welcome here!" he said, feeling angry. Major Hardy climbed out of his buckboard and stood firm in front of Joe. "I am not here to cause trouble Jones."

"Well what do you want?" Joe held Sarah's arm tight. They already had a discussion with Major Hardy on the trail over a week ago and thought things had been sorted. He hadn't been invited to the wedding but sent his men in with a freshly killed steer. They set it up over a firepit in the street, and the meat was still roasting. The aroma wafted over the town. The wedding guests couldn't wait to tuck into the beef.

"I want to give Sarah a wedding gift," Major Hardy said opening a black box he held in his hands. Keeping a tight grip on Joe's arm, Sarah and Joe, both gazed at the ruby and diamond necklace, sitting on a bed of black velvet, sparkling in the afternoon sun. "This was to be my gift to Elizabeth on our wedding day, now I would like you to have it." Sarah looked up at Major Hardy, and saw how he appeared sad. "I can't accept this Major," she said keeping her eyes on him. "It was to be your mother's Sarah ...please, accept it for her." When Major Hardy's eyes welled, Sarah could see he was still in love with her mother. "Would you put it on me Major?" Removing her hand from Joe's arm, and reaching behind her, she removed her gold locket and handed it to Joe who put it in his coat pocket. "Keep it safe for me Joe," she said as she turned her back on the Major. Taking the necklace out of the box, Major Hardy handed the box to Joe and did up the necklace around Sarah's slender neck. When Sarah faced him, she looked more like Elizabeth than ever before. "You look lovely

Sarah, congratulations on your wedding." Finding it difficult to speak, he turned and hurried back to his buckboard.

Down on the grassed area where everyone was waiting, Christian wondered what could be taking Sarah and Joe so long, and hoped Sarah hadn't changed her mind about marrying him again. Thomas looked at his silver timepiece he had taken out of his treasure box just for this occasion, he would make sure to put it back when the celebrations were over. He looked up at Christian. "It sure is taking Ma a long time, you want me to go take a look?"

"No, it's alright Thomas, give her a few more minutes," Christian replied nervously.

"Come on Sarah!" Joe said, leading Sarah down the trail. Major Hardy had just climbed into his buckboard when Sarah stopped Joe and turned back.

"Major Hardy!" she called. Remembering how she felt when he took Thomas from her, she understood how he must have felt when Frank was taken away by his mother, and again when Frank left him for her. It must have been unbearable, and so coming to the realization he loved his son and didn't mean to hurt him, Sarah made up her mind. Although she could not yet forgive him for the grief he caused, she realized she didn't hate him at all.

She had once been afraid of him, but not anymore, now all she wanted was for everything to be perfect when she married Christian.

When Major Hardy heard Sarah, he turned in his seat to see her smiling at him. "I would like you to come to my wedding ...we can talk later." On hearing Sarah's invitation, Major Hardy eagerly stepped out of his buckboard. Joe hadn't heard Sarah when they were out on the trail tell the Major, he and Thomas could get to know one and other. "Do you know what you are doing?" he queried. "I think I do Joe ...I hope so!" Major Hardy walked quickly toward Sarah and Joe. "Thank you, Sarah," he said, his eyes swimming. Following Sarah and Joe down to the grassed area, he sat on a stool at the back of the crowd where he could see Thomas standing near Christian. Convinced Christian would make a good Pa to Thomas, he hoped by getting to know Thomas himself, he could make up for all the years he lost with Frank.

When everyone stood up to watch Sarah coming along the track toward them, they oohed! and aahed! The organ player played the Wedding March and Christian moved out in the open so he could see who everyone was looking at. The trappers fell silent as Sarah walked past. After surprising them with how beautiful she looked wearing a dress, all bets were off. They all thought Christian a lucky man to have won Sarah's affection.

Christian felt his eyes beginning to sting as he watched Sarah approaching. Sarah was wearing the dress Joe held up that night in the lodge when he showed him the portrait of Elizabeth. The necklace around her neck sparkled when the sun danced off it. As Joe and Sarah stopped in front of Christian, Joe held her for a moment. "You have to promise me you will take care of Sarah Chris, or I won't hand her over to you."

"I prom..." Christian started to say. But before he could make his promise, he saw Major Hardy at the back of the crowd. "What is he doing here?" he asked. Sarah and Joe looked at Major Hardy, then Sarah looked at Christian. "It's alright ...I invited him." Christian raised his eyebrows. "He is Thomas's grandfather and it is time for him and Thomas to get to know each other," Sarah whispered. "I love you ...Sarah Cole." Christian bent his head and kissed her. "Hey you two! you ain't married yet!" Reece, one of the trappers called, causing the crowd to laugh. "Shut up Reece!" both Christian and Sarah said together, then laughing, they turned to Preacher Barnes.

The wedding ceremony went off without a hitch and the reception was in full swing. Major Hardy and Thomas were seated beside each other talking. Major Hardy laughed at something Thomas told him and Sarah, watching them, felt sad that Frank wasn't with them, but then if he was, she realized, she wouldn't be married to Christian. She vowed she would love Christian 'till death do them part' and Christian made the same vow to her. Wanting to spend as much time as she could with Christian, she prayed death would not come until they were both very old.

The men were standing in a group talking and drinking and Sarah felt strangely remote from everyone. Walking away from the celebration, she was standing at the top of the trail leading to her old camp where Major Hardy found her. "Sarah?" Turning when she heard his voice, her stomach fluttered. It wasn't fear she felt, it was more pity than anything. She didn't speak but watched Major Hardy's face intently. "Thomas is a fine boy, you have done a wonderful job raising him."

"It hasn't been easy Major!" Major Hardy bent his head and looked at the ground. "No …I imagine it hasn't been easy for you …and I didn't help, did I?" Sarah was curt when she answered, "no …you didn't!"

Ignoring her sarcasm Major Hardy went on. "I have given a lot of thought to you and Frank …and I have come to realize how wrong I was …he was happy with you, wasn't he?"

Sarah's eyes misted. "I think he was …I know I was happy with him …he gave me a gift in Thomas…" Sarah paused for a moment. "And Major! everyone knows I would never use my knife to skin a person, but …if you ever do anything to hurt Thomas …I will hurt you, in a way you can only imagine!" Sarah looked him squarely in the eyes. "That …I promise you!" Sarah didn't need to make her promise on the mountain. If anything were to happen to Thomas, she would keep her promise regardless of where she made it.

Christian and Joe saw Sarah and the Major standing together at the top of the trail. "You want me to come with you Chris?" Joe asked. "No, I can handle it …but keep your eyes open …if there is any trouble …come running!" Christian walked up to Sarah and standing beside her, wrapped his arm around her waist and held her against him. "Is everything alright Sarah?" he asked, eyeing Major Hardy. Without taking her eyes off Major Hardy, Sarah replied. "Everything is fine …just fine!"

To be continued….

'The Trappers Promise' concludes with
Book Three - Sarah's Mountain.

About the Author – Bronwyn Trotter

Being a new author, my inspiration for writing comes from a lifetime of growing up in a family that enjoyed western movies and reading a variety of novels. My father especially loved westerns and whenever I and my three brothers visited, I could guarantee dad would be watching a western or reading a western novel. I loved to sit and watch them with him, enjoying the posse chasing the baddies, the hero saving the little ranchers from the big. Forget about superheroes, modern romance stories, robots fighting robots or fighting monsters. Don't get me wrong, I like those stories (and movies) and I love to read a variety of different genres - Dan Brown, Jeffrey Archer, Jack Higgins, John Grisham, Markus Zusak, Stephen King, Nora Roberts, Di Morrisey, J R R Tolkien to name a few. As you can see, they are varied but not westerns. My collection of books is extensive, consisting of the above authors and others. My writing is new, The Trappers Promise is my first attempt at telling a story. My writing stems from my own personal memories and love of a good western. When I sat down to write, my story just came to me, so I put pen to paper, yes literally. After filling an exercise book with what I wanted to say I decided using a computer was much easier. My brain just ticked over with recollection after recollection of those days watching movies and dad getting to the exciting part in a western book. (I could always tell when the action started, dad had a way of making a noise with his teeth that sounded like a horse galloping and when it was really galloping the noise got faster. We children laughed because we knew the posse was on the chase).